Thomas Earl of Dundonald

**The Autobiography of a Seaman**

Thomas Earl of Dundonald

**The Autobiography of a Seaman**

ISBN/EAN: 9783337031053

Printed in Europe, USA, Canada, Australia, Japan

Cover: Foto ©Raphael Reischuk / pixelio.de

More available books at **www.hansebooks.com**

THE

# UTOBIOGRAPHY OF A SEAMAN.

BY

## THOMAS, TENTH EARL OF DUNDONALD, G.C.B.

ADMIRAL OF THE RED; REAR-ADMIRAL OF THE FLEET,
ETC. ETC.

VOLUME THE FIRST.

LONDON:

RICHARD BENTLEY, NEW BURLINGTON STREET,

Publisher in Ordinary to Her Majesty.

1860.

TO

# THE ELECTORS OF WESTMINSTER,

BY WHOSE GENEROUS SUPPORT, NEARLY HALF A CENTURY AGO,

I WAS RESCUED FROM DESPAIR,

THE RESULT OF UNMERITED INJURIES INFLICTED

BY HOSTILE POLITICAL FACTION

IN RETALIATION FOR

MY ADVOCACY OF NAVAL AND ADMINISTRATIVE REFORMS;

AND TO WHOSE HONOUR BE IT RECORDED

THAT IN NO INSTANCE

DURING OUR LONG POLITICAL CONNEXION

DID ANY OF THEIR BODY EVER ASK ME

TO PROCURE FOR HIM PLACE, BENEFIT, OR EMOLUMENT,

## This Volume is Inscribed

BY THEIR FAITHFUL SERVANT,

DUNDONALD.

# PREFACE.

THE present Volume narrates my services in the British Navy, from my entrance into it, and including, the action in Aix Roads, on the 11th, 12th, and 13th of April, 1809. The result of that action, viz., the court-martial on Lord Gambier — virtually a prosecution of myself; my non-employment thenceforward in the navy; the unscrupulous plot by which I was driven from that noble service; my restoration to rank by his late Majesty William IV., and to the honours which had accompanied that rank by my present most gracious Sovereign Queen Victoria; form subjects, which, together with many others, will be concisely set forth in the succeeding portion of this Work.

To one of these points I shall, however, here briefly allude,—my restoration to the naval service; not for the purpose of pre-judging the subject, but with the intention of embracing the first opportunity which has been afforded me, of paying a tribute of thanks to those who, convinced of the injustice of the sentence, were mainly instrumental in procuring its reversal.

Amongst these I am proud to rank one, the soundness of whose judgment, and the disinterestedness of whose patriotism, have throughout a long life never failed to secure the highest respect amongst men of every shade of political party — the Marquis of Lansdowne; who, from the commencement of my unmerited troubles, has to this day manifested the most generous confidence in my honour, and has as generously supported my cause when my character has been called in question. If proof were wanted of my entire innocence of the accusation laid to my charge forty-five years ago, no prouder testimony of incapability to have committed the imputed offence could be adduced than the unabated friendship of the Marquis of Lansdowne; simply because no man with a stain on his character could have retained any place in that illustrious nobleman's consideration.

To another nobleman, whose name will descend to the remotest posterity as the promoter of everything rationally liberal in politics, and the untiring advocate of measures calculated to promote social

advancement, my warmest thanks are no less due.
First my counsel, and for half a century my friend,
—to the long-continued esteem of Lord Brougham,
I owe no small portion of that consolation which for
so many years formed my only support under a
weight of persecution enough to have bowed any man,
not so supported, to the earth; into which, had it not
been for the disinterested countenance thus afforded
by men above reproach I must have prematurely
sunk.

One testimony of my venerated friend I may be
allowed to adduce * : —

"I must be distinctly understood to deny the accuracy of
the opinion which Lord Ellenborough appears to have formed
in Lord Cochrane's case, and deeply to lament the verdict
of Guilty, which the jury returned after three hours' consulting and hesitation.

"Our own complaint was his Lordship's refusal to adjourn
after the prosecutor's case closed, and his requiring us to
enter upon our defence at so late an hour—past nine o'clock—
so that the adjournment took place at midnight and before we
had called our witnesses. I speak of the trial at Guildhall
only. Lord Ellenborough was *equally to blame with his
brethren in the Court of King's Bench for that most cruel and
unjustifiable sentence* which at once secured Lord Cochrane's
re-election for Westminster.

* See Lord Brougham's "Historic Sketches of Statesmen of the
Reign of George III."

"In 1833 the Government of which I was a member restored this great warrior to his rank of admiral in our navy. The country, therefore, in the event of hostilities, would now have the inestimable benefit of his services, whom none perhaps ever equalled in heroic courage, and whose fertility of resources, military as well as naval, places him high among the very first of commanders. That his honours of knighthood, so gloriously won, should still be withholden, is a stain, *not upon him*, but upon the councils of his country; and after his restoration to the service, it is as inconsistent and incomprehensible as it is cruel and unjust."*

To many others, high in public estimation and in the councils of their Sovereign, I have been equally indebted for countenance and support, but as it has been my lot to outlive them, they are beyond the reach of thanks. Amongst these may be mentioned the late Duke of Hamilton, the Earl of Auckland, Sir Francis Burdett, — my late warm-hearted friend and colleague; Mr. Whitbread, Mr. Hume, and others whose names have escaped my memory rather than my gratitude.

Last, though foremost in estimation, is another friend, found where man will seldom look for a

* On the accession of Her present Most Gracious Majesty those honours were restored; every attempt to obtain their restoration during the reign of His late Majesty having failed, from causes which will be stated in the next Volume; and notwithstanding that His Majesty himself warmly espoused my cause.

friend in vain,—at home ; the Countess of Dundonald,
my wife. Knowing the opinion of her Sovereign
with regard to the persecution which had entailed
on me so many years of misery, and equally well
aware that in the first years of his Majesty's reign
the non-reversal of that unjust sentence was owing
to the influence of some in His Majesty's councils,
whose political animosity sixteen years before had
no small share in its infliction,—that ardent and
heroic lady determined to penetrate to the foot of
the throne, and learn from the lips of the Sovereign
himself whether it was consistent with the dignity
of his crown, that its attribute of mercy should be
the sport of an almost extinct political faction.

The step was a bold one; but the ardour which
had conceived it to be necessary lacked not the energy
to carry out its resolve. In spite of the coolness of
some about the court, and the positive rudeness of
others whose names it is not worth while to resus-
citate, this devoted lady gained an interview with
her Sovereign, and with the greatest respect besought
His Majesty not to permit the benevolence of his disposition, and his own belief in the innocence of her
unjustly maligned husband, to be thwarted by those
whose office it was to advise, but not to control, his
better judgment.

His Majesty graciously listened, and his reply was

kingly, that " he would no longer allow the reparation which was her husband's due, to be withheld."
A change of Ministry shortly afterwards followed,
and, as already quoted in an extract from the
writings of Lord Brougham, my restoration to rank
rewarded the heroic efforts of my devoted wife.
Nevertheless, a leaven of former political malice
remained, sufficiently powerful to prevent my restoration to the honours with which a previous Sovereign had invested me, but of which I had been
despoiled with every mark of degradation which
political animosity could invent.*

This gracious act of restoring my honours
was reserved for Her present Majesty, who unsolicited, and with the delicacy which is one of Her
Majesty's noblest characteristics, gave back the boon
of which I had for so many years been wrongfully
deprived ; and subsequently conferred upon me, at
the age of seventy-three, my first command of a
British fleet. For both marks of Her Majesty's kindness and appreciation of my former services, I am
deeply grateful. But alas ! reparation came too late
to compensate for the early hopes and just expecta-

---

* Viz., a forcible intrusion into my apartments in the King's
Bench Prison in the dead of night, with a demand for their immediate surrender.

tions of a life forcibly wasted as regarded myself or
my country.

The moral — to use an old-fashioned phrase — of
my chequered career, is this: — That they who, in
political matters, propose to themselves a strict and
rigid adherence to the truth of their convictions,
irrespective of personal consequences, must expect
obloquy rather than reward; and that they who
obstinately pursue their professional duty in the face
of routine and official prejudice, may think themselves lucky if they escape persecution. Such a
moral may be derogatory in a national point of view,
but it is the result of my own bitter experience:
notwithstanding which, were my life to begin anew,
I would pursue the same unflinching course with
regard to naval abuses, of following out my own
convictions,— a course which would produce the same
result to myself, the consolation of my own rectitude,
even though I might be deprived of all other reward.

Still all is not dark. I have survived malignity,
and its chief cause, viz. the enmity arising from my
zealous advocacy of departmental and political
reform. The latter has been achieved to a greater
extent than the early political reformers, amongst
whose ranks I was enrolled, ever dreamed of; and
even departmental reform has become fashionable,
though it may not have advanced far beyond that point.

In one respect I will boldly assert that this narrative of my life is worthy of example. It will show the young officer that, in spite of obstacles, warm attachment and untiring devotion to my noble profession enabled me to render some services to my country upon which I may be allowed to reflect with satisfaction, even though this be accompanied with bitter reflection as to what the all-powerful enmity of my political opponents cruelly deprived me of further opportunity to accomplish.

In conclusion, I must express my thanks to Mr. Earp, whose zeal has exhumed from documents almost, in my own estimation, beyond comprehension or arrangement*, the mass of facts condensed within the compass of this volume.

In the succeeding portion of this work, should God spare me to see its completion, I trust to render additional service, by an attempt to deduce from past

* In the great earthquake at Valparaiso in 1822 my house shared the common destruction, and from the torrents of rain which accompanied the unusual atmospheric disturbance, my papers were saturated with water, to such an extent that it became necessary to lay them to dry in the sun. Whilst undergoing this process one of the whirlwinds common on the Chilian coast suddenly came on, and scattered them in all directions. Many were lost, but more torn, and rendered almost undecipherable; whilst all that remained have been ever since in confusion. The labour of accurate compilation from such materials may be imagined.

naval experience the best means of preserving un-
impaired our future maritime efficiency.    Should
the attempt be the means of awakening national
attention, the gratification will be mine of having
left no unworthy legacy to my country.

DUNDONALD.

December 14. 1859.

# CONTENTS

OF

# THE FIRST VOLUME.

---

INTRODUCTORY.

## CHAPTER I.

## CHAP. II.

## CHAP. XVIII.

### CRUISE OF THE *IMPÉRIEUSE* CONTINUED.

## CHAP. XIX.

### APPOINTMENT TO COMMAND FIRE-SHIPS IN BASQUE ROADS.

## CHAP. XX.

## CHAP. XXI.

## CHAP. XXII.

### ARRIVAL IN ENGLAND.

## CHAP. XXIII.

### LORD GAMBIER'S DESPATCH.

# AUTOBIOGRAPHY OF A SEAMAN.

## INTRODUCTORY.

### SOME ACCOUNT OF THE DUNDONALD FAMILY.

TRADITION has assigned to the Cochranes a derivation from one of the Scandinavian sea-rovers, who, in a remote age, settled on the lands of Renfrew and Ayr. There is reason to believe the tradition well founded; but to trace its authenticity would be foreign to the purpose of the present work.

In later times, incidents of historic interest connected with the family, justify allusion, as forming contributions not only to the national annals of Scotland, but to those of England also. The earliest authentic record of our house is contained in the subjoined extract from Crawfurd's "Peerage of Scotland."

"This family, which originally took its surname from the Barony of Cochran, in Renfrewshire*, is of great antiquity;

* "Opposite to Johnstoun, upon the east side of the river, lye the house and barony of Cochran, the principal manour of the Cochrans, a family of great antiquity in this shire, whose ancestors

and though none of the family arrived to the dignity of peerage till the reign of King Charles I., yet it is undeniable that they were barons of special account for many ages before, and endowed with large possessions in these parts and elsewhere.

"The first of whom I have found upon record is Waldenus de Coveran, *i.e.* Cochran, who, in 1262, is witness to the grant which Dungal, the son of Suayn, made to Walter Stewart Earl of Monteith of sundry lands in the county of Argyle, which came in aftertimes to be transmitted to Forrester of Carden. Another William de Coveran is mentioned by Pryn, as a person of account in this county, who makes his submission to King Edward I. Anno Dom. 1296, in the Ragman Roll; also John de Coveran is witness in the regular election of James, Abbot of Paisley, 17th of David II. Anno 1346.

"The next remarkable person of the family is Gosiline de Cochran, who flourished under King David Bruce; he is witness to several grants made by Robert II. when Earl of Strathern, to the religious of Paisley, an abbacy he assumed into his particular patronage, wherein his ancestors' donations being made to the glory of God are particularly narrated. He left issue, William de Cochran, of that Ilk, his son, who obtained from King Robert II. a charter of the lands of Cochran, to be held in as ample a manner as any of his progenitors held the same of the Lord High Steward of Scotland, dated on the 22nd of September 1389. As he stood in special favour with this king, so was he in no less with Robert III. his son, to whom it seems he had been serviceable; for when he came to the crown he had so grateful a sense thereof, that in the second year of his reign, Anno 1392, he made him a grant of forty shillings sterling in annuity, arising out of the profits of the Burgh of Rutherglen. He

have possessed these lands well nigh 500 years, and, without doubt, have taken appellation from their hereditary lands, when fixed surnames came to be used."—*Crawfurd's Description of Renfrew*, p. 82.

was succeeded by Robert his son who, in 1456, resigned his estates in favour of Allan his son."

This surrender of his estate appears to have been made for no other purpose than to devote himself to the study and practice of architecture, in which, as an art, Scotland was, at that time, behind other nations. In the exercise of his self-imposed profession, Robert Cochran is said to have displayed great skill in the erection of several edifices*, and when, by the favour of the King James III. he afterwards rose to power, his architectural eminence procured for him, amongst the host of enemies created by his elevation, the contemptuous appellation of the " mason chiel."

It was not, however, his architectural skill alone which gave him a place in his sovereign's estimation, but his good broadsword and powerful arm, the efficacy of which having been displayed in a combat in the king's presence† attracted his majesty's attention ; so much so, that the king, finding him to be of good family, and possessed of great talent, placed him near his person ;

* Pinkerton.

† " He came to be known to the king by a duel which he fought with another; and presently from an architect came to be made a courtier, and was put in a fair way of rising to some greater advancement; for, having performed some lighter matters, intrusted to him, with diligence, and also accommodating himself to the king's humour, he was soon admitted to advise concerning the grand affairs of the kingdom; insomuch that Preston chose him to be his son-in-law."—*Buchanan*, vol. ii. p. 301. " But that which made Cochran most envied was his earldom of March; which country the king had either given to him, or at least committed to his trust, upon the death of the king's younger brother."—*Buchanan*, vol. ii. p. 309.

the result being that in a brief space of time he became his chief adviser, and the great opponent of the Scottish nobility, who sought to hold the king in their power.

In short, Robert Cochran appears to have become to James something like what Wolsey subsequently was to Henry VIII. not in power only, but also in ostentation. In the latter respect, Lindsay says of him, that " even his pavilions were of silk, and the fastening chains thereof richly gilt." Pinkerton says he " became the fountain of royal favour, and was elevated to a giddy and invidious height of power — this being the earldom of Mar."*

This advancement to the earldom of Mar, says Buchanan, " was the chief source of the hatred of the nobility, who were disgusted with James, partly by

---

* The following extract from Crawfurd shows that the title and revenues of the earldom of Mar were in the hands of James at this time : —

"ERSKINE EARL OF MAR.

" Which Thomas [Erskine Earl of Mar,] did prosecute his father's claim to the earldom of Mar with all the vigour imaginable, but having a powerful party, the king, to deal with, at length a final sentence was given against him in parliament, on the 5th November 1457, which he was obliged to acquiesce in; but notwithstanding the hard measure he had undergone from the king, and which might have been thought would have made him ready to have taken all occasions of being severe of it, yet he was a person of so much honour and virtue that in the succeeding reign of James III., when he had a very fair opportunity to be revenged, yet he no sooner saw the ways of duty towards the king decline, and his power *envied by a strong party of the nobility*, than out of pure conscience to serve his Majesty when he was in distress he fairly engaged in his quarrel, and when the war broke out accepted a command in the army in which he continued till the very end that the king was miserably killed in the field of Stirling on the 11th of June 1488."

reason of his familiarity with that rascally sort of people, but chiefly because *he slighted the nobility*, and chose mean persons to be his counsellors and advisers, the chief of these being Thomas Preston, one of a good family, and Robert Cochran, a man endued with great strength of body and equal audacity of mind."

In classing Thomas Preston and Robert Cochran amongst " that rascally sort of people," Buchanan contradicts himself, for he admits that Preston was of good family, and he must have known that Cochran's family was still more ancient, so that the historian only gives evidence of his own tufthunting tendencies. What were the feelings of the nobility towards Robert Cochran, may be gathered from the titles to the chapters of a scurrilous book subsequently written in their interest for the purpose of denouncing his memory.

1. " This minister's (Robert Cochran) raising himself, first by his impudence, and next by his alliance with a noble lord, whom he wormed out of power."

2. " His poor condition when he first came to court."

5. " His buildings and passion for hunting."

7. " *His working the disgrace of all the great men,*" &c.

This last head, " *working the disgrace of all the great men,*" appears to form the key to their whole hatred, but it implies patriotism towards a monarch and a country whom the " great men" had previously oppressed. I am quite content to rest the reputation of my ancestor upon the libellous evidence of his adversaries, or the showing of the Scottish historians, that he attempted to abridge the power of the nobles, *and succeeded* to such an extent as to secure his own murder.

To enter at length into such matters would, however, be to substitute my ancestor's biography for my own, and therefore it will only be necessary to abridge from Pinkerton a few interesting extracts relative to this romance of Scottish history.

"The new Earl of Mar, unconscious that his extreme elevation was an infallible step to the deepest ruin, continued to abuse his power, and that of his sovereign. The nobles beheld the places, *formerly given to their sons,* now sold (?) to Mar's followers. The prelates and other dignitaries of the church *sighed at the increase of simony!* &c. &c. In short, the whole honour and welfare of the king and kingdom were sacrificed on the domestic altar of this base and covetous minion!

"Some of the peers assembled, and consulted upon the means of delivering the realm from the disgrace and destruction inflicted by Cochran and the other royal favourites. A noble deputation had even been sent to the king, requesting that he would dismiss these pernicious councillors, and restore the confidence placed by his ancestors *in the loyalty of the nobility.* The answer of James was far from satisfactory, but the peers assented to delay, and dissembled till some decisive occasion should arise.

"The Scottish array, amounting to about fifty thousand, had crowded to the royal banner at Burrough-muir, near Edinburgh, whence they marched to Sontray and to Lauder, at which place they encamped between the church and the village. Cochran, Earl of Mar, conducted the artillery, and his presence and pomp were additional insults. On the morning after their arrival at Lauder, the peers assembled in a secret council, in the church, and deliberated upon their designs of revenge. The Earls of Angus, Argyle, Huntley, Orkney or Caithness, Crawford, the Lords Home, Fleming, Gray, Drummond, Hales, and Seton, are chiefly mentioned upon this occasion; and the discontent must have spread far when we find Evandale the chancellor, and some bishops united to the above names.

"In the course of the debate Gray took occasion to introduce an apologue: 'The mice consulted upon the means of deliverance from their tyrannic enemy the cat, and agreed that a bell should be suspended about her neck, to notify her approach and their danger; but what mouse has courage sufficient to fasten the bell?' 'I shall bell the cat,' exclaimed the impatience of Angus, in whom a current of the blood of Douglas flowed; and the homely times conferred upon him the appellation of Archibald Bell the Cat. It was concluded that the king *should be put in a gentle imprisonment* in the castle of Edinburgh, and that all his favourites should be instantly hanged over the bridge of Lauder.

"Cochran, ignorant of their designs, at length left the royal presence to proceed to the council. The earl was attended by three hundred men, armed with light battle-axes, and distinguished by his livery of white with black fillets. He was clothed in a riding cloak of black velvet, and wore a large chain of gold around his neck; his horn of the chase, or of battle, was adorned with gold and precious stones; and his helmet, overlaid with the same valuable metal, was borne before him. Approaching the door of the church, he commanded an attendant to knock with authority; and Sir Robert Douglas of Lochleven, who guarded the passage, inquiring the name, was answered, ''Tis I, the Earl of Mar.' Cochran and some of his friends were admitted. Angus advanced to him, and pulling the golden chain from his neck, said, 'A rope will become thee better;' while Douglas of Lochleven seized his hunting-horn, declaring that he had been too long a hunter of mischief. Rather astonished than alarmed, Cochran said: 'My lords, is it jest or earnest?' To which it was replied, 'It is good earnest, and so thou shalt find it, for thou and thy accomplices have too long abused our prince's favour; but no longer expect such advantage, for thou and thy followers shall now reap the deserved reward.'

"Having secured Mar, the lords dispatched some men-at-arms to the king's pavilion, conducted by two or three moderate leaders, who amused James while their followers seized the favourites. Sir William Roger, the English musician; Preston, a gentleman, Hommil, Torphichan, Leonard, and others, were instantly hanged over the bridge at Lauder. John Ramsay of Balmain having clasped the king's person, was alone spared. Cochran was now brought out, his hands bound with a rope, and thus conducted to the bridge, and hanged above his companions."

Even the privilege of being hanged with one of the silken cords of his pavilion was denied him; and his making such a request Pinkerton attributes to "weak pride," though it certainly looked more like "cool pride," which would not condescend to beg life, and only asked to die like a gentleman.

Much in the same spirit, but showing the abilities of the man, are the following extracts from "A Detection of the Falsehood, Abuse, and Misrepresentations in a late Libel, entitled, The Life of Sir Robert Cochran, Prime Minister in Scotland to James the Third."

"This COCHRAN, [Sir Robert] according to the greatest of the Scottish Writers, lived at a Time when a Faction in England made War on their lawful Sovereign, and imposed it on the King by Force of Arms, that he should bear the Name and Ensigns, or Badges of a King, but the Power of the Government should be in the Heads of their Faction, against which Violence and Tyranny the Queen drew the Sword for her Husband's (Henry the 6th) Deliverance with such Vigour and Success, as rescued him from his Enemies, slew their Chiefs in Battle, destroyed two Armies, gaining two compleat Victories; and even when Fortune deserted this masculine Princess, in her final Overthrow Six and thirty thousand men were slain before she lost the Field.

"These were the Times when Cochran became the Minion of the King of Scotland, who departing from the Counsels of his ancient Servants, and withdrawing Himself from the Nobility, chose mean and infamous Persons to be the Companions of his Pleasures, and the Advisers of his Reign.

"Of these one *Preston* was Chief, though born of a better Family than any of his Comrades, who abandoned himself to indulge the King's Humour in all Things. And Cochran came next, who, of a Builder was instantly made Courtier! History describes Him as a Man of great Bodily Strength, and of equal Impudence! who, making Himself known to the King by a Duel which He fought, was admitted at Court with great Expectations of Advancement. Having been employ'd in Matters of small Concern, which He performed with great Application, and insinuating Himself into the King's Favour by constant Assiduity, He became immediately advised with in the most important and the most intimate Councils of the Kingdom. Preston upon this made Him his Son, by giving him his Daughter in Marriage * . . . ."

To return to the descendants of the murdered minister : —

"This Allan (son of the murdered Robert), in 1452, is witness to the mortification which Robert Lord Lyle made to

---

* Buchanan speaks of Preston's alliance with Cochran as "one solicited to strengthen himself, which was not the cause but the effect of Cochran's power at Court . . . . Again, the immediate Acquisition of Crown Lands which rendered Cochran most odious, is highly spoken of, notwithstanding that he obtained a Grant of the Lands belonging to a Prince of the Blood, even the Revenue of an Earl! and by such Grants *outvied the Splendour of the ancient Nobility!* who beheld Persons of the meanest extraction eclipse them in Lustre! "

the abbot and conventual brethren of the monastery of Paisley, of the fishing on the river of Clyde, at the place called Crokatshot, for the help of their prayers to advance his spiritual estate, in which deed he is designated Allanus Cochran, Armiger, his father being then alive, and to whom he succeeded before the 1480. He married . . . . . . , daughter of . . . . . . , by whom he had Robert, a son, who was father of John Cochran of that Ilk, who immediately succeeded his grandfather upon his death.

"Which John, for some consideration I know not, obtained a licence from his sovereign Lord King James IV. under the Great Seal, impouring him to dispose of either his lands of Easter Cochran in Renfrewshire, or his lands of Pitfour in Perthshire. Accordingly, he alienated a part of his lands of Cochran to James Archbishop of Glasgow, Anno 1519; to which deed he appends his seal, the impression bearing *three Boars' Heads eraz'd*, and circumscribed *Sigillum Johannis de Cochran*. His wife was Elizabeth, daughter of John Simple of Fullwood, who bore him a son, John, who was served and retourned heir to his father on the 12th of May, 1539; he, dying in the 1557, left issue by Mary, his wife, daughter of Lindsay of Dunrod, *in Vicecomitatu de Renfrew*, a son,

"William, who succeeded him. In 1593, he erected from the foundation at Cochran, the ancient seat of his family, a very high tower of free-stone, and adorned it with large plantations; he marrying Margaret, daughter of Robert Montgomery of Skelmurly, *in Vicecomitatu de Air*, by Mary, his wife, daughter of Robert, Lord Semple, had a daughter Elizabeth, his sole heir.

"He wisely considering the proper way of supporting his family was to settle his daughter in his own time, and declining to marry her into a richer family than his son, he made a prudent and discreet match for her with Alexander Blair, a younger son of an ancient and genteel family in Airshire, whose ancestors had been seated in the country foresaid for many ages before, so that beside a noble alliance, and a competent patrimony, he yielded to change his name to Cochran, which was almost the only condition the old gentleman required. This Alexander, so taking upon him the surname of Cochran, was a virtuous and frugal man, and studied as much the good of the family as if he himself had been born the heir thereof. In 1622, he acquired the lands of Cowdoun with an intention to unite them to the ancient patrimonial inheritance of Cochran; but he afterwards sold them to Sir William, his second son, as a fund to provide his younger children; for, besides Sir John, his eldest son, he had six other sons, and two daughters:

" Sir William Cochran of Cowdoun.

" Alexander, a colonel in the king's service, in the wars of Ireland, which commenced, in 1641, with the murder of upwards of fifty thousand Scots and English by the native Irish.

" Hugh, author of the branch of Fergusly; he was a colonel, first under the renoun'd Gustavous Adolphus King of Sweden, and afterward to King Charles I. in the time of the Civil War in Ireland.   .

" Bryse, a colonel in the time of the Civil War, who lost his life in the king's service, Anno 1650.

" Captain Ochter Cochran.

" Gavin Cochran of Craigmure, was the seventh and youngest son.

" Elizabeth, married to John Lennox of Woodhead in Stirlingshire.

" Grisel, to Thomas Dunlop of Housle.

" Which Sir John, in the time of the unhappy Civil War in Britain, firmly adhered to the interest of King Charles I. and had a colonel's commission in the army. In the year 1644, he was sent ambassador to several princes to solicit their assistance in his Majesty's behalf, which he performed with such diligence and conduct, that in the treaty of peace which was set on foot betwixt the king and the Parliament of England and the Estates of Scotland, Anno 1646, he was, together with the Marquis of Huntly and Montrose, the Earls of Nithsdale, Crawfurd, Traquair, &c. proposed to be excepted from the king's pardon, which His Majesty generously refused. Upon the murder of the king, he attended King Charles II. into foreign parts, and in the 1650 was sent into Poland to crave aid of the Scots merchants there; but before his return the king and the Scots army were defeated at Worcester; he continuing with the king during his exile, dyed about the time of the Restoration, without issue; so that his next brother, Sir William, became his heir.

"Which Sir William was very carefully educated in grammar learning in his youth, whence he was removed to the university; where having applied himself indefatigably to his studies, and highly improved his natural endowments with academical learning, he removed from thence after he had taken the degree of Master of Arts, and studied our laws; in which profession he attained to an uncommon perfection. Soon after his entering on the stage of business, he became much famed for his prudent management and conduct, by which he acquired a fair estate, both in the shires of Renfrew and Air, for the last of which he had the honour to serve as a member in the Parliament, 1647, wherein his abilities were soon discovered by the great and leading men of the House, and he showed himself, thro' the course of the sitting of that Parliament, a good and even patriot, wholly intent upon the honour and safety of the king, whose interest he did visibly advance, and the welfare and tranquillity of the nation then in no small ferment."

On the visit of Charles I. to his Scottish dominions in 1641, for the purpose of allaying the hostile feelings which his arbitrary acts had there excited, Sir William Cochrane of Cowden had sufficient influence to be instrumental in reconciling the monarch and his angry subjects; together with sufficient substance and loyalty to minister to the necessities of his sovereign. For these and other services Sir William was at this time elevated to the peerage under the title of Lord

Cochrane of Cowden ; the gratitude of Charles, however, not being openly manifested until some years afterwards a prisoner in Carisbrook Castle.*

As this circumstance is, to the best of my knowledge, unique, and is at variance with the statements of some Scottish genealogists, who give the date of the letters-patent as at Scarborough, Dec. 27, 1647, an extract from the " Acts " of the Privy Council in Edinburgh, confirming the original patent, may be gratifying to the historian.

"*At Edinburgh, the 1st day of April*, 1648.

" The which day and year of our Lord, at his Majesty's Privy Council, John Earl of Crafurd and Lindsay produced a patent under his Majesty's Great Seal, dated at Carisbrook, the 26th day of December 1647 — by which his Majesty, considering the faithfulness and good affection of Sir William Cochran of Cowden towards his Majesty's service — and his Majesty, being willing, for his further encouragement to continue therein, to bestow some token of his royal favor on him, hath given and granted to the said Sir William Cochrane, and his heirs male lawfully begotten, the title and dignity of a Lord of Parliament within this kingdom, to be called in all time coming Lord Cochrane of Dundonald, and to have exercise, and enjoy all the privileges, liberties, and preeminences belonging thereto, &c. &c. In token whereof, Archibald Marquis of Argyll, President of the Council at

---

* That the peerage was considered to have been conferred in 1641, appears from a subsequent order of Charles II. for the elevation of Lord Cochrane to the earldom of Dundonald (see p. 22); but for some cause or other the making out of the patent had been neglected or omitted till 1647. It would almost seem that Charles, whilst a prisoner at Carisbrook had some presentiment of his approaching fate, and had hastened to remedy the neglect before it was too late.

this time deliberate—in the name of Lord Cochrane—received the same on his knees," &c. &c. — *Extractum de Libris Actorum.*

It is not my intention to dilate upon the course pursued by Lord Cochrane, in promoting the reconciliation of Charles and his hereditary liegemen. Suffice it to say that, whilst his lordship's predilections and services were in favour of the constitutional power of the king, he made a firm stand against his despotic tendencies, especially when meditating the subversion of the Scottish Church, under the guise of ecclesiastical reform.*

In the national struggle which ensued after the death of Charles I. Lord Cochrane was amongst the most active in raising troops to assert the right of Charles II. to the throne. The subjoined letter from that monarch, divested of its antique orthography, will show the nature of the services rendered.

### CHARLES R.

"Right trusty and well-beloved—we greet you well. We have seen your letter to the Duke of Hamilton, whom you give no encouragement; so hope that sometime you, with the horse raised upon the baronies of Ayr and Renfrew, shall soon be in arms.

"Having been engaged to give to General-Major Vandrosk the first regiment of horse raised within our kingdom of Scotland, we could not possibly break our promise to so deserving a person. But seeing your brother was appointed

---

* "Charles and Laud determined to force on the Scots the English Liturgy—or rather a liturgy which, whenever it differed from that of England, differed, in the judgment of all rigid Protestants, for the worse."—*Lord Macaulay.*

to have the command of one of the regiments of foot before they were converted into horse, he will now be disappointed, as likewise will Col. Cunninghame, of their expectations. We have, therefore, thought fit to desire you to shift your brother up to the army to us, and we do oblige ourselves to take him into our particular favor, and to give him the command of a regiment either of horse or foot.

" We likewise find you desire the removing of the garrison from Newark, but having advised twice with our Committee of Estate, we find it is not for the good of the service to remove the said garrison; but we are content that the strength be reduced to the number of threttie soldiers only.

" We shall desire that you would be assisted in hasting these levies, and continue in your barony all public despatch, so as you may be in continual receipt of our respects to you.

" So we bid you now heartily farewell, from our Camp Royal at Woodhend, the fifth of August, 1651.

" To our right trusty and well-beloved,
        the Lord Cocorane."

The preceding letter marks the dawn of that ingratitude towards his tried adherents of which Charles has been, not without reason, accused. Lord Cochrane's reward for raising " the first regiment of horse in Scotland " was the displacement of his brother from the command, in favour of a Dutchman ; notwithstanding that the whole expenditure had been borne by his lordship, whose fate it subsequently was that the Stuarts should draw largely upon resources which, to the injury of his descendants, his loyalty ungrudgingly supplied.

Passing over the defeat which followed, I select from others a letter addressed by Charles, when in exile, to Lord Cochrane, under the assumed name of " Lenos and Richmond ; " its purport being to show that the unfortunate royal family depended upon Lord Cochrane's management not only for advice, but, what was more to the purpose, for the means of subsistence.

"February 2nd, 1657.

"MY LORD,—I find myself very much obliged to your lordship by your great care of my dear son's interests and mine, and have seen your letter concerning the gentleman recommended for a commissioner, who, though a stranger to me—yet, since it is the opinion of your lordship that he be added to the number of the commissioners, I do in this, as in all other things, hearken to your lordship's advice; relying on your lordship's favour to me, and therefore do hereby invite him, if he will accept the trouble, with many thanks to your lordship and to him.

"I must further beseech of your lordship to intend the raising five thousand pounds upon Glasgow, and to labour the sale of Methuen and Killmorocate, both with all possible expedition.*

"I hope to have the happiness of seeing your lordship in these parts ere long, that I may have a larger conveniency of making my acknowledgments to your lordship for your eminent favour to

"Your lordship's most humble servant,

"C. R. LENOS and RICHMOND.

"For my Lord Cochrane."

Whether Lord Cochrane visited the exiled court or not, I have no documents to decide; nor is it at all material; these letters being adduced to show the nature of his connection with the Stuarts in their day of humiliation, which only appeared to add to his zeal for their welfare.

* This letter appears to mix up the affairs of Charles and the Duke, probably with a view to avert danger to Lord Cochrane, if intercepted.

The " son " alluded to in the preceding letter was the Duke of Monmouth *, for espousing whose cause, in the subsequent reign of James II., the Cochrane family suffered severely.

Soon after the Restoration in 1660, Lord Cochrane was sworn a privy councillor; and by his Majesty's special choice was constituted one of the Commissioners of the Treasury and Exchequer, which great and weighty employment, says Crawfurd, " he discharged with admirable prudence and integrity, to the general satisfaction of the whole nation. Increasing still more in wealth and honour, he acquired the lordship of Paisley, where he fixed his seat, and lived with great splendour and hospitality for many years. After the barbarous murder of the late king, his lordship contributed his best and hearty endeavours towards bringing home Charles II. to inherit the rightful possession of the throne of these realms; which, no doubt, was the cause, when Oliver Cromwell came to be called protector, why he fined my Lord Cochrane, among other royalists, in 5000l. sterling, by special ordinance of the Commonwealth of England, dated April 12th, 1654."

---

* " Charles, when a wanderer on the Continent, had fallen in at the Hague with Lucy Walters, a Welsh girl of great beauty, but of weak understanding. She became his mistress, and presented him with a son, upon whom he poured forth such an overflowing fondness as seemed hardly to belong to his cool and careless nature. Soon after the Restoration the young favourite made his appearance at Whitehall, where he was lodged in the palace and permitted to enjoy distinctions till then confined to princes of the blood royal." *Lord Macaulay.*

The following letters from the Dukes of Lenox and Monmouth are still in my possession, and from historic interest alone require no apology for their introduction in this place.

"London, Dec. 27, 1662.

"My Lord,—I received a discharge from your lordship, which being ill-drawn, I have forborne to sign it; but shall readily perform it so soon as it comes to my hands corrected by Mr. Graham.

"I must intreat of your lordship's endeavours to raise fifteen hundred pounds upon the two years' rent of Jyla and my other lands for the year 1661; with which I would desire your lordship to discharge the six hundred pounds you borrowed for me when I was at Edinburgh, and the seven hundred pounds I borrowed of Sir James Stuart at the same time. The rest to be returned to me, who am

"Your lordship's humble servant,

"Lenos and Richmond.

"For my Lord Cochrane."

"P.S.—I desire your lordship to excuse my own writing, for nothing but illness should make me make use of another."

"London, Feb. 26th, 1663.

"My Lord,—Give me leave to add this trouble to your lordship's favours, in desiring that you will be pleased to send me a full account of all you know of the condition of my affairs in Scotland. And wherein and how you conceive any part of my estate proper or casual may be better improved to my advantage, with your lordship's advice for the management thereof for the future. If you know of any grants made by me to any person in Scotland when I was there, which may be prejudicial to or on my estates, you will be pleased to acquaint me with it; for I am resolved to repose all my confidence upon your lordship's directions, and to take measures of all the management of my affairs from them.

" I shall wholly trust to your lordship, and therefore entreat you will not impart this to anybody, but conceal the request of

"Your lordship's very humble servant,

"LENOS and RICHMOND.

" For my Lord Cochrane."


"Whitehall, Aug. 25th, 1663.

"MY LORD,—I must desire your lordship to give yourself the trouble of sending me word how my engagements stand to my estate mortgaged in Scotland, that I may know whether it be convenient that the several persons to whom it is mortgaged should receive the profits of the lands mortgaged to them till both principal and interest is satisfied. Or whether it be convenient if one person, in the name of the rest, should receive the whole profits of the estate, and engage to pay all the debts, both principal and interest, in so many years, and then to return the estate to me again. I must beg your lordship's faithful advice in this, having found it so formerly. And, good my lord, let me know in how many years my estate will pay the debt upon it, both principal and interest. I cannot believe anybody will be so warm in my concerns as yourself, and therefore wholly repose this trust in you, desiring you to send me in writing a conveyance of my estate to yourself for the payment of the debt in the aforesaid years, with the return of the estate into my hands, who am, my lord,

"Your lordship's most obliged servant,

"LENOS and RICHMOND."


The following letter, written to Lord Cochrane after the removal of the Court to Oxford on account of the plague raging in London, will show the straits to which even the wealthiest of the Scottish nobility had been reduced.

"Oxford, November 11th, 1665.

"My Lord,—I had written to your lordship before this had I not an intention of coming to Scotland myself. But being now prevented by other affairs, I must desire your lordship to make all the possible speed that may be to return me five hundred pounds out of the thousand pounds that are due to me.

"My lord, *I never was in a greater strait in my life*, the plague having prevented my tenants' payment. If you ever did intend to oblige me, I am sure you could never have a better opportunity than making me a present payment.

"Good, my lord, do not fail me, who am,

"Your most humble servant,

RICHMOND and LENOS.

"For my Lord Cochrane."

"*P.S.*—My uncle Aubigny is very sick at Paris, and we expect to hear he is dead by every post,—the last letters assuring that he was past recovery."

"July 1666.

"My Lord,—I need not acquaint your lordship how great a confidence I have of your lordship's friendship and assistance. Having now sent Boreman into Scotland to attend and follow your lordship's directions, and my Lord Newburgh's, for the completing and settling the whole affairs of the Admiralty. If my Lord Macdonnel goes on in his intended bargain, I shall expect 6000l. to be paid and returned to me by Michaelmas. Please to remember the 100l. you reserved till Boreman's coming. I shall trouble your lordship with nothing more at present, but the assurance of being,

"Your lordship's very humble servant,

"RICHMOND and LENOS.

"For my Lord Cochrane."

"London, 18th Sept. 1666.

"My Lord,—Though I consider that 5000l. is too small a sum for so considerable and convenient an estate to my Lord

Macdonald, yet I am satisfied to be ruled by the market and the exigency of my own affairs, but especially by your lordship's judgment and kindness, of which I have had so good experience.

"My lord, the sad accident of fire which hath lately happened in London *hath almost ruined us all.* I must therefore earnestly entreat you to return me what money you have in your hands of. mine, with all possible speed, not knowing which way to turn myself at present, there being no such thing as money here. Pray, likewise hasten Boreman in returning what money is due to me on the prizes, in doing all which, you will very much oblige

"Your lordship's humble servant,

" RICHMOND and LENOS.

" For my Lord Cochrane, at Edinburgh."

I have purposely refrained from comment on these letters, as being foreign to the purpose of this introductory chapter, which is not to dilate on immaterial subjects, but simply to point out the connection of the Cochrane family with the Stuarts, and their faithful adherents. The subjoined, from the Duke of Monmouth, is also curious, as alluding to the disaster of invasion, in addition to those of plague and fire.

" June 28th, 1667.

" MY LORD,—So soon as I received your lordship's of the 26th of May I was commanded by the king for Harwich, and have ever since been so hurried about in this confusion upon the arrival of the Dutch, that I have not had time to answer your lordship, to whom I do acknowledge myself very much obliged for your care of my affairs; and if it lies in my power to acknowledge it otherwise than in words, your lordship shall ever find me really to be, my lord,

"Your lordship's real friend and servant,

" MONMOUTH and BUCCLEUCH.

" These for my Lord Cochrane."

c 3

On the 12th of May 1669, Lord Cochrane was created Earl of Dundonald. The annexed is His Majesty's order for the patent:—

"Our sovereign Lord, considering that it hath been always the ancient, constant, and worthy practice of all kings to confer titles and degrees of honour and dignity upon such of those subjects whose good services and worth have so deserved, and that his Majestie's father of blessed memory did, in the year 1641, dignify and confer upon his right trusty and well-beloved William Lord Cochrane, the title of Lord Cochrane. And now his Majesty—in consideration of his faithful services, and for the better encouragement of him and his family to continue in their constant and affectionate adhering to his interest and service for the future—being graciously pleased to confer a further mark of his royal favour upon him, doth therefore, of his royal and princely power, ordain a letter patent to be made and decreed under the great seal of his ancient kingdom of Scotland, in due form, making, constituting, and creating the said William Lord Cochrane, and his heirs male, which failing, the oldest heirs female, without division, already procreate or to be procreate, of the body of the said William Lord Cochrane, &c. &c. &c., to be called and designed now and for ever hereafter Earl of Dundonald, Lord Cochrane of Paisley and Ochiltree, &c. &c. (Then follow the usual technical formalities.)

"MAY IT PLEASE YOUR MAJESTY.—This contains your Majesty's warrant for a patent to be passed under the great seal of Scotland, for creating William Lord Cochrane Earl of Dundonald, Lord Cochrane of Paisley and Ochiltree, with power, &c. &c. &c. For subscription.

"LAUDERDAILL.'

"Sit supra scribitur,
"CHARLES R."

The subjoined letters from the Duke and Duchess of

Monmouth, the latter the heiress of Buccleuch*, are not without historical interest.

"Whitehall, May 2nd, 1671.

"My Lord,—This is expressly to beg your lordship's pardon, that I writ not to you by the person that brought you my commission concerning my lands, in which I was confident to put your lordship's and Lord Cochrane's names; being assured that neither yourself nor any of your family would deny me the favour of your assistance in the management of my estate, which I have now taken into my own possession, and hope to see the good effects of it.   I beseech your lordship to give my service and excuse to my Lord Cochrane, and tell him I hope he will be no worse a friend to me than you have been, who, I must acknowledge, have obliged me ever to be, my lord,

"Your very humble servant,
"Monmouth and Buccleuch.

"For Lord Dundonald."

"Whitehall, May 25, 1671.

"My Lord,—I know not how to express my thanks to your lordship for the trouble I have put upon you in your journey to Branxholme, where your presence hath been of that advantage to my affairs, as could not, without you, have been expected.   I thank your lordship most heartily for this and all other your kindnesses to me, and particularly your advice concerning Orkney, &c. and to refraine the signing of anything but what shall be most maturely advised by your lordship, and such other my friends to whose counsel and advice,

---

* "Monmouth was married while still in tender youth, to Anna Scott, heiress of the noble house of Buccleuch.  He took her name, and received with her hand possession of her ample domains.  The estate which he acquired by this match was popularly estimated at not less than 10,000l. a-year."—*Lord Macaulay.*

as always faithful to me, I shall firmly adhere, and constantly remain, my lord,

    " Your very affectionate friend and humble servant,

                     " MONMOUTH and BUCCLEUCH."

" For the Right Hon. the Earl of Dundonald."

                                   " Oct. 31, 1671.

" MY LORD, — Being very sensible of your constant care and industry to promote and advance all our interests in Scotland, and receiving daily demonstrations of your particular kindness and friendship to us, we are the more confident on all occasions to depend wholly upon you, for resolution in doubtful, and assistance in difficult cases, and do entreat your lordship to take them seriously into your consideration, and weighing all circumstances deal freely and candidly with us, and declare truly to us your opinion what you do conceive fit for us to do to extricate ourselves out of those dangers both we and our estate lie under.

" We are now both of us so near the time of our majority, and are told that it is very necessary for us to undertake a journey to Scotland this next spring. If your lordship be of the same judgment, we must (if possible) find out some expedient to effect it.

" My lord, we are informed that many of our late chamberlains are resolved to stand trial with us for 3000l. yet remaining in their hands upon the balance of their accounts, unless they may have such discharge as they please.

" We do, therefore, very earnestly recommend it to your lordship's care to proceed vigorously against them, not only for that, but also for the great waste and destruction they have made of the woods. A letter is also written to the Lord President Stair and the rest of the lords of the session's favour for a speedy dispatch of our concerns before them. We shall have the satisfaction that in the place where we have received so great obligations from your lordship and the rest of our friends—even there we shall express with much sincerity that we are, my lord,

" Your lordship's very affectionate and humble servants,
              " BUCCLEUCH and MONMOUTH.
              " ANNA BUCCLEUCH and MONMOUTH.

" For the Right Hon. the Earl of Dundonald."


                    " March 14th, 1674.

MY LORD, — The great assurance we have had of your affection and kindness to us, which upon all occasions you have given sufficient testimonies of in your adherence to and promoting our interest in Scotland, encourages us to entreat and, indeed, earnestlie to desire your continuance thereof, but especially at this time, when we find our tenants like to be ruined and undone by the severity of continued frost and snow. How mischievous the consequences thereof may be to us, we are not able at this distance to conjecture, only we have just reason to fear the worst.

" But we, depending very much if not solely upon your lordship's wisdom and good conduct at this juncture, and very well knowing how prevalent your countenance and authority will be among our tenants, and what encouragement they will receive from your presence, must needs desire and entreat your lordship that you will not fail to be at the next land settling, for it is your discretion and prudence that shall be our guide and measure in the regulation of our own interests, or that of any of our tenants who shall be held fit objects of our consideration and favour in so general a calamity, if they be recommended by your lordship unto, my lord,

    " Your lordship's most affectionate friends and servants,
              " BUCCLEUCH and MONMOUTH.
              " ANNA BUCCLEUCH and MONMOUTH.

" For Lord Dundonald."

"September 29th, 1674.

"My Lord,—Upon all occasions my wife and I do receive new testimonies and proofs of your continued kindness to us, and of your unwearied care and industry to do all good offices which may any wise conduce to our profit and advantage. And, in truth, the great pains you have taken about our affairs, and the trouble you took upon you of an inconvenient journey to be at our land settling, are sufficient assurances of your zeal and affection for our welfare and prosperity, for which we owe you a particular acknowledgment. And I do assure your lordship, I am so extremely sensible of these and all other the kindnesses which you have done for us, that it shall never be my fault if I do not make it appear how much I am, my lord,

"Your lordship's most affectionate friend and servant,
"BUCCLEUCH and MONMOUTH.
"For Lord Dundonald."

"Whitehall, March 19th, 1676.

"My Lord,—We are truly sorry to understand by your letter that you are unable to ride by reason of your age and weakness, and that you cannot go all the way in your coach to our land settling. We know very well, and have had long and great experience, how useful you have been in that affair for many years together; and we may have just reason to fear that we may suffer very much by your absence from that service, so many of our lands lying at this time waste. The tenants will be apt to be discouraged, when they want your countenance to whom they are so well known. But, my lord, we do not think it reasonable to press you with arguments to undertake anything, how necessary soever it may be for our service, if it be in the least prejudicial to your health and safety.

"Therefore, if your infirmities cannot well dispense with your own going that journey, we do entreat your lordship to prevail with your son, my Lord Cochrane, to supply your place. For we are very sure that there is not any one related to you, but will have a great influence on our tenants; and, next to yourself, we can desire none more considerable than your son.

" We need not tell you how much the present necessity of our affairs requires all the prudence, all the countenance and authority, and all the diligence of ourselves, and of my lords, our commissioners, to bring our estate out of that waste, ruinous, and scandalous condition under which it hath lain, and we do know that your lordship will contribute as much pains, and be as instrumental to bring this to pass as any person whatsover.   And in this assurance we do subscribe ourselves, as in truth we are, my lord,

" Your lordship's most affectionate friends and servants,
" BUCCLEUCH and MONMOUTH.
" ANNA BUCCLEUCH and MONMOUTH.
" For Lord Dundonald."

The Earl of Dundonald was subsequently appointed by James the Second one of the Privy Council of Scotland. As the place from which the patent was dated, viz. Hounslow Heath, is of historical significance, I shall give the document entire :—

" JAMES R.

"Right trusty and right entirely-beloved cousin and council-lor !  Right trusty and right well-beloved cousin and councillor !  Right trusty and entirely-beloved cousins and councillors !  Right trusty and right well-beloved cousins and councillors !  Right trusty and well-beloved cousins and councillors !  Right trusty and well-beloved councillors, and trusty and well-beloved councillors !

" We greet you well.

" Whereas we are fully satisfied of the loyalty, abilities, and dutiful affection to our service, of our right trusty and well-beloved Earl of Dundonald, we have therefore thought fit to add him to our Privy Council of that our ancient kingdom, and do authorise and require you to admit him accordingly.

"And we do hereby dispense with him from taking the test, oath of allegiance, or any other oath, except that of Privy Councillor only. For doing whereof this shall be your warrant, and to him a full and ample security.

"Given at our camp on Hounslow Heath, the 10th day of June 1686, and of our reign the second year.

"By His Majesty's command,

"MELFORT."

In the subsequent rebellions of Argyle and Monmouth the Cochranes again suffered severely: John, the second son of the Earl of Dundonald, being deeply implicated therein; and only escaping with his life by the earl satisfying, first, the greed of James the Second's popish priests, and secondly, that of James himself.

The annexed extracts from Burnet will show all that needs be said on this head :—

"Cochran, another of those who had been concerned in this treaty [as to an insurrection in Scotland], was complained of, as having talked very freely of the duke's government of Scotland. Upon which the Scottish secretary sent a note to him, desiring him to come to him; for it was intended only to give him a reprimand, and to have ordered him to go to Scotland. But he knew his own secret; so he left his lodgings, and got beyond sea. This shewed the court had not yet got full evidence, otherwise he would have been taken up, as well as others were."—Vol. i. folio, p. 548.

"The deliberations in Holland, among the English and Scotch that fled thither, came to ripen faster than was expected. Lord Argile had been quiet ever since the disappointment in the year eighty-three. He had lived for most part in Frizeland, but came oft to Amsterdam, and met with the rest of his countrymen that lay concealed there; the chief of whom were the Lord Melvill, Sir Patrick Hume, and Sir John Cochran. [The first of these (Melvill) was a fearful and mean-spirited man, a zealous presbyterian, but more zealous in preserving his person and estate. Hume was a hot and eager man, full of passion and resentment; and instead of minding the business then in hand, he was always forming schemes about the modelling of matters, when they should prevail, in which he was so earnest, that he fell into perpetual disputes and quarrels about it; Cochran was more tractable.*] With these Lord Argile communicated all the advices that were sent to him."—On margin, "Argile designed to invade Scotland."—Vol. iii. 27; fol. vol. i. 632.

Argile landed in the Isle of Bute with his adherents. "He had left his arms in a castle, with such a guard as he could spare; but they were routed by a party of the king's forces. And with this he lost both heart and hope. And then, apprehending that all was gone, he put himself in a disguise, and had almost escaped; but he was taken. A body of gentlemen that had followed him stood better to it, and forced their way through, so that the greater part of them escaped. Some of these were taken; the chief of them were Sir John Cochran, Ailoffe, and Rumbold. These last two were Englishmen; but I knew not upon what motive it was that they chose rather to run fortunes with Argile than with the Duke of Monmouth. Thus was this rebellion brought to a speedy end, with the effusion of very little blood."—Vol. i. fol. p. 629.

"Cochran had a rich father, the Earl of Dundonald, and he offered the priests 5000l. to save his son. They wanted a stock of money for managing their designs, so they interposed so effectually that the bargain was made. But to

* Original note.

cover it, Cochran petitioned the council that he might be
sent to the king; for he had some secrets of great importance
which were not fit to be communicated to any but to the king
himself.  He was upon that brought up to London; and
after he had been for some time in private with the king,
the matters he had discovered were said to be of such importance, that in consideration of that the king pardoned
him.  It was said he had discovered all their negotiations
with the Elector of Brandenburg and the Prince of Orange.
But this was a pretence only, given out to conceal the bargain; for the prince told me he had never once seen him.
The secret of this came to be known soon after."—Vol. i.
fol. 634.

Lord Macaulay's account of the same event as regarded my ancestor, for it is from this Sir John Cochrane that the present branch of our family is descended,
will complete all which is necessary to be alluded to in
this place.

"With Hume (Sir Patrick) was connected another Scottish
exile of great note, Sir John Cochrane, second son of the
Earl of Dundonald.  The great question was, whether the
Highlands or the Lowlands should be the seat of war.  The
Earl (Argyle) wished to establish his authority over his own
domains, and to take possession of the ancient seat of his
family, at Inverary.  But Hume and Cochrane were impracticable, seeing that amongst his own mountains and lakes,
and at the head of an army of his own tribe, he would be able
to bear down their opposition, and to exercise the full authority of a general.  They said that the Campbells took up
arms neither for liberty nor for the Church of God, but for
Mac Callum More alone.  Cochrane declared he would go to
Ayrshire, if he went by himself, and with nothing but a pitch-
fork in his hand.  Argyle, after long resistance, consented,
and Cochrane and Hume were at the head of a force to invade
the Lowlands.

" Ayrshire was Cochrane's object, and the coast was guarded
by English frigates.  A party of militia lay at Greenock, but
Cochrane, who wanted provisions, was determined to land.
Hume objected, but Cochrane was peremptory.  Cochrane
entered Greenock, and procured a supply of meal, but found
no disposition to insurrection.

" Cochrane, having found it impossible to raise the population on the south of the Clyde, rejoined Argyle in Bute.  The
Earl again proposed to make an attempt on Inverary, and
again encountered pertinacious opposition.  The seamen sided
with Hume and Cochrane.  The Highlanders were absolutely
at the command of their chieftain.

*     *     *     *     *     *

" Cochrane was taken and sent to London . . . . . He held
amongst the Scotch rebels the same rank which had been
held by Grey in the West of England.  That Cochrane should
be forgiven by a prince vindictive beyond all example seemed
incredible.  But Cochrane was the younger son of a rich
family; it was, therefore, only by sparing him *that money
could be made out of him.*  His father, Lord Dundonald,
offered a bribe to the priests of the royal household, and a
pardon was granted."

The history of the succeeding Earls of Dundonald,
down to the failure of issue in the first branch, is thus
detailed by Crawfurd.

" William, first Earl of Dundonald, married Euphemie,
daughter of Sir William Scot of Ardross, *in comitatu de Fife,*
by whom he had two sons and a daughter.

" 1. William Lord Cochran, who dyed in the flower of his
Age, Anno 1680, leaving Issue by the Lady Catherine his
Wife, Daughter of John Earl of Cassils, John who succeeded
his Grand-father in the Honour, William Cochran, of Kil-
maronock, a Member of Parliament for the Burgh of Wigtoun,
and the other towns in that District and one of the Commissioners for keeping her Majesty's Signet, Sir Alexander

Erskin, Lord Lyon, and John Pringle, of Haining, being joined in Commission with him. He married Grisel, Daughter of James, second Marquis of Montrose, and has issue; Thomas Cochran of Polkely, third Son, dyed without children; Alexander Cochran, of Bonshaw, the youngest; also three Daughters; 1st. Margaret, married to Alexander Earl of Eglintoun. 2nd. Helen, to John Earl of Sutherland. 3rd. Jean, to John Viscount of Dundee, and afterward to William Viscount of Kilsyth.

"2nd. son, Sir John Cochran of Ochiltree, in Air-shire, Likewise a Daughter Grisel, married to George Lord Ross.

"This Earl gave way to Nature in the spring of the Year 1686, and was by his own Direction interr'd in the Paroch Church of Dundonald, without any Funeral Monument, but upon his Escutcheon I find the Arms of these noble and ancient Families.

"PATERNAL SIDE.

"Cochran of that Ilk.
"Lord Semple.
"Cunningham of Glengarnock.
"Lord Cairlyle of Torthorald.

"MATERNAL SIDE.

"Cochran of that Ilk.
"Montgomery of Skelmurly.
"Lindsay of Dunrod.
"Lord Semple.

"To William Earl of Dundonald succeeded John his Grandson and Heir, a nobleman of great Goodness and excellent Parts; he dyed in the prime of his Years, Anno 1691, regrated by all those who knew him, leaving Issue by the Lady Susanna his Wife, Daughter of William Duke of Hamilton, two Sons, William who succeeded in the Honours, but dyed unmarried the 19th of November 1705. And

"John married Anne Daughter of Charles Earl of Dun-

more, a Lady who wanted no Vertue to make her an accep-
table Wife; she dyed in 1711, universally lamented, whose
Conduct in all Conditions of Life render'd her Loss a lasting
Grief to her Relations, he had by her a Son and three
Daughters.

"William Lord Cochran,
" Lady Anne,
" Lady Catherine,
" Lady Susanne.

### " ARMS.

"Argent, a chiveron; Gules, betwixt three Boars Heads,
Azure, supported by two Ratch Hounds of the first; Crest, a
Horse, Argent, Motto, Virtute et Labore."

# CHAPTER I.

### MY BOYHOOD, AND ENTRANCE INTO THE NAVY.

YOUNGER BRANCH SUCCEEDS TO EARLDOM. — ALIENATION OF FAMILY
ESTATES. — MY FATHER'S SCIENTIFIC PURSUITS. — HIS RUINOUS MA-
NUFACTURING PROJECTS.— A NEGLECTED DISCOVERY.—COMMUNICATED
TO JAMES WATT. — LORD DUNDONALD'S AGRICULTURAL WORKS STILL
HELD IN ESTIMATION. — EARLY REMINISCENCES. — MY FIRST VISIT
TO LONDON. — MY FATHER DESTINES ME FOR THE ARMY. — A COM-
MISSION PROCURED.— MY AVERSION TO THE MILITARY PROFESSION.—
OUR RETURN TO SCOTLAND.—I AM PERMITTED TO ENTER THE NAVY.

MY birth is recorded as having taken place on the
14th of December 1775, at Annsfield in Lanarkshire.
My father was Archibald, ninth Earl of Dundonald;
my mother, Anna Gilchrist, daughter of Captain Gilchrist, a distinguished officer of the Royal Navy.*

My father was descended from John, the younger son
of the first earl—noticed in the introductory chapter as the
compatriot of Argyll. On default of issue in the elder
branch of the family the title devolved on my grand-

* One action of my maternal grandfather is worthy of record.
On March 28th 1758, upwards of a century ago, he commanded the
*Southampton*, 32, and when in company with the *Melampe*, 24,
Captain Hotham, fell in with two French frigates off Yarmouth.
The *Melampe*, being the faster sailer, came up first, and was so dis-
abled that she fell astern before the *Southampton* got within range.
On the *Melampe* falling off, one of the frigates made sail, and got
away. The *Southampton* then engaged the other, and after a six
hours' contest, carried on with equal bravery on both sides, she

father, Thomas, who married the daughter of Archibald Stuart, Esq., of Torrence, in Lanarkshire, and had issue one daughter and twelve sons, the most distinguished amongst whom, in a public capacity, was Admiral the Honourable Sir Alexander, father of the present Admiral Sir Thomas Cochrane.*

Some of my father's earlier years were spent in the Navy, in which he became acting lieutenant. A cruise on the coast of Guinea gave him a distaste for

boarded. and captured the *Danaë*, of 40 guns and 340 men, com- manded by one of the bravest officers in the French navy.

The loss of the *Danaë* was her first and second captains, and eighty men killed. The *Southampton* had only one killed and ten wounded; amongst whom was my grandfather, whose shoulder was shattered by a grape-shot.

* Thomas Cochrane, eighth Earl of Dundonald, was a major in the army, and M.P. for Renfrewshire. He died in 1778, at the age of eighty-seven, and was married, first, to Elizabeth, daughter of James Kerr, Esq. of Moris Town, Berwickshire, by whom he had two children, Thomas, who died young, and a daughter, Grizel, who died unmarried.

By his second countess, he had issue—1. Argyle, died in infancy; 2. Archibald, my father, died in 1823; 3. Charles, a colonel in the army, killed in 1781, at York Town, in Virginia, during the American war of Independence; 4. John, died in 1802; 5. James Athol, rector of Mansfield in Yorkshire; 6. Basil, in the civil ser- vice of the East India Company; 7. and 8. Thomas and George, died young; 9. Alexander Forrester, Knight of the Bath, and rear- admiral in the navy; 10. ———, died young; 11. George Au- gustus Frederick, M.P. for Grampound; 12. Andrew, also M.P. for Grampound, who, on his marriage, assumed the surname of John- stone, and was the father of the present dowager Lady Napier, relict of the late Lord Napier; 13. Elizabeth, married to Patrick Heron, Esq. of Heron.

The issue of my father, Archibald, ninth Earl of Dundonald, was as follows: 1. myself; 2. a daughter, died young ; 3. James, died the naval profession, which, in after years, postponed my entrance therein far beyond the usual period.  On his return home he quitted the navy for a commission in the army, which was, after a time, also relinquished.

Of our once extensive ancestral domains I never inherited a foot.  In the course of a century, and before the title descended to our branch, nearly the whole of the family estates had been alienated by losses incurred in support of one generation of the Stuarts, rebellion against another, and mortgages, or other equally destructive process, — the consequence of both.  A remnant may latterly have fallen into other hands from my father's negligence in not looking after it, and his unentailed estates were absorbed by expensive scientific pursuits presently to be noticed.  So that my outset in life was that of heir to a peerage, without other expectations than those arising from my own exertions.

My father's day was that of Cavendish, Black, Priestley, Watt, and others, now become historical as the forerunners of modern practical science.  Imbued with like spirit, and in intimate communication with these distinguished men, he emulated their example with no mean success, as the philosophical records of that period testify.  But whilst they prudently confined their attention to their laboratories, my father's sanguine expectations of retrieving the family estates

young; 4. Basil, lieutenant-colonel of the 36th Regiment; 5. William Erskine, major in the 15th Light Dragoons, my only surviving brother; 6. Archibald, captain in the Royal Navy; 7. Charles, died young.

by his discoveries led him to embark in a multitude of manufacturing projects. The motive was excellent; but his pecuniary means being incommensurate with the magnitude of his transactions, its object was frustrated, and our remaining patrimony melted like the flux in his crucibles; his scientific knowledge, as often happens, being unaccompanied by the self-knowledge which would have taught him that he was not, either by habit or inclination, a " man of business." Many who were so, knew how to profit by his inventions without the trouble of discovery, whilst their originator was occupied in developing new practical facts to be turned to their advantage, and his consequent loss.

An enumeration of some of my father's manufacturing transactions, extensively and simultaneously carried on, will leave no doubt as to their failure in a pecuniary sense. First, the preparation of soda from common salt, as a substitute for *barilla*,—till then the only alkali available for soap and glass making. Secondly, a manufactory for improvement in the production of *alumina*, as a mordant for silk and calico printers. Thirdly, an establishment for preparing British gum as a substitute for *gum Senegal*, these products being in use amongst calico-printers to the present day; the latter especially being at that distant period of great utility, as the foreign gum was scarce and expensive. A fourth manufactory had for its object the preparation of *sal ammoniac*. At a fifth was carried on the manufacture of *white lead*, by a process then new to productive science. A sixth establishment, on a ruinous scale as compared with his resources, was for a new process of extracting tar and other products from pit-coal; the former as an effective agent in protecting timber from decay, whilst the refuse coke was in request amongst ironfounders, whose previous operations for its manufacture were wasteful and unsatisfactory.*

After this enumeration, it is unnecessary to dilate on its ruinous results. It is simply the old adage of " too many irons in the fire." One by one, his inventions fell into other hands, some by fair sale, but most of them by piracy, when it became known that he had nothing left wherewith to maintain his rights. In short, with seven children to provide for, he found himself a ruined man.

In the present state of manufacturing science, by which the above objects are accomplished through improved means, the mention of such matters may, at first sight, appear unnecessary. Yet, seventy years ago they bore the same relation to the manufacturing processes of our time as at that period did the crude attempts at the steam engine to its modern perfection. In this point of view—

* Whilst serving on the west coast of Africa, my father remarked the destructive ravages made on ships' bottoms by worms, and, from his chemical knowledge, it occurred to him that an extract from pit-coal, in the form of tar, might be employed as a preventive of the evil. On his return home, the experiment was tried, and found to answer perfectly. Notwithstanding the subsequent refusal of the Admiralty to make use of his preservative, it was at once adopted by the Dutch and elsewhere in the North, and in the case of small coasting vessels is to this day used in our own country, as less expensive than coppering. Had not the coppering of vessels become common shortly afterwards, the discovery must have proved of incalculable value.

which is the true one—reference to my father's patents, though now superseded by improvements, will fairly entitle him to no mean place amongst other inventors of his day, who deservedly rank as benefactors to their country.

One of my father's scientific achievements must not be passed over. Cavendish had some time previously ascertained the existence of hydrogen. Priestley had become acquainted with its inflammable character ; but the Earl of Dundonald may fairly lay claim to the practical application of its illuminating power in a carburetted form.

In prosecution of his coal-tar patent; my father went to reside at the family estate of Culross Abbey, the better to superintend the works on his own collieries, as well as others on the adjoining estates of Valleyfield and Kincardine. In addition to these works, an experimental tar-kiln was erected near the Abbey, and here coal-gas became accidentally employed in illumination. Having noticed the inflammable nature of a vapour arising during the distillation of tar, the Earl, by way of experiment, fitted a gun-barrel to the eduction pipe leading from the condenser. On applying fire to the muzzle, a vivid light blazed forth across the waters of the Frith, becoming, as was afterwards ascertained, distinctly visible on the opposite shore.

Strangely enough, though quick in appreciating a new fact, Lord Dundonald lightly passed over the only practical product which might have realised his expectations of retrieving the dilapidated fortunes of our house ; considering tar and coke to constitute the legitimate objects of his experiments, and regarding the illuminating property of gas merely as a curious natural phenomenon. Like Columbus, he had the egg before him, but, unlike Columbus, he did not hit upon the right method of setting it on end.

The incident just narrated took place about the year 1782, and the circumstances attending it are the more vividly impressed on my memory from an event which occurred during a subsequent journey with my father to London. On our way we paid a visit to James Watt, then residing at Handsworth, near Birmingham, and amongst other scientific subjects discussed during our stay were the various products of coal, including the gaslight phenomenon of the Culross Abbey tar-kiln. This gave rise to some interesting conversation, which, however, ended without further result.

Many years afterwards, Mr. Murdoch, then one of Watt's assistants at Soho, applied coal-gas to the illumination of that establishment, though even with this practical demonstration its adoption for purposes of general public utility did not keep pace with the importance of the fact thus successfully developed, until, by the persevering endeavours of Mr. Winsor, its advantages overcame prejudice.*

---

* A paper on the " Utility and Advantages of Gas-lights," written by Mr. Murdoch, and transmitted by him to Sir Joseph Banks, was read before the Royal Society on the 25th of February 1808, detailing the lighting of Messrs. Phillips and Lee's manufactory at Manchester, and describing the process of gas-manufacture. In this paper Mr. Murdoch alludes to a memorial presented by Mr. Winsor to George III., pointing out the utility of gas for lighting the public streets, &c.

It is no detraction from Mr. Murdoch's merit of having been the first to turn coal-gas to useful account, to infer that Watt might, at some period during the interval, have narrated to him the incident just mentioned, and that the fact accidentally developed by my father had thus become the subject of long and careful experiment; for this must have been the case before the complete achievement shone forth in perfection. Mr. Murdoch, so far as I am aware, never laid claim to a discovery of the illuminating property of coal-gas, but to its useful application only, to which his right is indisputable.   As it is not generally known to whom an earlier practical appreciation of gas-light was in reality due, I have placed these facts on record.

One notice more of my father's investigations may be permissible.   To Sir Humphry Davy is usually ascribed the honour of first pointing out the relation between Agriculture and Chemistry.   Reference to a work published in 1795, entitled "*A Treatise showing the intimate connection between Agriculture and Chemistry, by the* EARL OF DUNDONALD," will decide the priority. Davy's work may in a theoretical point of view surpass that of my father, inasmuch as the analytical chemical science of a more modern date is more minute than that of the last century; but in point of patient investigation from countless practical experiments, my father's work is more than equal to that of his distinguished successor in the same field, and is, indeed, held in no small estimation at the present time.*

* I may mention three points contained in this work, to the discovery of which claim has been laid by modern writers, viz. the

The reader will readily pardon me for thus devoting a few pages by way of a tribute to a parent, whose memory still exists amongst my most cherished recollections; even though his discoveries, now of national utility, ruined him, and deprived his posterity of their remaining paternal inheritance.

During boyhood, we had the misfortune to lose our mother *, and as our domestic fortunes were even then at a low ebb, great difficulty was experienced in providing us with the means of education—four of us being then at an age to profit by more ample opportunities. In this emergency, temporary assistance was volunteered by Mr. Rolland, the minister of Culross, who thus evinced his gratitude for favours received in the more auspicious days of the family. Highly as was the offer appreciated, family pride prevented our reaping from it the advantage contemplated by a learned and truly excellent man.

Perceiving our education imperilled, the devotedness of my maternal grandmother, Mrs. Gilchrist, prompted her to apply her small income to the exigencies of her grandchildren. By the aid thus opportunely afforded,

malting of grain for the purpose of feeding cattle, the converting of peat moss into good soil, and the benefit of a judicious use of salt refuse as a manure; the latter suggestion being made by my father in a treatise published in 1785, nearly seventy-five years ago. Other discoveries might be enumerated, but from those adduced it will be seen that most of my father's experiments were far in advance of the age in which he lived. With slight modifications only not a few rank as modern discoveries, though little more than plagiarisms without acknowledgment.

* Anna, Countess of Dundonald, died at Brompton, on the 13th of November 1784.

a tutor was provided, of whom my most vivid recollection is a stinging box on the ear, in reply to a query as to the difference between an interjection and a conjunction; this solution of the difficulty effectually repressing further philological inquiry on my part.

We were, after a time, temporarily provided with a French tutor, a Monsieur Durand, who, being a Papist, was regarded with no complacent eye by our not very tolerant Presbyterian neighbours. I recollect this gentleman getting into a scrape, which, but for my father's countenance, might have ended in a Kirk Session.

As a matter of course, Monsieur Durand did not attend church. On one side of the churchyard was the Culross Abbey cherry-garden, full of fine fruit, of which he was very fond, as were also the magpies which swarmed in the district. One Sunday, whilst the people were at church, the magpies, aware no doubt of their advantage, made a vigorous onslaught on the cherries—provoking the Frenchman, who was on the watch, to open fire on the intruders, from a fowling-piece. The effect of this reached farther than the magpies. To fire a gun on the Sabbath was an abomination which could only have emanated from a disciple of the Scarlet Lady, and neither before nor after did I witness such a hubbub in the parish. Whatever pains and penalties were to be found in Scottish church law were eagerly demanded for Monsieur Durand's benefit, and it was only by my father's influence that he was permitted to escape the threatened martyrdom. Annoyed at the ill-feeling thus created, he relinquished his engagement before we had acquired the rudiments of the French language.

Even this inadequate tuition was abruptly ended by my father taking me with him to London. His object in visiting the metropolis, was to induce the Government to make use of coal-tar for protecting the bottoms of inferior ships of war—for in those days copper sheathing was unknown. The best substitute—by no means a general one—was to drive large-headed iron nails over the whole ship's bottom, which had thus the appearance of being "hobnailed." Even this indifferent covering was accorded to superior vessels only, the smaller class being entirely left to the ravages of the worm. It was for the protection of these small vessels that my father hoped to get his application adopted, and there is no doubt of the benefit which would have resulted had the experiment been permitted.

But this was an innovation, and the Board of Admiralty being then, as too often since, opposed to everything inconsistent with ancient routine, refused to entertain his proposal. It was only by means of political influence that he at length induced the Navy Board to permit him, at his own expense, to cover with his composition one side of the buoy at the Nore. The result was satisfactory, but he was not allowed to repeat the process. As compared with the exposure at that time of ships' bottoms to rapid destruction, without any effort to protect them, my father's plan was even a greater improvement than is the modern substitution of copper-sheathing for the "hobnail" surface which it tardily superseded.

Failing to induce the Government to protect their ships of war, he applied to the mercantile interest,

but with no better success.   I remember going with
my father to Limehouse, in the hope of inducing a
large shipbuilder there to patronise his composition ;
but the shipbuilder had even a greater horror of innovation than the Admiralty authorities.   His reply was
remarkable.   " My Lord," said he, " we live by repairing
ships as well as by building them, and the worm is our
best friend.   Rather than use your preparation, I would
cover ships' bottoms with honey to attract worms ! "

Foiled in London, my father set on foot agencies at
the outports, in the hope of inducing provincial ship-
builders to adopt his preservative.   Prejudice, however,
was not confined to the metropolis, and the objection
of the Limehouse man was everywhere encountered.
Neither they, nor any artisans in wood, would patronise
a plan to render their work durable.

Unsuccessful everywhere, my father turned his attention to myself.   My destination was originally the army,
whether accordant with my taste or not—for he was not
one of those who considered it necessary to consult the
inclinations of his children in the choice of a profession;
but rather how he could best bring family influence to
bear upon their future interests.   Unfortunately for his
passive obedience theory, my *penchant* was for the sea ;
any hint, however, to this effect was peremptorily
silenced by parental authority, against which it was useless to contend.

My uncle, the Hon. Captain, afterwards Admiral,
Sir Alexander Cochrane, had, the sagacity to perceive, that as inclination became more rooted with
my growth, passive obedience on this point might

one day come to an end. Still further, he was kind
enough to provide against such contingency, should it
arise. Unknown to my father, he had entered my
name on the books of various vessels under his command ; so that, nominally, I had formed part of the
complement of the *Vesuvius, Carolina, La Sophie,* and
*Hind ;* the object—common in those days—being, to
give me a few years' standing in the service, should it
become my profession in reality.

Having, however, a relative in the army, who possessed influence at the Horse Guards, a military com-    ✗
mission was also procured for me; so that I had
simultaneously the honour of being an officer in his
Majesty's 104th Regiment, and a nominal seaman on
board my uncle's ship.

By way of initiation into the mysteries of the military
profession, I was placed under the tuition of an old
sergeant, whose first lessons well accorded with his instructions, not to pay attention to my foibles. My hair,
cherished with boyish pride, was formally cut, and
plastered back with a vile composition of candle-grease
and flour, to which was added the torture incident to
the cultivation of an incipient *queue.* My neck, from
childhood open to the lowland breeze, was encased in
an inflexible leathern collar or stock, selected according
to my preceptor's notions of military propriety ; these
almost verging on strangulation. A blue semi-military
tunic, with red collar and cuffs, in imitation of the
Windsor uniform, was provided, and to complete the
*tout ensemble,* my father, who was a determined Whig
partisan, insisted on my wearing yellow waistcoat and

breeches; yellow being the Whig colour, of which I was admonished never to be ashamed. A more certain mode of calling into action the dormant obstinacy of a sensitive, high-spirited lad, could not have been devised than that of converting him into a caricature, hateful to himself, and ridiculous to others.

As may be imagined, my costume was calculated to attract attention, the more so from being accompanied by a stature beyond my years. Passing one day near the Duke of Northumberland's palace at Charing-Cross, I was beset by a troop of ragged boys, evidently bent on amusing themselves at the expense of my personal appearance, and, in their peculiar slang, indulging in comments thereon far more critical than complimentary.

Stung to the quick, I made my escape from them, and rushing home, begged my father to let me go to sea with my uncle, in order to save me from the degradation of floured head, pigtail, and yellow breeches. This burst of despair aroused the indignation of the parent and the Whig, and the reply was a sound cuffing. Remonstrance was useless; but my dislike to everything military became confirmed; and the events of that day certainly cost His Majesty's 104th Regiment an officer, notwithstanding that my military training proceeded with redoubled severity.

At this juncture, my father's circumstances became somewhat improved by a second marriage*, so that my

---

* My father's second countess was Mary, daughter of Samuel Raymond, Esq., and relict of the Rev. Mr. Mayne. This lady died, without issue, in December 1808.

brother Basil and myself were sent to Mr. Chauvet's academy in Kensington Square, in order to perfect our military education—Basil, like myself, being destined for the army. At this excellent school we only remained six months; for with slightly increased resources my father resumed his ruinous manufacturing pursuits, so that we were compelled by the "*res angusta domi*" to return to Scotland.*

Four years and a half were now wasted without further attempt to secure for us any regular training. We had, however, during the short advantage enjoyed at Kensington, studied diligently, and were thus enabled to make some progress by self-tuition, our tutor's acquirements extending only to teaching the rudiments to the younger branches of the family. Knowing that my future career depended on my own efforts, and more than ever determined not to take up my military commission, I worked assiduously at the meagre elements of know-

* Lord Dundonald about this time entered upon a series of experiments which, as usual, were productive of more benefit to his country than himself, viz. an improved mode of preparing hemp and flax for the manufacture of sailcloth. For this he subsequently took out a patent, and submitted his process, together with samples of the manufacture, to the Admiralty. So sensible was the Board of the advantages of the plan, that it was subsequently stipulated in every contract that hemp should be steeped and boiled in the way recommended in his lordship's patent. Since that period, the use of sailcloth so manufactured has become general. Formerly, it was sold by weight, the worthless material of which it was composed being saturated with a composition of flour and whitening, so that the first shower of rain on a new sail completely white-washed the decks. Of so flimsy a nature were the sails when this composition was washed out, that I have taken an observation of the sun through the fore-topsail, and brought it to a horizon through the foresail.

ledge within my reach, in the hope that by unremitting industry my father might be convinced that opposition to his views was no idle whim, but the result of conviction that I should not excel in an obnoxious profession.

Pleased with my progress, and finding my resolution in favour of the naval service unalterable, he at length consented that my commission should be cancelled, and that the renewed offer of my uncle to receive me on board his frigate should be accepted.

The difficulty was to equip me for sea, but it was obviated by the Earl of Hopetoun considerately advancing 100*l.* for the purpose. With this sum the requisite outfit was procured, and a few days placed me in a position to seek my fortune, with my father's gold watch as a keepsake—the only patrimony I ever inherited.

The Dowager Countess of Dundonald, then meditating a journey to London, offered to take me with her. On our arrival in the metropolis, after what was at that time the formidable achievement of a tour through Wales, her ladyship went to reside with her brother, General James Stuart, in Grosvenor Street; but, anxious to become initiated in the mysteries of my profession, I preferred going on board the *Hind* at Sheerness; joining that ship on the 27th of June 1793, at the mature age, for a midshipman, of seventeen years and a half.

# CHAP. II.

## CRUISE OF THE *HIND*.

A LIEUTENANT OF THE OLD SCHOOL. — HIS IDEAS ON SEA-CHESTS. —
DOCKYARDS SIXTY YEARS AGO. — PRIZE-MONEY, THE LEADING MOTIVE
OF SEAMEN. — VOYAGE TO NORWAY. — NORWEGIAN CUSTOMS. — A
MIDSHIPMAN'S GRIEVANCES. — A PARROT TURNED BOATSWAIN. — IN-
EFFECTIVE ARMAMENTS. — MEN BEFORE DOCKYARDS. — TRAINING OF
OFFICERS.

My kind uncle, the Hon. John Cochrane, accompanied
me on board the *Hind* for the purpose of introducing me
to my future superior officer, Lieutenant Larmòur, or,
as he was more familiarly known in the service, Jack
Larmour—a specimen of the old British seaman, little
calculated to inspire exalted ideas of the gentility of
the naval profession, though presenting at a glance a
personification of its efficiency. Jack was, in fact, one
of a not very numerous class, whom, for their superior
seamanship, the Admiralty was glad to promote from
the forecastle to the quarter-deck, in order that they
might mould into ship-shape the questionable materials
supplied by parliamentary influence—even then paramount in the Navy to a degree which might otherwise
have led to disaster. Lucky was the commander who
could secure such an officer for his quarter-deck.

On my introduction, Jack was dressed in the garb

of a seaman, with marlinspike slung round his neck,
and a lump of grease in his hand, and was busily
employed in setting up the rigging.   His reception of
me was anything but gracious.   Indeed, a tall fellow,
over six feet high, the nephew of his captain, and
a lord to boot, were not very promising recommenda-
tions for a midshipman.   It is not impossible that he
might have learned from my uncle something about
a military commission of several years' standing; and
this, coupled with my age and stature, might easily
have impressed him with the idea that he had caught
a scapegrace with whom the family did not know what
to do, and that he was hence to be saddled with a
" hard bargain."

After a little constrained civility on the part of the
first lieutenant, who was evidently not very well pleased
with the interruption to his avocation, he ordered me
to " get my traps below."   Scarcely was the order
complied with, and myself introduced to the midshipman's berth, than I overheard Jack grumbling at the
magnitude of my equipments.   " This Lord Cochrane's
chest?   Does Lord Cochrane think he is going to bring
a cabin aboard?   The service is going to the devil!
Get it up on the main-deck."

The order being promptly obeyed, amidst a running
fire of similar objurgations, the key of the chest was
sent for, and shortly afterwards the sound of sawing
became audible.   It was now high time to follow
my property, which, to my astonishment, had been
turned out on the deck — Jack superintending the
process of sawing off one end of the chest just be-

yond the keyhole, and accompanying the operation
by sundry uncomplimentary observations on midshipmen in general, and on myself in particular.

The metamorphose being completed to the lieutenant's satisfaction, though not at all to mine, for
my neat chest had become an unshapely piece of
lumber, he pointed out the "lubberliness of shore-
going people in not making keyholes where they could
be most easily got at," viz. at the end of a chest instead
of the middle! The observation was, perhaps, made
to test my temper, but, if so, it failed in its object. I
thanked him for his kindness in imparting so useful a
lesson, and left him evidently puzzled as to whether I
was a cool hand or a simple one.

Poor Jack! his limited acquaintance with the world
—which, in his estimation, was bounded by the taffrail
and the bowsprit—rendered him an indifferent judge of
character, or he might have seen in me nothing but an
ardent desire diligently to apply myself to my chosen
profession—with no more pride in my heart than money
in my pocket. A short time, however, developed this.
Finding me anxious to learn my duty, Jack warmly
took me by the hand, and as his only ideas of relaxation were to throw off the lieutenant and resume the
functions of the able seaman, my improvement speedily
rewarded my kind though rough teacher, by converting into a useful adjunct one whom he had, perhaps,
not unjustifiably, regarded as a nuisance. We soon became fast friends, and throughout life few more kindly
recollections are impressed on my memory than those
of my first naval instructor, honest Jack Larmour.

Another good friend in need was Lieutenant Murray, a son of Lord Dunmore, who observing that my kit had been selected rather with a regard to economy than fitness, kindly lent me a sum of money to remedy the deficiency.

The period at which I joined the service was that during which events consequent on the first French revolution reached a crisis, inaugurating the series of wars which for twenty years afterwards devastated Europe. Whatever might have been the faults of the British Government in those days, that of being unprepared for the movements of revolutionary neighbours was not amongst them, for the energy of the Government kept pace with the patriotism of the nation. That fearful system of naval jobbery, which unhappily characterised the subsequent progress of the war, crowding the seas with worthless vessels, purchased into the service in exchange for borough influence—had not as yet begun to thwart the unity of purpose and action by which the whole realm was at first roused into action.

With few of those costly appliances in the dockyards which at the present day absorb vast sums voted by the nation for the support of the Navy, to the exclusion of its real strength—*trained men*, the naval ports presented a scene of activity in every way commensurate with the occasion by which it had been called into existence. Their streets abounded with seamen eager to share in anticipated prize-money—for whatever may be the ideas of modern statesmen on this subject, prize-money formed then, as it will ever form, the principal motive of seamen to encounter the perils of war.

On this point, there is, at the present day, a tendency to dangerous doctrine; and a word respecting it will not be out of place. I have seen it openly proclaimed that seamen will fight for fighting's sake, and without expectation of reward. If the propounders of such an opinion were to ask themselves the question, whether they engage in professional or commercial pursuits from pure patriotism, and without hope of further remuneration, their own reply would show them the fallacy of ascribing to seamen a want of those motives which impel all men to adventure and exertion. Human nature is the same in all its grades, and will remain so, despite romantic notions of its disinterestedness and patriotism. The result of my own experience is, that seamen fight from two leading motives: 1st. Prize-money; 2nd. From a well-grounded belief in their own physical and disciplinary superiority, which refuses to be beaten, and is not satisfied with less than conquest. Take away the first motive, and we may find difficulty, on an emergency, in getting men to accomplish the second.

The bounty system, which has superseded the press-gang, is a direct proof of money being admitted as the seaman's inciting motive to engage in war. The press-gang itself was a no less decisive proof, for it rarely had to be resorted to, except in case of unpopular officers, inefficient vessels, or out-of-the-way stations, where the chances of prize-money were few. For ships commanded by well-known officers, and with a favourable chance of making prizes, the press-gang was unnecessary. This circumstance forms no indifferent comment on the real motives which induce seamen voluntarily to enter the service. On this most important subject more will be said hereafter.

To return to our cruise. The destination of the *Hind* was the coast of Norway, to the *fiords* of which country the Government had reason to suspect that French privateers might resort, as lurking-places whence to annoy our North Sea and Baltic commerce. To ascertain this was our primary object. The second was to look out for an enemy's convoy, shortly expected from the West Indies by the northern route round the Orkneys.

We had not, however, the luck to fall in with either convoy or privateers, though for the latter every inlet was diligently searched. The voyage was, therefore, without incident, further than the gratifying experience of Norse hospitality and simplicity; qualities which, it is to be feared, may have vanished before the influence of modern rapidity of communication, without being replaced by others equally satisfactory.

To us youngsters, this Norwegian trip was a perpetual holiday, for my uncle, though a strict disciplinarian, omitted no opportunity of gratifying those under his command, so that we spent nearly as much time on shore as on board; whilst the few hours occupied in running along the coast from one inlet to another supplied us with a moving panorama, scarcely less to our taste than were the hospitalities on shore.

Our great amusement was sleighing at racing speed, to the musical jingling of bells, without a sound from the catlike fall of the horse's feet on the snow. Other variations in the routine of pleasure, were

shooting and fishing, though these soon became secondary objects, as the abundance of fish and game
rendered their capture uninteresting.

But the principal charm was the primitive aspect of
a people apparently sprung from the same stock as ourselves, and presenting much the same appearance as
our ancestors may be supposed to have done a few cen-
turies before, without any symptoms of that feudal
attachment which then prevailed in Britain. I have
never seen a people more contented and happy; not
because their wants were few, for even luxuries were
abundant, and in common use.

Much, however, cannot be said for Norwegian gallantry
at that period. On one occasion my uncle took me to
a formal dinner at the house of a magnate named Da
Capa. The table literally groaned beneath the feast;
but a great drawback to our enjoyment of the good
things set before us, was that, during a five hours' succession of dishes, the lady of the house stood at the
head of the table, and performed the laborious duty of
carver throughout the tedious repast. Her flushed countenance after the intervals between the various removes,
moreover, warranted the suspicion that the very excellent cookery was the result of her supervision. It is to
be hoped that the march of civilisation has altered this
custom for the better.

It is possible that these remarks may be considered
somewhat profound for a midshipman of three months'
standing; but it must be remembered that, from previous
hard necessity, no less than maturity, they are those of a
reflective midshipman. At any rate, the remarks were

duly jotted down, and to this day their reperusal calls forth somewhat of the freshness of boyhood to a mind worn down, not so much with age as with unmerited injuries, which have embittered a long life, and rendered even the failings of age premature.

From boyish impressions to a midshipman's grievances is but a step. At the first moment of my setting foot on board the *Hind* it had been my determination never to commit an act worthy of punishment; but it was equally the determination of Jack Larmour to punish me for my resolution the first time he caught me tripping. This was certain, for Jack was open and above board, and declared that "he never heard of such a thing as a faultless midshipman!" For a long time he watched in vain, but nothing occurred more than to warrant his swearing twice as much at me as at any other of my messmates, Jack never troubling himself to swear at a waister. To use his own words, it "was expending wind for nothing."

One day, when his back was turned, I had stolen off deck for a few minutes, but only to hear on my return the ominous words, "Mast-head, youngster!" There was no alternative but to obey. Certainly not cheerfully—for the day was bitterly cold, with the thermometer below zero. Once caught, I knew my punishment would be severe, as indeed it was, for my sojourn at the mast-head was protracted almost to the limit of human endurance, my tormentor being evidently engaged in calculating this to a nicety. He never mast-headed me again.

By way of return for the hospitality of the Norwegian

people, the frigate was freely thrown open to their inspection.   On one of their frequent visits, an incident
occurred not unworthy of record.

On board most ships there is a pet animal of some
kind. . Ours was a parrot, which was Jack Larmour's
aversion, from the exactness with which the bird had
learned to imitate the calls of the boatswain's whistle.
Sometimes the parrot would pipe an  order so correctly
as to throw the ship into momentary confusion, and the
first lieutenant into a volley of imprecations, consigning
Poll to a warmer latitude than his native tropical forests.
Indeed, it was only by my uncle's countenance that the
bird was tolerated.

One day a party of ladies paid us a visit aboard, and
several had been hoisted on deck by the usual means of
a " whip " on the mainyard.   The chair had descended
for another " whip," but scarcely had its fair freight
been lifted out of the boat alongside, than the unlucky
parrot piped "*Let  go!*"   The order being instantly
obeyed,  the unfortunate lady, instead of being com-
fortably seated on deck, as had been those who preceded
her, was soused overhead in the sea !  Luckily for Poll,
Jack Larmour was on shore at the time, or this unseasonable assumption of the boatswain's functions might
have ended tragically.

On the return of the *Hind* from Norway, my uncle
was appointed to the *Thetis*, a more powerful frigate ;
for though the *Hind* carried 28 guns, they were only
9-pounders ; an armament truly ridiculous as compared
with that of frigates of the present day.   It may almost
be said, that the use of such an armament consisted in

rendering it necessary to resort to the cutlass and boarding-pike—weapons to be relied on. Had such been the object of the Board of Admiralty as regarded the smaller class of frigates, it could not have been better carried out. The lighter class of vessels were even worse provided for. Seven years later a sloop was placed under my command, armed with 4-pounders only. One day, by way of burlesque on such an equipment, I walked the quarter-deck with a whole broadside of shot in my coat pockets.

The *Thetis* was ordered to equip at Sheerness, and knowing that her first lieutenant, instead of indulging himself ashore, would pursue his customary relaxation of working hard aboard, I begged permission to remain and profit by his example. This was graciously conceded, on condition that, like himself, I would put off the officer and assume the garb of a seaman. Nothing could be more to my taste; so, with knife in belt and marlinspike in hand, the captain of the forecastle undertook my improvement in the arts of knotting and splicing; Larmour himself taking charge of gammoning and rigging the bowsprit, which, as the frigate lay in dock, overhung the common highway. So little attention was then paid to the niceties of dockyard arrangement.

Dockyards in those days were secondary objects. At Sheerness the people lived, like rabbits in a warren, in old hulks, hauled up high and dry; yet everything was well done, and the supervision perfect. It would be folly to advocate the continuance of such a state of things, yet it may be doubted whether the naval efficiency

of the present day keeps pace with the enormous out-
lay on modern dockyards, almost (as it appears to me)
to ignoring the training of men.   I would rather see a
mistake in the opposite extreme—men before dockyard
conveniencies; and am confident that had such been
our practice, we should not have recently heard humi-
liating explanations, that we were without adequate
naval protection, and that our national safety depended
on the forbearance of a neighbouring state.

Precision in stone and mortar is no more naval efficiency, than are the absurd coast fortifications (to which
there is an evident leaning) national safety.   The true
fortification of England is, always to be in a position to
strike the first blow at sea the moment it may become
necessary.   To wait for it would, under any circumstances, be folly — to be unprepared for it national
suicide.

The service now seems to savour too much of the
dockyard, and too little of the seaman.   Formerly, both
officers and men had to lend a hand in everything, and
few were the operations which, unaided by artificers,
they could not perfectly accomplish.   On two occasions
my own personal skill at pump-work has saved ships
and crews when other assistance was not available.

The modern practice is to place ships in commission,
with everything perfect to the hands of the officers and
crew, little being required of them beyond keeping the
ship in order whilst at sea.   The practice is to a certain
extent praiseworthy; but it has the disadvantage of
impressing officers with the belief that handicraft skill
on their part is unnecessary, though in the absence of

practically acquired knowledge it is impossible even to direct any operation efficiently.

Without a certain amount of this skill, as forming an important part of training, no man can become an efficient naval officer. It would be gratifying to me should these remarks lead to inquiry on the subject. I must confess my inability to peruse the accounts of inexperience in the fleet at the outbreak of the late war with Russia, without grave misgivings that the supervision of the navy in the present day is not that of old time.

# CHAP. III.

## THE VOYAGE OF THE *THETIS*.

As soon as the *Thetis* had obtained her complement, she was ordered to join the squadron of Admiral Murray, which was being fitted out for North America; whither, soon after the declaration of war against England by the French Convention, the Government had despatched orders to seize the islands of St. Pierre and Miguilon, previously captured from the French in 1778, but restored at the termination of the American war.

It was in order to regain these islands, and for the protection of our commerce and fisheries generally, that a stronger force on the Nova Scotia station was deemed essential. The conduct of the American people was doubtful, as, from the assistance rendered by the French in the War of Independence, and still more from the democratic institutions recently established in France, little doubt existed that their leaning would be upon the side of the enemy. The United States Government, however, did all in its power to preserve neutrality by proclamations and addresses, but as its authority was little more than nominal throughout the various states, a disposition on the part of American shipowners to assist the French in providing stores of every kind was manifested very soon after the declaration of war. On our return from Leith to Plymouth to join the admiral, we detained several American vessels laden with corn and other provisions for French ports ; one of the objects of Admiral Murray's squadron being to intercept traffic of this nature.

The squadron sailed from Plymouth ; and when about midway across the Atlantic an incident occurred worth relating, as bearing upon a conjecture made a few years ago, by the master and passengers of a merchant vessel, regarding some vessels, supposed, though erroneously, to form part of Sir John Franklin's expedition.

One night finding the temperature of the atmosphere rapidly decreasing, the squadron was proceeding under easy sail, with a vigilant look-out for icebergs. At dawn we were close to a block of these, extending right across our path as far as the eye could reach. The only alternative was to alter our course and pass to leeward of the group, to which, from the unwonted sublimity of the sight, we approached as nearly as seemed consistent with safety. The appearance of icebergs is now so well known that it would be superfluous to describe them. I shall only remark that on passing one field of great extent we were astonished at discovering on its sides three vessels, the one nearest to us being a polacca-rigged ship, elevated at least a hundred feet ; the berg having rolled round or been lightened by melting, so that the vessel had the appearance of being on a hill forming the southern portion of the floe. The story of two vessels answering the description of Sir John Franklin's ships having a few years ago been seen on an iceberg was scarcely credited at the time, but may receive corroboration from the above incident.

Nothing can exceed the extraordinary aspect of these floating islands of ice, either as regards variety of form, or the wonderful display of reflected light which they present. But, however they may attract curiosity, ships should always give them a wide berth, the in-draught of water on their weather side being very dangerous. A singular effect was experienced as we passed to leeward of the field; first, the intense cold of the wind passing over it, and occasionally, the heat caused by the reflection of the sun's rays from the ice whenever the ship came within the angle of incidence.

On our arrival at Halifax we found many American vessels which had been detained, laden with corn and provisions. These had been seized by our predecessors on the station, the act by no means tending to increase our popularity on subsequent visits along the United States coast. Another practice which was pursued has always appeared to me a questionable stretch of authority towards a neutral nation, viz., the forcible detention of English seamen whenever found navigating American ships. Of this the Government of the United States justly complained, as inflicting severe losses on their citizens, whose vessels were thus delayed or imperilled for want of hands.

The practice was defended by the British Government, but on what grounds I am not jurist enough to comprehend.  Certain it is, that should another Continental war arise, such a course would be impracticable ; for as American ships, whether of war or commerce, are now for the most part manned by British seamen, driven from the service of their country by an unwise abrogation of that portion of the navigation laws which fostered our own nursery for the Navy—the effect of such an order would be to unman American ships; and it is questionable whether the United States Government would submit to such a regulation, even if we were inclined to put it in execution.

On the 14th of January 1795, Admiral Murray appointed me acting third lieutenant of the *Thetis*, though not eighteen months had elapsed since my entrance into the service.  Thanks to my worthy friend Jack Larmour, and to my own industry, it may be stated, without vanity, that I was not incompetent to fill the station to which the admiral had promoted me.  This unlooked-for reward redoubled my zeal, and on the 13th of April following, I was made acting lieutenant of the *Africa*, Captain Rodham Home, who applied to the admiral for my services.  This additional promotion was followed on the 6th of July by a provisional commission confirming my rank.

The *Africa* was sent to scour the seaboard of the States in search of enemy's vessels, but not falling in with any, we ran on to Florida, with similar ill-success.  An accident here occurred to me which left its mark through life.  I had contrived a ball of lead studded with

barbed prongs, for the purpose of catching porpoises.
One day the doctor laid me a wager against hurling the
missile to a certain distance, and in the attempt a hook
nearly tore off the fore-finger of my right hand. A perhaps not very judicious course of reading had at that
time led me to imbibe the notion of a current spurious
philosophy, that there was no such thing as pain, and few
opportunities were lost of parading arguments on the
subject. As the doctor was dressing my hand, the pain
was so intense that my crotchet was sadly scandalised
by an involuntary exclamation of agony. "What!"
said the doctor, "I thought there was no such thing as
pain!" Not liking to have a favourite theory so pal-
pably demolished, the ready reply was that "my exclamation was not one of pain, but mental only, arising
from the sight of my own blood!" He laughed, whilst
I writhed on, but the lesson knocked some foolish
notions out of my head.

On the 5th of January 1796, the first lieutenant of
the *Thetis* having been promoted, an order was transmitted for me to quit the *Africa*, and rejoin my uncle's
ship, which I did in the *Lynx*, Captain Skene. An incident occurred during the passage worth relating.

The *Lynx* one day overhauled an American vessel
from France to New York, professedly in ballast. At
first, nothing was found to warrant her detention, but
a more minute search brought to light from amongst
the shingle ballast, a number of casks filled with costly
church plate; this being amongst the means adopted by
the French Convention to raise supplies, an intention in
this case thwarted by the vigilance of Captain Skene.

The sagacity of Captain Skene was exemplified in another instance. Observing one day a quantity of stable litter on the surface of the sea, it was obvious that it could only arise from the transport of animals. Tracking the refuse to the southward, we overtook and captured a vessel laden with mules for the use of one of the French possessions.

The period having arrived at which the Admiralty regulations permitted young officers to offer themselves for examination—on rejoining the *Thetis* I was ordered up, and passed for lieutenant accordingly; my time as a midshipman being made up from my nominal rating on board the *Vesuvius*, &c., as narrated in a former chapter.

The mention of this practice will, perhaps, shock the purists of the present day, who may further regard me as a stickler for corruption, for pronouncing its effect to have been beneficial. First, because—from the scarcity of lieutenants — encouragement was often necessary; secondly, because it gave an admiral a power which he does not now possess, viz. that of selecting for commissions those who exerted themselves, and on whom he could rely, in place of having forced upon him young men appointed by parliamentary or other influence; of whom he could know nothing, except that they did not owe their commissions to practical merit.

In my own subsequent career as captain of a man-of-war, there never was the slightest difficulty as regarded men; yet no commander could, in this respect, be more particular; but of many officers furnished to me through parliamentary influence, it can only be said that they were seldom trusted, as I considered it preferable, on pressing occasions, to do their duty myself; and this, as some of them had powerful influence, no doubt made me many enemies amongst their patrons. It is all very well to talk of the inordinate power exercised by commanding officers in former times, but whilst the Admiralty, even in our day, appears to extend a system in which influence has everything and experience nothing to do, the so-called corruption of old, which was never made use of but to promote merit, had its advantages; no instance in which the power then indirectly pertaining to admirals commanding having, to my knowledge, been abused.*

During my absence in the *Africa*, I lost the chance of participating in a gallant attack made by the Hon. Captain Cochrane, in the *Thetis*, and Captain Beresford, in the *Hussar*, on five French ships, which they had been watching near the mouth of the Chesapeake. These ships were fallen in with at sea off Cape Henry, and on the approach of the *Thetis* and *Hussar* formed in line to receive them. The *Hussar*, being the smaller vessel, encountered the two leading ships, whilst the *Thetis* opened her broadside on the centre vessel, and the two

---

* This adoption, for political purposes, of a baneful system may, in an unforeseen emergency, tend to the overthrow of the state; and nothing, in my opinion, can be more injurious to the Navy than the usurpation of all distributive power by a ministry in exchange for parliamentary votes. In civil offices this may be merely obstructive—in the Navy it is destructive. Systems like these are such as no state can long exist under securely, and history warns us that from perversion of patronage great states have fallen.

in the rear.   In half an hour, the French commodore
and the second in the line gave up the combat, and
made sail, leaving the others to the mercy of the two
English frigates, which in another half hour compelled
them to surrender, one of them, however, contriving to
escape.   Two, the *Prévoyant*, 36, and the *Raison*, 18,
were secured and taken to Halifax, where they were
fitted out as cruisers, and afterwards returned with the
squadron to England.   This action was the only one of
any importance which occurred during the dreary five
years that we were employed on the North American
coast, and is here mentioned because it has been said
I was present, which was not the case.

In the year 1797, Admiral Murray was succeeded in
the command by Admiral Vandeput, who, on the 21st
of June, appointed me lieutenant in his flag-ship the
*Resolution*.   On joining this ship a few days afterwards,
my reception was anything but encouraging.

Being seated near the admiral at dinner, he inquired
what dish was before me.   Mentioning its nature, I
asked if he would permit me to help him.   The un-
courteous reply was—that whenever he wished for anything he was in the habit of asking for it.   Not knowing what to make of a rebuff of this nature, it was
met by an inquiry if he would allow me the honour
of taking wine with him.   " I never take wine with
any man, my lord," was the unexpected reply, from
which it struck me that my lot was cast among Goths,
if no worse.

Never were first impressions more ill-founded.   Admiral Vandeput had merely a habit of showing his

worst features first, or rather of assuming those which were contrary to his nature. A very short time developed his true character,—that of a perfect gentleman, and one of the kindest commanders living. In place of the hornet's nest figured to my imagination, there was not a happier ship afloat, nor one in which officers lived in more perfect harmony.

The only drawback was that of wanting something better to do than cruise among the fogs of Newfoundland and Nova Scotia,—an inglorious pursuit, the more severely felt, from the fact that each succeeding packet brought accounts of brilliant naval victories achieved in European waters. The French, after my uncle's capture of their store-ships, gave up all attempts to get supplies from America by means of their own vessels ; and the United States Government concluded a treaty with England, in which both sides disclaimed all wish to pass the bounds observed by neutral nations, so that the squadron was without beneficial employment.

Tired of the monotony of Halifax, Admiral Vandeput determined to winter in the Chesapeake, where he resided ashore. As it was his practice to invite his officers by turns to remain a week with him, our time was agreeably spent, the more so that there were several families in the vicinity which retained their affection for England, her habits, and customs. Even the innkeeper of the place contrived to muster a tolerable pack of hounds which, if not brought under the perfect discipline of their British progenitors, often led us into more danger than is encountered in an English field, in consequence of our runs frequently taking us amongst thick forests, the overhanging branches of which compelled us to lay ourselves flat on the horses' backs, in order to avoid the fate intended for the objects of the chase.

Another of our amusements was shooting; and one day a circumstance took place of which I did not for a long time hear the last. Being invited to pass a week with the admiral, who was about to give a dinner to his neighbours, it was my wish to add a delicacy to his table; and having heard that a particular locality abounded with wild hogs, it seemed practicable that a boar's head might grace the feast. On reaching the forest, nearly the first object encountered was a huge wild-looking sow with a farrow of young pigs, and as the transition from boar's head to sucking pig was not great, a shot from my rifle speedily placed one in a pre-liminary condition for roasting. But porcine maternal affection had not entered into my calculations. The sow charged me with such ferocity that prompt retreat, however undignified, became necessary, for my weapon was now harmless. In short, so vigorous was the on-slaught of the enemy, that it became necessary to shelter myself in the fork of a tree, my gun being of necessity left at the bottom. The enraged animal mounted guard, and for at least a couple of hours waited for my descent; when, finding no symptoms of unconditional surrender, she at length moved slowly off with the re-mainder of her family. As the coast was now clear, I came down and shouldered the defunct pig, hoping to be in time to add it to the admiral's table, for which, however, it was too late.

Having told the story with great simplicity, I found myself at dinner roasted instead of the pig; the changes on this theme being rung till it became rather annoying. By way of variation the admiral asked me for a toast, and on my pleading ignorance of such customs insisted on my giving a sentiment; whereupon I gave " the Misses Tabbs,"— the point consisting in the fact that these ladies were each over six feet high, and in the gossip of the place were understood to be favourites of the admiral. For a moment Admiral Vandeput looked grave, but thinking, no doubt, the retort a fair one, he joined in the laughter against himself; though from that day he never asked me for a toast.

Those were days when even gentlemen did not consider it a demerit to drink hard. It was then, as it is now, a boast with me never in my life to have been inebriated, and the revenge was that my boast should be at an end. Rapid circulation of the bottle accordingly set in; but this I managed to evade by resting my head on my left hand, and pouring the wine down the sleeve of my uniform coat. The trick was detected, and the penalty of drinking off a whole bottle was about to be enforced when I darted from the room, pursued by some of the company, who at length got tired of the chase, and I passed the night at a farm-house.

Having paid so lengthened a visit to the United States at a period almost immediately following their achievement of independence, a few remarks relative to the temper and disposition of the American people at that period may not be uninteresting. Thoroughly English in their habits and customs, but exasperated by the contumely with which they had been treated by former British governments, their civility to us was somewhat constrained, yet so thoroughly English as to convince us that a little more forbearance and common sense on the part of the home authorities might have averted the final separation of these fine provinces from the mother country. There is every reason to believe that the declaration of the Confederation of the United Colonies in 1775 was sincere; viz. that on the concession of their just demands, " the colonies are to return to their former connections and friendship with Great Britain ; but on failure thereof this Confederation is to be perpetual." *

In vain, however, did the more far-sighted of the English public remonstrate with the Government, and in vain did the City of London by their chief magistrate urge the wrongs and loyalty of the colonists, even to memorialising the king to dismiss from his councils those who were misleading him. A deaf ear was turned to all remonstrance, and a determination to put down by force what could not at first be called rebellion was the only reply vouchsafed ; it was not till all conciliatory means had failed that the first Congress of Philadelphia asserted the cause and necessity of taking up arms in the defence of freedom; the second Congress of the same place confederating the provinces under the title of the " United States of America."

The failure of those employed in conciliation to in-

* " Articles of Confederation between New Hampshire, Massachusetts," &c. &c., May 20th, 1775.

duce the colonists to return to their allegiance—the co-operation of the King of France in aid of the revolt—the discreditable war which followed—and the singular recoil of his own principles on the head of Louis XVI. himself, are matters of history and need not here be further alluded to.

When the *Thetis* was first on the coast, the American republic was universally recognised, and it must be admitted that our treatment of its citizens was scarcely in accordance with the national privileges to which the young republic had become entitled. There were, no doubt, many individuals amongst the American people who, caring little for the Federal government, considered it more profitable to break than to keep the laws of nations, by aiding and supporting our enemy, and it was against such that the efforts of the squadron had been chiefly directed; but the way in which the object was carried out was scarcely less an infraction of those international laws which we were professedly enforcing.

The practice of taking English seamen out of American vessels, without regard to the safety of navigating them when thus deprived of their hands, has been already mentioned. To this may be added, the detention of vessels against which nothing contrary to international neutrality could be established, whereby their cargoes became damaged; the compelling them, on suspicion only, to proceed to ports other than those to which they were destined, and generally treating them as though they were engaged in contraband trade.

Of these transactions the Americans had a right to complain; but in other respects their complaints were indefensible; such as that of our not permitting them to send corn and provisions to France, a violation of neutrality into which, after declaration of blockade, none but an inexperienced government could have fallen; though there was perhaps something in the collateral grievance that American ships were not permitted to quit English ports without giving security for the discharge of their cargoes in some other British or. neutral port.

It would be wearisome to enter into further details respecting the operations of a squadron so ingloriously employed, or to notice the subordinate part which a junior lieutenant could take in its proceedings. Suffice it to say, that after remaining five years on the North American station, the *Thetis* returned to England.

## CHAP. IV.

### SERVICES IN THE MEDITERRANEAN.

I JOIN LORD KEITH'S SHIP. — AN UNPLEASANT ALTERCATION, ENDING
IN A COURT-MARTIAL. — THE BLOCKADE OF CADIZ. — FRENCH FLEET
IN THE OFFING. — PURSUED BY LORD KEITH. — ENEMY'S VESSELS
BURNT AT TOULON. — LORD KEITH RECALLED BY LORD ST. VINCENT.
— LORD ST. VINCENT RESIGNS THE COMMAND. — LORD KEITH PUR-
SUES THE FRENCH FLEET TO BREST, AND FROM THENCE TO THE
MEDITERRANEAN. — STATE OF THE FRENCH MARINE. — LORD KEITH
APPOINTS ME TO THE GENEREUX. — BURNING OF THE QUEEN CHAR-
LOTTE. — ACTION WITH PRIVATEERS OFF CABRITTA POINT. — RECOM-
MENDED FOR PROMOTION.

TOWARDS the close of the autumn of 1798, Lord Keith
was appointed to relieve Lord St. Vincent in the command of the Mediterranean fleet, and kindly offered to
take me with him as a supernumerary. I therefore
embarked, by his lordship's invitation, in the flag-ship.

We arrived at Gibraltar on the 14th of December,
and found Lord St. Vincent residing on shore, his flag
flying on board the *Souverain* sheerhulk.

His lordship's reception of me was very kind, and
on the 24th of December, at Lord Keith's request, he
gave an order for my appointment to the *Barfleur*, to
which ship Lord Keith had shifted his flag. This
appointment, from a certain dissatisfaction at my having
received such a commission after being so short a time
at sea, afterwards brought me into trouble.

Lord St. Vincent did not, as was expected, immediately transfer to Lord Keith the command of the Mediterranean fleet, but remained at Gibraltar, giving orders to his lordship to blockade the Spanish fleet in Cadiz.

The first part of the year was spent in this employment, Lord Keith's force varying from eleven to fifteen sail of the line, but without frigates, though the commander-in-chief had a considerable number under his orders. The omission was the more remarkable, as the blockaded Spanish force numbered upwards of twenty ships of the line, with frigates and smaller vessels in proportion.

The British force, for upwards of four months, was anchored some seven or eight miles from Cadiz, but without rousing the national spirit of the Spaniards, who manifested no disposition to quit their shelter, even though we were compelled from time to time to leave our anchorage for the purpose of procuring water and cattle from the neighbouring coast of Africa. It was during one of these trips in the *Barfleur* that an absurd affair involved me in serious disaster.

Our first lieutenant, Beaver, was an officer who carried etiquette in the wardroom and on deck almost to despotism. He was laudably particular in all matters visible to the eye of the admiral, but permitted an honest penny to be turned elsewhere by a practice as reprehensible as revolting. On our frequent visits to Tetuan, we purchased and killed bullocks *on board the Barfleur*, for the use of the whole squadron. The reason was, that raw hides, being valuable, could be stowed away in her hold in empty beef-casks, as especial perquisites to certain persons connected with the flag-ship; a natural result being, that, as the fleshy parts of the hides decomposed, putrid liquor oozed out of the casks, and rendered the hold of the vessel so in-tolerable, that she acquired the name of " The stinking Scotch ship."

As junior lieutenant, much of the unpleasantness of this fell to my share, and as I always had a habit of speaking my mind without much reserve, it followed that those interested in the raw hide speculation were not very friendly disposed towards me.

One day, when at Tetuan, having obtained leave to go ashore and amuse myself with shooting wild-fowl, my dress became so covered with mud, as to in-duce me not to come off with other officers in the pinnace which took me on shore, preferring to wait for the launch, in which the filthy state of my apparel would be less apparent. The launch being delayed longer than had been anticipated, my leave of absence expired shortly before my arrival on board—not without attracting the attention of Lieutenant Beaver, who was looking over the gangway.

Thinking it disrespectful to report myself on the quarter deck in so dirty a condition, I hastened to put on clean uniform, an operation scarcely completed when Lieutenant Beaver came into the wardroom, and in a very harsh tone demanded the reason of my not having reported myself. My reply was, that as he saw me come up the side, he must be aware that my dress was not in a fit condition to appear on the quarter deck, and that it had been necessary to change my clothes before formally reporting myself.

Lieutenant Beaver replied to this explanation in a manner so offensive, that it was clear he wanted to surprise me into some act of insubordination. As it would have been impossible to be long cool in opposition to marked invective, I respectfully reminded him that by attacking me in the wardroom he was breaking a rule which he had himself laid down; viz., that "Matters connected with the service were not there to be spoken of." The remark increased his violence, which, at length, became so marked as to call forth the reply, "Lieutenant Beaver, we will, if you please, talk of this in another place." He then went on deck, and reported to Captain Elphinstone that in reply to his remarks on a violation of duty, he had received a challenge!

On being sent for to answer the charge, an explanation of what had really taken place was given to Captain Elphinstone, who was kindly desirous that the first lieutenant should accept an apology, and let so disagreeable a matter drop. This was declined on my part, on the ground that, in the conversation which had passed, I had not been in the wrong, and had, therefore, no apology to make. The effect was, that Beaver demanded a court-martial on me, and this, after manifest reluctance on the part of Lord Keith, was ordered accordingly; the decision of which was an admonition to be "more careful in future "— a clear proof that the court thought great provocation had been given by my accuser, or their opinion would have been more marked.

The Judge-Advocate on this occasion was the admiral's secretary, one of those who had taken offence about the raw hides before mentioned! After the business of the court was concluded, Lord Keith, who was much vexed with the whole affair, said to me privately: "Now, Lord Cochrane, pray avoid for the future all flippancy towards superior officers." His secretary overheard and embodied the remark in the sentence of the court-martial; so that shortly afterwards his officiousness or malice formed an impediment to my promotion, though the court had actually awarded no censure.

Lord Keith, who had in vain used every endeavour to induce the Spaniards to risk an engagement, began to get tired of so fruitless an operation as that of watching an enemy at anchor under their batteries, and resolved to try if he could not entice or force them to quit their moorings. With this view, the British force, though then consisting of twelve ships only, without a single frigate to watch the enemy meanwhile, proceeded to water, as usual, at Tetuan, so as to be in readiness for any contingencies that might arise. As the events which followed have been incorrectly represented by naval historians, if not in one instance misrepresented, it is necessary, in order to do justice to Lord Keith, to detail them at some length.

Immediately after our return from Tetuan, the *Childers* arrived with intelligence that five Spanish sail of the line had got out of Ferrol, and she was followed on the same day by the *Success* frigate, which had been chased by a French fleet off Oporto. Lord Keith at

once despatched the *Childers* to Gibraltar, to inform
Lord St. Vincent, as was understood in the squadron,
that he intended, if the French fleet came to Cadiz, to
engage them, notwithstanding the disparity of numbers.
Lord Keith's force, by the arrival of three additional
ships of the line and one frigate, now amounted to sixteen sail; viz. one 112-gun ship, four 98's, one 90, two
80's, seven 74's, and one frigate, and these were immediately got under weigh and formed in order of battle,
standing off and on in front of the harbour.

About 8 A.M. on the 6th of May the French fleet was
signalled in the offing, and was made out to consist of
thirty-three sail, which with the twenty-two sail of
Spaniards in Cadiz made fifty-five, besides frigates, to
be encountered by the comparatively small British
force. The French fleet was on the larboard tack, and
our ships immediately formed on the same tack to
receive them. To our surprise they soon afterwards
wore and stood away to the south-west; though from
our position between them and the Spaniards they had
a fair chance of victory had the combined fleets acted
in concert. According to Lord Keith's pithily expressed
opinion, we lay between " the devil and the deep sea."

Yet there was nothing rash. Lord Keith calculated
that the Spaniards would not move unless the French
succeeded in breaking through the British line, and this
he had no doubt of preventing. Besides which, the
wind, though not dead on shore, as has been said, was
unfavourable for the Spaniards coming out with the
necessary rapidity. The great point to be gained was
to prevent the junction of the enemies' fleets, as was

doubtless intended; the attempt was however completely frustrated by the bold interposition of Lord Keith, who, strange to say, never received for this signal service the acknowledgment of merit which was his due.

It has been inferred by naval historians that a gale of wind, which was blowing on the first appearance of the French fleet, was the cause of their standing away. A better reason was their disinclination to encounter damage, which they knew would defeat their ultimate object of forming a junction with the Spanish fleet elsewhere.

At daylight on the 7th we were still standing off and on before Cadiz, expecting the enemy to return; when shortly afterwards four of their ships were seen to windward of the British force, which immediately gave chase; but the enemy outstripping us, we returned to the coast, to guard every point by which they might get into Cadiz. Seeing no symptoms of the main body of the French fleet, Lord Keith concluded that the four ships just noticed had been left as a decoy to draw his attention from their real object of running for Toulon, now that they had been foiled in their expectation of carrying with them the Spanish fleet. We accordingly made all sail for Gibraltar.

From the intelligence forwarded by the *Childers*, there was reason to suppose that Lord St. Vincent would have prepared for instant pursuit. To our surprise, the signal was made to anchor and obtain water and provision. Three entire days were consumed in this operation; with what effect as regarded the other ships I do not know, but so far as the *Barfleur* was concerned, and as far as I know of the other ships, the delay was unnecessary. The fleet was greatly disappointed at being thus detained, as the enemy would thereby reach Toulon without molestation, and for any good which could be effected we might as well remain where we lay.

This impatience was, after a lapse of three days, ended by Lord St. Vincent hoisting his flag on board the *Ville de Paris ;* when, reinforced by the *Edgar*, 74, the fleet shaped its course up the Mediterranean.

After we had proceeded as far as the Bay of Rosas, Lord St. Vincent, having communicated with Lord Keith, parted company in the *Ville de Paris* for Minorca, leaving Lord Keith to pursue the enemy with the remaining ships. We now made straight for Toulon, where we learned from some fishing boats that the enemy's fleet had embarked spars, cordage, anchors, and other heavy articles for the equipment of their ships of war built or building at Spezzia—and had sailed to the eastward.

After burning some merchant vessels working into Toulon, we again started in chase. It was now of even greater importance to overtake the French fleet, in order to frustrate a double mischief; first, their escape ; and secondly, their getting to Spezzia with the materials for so important an addition to their force. With this object the British ships crowded all sail in the direction the enemy had taken, and at length came in sight of their look-out frigates between Corsica and Genoa.

Just as we were upon the point of seeing the fleet also, a fast sailing transport arrived from Lord St. Vincent, with orders to return to Port Mahon; intelligence of the sailing of the French fleet having reached that port, which, Lord St. Vincent feared, might become the object of attack. Lord Keith, however, knowing exactly the position of the enemy, within reach of whom we now virtually were, persevered in the pursuit.

Shortly afterwards another fast sailing transport hove in sight, firing guns for Lord Keith to bring to, which having done, he received peremptory orders to repair immediately to Minorca; Lord St. Vincent still imagining that as the enemy had left Toulon they might catch him in Port Mahon; the fact of their having gone to Spezzia, though known to us, being unknown to him. Compliance with this unseasonable order was therefore compulsory, and Lord Keith made the signal for all captains, when, as reported by those officers, his lordship explained that the bearing up was no act of his, and the captains having returned on board their respective ships, reluctantly changed the course for Minorca, leaving the French fleet to proceed unmolested to Spezzia.

On Lord Keith receiving this order, I never saw a man more irritated. When annoyed, his lordship had a habit of talking aloud to himself. On this occasion, as officer of the watch, I happened to be in close proximity, and thereby became an involuntary listener to some very strong expressions, imputing jealousy on the part of Lord St. Vincent as constituting the motive for recalling him. The actual words of Lord Keith not being meant for the ear of any one, I do not think proper to record them. . The above facts are stated as coming within my own personal knowledge, and are here introduced in consequence of blame being cast on Lord Keith to this day by naval historians, who could only derive their authority from *data* which are certainly untrue — even if official. Had the command been surrendered to Lord Keith on his arrival in the Mediterranean, or had his lordship been permitted promptly to pursue the enemy, they could not have escaped.

The French fleet, after we were compelled to relinquish the chase (when in sight of their look-out frigates), were reported to have landed 1000 men at Savona, and convoyed a supply of wheat to Genoa, as well as having landed their naval stores at Spezzia, not one of which services could have been effected had it not been for the unfortunate delay at Gibraltar and the before-mentioned recall of the pursuing fleet.

Immediately after our departure from Gibraltar, the Spanish fleet quitted Cadiz for the Mediterranean, and as no force remained to watch the Straits, they were enabled to pass with impunity, the whole, after suffering great damage by a gale of wind, succeeding in reaching Carthagena.

On our arrival at Minorca, Lord St. Vincent resumed the command, and proceeded for some distance towards Toulon. On the 2nd of June, his lordship again quitted the fleet for Mahon, in the *Ville de Paris*. On the 14th Lord Keith shifted his flag from the *Barfleur* to the *Queen Charlotte*, a much finer ship, to which I had the honour to accompany him.

We once more proceeded in quest of the French fleet, and on the 19th the advanced ships captured

three frigates and two brigs of war on their way from
Egypt to Toulon, but learned nothing of the fleet we
were in search of. On the 23rd of June, Lord St.
Vincent at length resigned the Mediterranean command and sailed for England, so that Lord Keith had
no alternative but to return to Port Mahon to make the
necessary arrangements.

Scarcely had we come to an anchor when we received
intelligence that the French fleet had passed to the
westward to join the Spanish fleet at Carthagena!

Without even losing time to fill up with water, every
exertion was made for immediate pursuit, and on the
10th we started for Carthagena, but finding the enemy
gone, again made sail, and on the 26th reached Tetuan,
where we completed our water. On the 29th Lord
Keith communicated with Gibraltar, but as nothing was
heard of the combined fleets, it was evident they had
gone through the Straits in the dark; we therefore followed and examined Cadiz, where they were not. Pursuing our course without effect along the Spanish and
Portuguese coasts — on the 8th of August we fell in
with a Danish brig off Cape Finisterre, and received
from her information that she had two days before
passed through the combined French and Spanish fleets.
We then directed our course for Brest, hoping to be
in time to intercept them, but found that on the day
before our arrival they had effected their object, and
were then safely moored within the harbour. We
now shaped our course for Torbay, and there found
the Channel fleet under Sir Alan Gardner—the united
force being nearly fifty ships of the line.

On our arrival at Torbay, Lord Keith sent me with despatches on board the commander-in-chief's ship, where, after executing my commission, it was imperiously demanded by her captain whether I was aware that my coming on board was an infringement of quarantine regulations? Nettled at the over-bearing manner of an uncalled-for reprimand to an inferior officer, my reply was that, having been directed by Lord Keith to deliver his despatches, his lordship's orders had been executed accordingly; at the same time, however, assuring my interrogator that we had no sickness in the fleet, nor had we been in any contagious localities. From the captain's manner, it was almost evident that, for being thus plain spoken, he intended to put me under arrest, and I was not sorry to get back to the *Queen Charlotte;* even a show of resistance to an excess of authority being in those days fatal to many an officer's prospects.

I shall not enter into detail as to what occurred in the Channel; suffice it to say that despite the imposing force lying at Torbay, the combined French and Spanish fleets found no difficulty in getting out of Brest, and that on the 6th of December Lord Keith returned in pursuit to Gibraltar, where he resumed the Mediterranean command, administered by Lord Nelson during his absence.

It is beyond the province of this work to notice the effectual measures taken by Lord Nelson in the Mediterranean during our absence, as they are matters in which I bore no part. But whilst Nelson and Lord Keith had

been doing their best there, little appeared to be done
at home to check the enemy's operations.

From Gibraltar we proceeded to Sicily, where we
found Lord Nelson surrounded by the *élite* of Neapolitan society, amongst whom he was justly regarded as
a deliverer.  It was never my good fortune to serve
under his lordship, either at that or any subsequent
period.  During our stay at Palermo, I had, however,
opportunities of personal conversation with him, and
from one of his frequent injunctions, "Never mind
manœuvres, always go at them," I subsequently had
reason to consider myself indebted for successful attacks
under apparently difficult circumstances.

The impression left on my mind during these opportunities of association with Nelson was that of his being
an embodiment of dashing courage, which would not
take much trouble to circumvent an enemy, but being
confronted with one would regard victory so much a
matter of course as hardly to deem the chance of defeat worth consideration.

This was in fact the case; for though the enemy's
ships were for the most part superior to ours in build,
the discipline and seamanship of their crews was in
that day so inferior as to leave little room for doubt of
victory on our part.  It was probably with the object
of improving his crews that Admiral Bruix had risked
a run from the Mediterranean to Brest and back, as
just now detailed.  Had not Lord Keith been delayed
at Gibraltar, and afterwards recalled to Minorca, the
disparity of numbers on our side would not have been
of any great consequence.

Trafalgar itself is an illustration of Nelson's peculiar dash. It has been remarked that Trafalgar was a rash action, and that had Nelson lost it and lived he would have been brought to a court-martial for the way in which that action was conducted. But such cavillers forget that, from previous experience, he had calculated both the nature and amount of resistance to be expected; such calculation forming as essential a part of his plan of attack as even his own means for making it. The result justified his expectations of victory, which were not only well founded but certain.

The fact is, that many commanders in those days committed the error of overrating the French navy, just as, in the present day, we are nationally falling into the still more dangerous extreme of underrating it. Steam has, indeed, gone far towards equalising seamanship; and the strenuous exertions of the French department of Marine have perhaps rendered discipline in their navy as good as in ours. They moreover keep their trained men, whilst we thoughtlessly turn ours adrift whenever ships are paid off—to be replaced by raw hands in case of emergency!

To return from this digression. After quitting Palermo, and when passing the Straits of Messina, Lord Keith placed me as prize-master in command of the *Généreux,* 74—shortly before captured by Lord Nelson's squadron—with orders to carry her to Port Mahon. A crew was hastily made up of sick and invalided men drafted from the ships of the fleet, and with these we proceeded on our voyage, but only to find ourselves in imminent danger from a gale of wind. The rigging

not having been properly set up, the masts swayed
with every roll of the ship to such a degree that it
became dangerous to go aloft; the shrouds alternately
straining almost to breaking, or hanging in festoons,
as the masts jerked from side to side with the roll
of the vessel.    It was only by going aloft myself
together with my brother Archibald, whom Lord Keith
had permitted to accompany me, that the men could be
induced to furl the mainsail.    Fortunately the weather
moderated, or the safety of the ship might have been
compromised; but by dint of hard work, as far as the
ill-health of the crew would allow, we managed, before
reaching Mahon, to put the *Généreux* into tolerable
order.

It has been stated that Lord Keith permitted my
brother to accompany me in the *Généreux*.    By this
unexpected incident both he and myself were, in all
probability, saved from a fate which soon afterwards
befel most of our gallant shipmates.    On our quitting
the *Queen Charlotte*, Lord Keith steered for Leghorn,
where he landed, and ordered Captain Todd to reconnoitre the island of Cabrera, then in possession of the
French.    Whilst on his way, some hay, hastily embarked and placed under the half-deck, became ignited,
and the flame communicating with the mainsail set the
ship on fire aloft and below.    All exertions to save her
proved in vain, and though some of the officers and
crew escaped, more than three-fourths miserably perished, including Captain Todd, his first lieutenant
Bainbridge, three other lieutenants, the captain of
marines, surgeon, more than twenty master's mates

and petty officers, and upwards of 600 marines and seamen.

On our return from England to Gibraltar I had been associated with poor Bainbridge in an affair which — except as a tribute to his memory — would not have been worth mentioning.   On the evening of the 21st of September, 1799, we observed from the *Queen Charlotte*, lying in Gibraltar Bay, the 10-gun cutter *Lady Nelson*, chased by some gun-vessels and privateers, all of which simultaneously commenced an attack upon her.   Lord Keith instantly ordered out boats, Bainbridge taking command of the barge, whilst another of the boats was put under my orders.   Lord Keith's intention was, by this prompt aid, to induce the *Lady Nelson* to make a running fight of it, so as to get within range of the garrison guns ;  but before the boats could come up she had been captured; Lieutenant Bainbridge, though with sixteen men only, dashed at her, boarded, and retook her, killing several and taking prisoners seven French officers and twenty-seven men ;  but not without himself receiving a severe sabre cut on the head and several other wounds.

The boat under my command was the cutter with thirteen men.   Seeing two privateers which had chiefly been engaged in the attack on the *Lady Nelson* running for Algesiras, we made at the nearest, and came up with her at dark.   On laying the cutter alongside, I jumped on board, but the boat's crew did not follow, this being the only time I ever saw British seamen betray symptoms of hesitation.   Regaining the cutter, I upbraided them with the shamefulness of their conduct, for

the privateer's crew had run below, the helmsman alone
being at his post.   Their excuse was that there were
indications of the privateer's men having there fortified
themselves.   No reasoning could prevail on them to
board.   If this boat's crew perished in the *Queen
Charlotte*, their fate is not nationally to be regretted.

On the destruction of the *Queen Charlotte* Lord Keith
hoisted his flag in the *Audacious*.   His lordship was
so well satisfied with my conduct of the *Généreux* as to
write home to the Admiralty recommending my promotion, at the same time appointing me to the command
of the *Speedy*, then lying at Port Mahon.

The vessel originally intended for me by Lord Keith
was the *Bonne Citoyenne*, a fine corvette of eighteen
guns; but the brother of his lordship's secretary hap-
pening at the time to arrive from Gibraltar, where he
had been superseded in the command of the sheer
hulk, that functionary managed to place his brother in
one of the finest sloops then in the service, leaving to
me the least efficient craft on the station.

# CHAP. V.

## CRUISE OF THE *SPEEDY*.

THE *Speedy* was little more than a burlesque on a
vessel of war, even sixty years ago. She was about
the size of an average coasting brig, her burden being
158 tons. She was crowded, rather than manned, with
a crew of eighty-four men and six officers, myself included. Her armament consisted of fourteen *4-pounders !*
a species of gun little larger than a blunderbuss, and
formerly known in the service under the name of
" miñion," an appellation which it certainly merited.

Being dissatisfied with her armament, I applied for
and obtained a couple of 12-pounders; intending them
as bow and stern chasers, but was compelled to return
them to the ordnance wharf, there not being room on
deck to work them ; besides which, the timbers of the
little craft were found on trial to be too weak to

withstand the concussion of anything heavier than the guns with which she was previously armed.

With her rig I was more fortunate. Having carried away her mainyard, it became necessary to apply for another to the senior officer, who, examining the list of spare spars, ordered the *foretopgallant-yard* of the *Généreux* to be hauled out *as a mainyard for the Speedy !*

The spar was accordingly sent on board and rigged, but even this appearing too large for the vessel, an order was issued to cut off the yard-arms and thus reduce it to its proper dimensions. This order was neutralised by getting down and planing the yard-arms as though they had been cut, an evasion which, with some alteration in the rigging, passed undetected on its being again swayed up ; and thus a greater spread of canvas was secured. The fact of the foretopgallant-yard of a second-rate ship being considered too large for the mainyard of my " man-of-war " will give a tolerable idea of her insignificance.

Despite her unformidable character, and the personal discomfort to which all on board were subjected, I was very proud of my little vessel, caring nothing for her want of accommodation, though in this respect her cabin merits passing notice. It had not so much as room for a chair, the floor being entirely occupied by a small table surrounded with lockers, answering the double purpose of storechests and seats. The difficulty was to get seated, the ceiling being only five feet high, so that the object could only be accomplished by rolling on the locker, a movement sometimes attended with unpleasant failure. The most singular discomfort, however, was that my only practicable mode of shaving consisted in removing the skylight and putting my head through to make a toilet-table of the quarter-deck.

In the following enumeration of the various cruises in which the *Speedy* was engaged, the boarding and searching innumerable neutral vessels will be passed over, and the narrative will be strictly confined — as in most cases throughout this work—to log extracts, where captures were made, or other occurrences took place worthy of record.

" *May* 10. — Sailed from Cagliari, from which port we had been ordered to convey fourteen sail of merchantmen to Leghorn. At 9 A.M. observed a strange sail take possession of a Danish brig under our escort. At 11·30 A.M. rescued the brig, and captured the assailant. This prize — my first piece of luck — was the *Intrépide,* French privateer of six guns and forty-eight men.

" *May* 14. — Saw five armed boats pulling towards us from Monte Cristo. Out sweeps to protect convoy. At 4 P.M. the boats boarded and took possession of the two sternmost ships. A light breeze springing up, made all sail towards the captured vessels, ordering the remainder of the convoy to make the best of their way to Longona. The breeze freshening we came up with and recaptured the vessels with the prize crews on board, but during the operation the armed boats escaped.

" *May* 21.—At anchor in Leghorn Roads. Convoy all safe. 25. — Off Genoa. Joined Lord Keith's squadron of five sail of the line, four frigates and a brig.

" 26, 27, 28. — Ordered by his lordship to cruise in the offing, to intercept supplies destined for the French army under Massena, then in possession of Genoa.

" 29. — At Genoa some of the gun-boats bombarded the town for two hours.

" 30. — All the gun-boats bombarded the town. A partial bombardment had been going on for an hour a day, during the past fortnight, Lord Keith humanely refraining from continued bombardment, out of consideration for the inhabitants, who were in a state of absolute famine."

This was one of the *crises* of the war. The French, about a month previous, had defeated the Austrians with great slaughter in an attempt, on the part of the latter, to retake Genoa ; but the Austrians, being in possession of Savona, were nevertheless able to intercept provisions on the land side, whilst the vigilance of Lord Keith rendered it impossible to obtain supplies by sea.

It having come to Lord Keith's knowledge that the French in Genoa had consumed their last horses and dogs, whilst the Genoese themselves were perishing by famine, and on the eve of revolt against the usurping force—in order to save the carnage which would ensue, his lordship caused it to be intimated to Massena that a defence so heroic would command honourable terms of capitulation. Massena was said to have replied that if the word " capitulation " were mentioned his army should perish with the city ; but, as he could no longer defend himself, he had no objection to " treat." Lord Keith, therefore, proposed a treaty, viz. that the army might return to France, but that Massena himself must remain a prisoner in his hands. To this the French general demurred ; but Lord Keith insisting—with the complimentary observation to Massena that " he was worth 20,000 men "—the latter reluctantly gave in, and on the 4th of June 1800 a definitive treaty to the above effect was agreed upon, and ratified on the 5th, when the Austrians took possession of the city, and Lord Keith of the harbour, the squadron anchoring within the mole.

This affair being ended, his lordship ordered the *Speedy* to cruise off the Spanish coast, and on the 14th of June we parted company with the squadron.

"*June* 16. — Captured a tartan off Elba. Sent her to Leghorn, in the charge of an officer and four men.

" 22.—Off Bastia. Chased a French privateer with a prize in tow. The Frenchman abandoned the prize, a Sardinian vessel laden with oil and wool, and we took possession. Made all sail in chase of the privateer; but on our commencing to fire she ran under the fort of Caprea, where we did not think proper to pursue her. Took prize in tow, and on the following day left her at Leghorn, where we found Lord Nelson, and several ships at anchor.

" 25. — Quitted Leghorn, and on the 26th were again off Bastia, in chase of a ship which ran for that place, and anchored under a fort three miles to the southward. Made at and brought her away. Proved to be the Spanish letter of marque *Assuncion*, of ten guns and thirty-three men, bound from Tunis to Barcelona. On taking possession, five gunboats left Bastia in chase of us; took the prize in tow, and kept up a running fight with the gun-boats till after midnight, when they left us.

" 29. — Cast off the prize in chase of a French privateer off Sardinia. On commencing our fire she set all sail and ran off. Returned and took the prize in tow; and the 4th of July anchored with her in Port Mahon.

" *July* 9. — Off Cape Sebastian. Gave chase to two Spanish ships standing along shore. They anchored under the protection of the forts. Saw another vessel lying just within range of the forts; — out boats and cut her out, the forts firing on the boats without inflicting damage.

"*July* 19. — Off Caprea. Several French privateers in sight. Chased, and on the following morning captured one, the *Constitution,* of one gun and nineteen men. Whilst we were securing the privateer, a prize which she had taken made sail in the direction of Gorgona and escaped.

" 27. — Off Planosa, in chase of a privateer. On the following morning saw three others lying in a small creek. On making preparations to cut them out, a military force made its appearance, and commenced a heavy fire of musketry, to which it would have answered no purpose to reply. Fired several broadsides at one of the privateers, and sunk her.

" 31. — Off Porto Ferraio in chase of a French privateer, with a prize in tow. The Frenchman abandoned his prize, of which we took possession, and whilst so doing the privateer got away.

"*August* 3. — Anchored with our prizes in Leghorn Roads, where we found Lord Keith in the *Minotaur.*"

Lord Keith received me very kindly, and directed the *Speedy* to run down the Spanish coast, pointing out the importance of harassing the enemy there as much as possible, but cautioning me against engaging anything beyond our capacity. During our stay at Leghorn, his lordship frequently invited me ashore to participate in the gaieties of the place.

Having filled up with provisions and water, we sailed on the 16th of August, and on the 21st captured a French privateer bound from Corsica to Toulon. Shortly afterwards we fell in with H.M.S. ships *Mutine* and *Salamine,* which, to suit their convenience, gave into our charge a number of French prisoners, with whom and our prize we consequently returned to Leghorn.

On the 14th of September we again put to sea, the interval being occupied by a thorough overhaul of the sloop. On the 22nd, when off Caprea, fell in with a Neapolitan vessel having a French prize crew on board. Recaptured the vessel, and took the crew prisoners.

On the 5th of October, the *Speedy* anchored in Port Mahon, where information was received that the Spaniards had several armed vessels on the look-out for us, should we again appear on their coast. I therefore applied to the authorities to exchange our 4-pounders for 6-pounders, but the latter being too large for the *Speedy's* ports, we were again compelled to forego the change as impracticable.

"*October* 12. — Sailed from Port Mahon, cruising for some time off Cape Sebastian, Villa Nova, Oropesa, and Barcelona; occasionally visiting the enemy's coast for water, of which the *Speedy* carried only ten tons. Nothing material occurred till November 18th, when we narrowly escaped being swamped in a gale of wind, the sea breaking over our quarter, and clearing our deck, spars, &c., otherwise inflicting such damage as to compel our return to Port Mahon, where we were detained till the 12th of December.

"*December* 15. — Off Majorca. Several strange vessels being in sight, singled out the largest and made sail in chase; shortly after which a French bombard bore up, hoisting the national colours. We now cleared for action, altering our course to meet her, when she bore up between Dragon Island and the Main. Commenced firing at the bombard, which returned our fire; but shortly afterwards getting closer in shore she drove on the rocks. Three other vessels being in the passage we left her, and captured one of them, the *La Liza* of ten guns and thirty-three men, bound from Alicant to Marseilles. Took nineteen of our prisoners on board the *Speedy*. As it was evident that the bombard would become a wreck, we paid no further attention to her, but made all sail after the others.

"*December* 18. — Suspecting the passage between Dragon Island and the Main to be a lurking-place for privateers, we ran in again, but found nothing. Seeing a number of troops lining the beach, we opened fire and dispersed them, afterwards engaging a tower, which fired upon us. The prisoners we had taken proving an incumbrance, we put them on shore.

"*December* 19.—Stood off and on the harbour of Palamos, where we saw several vessels at anchor. Hoisted Danish colours, and made the signal for a pilot. Our real character being evidently known, none came off, and we did not think it prudent to venture in."

It has been said that the *Speedy* had become the marked object of the Spanish naval authorities. Not that there was much danger of being caught, for they confined their search to the coast only, and that in the daytime, when we were usually away in the offing ; it being our practice to keep out of sight during the day, and run in before dawn on the next morning.

On the 21st, however, when off Plane Island, we were very near "catching a Tartar." Seeing a large ship in shore, having all the appearance of a well-laden merchantman, we forthwith gave chase. On nearing her she raised her ports, which had been closed to deceive us, the act discovering a heavy broadside, a clear demonstration that we had fallen into the jaws of a formidable Spanish frigate, now crowded with men, who had before remained concealed below.

That the frigate was in search of us there could be no doubt, from the deception practised. To have encountered her with our insignificant armament would have been exceedingly imprudent, whilst escape was out of the question, for she would have outsailed us, and could have run us down by her mere weight. There was, therefore, nothing left, but to try the effect of a *ruse*, prepared beforehand for such an emergency. After receiving at Mahon information that unusual measures were about to be taken by the Spaniards for our capture, I had the *Speedy* painted in imitation of the Danish brig *Clomer;* the appearance of this vessel being well known on the Spanish coast. We also shipped a Danish quartermaster, taking the further precaution of providing him with the uniform of an officer of that nation.

On discovering the real character of our neighbour, the *Speedy* hoisted Danish colours, and spoke her. At first this failed to satisfy the Spaniard, who sent a boat to board us. It was now time to bring the Danish quartermaster into play in his officer's uniform ; and to add force to his explanations, we ran the quarantine flag up to the fore, calculating on the Spanish horror of the plague, then prevalent along the Barbary coast.

On the boat coming within hail,—for the yellow flag effectually repressed the enemy's desire to board us— our mock officer informed the Spaniards that we were two days from Algiers, where at the time the plague was violently raging. This was enough. The boat returned to the frigate, which, wishing us a good voyage, filled, and made sail, whilst we did the same.

I have noted this circumstance more minutely than it merits, because it has been misrepresented. By some

of my officers blame was cast on me for not attacking
the frigate after she had been put off her guard by
our false colours, as her hands — being then employed
at their ordinary avocations in the rigging and elsewhere
— presented a prominent mark for our shot.   There is
no doubt but that we might have poured in a murderous
fire before the crew could have recovered from their
confusion, and perhaps have taken her, but feeling
averse to so cruel a destruction of human life, I chose
to refrain from an attack, which might not, even with
that advantage in our favour, have been successful.

It has been stated by some naval writers that this
frigate was the *Gamo*, which we subsequently captured.
To the best of my knowledge this is an error.

"*December* 24.—Off Carthagena.   At daylight fell in with
a convoy in charge of two Spanish privateers which came up
and fired at us; but being to windward we ran for the convoy,
and singling out two, captured the nearest, laden with
wine.   The other ran in shore under the fort of Port Genoese,
where we left her.

"25. — Stood for Cape St. Martin, in hope of intercepting
the privateers.   At 8 A.M. saw a privateer and one of the convoy
under Cape Lanar.   Made sail in chase.   They parted company; when on our singling out the nearest privateer, she
took refuge under a battery, on which we left off pursuit.

"30. — Off Cape Oropesa.   Seeing some vessels in shore,
out boats in chase.   At noon they returned pursued by two
Spanish gun-boats, which kept up a smart fire on them.
Made sail to intercept the gun-boats, on which they ran in
under the batteries.

"*January* 10, 1801. — Anchored in Port Mahon, and
having refitted, sailed again on the 16th.

"12.—Off Barcelona.   Just before daylight chased two
vessels standing towards that port.   Seeing themselves pur-

sued, they made for the battery at the entrance. Bore up and set steering sails in chase. The wind falling calm, one of the chase drifted in shore, and took the ground under Castel De Ferro. On commencing our fire, the crew abandoned her, and we sent boats with anchors and hawsers to warp her off, in which they succeeded. She proved to be the Genoese ship *Ns. Señora de Gratia*, of ten guns.

"22.—Before daylight, stood in again for Barcelona. Saw several sail close in with the land. Out boats and boarded one, which turned out a Dane. Cruising off the port till 3 A.M., we saw two strange vessels coming from the westward. Made sail to cut them off. At 6 P.M. one of them hoisted Spanish colours and the other French. At 9 P.M. came up with them, when after an engagement of half an hour both struck. The Spaniard was the *Ecce Homo* of eight guns and nineteen men, the Frenchman *L'Amitié* of one gun and thirty-one men. Took all the prisoners on board the *Speedy*.

"23. — Still off Barcelona. Having sent most of our crew to man the prizes, the number of prisoners on board the *Speedy* became dangerous; we therefore put twenty-five of the Frenchmen into one of their own launches, and told them to make the best of their way to Barcelona. As the prizes were a good deal cut up about the rigging, repaired their damages and made sail for Port Mahon, where we arrived on the 24th, with our convoy in company.

"28. — Quitted Port Mahon for Malta, not being able to procure at Minorca various things of which we stood in need; and on the 1st of February, came to an anchor at Valetta, where we obtained anchors and sweeps."

An absurd affair took place during our short stay at Malta, which would not have been worthy of notice, had it not been made the subject of comment.

The officers of a French royalist regiment, then at Malta, patronised a fancy ball, for which I amongst others purchased a ticket. The dress chosen was that

of a sailor — in fact, my costume was a tolerable imitation of that of my worthy friend, Jack Larmour, in one
of his relaxing moods, and personated, in my estimation, as
honourable a character as were Greek, Turkish, or other
kinds of Oriental disguises in vogue at such reunions.
My costume was, however, too much to the life to
please French royalist taste, not even the marlinspike
and the lump of grease in the hat being omitted.

On entering the ball-room, further passage was immediately barred, with an intimation that my presence
could not be permitted in such a dress. Good humour-
edly expostulating that, as the choice of costume was
left to the wearer, my own taste — which was decidedly
nautical — had selected that of a British seaman, a
character which, though by no means imaginary, was
quite as picturesque as were the habiliments of an
Arcadian shepherd; further insisting that as no rule
had been infringed, I must be permitted to exercise my
discretion. Expostulation being of no avail, a brusque
answer was returned that such a dress was not admis-
sible, whereupon I as brusquely replied that having
purchased my ticket, and chosen my own costume in
accordance with the regulations, no one had any right
to prevent me from sustaining the character assumed.

Upon this a French officer, who appeared to act as
master of the ceremonies, came up, and without waiting for further explanation, rudely seized me by the
collar with the intention of putting me out; in return
for which insult he received a substantial mark of
British indignation, and at the same time an uncomplimentary remark in his own language. In an instant

all was uproar; a French picket was called, which in a short time overpowered and carried me off to the guard-house of the regiment.

I was, however, promptly freed from detention on announcing my name, but the officer who had collared me demanded an apology for the portion of the *fracas* concerning him personally. This being of course re-fused, a challenge was the consequence; and on the following morning we met behind the ramparts and exchanged shots, my ball passing through the poor fellow's thigh and dropping him. My escape, too, was a narrow one — his ball perforating my coat, waistcoat, and shirt, and bruising my side. Seeing my adversary fall, I stepped up to him — imagining his wound to be serious — and expressed a hope that he had not been hit in a vital part. His reply — uttered with all the politeness of his nation — was, that " he was not mate-rially hurt." I, however, was not at ease, for it was impossible not to regret this, to him, serious *dénoue-ment* of a trumpery affair, though arising from his own intemperate conduct. It was a lesson to me in future, never to do anything in frolic which might give even unintentional offence.

On the 3rd of February we sailed under orders for Tripoli, to make arrangement for fresh provisions for the fleet. This being effected, the *Speedy* returned to Malta, and on the 20th again left port in charge of a convoy for Tunis.

24th.—At the entrance of Tunis Bay we gave chase to a strange sail, which wore and stood in towards the town, anchoring at about the distance of three miles. Suspecting some reason for this movement, I despatched an officer to examine her, when the suspicion was confirmed by his ascertaining her to be *La Belle Caroline*, French brig of four guns, bound for Alexandria with field-pieces, ammunition, and wine for the use of the French army in Egypt.

Our position was one of delicacy, the vessel being in a neutral port, where, if we remained to watch her, she might prolong our stay for an indefinite period or escape in the night; whilst, from the warlike nature of the cargo, it was an object of national importance to effect her capture. The latter appearing the most beneficial course under all circumstances, we neared her so as to prevent escape, and soon after midnight boarded her, and having weighed her anchor, brought her close to the *Speedy*, before she had an opportunity of holding any communication with the shore.

The following day was employed in examining her stores, a portion of her ammunition being transferred to our magazine, to replace some damaged by leakage. Her crew, now on board the *Speedy* as prisoners, becoming clamorous at what they considered an illegal seizure, and being, moreover, in our way, an expedient was adopted to get rid of them, by purposely leaving their own launch within reach during the following night, with a caution to the watch not to prevent their desertion should they attempt it. The hint was taken, for before daylight on the 27th they seized the boat, and pulled out of the bay without molestation, not venturing to go to Tunis lest they should be retaken. We thus got rid of the prisoners, and at the same time of what might have turned out their reasonable complaint to the Tunisian authorities, for that we had exceeded the bounds of neutrality there could be no doubt.

On the 28th we weighed anchor, and proceeded to sea with our prize. After cruising for some days off Cape Bon we made sail for Cagliari, where we arrived on the 8th of March, and put to sea on the 11th with the prize in tow. On the 16th, anchored in Port Mahon.

On the 18th we again put to sea, and towards evening observed a large frigate in chase of us. As she did not answer the private signal, it was evident that the stranger was one of our Spanish friends on the look-out. To cope with a vessel of her size and armament would have been folly, so we made all sail away from her, but she gave instant chase, and evidently gained upon us. To add to our embarrassment, the *Speedy* sprung her maintopgallant-yard, and lost ground whilst fishing it.

At daylight the following morning the strange frigate was still in chase, though by crowding all sail during the night we had gained a little upon her; but during the day she again recovered her advantage, the more so as the breeze freshening, we were compelled to take in our royals, whilst she was still carrying on with everything set. After dark, we lowered a tub overboard with a light in it, and altering our course thus fortunately evaded her. On the 1st of April we returned to Port Mahon, and again put to sea on the 6th.

" *April* 11.—Observing a vessel near the shoal of Tortosa, gave chase. On the following morning her crew deserted her, and we took possession. In the evening anchored under the land.

"13.—Saw three vessels at anchor in a bay to the westward of Oropesa. Made sail up to them and anchored on the flank of a ten-gun fort. Whilst the firing was going on, the boats were sent in to board and bring out the vessels, which immediately weighed and got under the fort. At 5·30 P.M. the boats returned with one of them; the other two being hauled close in shore, we did not make any further attempt to capture them. As the prize, the *Ave Maria*, of four guns, was in ballast, we took the sails and spars out of her, and set her on fire.

" On the following morning at daybreak, several vessels appeared to the eastward. Made all sail to intercept them, but before we could come up, they succeeded in anchoring under a fort. On standing towards them, they turned out to be Spanish gun-boats, which commenced firing at us. At 10 A.M. anchored within musket shot, so as to keep an angle of the tower on our beam, thus neutralising its effect. Commenced firing broadsides alternately at the tower and the gun-boats, with visible advantage. Shortly before noon made preparation to cut out the gun-boats, but a fresh breeze setting in dead on shore, rendered it impossible to get at them without placing ourselves in peril. We thereupon worked out of the bay.

" 15. Two strange sail in sight. Gave chase, and in a couple of hours came up with and captured them. Made sail after a convoy in the offing, but the wind falling light at dusk, lost sight of them.

" On the 26th we anchored in Mahon, remaining a week to refit and procure fresh hands, many having been sent away in prizes. On the 2nd of May put to sea with a reduced crew, some of whom had to be taken out of H.M.'s prison."

We again ran along the Spanish coast, and on the 4th of May were off Barcelona, where the *Speedy* captured a vessel which reported herself as Ragusan, though in reality a Spanish four-gun tartan. Soon after detaining her we heard firing in the W. N.-W., and steering for that quarter fell in with a Spanish privateer, which we also captured, the *San Carlos*, of seven guns. On this a swarm of gun-boats came out of Barcelona, seven of them giving chase to us and the prizes, with which we made off shore, the gun-boats returning to Barcelona.

On the following morning, the prizes were sent to Port Mahon, and keeping out of sight for the rest of the day, the *Speedy* returned at midnight off Barcelona, where we found the gun-boats on the watch; but on our approach they ran in shore, firing at us occasionally. Suspecting that the object was to decoy us within reach of some larger vessel, we singled out one of them and made at her, the others, however, supporting her so well that some of our rigging being shot away, we made off shore to repair, the gun-boats following. Having thus got them to some distance and repaired damages, we set all sail, and again ran in shore, in the hope of getting between them and the land, so as to cut off some of their number. Perceiving our intention, they all made for the port as before, keeping up a smart fight, in which our fore topgallant-yard was so much injured, that we had to shift it, and were thus left astern. The remainder of the day was employed in repairing damages, and the gun-boats not venturing out again, at 9 P.M. we again made off shore.

Convinced that something more than ordinary had actuated the gun-boats to decoy us — just before daylight on the 6th we again ran in for Barcelona, when the trap manifested itself in the form of a large ship, running under the land, and bearing E. S.-E. On hauling towards her, she changed her course in chase of us, and was shortly made out to be a Spanish xebec frigate.

As some of my officers had expressed dissatisfaction at not having been permitted to attack the frigate fallen in with on the 21st of December, after her suspicions had been lulled by our device of hoisting Danish colours, &c., I told them they should now have a fair fight, notwithstanding that, by manning the two prizes sent to Mahon, our numbers had been reduced to fifty-four, officers and boys included. Orders were then given to pipe all hands, and prepare for action.

Accordingly we made towards the frigate, which was now coming down under steering sails. At 9·30 A.M., she fired a gun and hoisted Spanish colours, which the *Speedy* acknowledged by hoisting American colours, our object being, as we were now exposed to her full broadside, to puzzle her, till we got on the other tack, when we ran up the English ensign, and immediately afterwards encountered her broadside without damage.

Shortly afterwards she gave us another broadside, also without effect. My orders were not to fire a gun till we were close to her; when, running under her lee, we locked our yards amongst her rigging, and in this position returned our broadside, such as it was.

To have fired our popgun four-pounders at a distance would have been to throw away the ammunition; but the guns being doubly, and, as I afterwards learned,

trebly, shotted, and being elevated, they told admirably
upon her main deck; the first discharge, as was subsequently ascertained, killing the Spanish captain and the
boatswain.

My reason for locking our small craft in the enemy's
rigging was the one upon which I mainly relied for
victory, viz. that from the height of the frigate out of
the water, the whole of her shot must necessarily go
over our heads, whilst our guns, being elevated, would
blow up her maindeck.

The Spaniards speedily found out the disadvantage
under which they were fighting, and gave the order to
board the *Speedy;* but as this order was as distinctly
heard by us as by them, we avoided it at the moment
of execution by sheering off sufficiently to prevent the
movement, giving them a volley of musketry and a
broadside before they could recover themselves.

Twice was this manœuvre repeated, and twice thus
averted. The Spaniards finding that they were only
punishing themselves, gave up further attempts to board,
and stood to their guns, which were cutting up our
rigging from stem to stern, but doing little farther
damage; for after·the lapse of an hour the loss to the
*Speedy* was only two men killed and four wounded.

This kind of combat, however, could not last. Our
rigging being cut up and the *Speedy's* sails riddled with
shot, I told the men that they must either take the
frigate or be themselves taken, in which case the
Spaniards would give no quarter—whilst a few minutes
energetically employed on their part would decide the
matter in their own favour.

The doctor, Mr. Guthrie, who, I am happy to say, is still living to peruse this record of his gallantry, volunteered to take the helm; leaving him therefore for the time both commander and crew of the *Speedy*, the order was given to board, and in a few seconds every man was on the enemy's deck—a feat rendered the more easy as the doctor placed the *Speedy* close along side with admirable skill.

For a moment the Spaniards seemed taken by surprise, as though unwilling to believe that so small a crew would have the audacity to board them; but soon recovering themselves, they made a rush to the waist of the frigate, where the fight was for some minutes gallantly carried on. Observing the enemy's colours still flying, I directed one of our men immediately to haul them down, when the Spanish crew, without pausing to consider by whose orders the colours had been struck, and naturally believing it the act of their own officers, gave in, and we were in possession of the *Gamo* frigate of thirty-two heavy guns and 319 men, who an hour and a half before had looked upon us as a certain if not an easy prey.

Our loss in boarding was Lieutenant Parker, severely wounded in several places, one seaman killed and three wounded, which with those previously killed and wounded gave a total of three seamen killed, and one officer and seventeen men wounded.

The *Gamo's* loss was Captain de Torres—the boatswain—and thirteen seamen killed, together with forty-one wounded; her casualties thus exceeding the whole number of officers and crew on board the *Speedy*.

Some time after the surrender of the *Gamo*, and when we were in quiet possession, the officer who had succeeded the deceased Captain Don Francisco de Torres, not in command, but in rank, applied to me for a certificate that he had done his duty during the action! whereupon he received from me a certificate that he had "conducted himself like a true Spaniard," with which document he appeared highly gratified, and I had afterwards the satisfaction of learning that it procured him further promotion in the Spanish service!

Shortly before boarding an incident occurred which, by those who have never been placed in similar circumstances, may be thought too absurd for notice. Knowing that the final struggle would be a desperate one, and calculating on the superstitious wonder which forms an element in the Spanish character, a portion of our crew were ordered to blacken their faces, and what with this and the excitement of combat, more ferocious looking objects could scarcely be imagined. The fellows thus disguised were directed to board by the head, and the effect produced was precisely that calculated on. The greater portion of the Spaniard's crew was prepared to repel boarders in that direction, but stood for a few moments as it were transfixed to the deck by the apparition of so many diabolical looking figures emerging from the white smoke of the bow guns; whilst our other men, who boarded by the waist, rushed on them from behind, before they could recover from their surprise at the unexpected phenomenon.

In difficult or doubtful attacks by sea,—and the odds of 50 men to 320 comes within this description, — no

device can be too minute, even if apparently absurd,
provided it have the effect of diverting the enemy's attention whilst you are concentrating your own. In this,
and other successes against odds, I have no hesitation
in saying that success in no slight degree depended on
out-of-the-way devices, which the enemy not suspecting, were in some measure thrown off their guard.

The subjoined tabular view of the respective force of
the two vessels will best show the nature of the contest.

| Gamo. | Speedy. |
|---|---|
| Main-deck guns. — Twenty-two long 12-pounders. | Fourteen 4-pounders. |
| Quarter-deck. — Eight long 8-pounders, and two 24-pounder carronades. | None. |
| No. of crew, 319. | No. of crew, 54. |
| Broadside weight of shot, 190 lbs. | Broadside weight of shot, 28 lbs. |
| Tonnage, 600 and upwards. | Tonnage, 158. |

It became a puzzle what to do with 263 unhurt prisoners now we had taken them, the *Speedy* having only
forty-two men left. Promptness was however necessary;
so driving the prisoners into the hold, with guns pointing down the hatchway, and leaving thirty of our men
on board the prize—which was placed under the command of my brother, the Hon. Archibald Cochrane, then
a midshipman—we shaped our course to Port Mahon
— not Gibraltar, as has been recorded — and arrived
there in safety; the Barcelona gun-boats, though spectators of the action, not venturing to rescue the frigate.
Had they made the attempt, we should have had some
difficulty in evading them and securing the prize, the

prisoners manifesting every disposition to rescue themselves, and only being deterred by their own main deck
guns loaded with cannister, and pointing down the
hatchways, whilst our men stood over them with
lighted matches.

The subjoined is Lord Keith's letter in reply to my
official announcement of our success.

"*Foudroyant*, off Arab's Tower,
"9th June, 1801.

"MY LORD,—I have received your lordship's letter of the
13th ult., enclosing a copy of your letter to Captain Dixon,
detailing your engagement with and capture of the Spanish
xebec of 32 guns; and cannot fail to be extremely gratified
with the communication of an event so honourable to the
naval service, and so highly creditable to your lordship's professional reputation, and to the intrepidity and discipline of
the *Speedy's* officers and men, to all of whom I request your
lordship will make my perfect satisfaction and approbation
known.

"I have the honour to be, My Lord,
"Your Lordship's most obedient servant,
(Signed)                    "KEITH.

"The Right Hon. Lord Cochrane,
"*Speedy.*"

As a matter of course, my report of the capture of
the *Gamo* was, in the first instance, made to the commandant at Port Mahon, the commander-in-chief being
in Egypt. It should have been forwarded by him to
the Secretary of the Admiralty, but was delayed for
upwards of a month, thus affording a pretence for not
promoting me to post rank, according to the recognised
rules of the service.

From information on the affair being thus delayed, it was generally believed at home, that the *Gamo* had been taken by surprise, instead of after a close engagement, deliberately decided on, and announced to the officers and crew of the *Speedy* at five o'clock in the morning, the hands being turned up for the purpose. The consequence of the delay was a postponement of my post commission for upwards of three months, viz. from the 6th of May to the 8th of August; and what was of more consequence, a misunderstanding with Lord St. Vincent, which bore most unfavourably upon all my future prospects. Upon this subject much will have to be said in a subsequent chapter.

The subjoined is a copy of my official report to the senior officer commanding at Port Mahon ; and also of his remarkably concise comment thereon, when tardily transmitting the same to the Secretary of the Admiralty.

*Copy of a letter from* Capt. M. DIXON, *of H. M. S. Genereux, to* E. NEPEAN, Esq., *Secretary of the Admiralty, dated Port Mahon, 9th June,* 1800.

" SIR, — I have the pleasure to transmit a copy of Lord Cochrane's letter relative to the very spirited and brilliant action with a Spanish xebec frigate.

' • " I have the honour, &c.<br>" MANLEY DIXON.

" E. Nepean, Esq."

" H. M. Sloop *Speedy*, off Barcelona,<br>" 6th May, 1800.

" SIR, — I have the pleasure to inform you, that the sloop I have the honour to command, after a mutual chase and warm action, has captured a Spanish xebec frigate of 32 guns, 22 long 12-pounders, 8 nines, and 2 heavy carronades, viz. the *Gamo*, commanded by Don Francisco de Torres, manned by 319 officers, seamen, and marines.

" The great disparity of force rendered it necessary to adopt some measure that might prove decisive. I resolved to board, and with Lieut. Parker, the Hon. A. Cochrane, the boatswain and crew, did so, when, by the impetuosity of the attack, we forced them to strike. I have to lament, in boarding, the loss of one man only; the severe wounds received by Lieut. Parker, both from musketry and the sword, one wound received by the boatswain, and one seaman.

" I must be permitted to say that there could not be greater regularity, nor more cool determined conduct shown by men, than by the crew of the *Speedy*. Lieut. Parker, whom I beg leave to recommend to their Lordship's notice, as well as the Hon. Mr. Cochrane, deserve all the approbation that can be bestowed. The exertions and good conduct of the boatswain, carpenter, and petty officers, I acknowledge with pleasure, as well as the skill and attention of Mr. Guthrie, the surgeon.

" I have the honour to be, &c.
" COCHRANE.

" M. Dixon, Esq."

*Speedy's force at commencement of action.*

Fifty-four officers, men, and boys, 14 4-pounders. Three killed and 8 wounded.

*Gamo's force at commencement of action.*

Two hundred and seventy-four officers, seamen, and supernumeraries. Forty-five marines. Guns, 32. Don Francisco de Torres, the boatswain, and 13 men killed, 41 wounded.

# CHAP. VI.

## CRUISE OF THE *SPEEDY* CONTINUED.

THE SPEEDY SENT TO ALGIERS. — INTERVIEW WITH THE DEY. — SPEEDY
RETURNS TO MINORCA. — ATTACK ON OROPESA. — ENEMY'S VESSELS
DESTROYED. — LETTER OF THANKS FROM LORD KEITH. — SPEEDY SENT
IN CONVOY OF A PACKET. — CAPTURED BY THREE FRENCH LINE OF
BATTLE SHIPS, AND TAKEN TO ALGESIRAS. — ATTACK BY SIR J.
SAUMAREZ'S SQUADRON. — LOSS OF THE HANNIBAL. — CAPTURE OF
DOCKYARD ARTIFICERS. — GALLANTRY OF CAPTAIN KEATS.

OUR success hitherto had procured us some prize money,
notwithstanding the peculations of the Mediterranean
Admiralty Courts, by which the greater portion of our
captures was absorbed.

Despite this drawback, which generally disinclined
officers and crews from making extraordinary exertions,
my own share of the twelvemonth's zealous endeavours
in our little sloop was considerable, and even the crew
were in receipt of larger sums than those constituting
the ordinary pay of officers ; a result chiefly owing
to our nocturnal mode of warfare, together with our
refraining from meddling with vessels ascertained to be
loading in the Spanish ports, and then lying in wait
for them as they proceeded on their voyage.

One effect of our success was no slight amount of ill
concealed jealousy on the part of officers senior to myself, though there were some amongst these who, being

in command of small squadrons instead of single vessels, might, had they adopted the same means, have effected far more than the *Speedy*, with an armament so insignificant, was calculated to accomplish.

After remaining some days at Port Mahon to refit, we prepared to return to our cruising ground, where, from private information, we knew that other prizes were at hand.  In place of being permitted so to do, the *Speedy* received an order to proceed to Algiers, for the purpose of representing to the Dey the illegality of his cruisers having taken a British vessel in retaliation for an Algerine captured whilst violating the law of blockade.

The mission was a singular one to be entrusted to the captain of one of the smallest and worst armed vessels in the British service.  Remonstrance, to be effectual with a piratical government, ought to have been committed to an officer armed with sufficient force at least to induce respect.  There was, however, no alternative but to obey, and a short time saw us at anchor off the mole of the predatory potentate.

The request for an interview with his highness occasioned no little dissatisfaction amongst his ministers, if those who were quite as much his masters as his subordinates could be so termed.  After some consultation, the interview was, however, granted, and a day was appointed to deliver my message.

The invariable Moslem preliminary of taking coffee having been gone through, I was ushered through a series of galleries lined with men, each bearing on his shoulder a formidable looking axe, and eyeing me with

an insolent scowl, evidently meant to convey the satisfaction with which they would apply its edge to my
vertebræ, should the caprice of their chief so will.

On reaching the presence of the Dey — a dignified
looking and gorgeously attired person, seated cross-
legged on an elevated couch in one corner of the gallery
and surrounded by armed people of most unprepos-
sessing appearance — I was marched up between two
janizaries, and ordered to make three salaams to his
highness.

This formality being complied with, he rudely demanded, through the medium of an interpreter, " What
brought me there?"   The reply was that " I was the
commander of an English vessel of war in the roads,
and had been deputed, on behalf of my government,
respectfully to remonstrate with his highness concerning
a vessel which his cruisers had taken contrary to the
laws of nations."   On this being interpreted the ferocious scowls of the bystanders were exchanged for expressions of injured innocence, but the Dey got in a
great passion, and told the interpreter to inform me
that " remonstrance came with an ill grace from us,
the British vessels being the greatest pirates in the
world, and mine one of the worst amongst them,"
which complimentary statement was acknowledged by
me with a formal bow.

"If I did right," continued the Dey, through his
interpreter, — " I should put you and your crew in
prison, till (naming a captured Algerine vessel) she was
restored ; and but for my great respect for the English
government, and my impression that her seizure was

unauthorised, you should go there. However, you may go, with a demand from me that the vessel unjustly taken from us shall be immediately restored."

This decision appeared to be anything but satisfactory to the oligarchy of which his court was composed, as savouring of a clemency to which they were little inclined. From the boisterous conversation which ensued, they were evidently desirous of prolonging my stay to an indefinite period, or perhaps of terminating it summarily through the instrumentality of the axemen who lined the galleries, as a few years afterwards they terminated the existence of the Dey himself.

To confess the truth, there was some room for self-congratulation on quitting the presence of such barbarians, to whom I was not fairly accredited for such a mission. However, the remonstrance confided to me being duly delivered, we returned to Minorca, to report progress, though not without being chased by an Algerine cruiser on our way. As the *Speedy* outsailed her, and as there was no beneficial object to be gained by interfering with her, we stood on without further notice.

On arriving at our former cruising ground, we encountered a Spanish privateer of six guns, which was captured. This vessel was fitted out at my own private expense, and my brother appointed to command her, as a tender to the *Speedy;* several enemy's vessels having previously escaped for want of such aid.

In a few days after this, we fell in with the *Kangaroo*, Captain Pulling, who, being senior to me, was therefore my commanding officer. Running down the coast in company, we attacked the fort of Almanara, and after silencing it, brought off a Spanish privateer of seven guns.

On the 8th of June, the *Speedy* ran into Oropesa, where, on the 13th and 14th of April, we had the previous action with the fort and gun-boats. Perceiving several vessels at anchor under the fort, it was deemed advisable to make off shore, with the intention of running in again at midnight, and cutting some of them out.

We had not proceeded far, before we again fell in with the *Kangaroo*, when informing Captain Pulling of what we had seen, he declined the night attack, preferring to postpone operations till the following day. Accordingly, at noon on the 9th, we went in, and made out a twenty-gun xebec and three gun-boats, with ten sail of merchantmen under their convoy. It was determined to attack them as they lay; the *Kangaroo* anchoring well up to and engaging the fort, whilst the *Speedy* and her tender under my brother's orders, encountered the xebec and the gun-boats — the *Speedy* anchoring in a line between those vessels and the *Kangaroo*.

For some hours an incessant cannonade was kept up on both sides, the *Kangaroo's* fire flanking the fort, whilst the slackened fire of the Spanish vessels showed that our shot had told. At this juncture, a twelve-gun felucca, and two more gun-boats having arrived from Valentia to their assistance, the Spaniards took heart, and the action became nearly as brisk as before.

The felucca and the newly arrived gun-boats were,

however, for a time beat off, and after an hour's additional firing, the xebec, two gunboats, and some of the convoy were sunk; the remaining gun-boats shortly afterwards sharing the same fate.

The action had now continued for upwards of nine hours; during which the *Speedy* had expended nearly all her ammunition, viz. 1400 shot, and the *Kangaroo* was much in the same predicament. As the felucca and gun-boats had again come up, it was necessary to effect something decisive. Captain Pulling, therefore, slipping his cable, shifted close to the fort, which was soon afterwards abandoned, and the *Speedy* closed with the felucca and her consorts, which forthwith fled. Had they remained, we had not half a dozen rounds left to continue the action.

Both vessels now hoisted out boats, and made for the merchantmen. Three of these had been sunk, and four others driven on shore; we, however, brought away the three still afloat. By this time a number of Spanish troops lined the beach for the protection of the vessels ashore, and as we had scarcely a shot left, it was impracticable to reply to the musketry, within range of which the boats must necessarily have been placed had the attempt been made. We therefore relinquished the endeavour to get off the stranded vessels.

It may be useful here to remark that on board the *Kangaroo* were some guns fitted on the non-recoil principle, and that during the action these broke from their breechings; one, if not more, endangering the vessel by bounding down the hatchways into the hold.

The subjoined letter of thanks for this affair was forwarded to Captain Pulling by Lord Keith, who was then at Alexandria, watching the movements of the French in Egypt.

"*Foudroyant*, Bay of Aboukir,
"10th July, 1801.

"SIR,—I have received your letter of the 10th of June, detailing the attack made by the *Kangaroo* and *Speedy* upon the fort of Oropesa and the enemy's armed vessels at anchor under its protection, on 9th of that month; as well as upon the tower of Almanara on a former day: and while I offer my congratulations upon the successful issue of your enterprise, I cannot withhold my approbation of the persevering and determined conduct manifested by you and by Captain Lord Cochrane, as well as by the officers and companies of both the sloops on these occasions, and I request that my satisfaction may be communicated by you to his lordship, and that you and he will make the same known to the officers and companies of the *Kangaroo* and the *Speedy*.

"I am, &c. &c.

"KEITH.

"Capt. Pulling, *Kangaroo*."

On our return to Port Mahon with the prizes, the *Gamo* had not been purchased by the Government; but, to my regret, this useful cruiser had been sold for a trifle to the Algerines, whilst I was condemned to continue in the pigmy and now battered craft by which she had been taken. To have obtained command of the *Gamo*, even as a means of deception on the enemy's coast, I would scarcely have changed place with an admiral.

But a more cruel thing still was in store for me. The commandant lived in the house of a Spanish merchant who had a contract for carrying the mails to

Gibraltar.  The vessel employed for this purpose was a notoriously bad sailer, and when the *Speedy* was ready for sea, instead of being permitted to return to our cruising ground, she was ordered to convoy this tub of a packet to Gibraltar, with further instructions to take the letter-bag on board the *Speedy*, protect the packet, put the mail on board her as soon as we arrived off the Rock, and return without holding any communication with the shore! the evident object of the last injunction being that the service which had been thrust upon us should not become known!

The expectation of the packet-master, doubtless, was that we should put to sea out of privateer reach.  In place of this, we ran along the Spanish coast, our superior sailing enabling us, without delay, to scrutinise every creek as we passed.  Nothing, however, occurred, till we were close in with a bay, or rather indentation of the shore near Alicant, where seeing some vessels at anchor, we made towards them, on which they weighed and deliberately ran ashore.  To have stopped to get them off would have been in excess of our instructions. To set fire to them was not, and as one was laden with oil, and the night following very dark, the result was a blaze which illumined the sky for many miles round.

Unluckily for us, three French line-of-battle ships, which afterwards turned out to be the *Indomptable*, the *Dessaix*, and the *Formidable*, were in the vicinity, and being attracted by the light of the burning vessels, ran in shore to see what was the matter.

At daybreak, on the morning of July 3rd, these large ships were observed in the distance, calling up to our imaginations visions of Spanish galleons from South America, and accordingly the *Speedy* prepared for chase.   It was not till day dawned that we found out our mistake, the vessels between us and the offing being clearly line-of-battle ships, forbidding all reasonable hope of escape.

It was about four o'clock in the morning when we made out the French ships, which immediately on discovering us gave chase.  Being to windward, we endeavoured to escape by making all sail, and, as the wind fell light, by using our sweeps.   This proving unavailing, we threw the guns overboard, and put the brig before the wind ; but notwithstanding every effort, the enemy gained fast upon us, and, in order to prevent our slipping past, separated on different tacks, so as to keep us constantly within reach of one or the other ; the *Dessaix*, being nearest, firing broadsides at us as she passed when tacking, at other times firing from her bow chasers, and cutting up our rigging.

For upwards of three hours we were thus within gunshot of the *Dessaix*, when finding it impossible to escape by the wind, I ordered all the stores to be thrown overboard, in the hope of being able, when thus further lightened, to run the gauntlet between the ships, which continued to gain upon us.

Watching an opportunity, when the nearest line-of-battle ship was before our beam, we bore up, set the studding sails, and attempted to run between them, the French honouring us with a broadside for this unexpected movement.  The *Dessaix*, however, immediately tacked in pursuit, and in less than an hour got within musket shot. At this short distance, she let fly at us a complete broadside of round and grape, the object evidently being to sink us at a blow, in retaliation for thus attempting to slip past, though almost without hope of escape.

Fortunately for us, in yawing to bring her broadside to bear, the rapidity with which she answered her helm carried her a little too far, and her round shot plunged in the water under our bows, or the discharge must have sunk us; the scattered grape, however, took effect in the rigging, cutting up a great part of it, riddling the sails, and doing material damage to the masts and yards, though not a man was hurt. To have delayed for another broadside would have been to expose all on board to certain destruction, and as further effort to escape was impotent, the *Speedy's* colours were hauled down.

On going aboard the *Dessaix*, and presenting my sword to the captain, Christie Pallière, he politely declined taking it, with the complimentary remark that " he would not accept the sword of an officer who had for so many hours struggled against impossibility," at the same time paying me the further compliment of requesting that " I would continue to wear my sword, though a prisoner "—a request with which I complied; Capt. Pallière at the same time good-naturedly expressing his satisfaction at having terminated our exploits in the cruising line, they having, in fact, special instructions to look out for us. After this reception it is scarcely necessary to add that I was treated with great kindness by my captors.

Thus ended the thirteen months' cruise of the *Speedy*,

during which we had taken and retaken upwards of 50 vessels, 122 guns, and 534 prisoners.

After the capture of the *Speedy*, the French line-of-battle ships, after a short cruise on the coast, proceeded with her, and the unlucky packet which had been the primary cause of the disaster, to Algesiras. During this cruise I had ample opportunity of observing the superior manner in which the sails of the *Dessaix* were cut, and the consequent flat surface exposed to the wind; this contrasting strongly with the bag reefs and bellying sails of English ships of war at that period.

As there was no force at Gibraltar adequate to an attack of the French squadron, the authorities lost no time in transmitting intelligence of their arrival to Sir James Saumarez, then blockading the Spanish squadron in Cadiz. The French meanwhile proceeded to water and refit, evidently with the intention of repassing the Straits with the first fair wind.

Quitting Cadiz, Sir James Saumarez immediately sailed for Algesiras with his squadron, consisting of the *Cæsar, Venerable, Audacious, Hannibal, Superb, Pompée, Spencer, Calpe,* and *Thames,* these reaching the bay on the 6th of July.

At the time of their first appearance I was conversing with Captain Pallière in his cabin, when a lieutenant reported a British flag over Cabritta point, and soon afterwards the top-gallant masts and pendants of a British squadron were reported visible. We at once adjourned to the poop, when the surprise of the French, at the sight of a more numerous squadron, became not unreasonably apparent; Captain Pallière asked me " if I thought an attack would be made, or whether the British force would anchor off Gibraltar?" My reply was " that an attack would certainly be made, and that before night both British and French ships would be at Gibraltar," at the same time adding that when there, it would give me great pleasure to make him and his officers a return for the kindness I had experienced on board the *Dessaix!*

The French admiral, however, determined that his ships should not be carried across the bay if he could help it. Before the British squadron had rounded the point, the French out boats, with kedges and stream anchors, for the purpose of warping in shore, so as to prevent the approaching squadron from cutting them out; but the order was so hurriedly executed, that all three ships were hauled aground with their sterns presented to the approaching British force; a position which could not have been taken by choice, for nothing could apparently be more easy than to destroy the French ships, which, lying aground stern on, could only use their stern chasers.

To employ their consequently useless hands to some purpose the French landed a considerable portion of their crews to man the Spanish batteries on the island, as the ship's guns could not be brought to bear. Two of the British ships anchored, and opened upon the French ships aground, but being exposed to the fire of some of the newly manned forts higher up the bay, the heavy guns of which were admirably handled by the French seamen, both the British vessels slipped their cables, and together with the remainder of the squadron, which did not anchor at all, backed their main-top-sails for the purpose of maintaining their position. The wind, however, blowing from the westward, with a rapid current sweeping round the bay, thwarted this intention, and the British squadron quickly drifted past the enemy, firing as they went.

Perhaps I ought previously to have mentioned an incident demonstrative of the *sang froid* of my captor. After having satisfied himself that an action with a superior force was inevitable, Capt. Pallière remarked, " that it should not spoil our breakfast," in which he had invited me to join him. Before the meal was ended, a round shot crashed through the stern of the *Dessaix*, driving before it a shower of broken glass, the *débris* of a wine bin under the sofa.

We forthwith jumped up from table, and went on the quarter-deck, but a raking shot from Sir James Saumarez's ship, sweeping a file of marines from the poop, not far from me, I considered further exposure on my part unnecessary, and went below to a position whence I could nevertheless, at times, see what was going on.

The *Hannibal*, having with the others forged past the enemy, gallantly filled and tacked with a view to get between the French ships and the shore, being evidently unaware of their having been hauled aground. The consequence was that she ran upon a shoal, and re-mained fast, nearly bow on to the broadsides of the French line-of-battle ships, which with the shore bat-teries and several gun-boats opened upon her a con-

centrated fire.   This, from her position, she was unable
to return.   The result was that her guns were speedily
dismounted, her rigging shot away, and a third of
her crew killed or wounded; Captain Ferris, who
commanded her, having now no alternative but to
strike his colours—though not before he had displayed
an amount of endurance which excited the admiration
of the enemy.

A circumstance now occurred which is entitled to
rank amongst the curiosities of war.   On the French
taking possession of the *Hannibal,* they had neglected
to provide themselves with their national ensign, and
either from necessity or bravado rehoisted the English
flag upside down.   This being a well-known signal of
distress, was so understood by the authorities at Gibraltar, who, manning all government and other boats with
dockyard artificers and seamen, sent them, as it was
mistakenly considered, to the assistance of the *Hannibal.*

On the approach of the launches, I was summoned on
deck by the captain of the *Dessaix,* who seemed doubtful what measures to adopt as regarded the boats now
approaching to board the *Hannibal,* and asked my
opinion as to whether they would attempt to retake the
ship.   As there could be no doubt in my mind about
the nature of their mission or its result, it was evident
that if they were allowed to board, nothing could prevent the seizure of the whole.   My advice, therefore,
to Captain Pallière was to warn them off by a shot—
hoping they would thereby be driven back and saved
from capture.   Captain Pallière seemed at first inclined
to take the advice, but on reflection—either doubting its

sincerity, or seeing the real state of the case—he decided to capture the whole by permitting them to board unmolested. Thus boat by boat was captured until all the artificers necessary for the repair of the British squadron, and nearly all the sailors at that time in Gibraltar, were taken prisoners!

In this action the French and Spaniards suffered severely both as regarded ships and men, their masts and hulls being much knocked about, whilst several Spanish gunboats were sunk. The wonder to me was, that the British squadron did not anchor, for the French ships being aground, stern on, could have offered little resistance, and must have been destroyed. It is true that the batteries on shore were admirably served, and thus constituted a formidable obstacle; but had not the squadron drifted past the French ships, the latter might have been interposed between the batteries and the British force, when the fire of the former would have been neutralised, and the enemy's ships aground destroyed with comparatively little loss. It is not, however, my purpose or province to criticise the action, but simply to give the details, as personally witnessed from that extraordinary place, for a British officer, the deck of a French ship!

Neither the imprisonment of the captured crews, nor my own were of long duration. The day after the action, Sir J. Saumarez sent Capt. Brenton into Algesiras Bay with a flag of truce, to endeavour to effect an exchange of the gallant Capt. Ferris, his officers, and crew. At that time there was no regulated system of exchange between the belligerent powers, but Capt.

Brenton succeeded in procuring the release of the crew of the *Hannibal* and the entrapped artificers, together with the officers and men of the *Speedy*. Admiral Linois would not at first give me up, but, on further consideration, allowed me to go with the other officers to Gibraltar on *parole*. My complete release was eventually effected for the second captain of the *St. Antonio*, taken shortly afterwards.

The French ships having lost no time in communicating with the Spanish admiral at Cadiz, he promptly appeared off Algesiras with a reinforcement of six ships of the line, several frigates, and gun-boats. The enemy having by this time warped off their grounded ships, as well as the *Hannibal*, and having by the 12th got them in sea-going order, the whole sailed from Algesiras, followed by the British squadron, which, by great exertions, had been got in readiness for pursuit.

Of the action which subsequently took place I have no personal knowledge, other than that of a scene witnessed by myself from the garden of the commissioner's house, in which I was staying.

The enemy were overtaken at dusk, soon after leaving the bay, and when it had become dark, Captain Keats, in the *Superb*, gallantly dashed in between the two sternmost ships, firing right and left, and passed on. Of course I do not assert myself to have been personally cognisant of the way in which the attack was made, the firing only being visible from the Rock, but that this is the correct version of the affair rests upon indisputable authority. The movement was so rapidly executed, that the *Superb* shot ahead before the smoke cleared away, and the Spanish ships, the *Real Carlos*, 112, and the *San Hermenegildo*, 112, mistaking each other for the aggressor, began a mutual attack, resulting in the *Real Carlos* losing her foretop-mast, the sails of which—falling over her own guns—caught fire. While in this condition the *Hermenegildo*—still engaging the *Real Carlos* as an enemy—in the confusion fell on board her and caught fire also. Both ships burned till they blew up, and nearly all on board perished; a few survivors only escaping on board the *Superb* as Captain Keats was taking possession of a *third* Spanish line-of-battle ship, the *San Antonio*—for whose second captain, as has been said, I was exchanged.

The remainder of the combined squadron got safely back to Cadiz after an encounter between the *Formidable* and *Venerable*. I am aware that the preceding account of the action with the French ships at Algesiras differs in some respects from that compiled by naval historians from the despatches; but this circumstance will not prevent me from giving my own version of a conflict in which it was my misfortune to be a reluctant spectator. The *Real Carlos*, one of the ships blown up, bore the flag of the Spanish Admiral, Moreno, who with Admiral Linois was said to be at the time on board a Spanish frigate.

# CHAP. VII.

## ADMIRALTY RELUCTANCE TO PROMOTE ME.

LETTER FROM SIR ALEXANDER COCHRANE. — SECOND LETTER FROM SIR
ALEXANDER.—BOTH WRITTEN UNKNOWN TO ME.—RELUCTANCE OF LORD
ST. VINCENT TO PROMOTE ME. — LETTER FROM MY FATHER TO LORD
ST. VINCENT, URGING MY RIGHT TO PROMOTION. — LORD ST. VIN-
CENT'S REPLY. — ITS FALLACY. — HIS LORDSHIP'S REASONING A SUB-
TERFUGE. — PROMOTION OF MY FIRST LIEUTENANT REFUSED. — MY
IMPRUDENT REMARK TO LORD ST. VINCENT, WHO BECOMES MY
ENEMY. — FURTHER EFFORT TO PROMOTE LIEUTENANT PARKER. —
ADMIRALTY REFUSAL ALSO. — LIEUTENANT PARKER'S EVENTUAL PRO-
MOTION, AND SUBSEQUENT SHAMEFUL TREATMENT.

IT has been already stated that not only was the action
with the *Gamo* for some time unnoticed in the customary manner, but the post rank to which the rule
of the service entitled me from the result of the
action, was withheld. My friends, being naturally surprised at the retention of what was no favour on the
part of Lord St. Vincent, but my unquestionable right,
respectfully pointed out to his lordship the nature of
the services rendered.

The subjoined letter addressed to Lord St. Vincent
by my kind uncle Sir Alexander Cochrane, in reference
to the *Speedy's* escape from a Spanish frigate (see
page 100), was written previous to that relating to the
capture of the *Gamo*, but is worthy of record on
grounds generally connected with the naval service.

"My Lord,—Yesterday we received accounts of your Lordship's being placed at the head of the Admiralty, on which occasion I beg to offer my congratulations. I never subscribed to the opinion that a naval officer ought not to be First Lord of the Admiralty, and from your Lordship's thorough knowledge of the service, we may now hope for that support on many occasions which we could not look for from those who—not having borne the brunt of the day, or being bred to the Navy — could be but bad judges either of officers' characters, or the motives which on many occasions actuate them.

"Doubtless your Lordship has already received numerous weighty applications for the promotion of young men in the service, nor would I presume to add to their number but from the obliging expressions your Lordship once made me in favour of Lord Cochrane, had you remained longer on this station. I have the less reserve on this occasion, as I think his Lordship has a claim to be made post, from the presence of mind by which he lately saved H.M.'s sloop *Speedy*, which he at present commands. This I beg leave to recount.

"He had taken several prizes off Carthagena, when, one morning, he found himself close under the guns of a Spanish frigate.

" His only chance of escape was, either to board the frigate, in the hope of finding her unprepared, or to pass off the *Speedy* as a Danish sloop of war.

"With one of these objects he stood towards her under Danish colours, but, on a near approach, found her too formidable to be carried by the few hands he had on board. On being hailed to know what brig it was, he gave, through the medium of a Danish quartermaster, the name of a Danish brig lately arrived on the station. On being ordered to come on board the frigate with his commission, he informed the Spaniards that his orders from the court of Denmark were not to send a boat on board any foreign man of war, but that if they had any doubts of his not being a Danish sloop of war, they were at liberty to board him.

"On this a boat left the frigate, but just as they were almost alongside the *Speedy*, they were informed that she was in quarantine, being only a few days from Algiers, where the plague at that time existed.   On this the Spanish officers in the boat refused to touch a rope, and returned to the frigate, when her captain told Lord Cochrane that he knew his brig, and wished him a pleasant voyage.*

"I have ever been of opinion that rewards for bold services cannot be too great, and I must confess that where one of his Majesty's ships is saved by presence of mind similar to what I have related, great praise is due to her commander.

"Your Lordship will, I hope, excuse me for trespassing a little longer in favour of my nephew, who is now twenty-five years old, a time of life that promotion can only be of use. His father has expended his whole fortune in discoveries which will be of great use to the public—but the real sufferer is Lord Cochrane.   The liberality of your Lordship's mind will see this in its true light, and also plead my excuse for the liberty I have taken.

"Hoping that your Lordship's health is reinstated, &c. &c.

"I am, your Lordship's, &c. &c.

"ALEXANDER COCHRANE.

"The Right Hon. Lord St. Vincent."

I was not aware till recently that Sir Alexander had kindly made this application on my behalf.   At the time the preceding letter was written he did not know of the capture of the *Gamo;* the *Ajax,* which he commanded, being then before Alexandria.   On learning our success, he again wrote to Lord St. Vincent as follows:—

* As the reader is aware, we had previously painted the *Speedy* in imitation of the Danish brig.

"*Ajax*, off Alexandria, June 10th, 1801.

"My Lord, — I some time ago wrote your Lordship in favour of my nephew Lord Cochrane, recommending his being made post.

"I hope your Lordship received my letter, and that you viewed Lord Cochrane's conduct in the light I did. But if my persuasions were not then judged of sufficient weight, I may now with much confidence come forward and claim for my nephew the palm of victory in both ways, by an act hardly equalled in this war of naval miracles, considering the great inequality of force between the *Speedy* with fifty-four men, and a xebec frigate of thirty-two guns and 319 men.

"Well knowing that nothing gives your Lordship more pleasure than having an opportunity of rewarding merit, let the rank of the person be what it may, I am confident your Lordship will, on the present occasion, do every justice to Lord Cochrane, though should his promotion have arisen from his former exploits it would be more grateful to my feelings more especially as his subsequent conduct will do honour to your Lordship's appointment.

"I believe I told your Lordship, in my former letter, that Lord Cochrane has the world before him. He has three younger brothers to take care of, one of whom boarded at his side* when the Spaniard was carried. Unfortunately he has not served his time; if he had I daresay your Lordship would think him worthy of promotion for his conduct on that occasion.

"It will give me much pleasure to hear that your Lordship's health is quite re-established, and that you may long live to enjoy it, is the sincere wish of
                "Your Lordship's
            "Most obedient and humble servant,
                        "A. Cochrane.

"P.S. I wish I could give your Lordship any pleasing intelligence from this quarter; but ever since the death of

* Archibald.

Sir R. Abercromby, procrastination has been the order of the day. Never was a gallant army so lost as the present. God grant some man of sense may come out to command them, and save the remnant from destruction. Delay in this climate is worse than death; five men fall a sacrifice to disease for one in the field, and yet I don't think it unhealthy; our troops suffer from being encamped on burning sands."

Even this request from a distinguished officer—preferred unknown to me—failed to obtain what was no favour, but my right according to the invariable rule of the service. There was even then clearly some sinister influence at work, of the real cause for which I am to this day ignorant, and can only surmise that it might have arisen from my, no doubt, freely expressed opinions on being appointed to convoy the wretched packet which led to my capture; or perhaps from the still more indiscreet plainness with which I had spoken of the manner in which the French fleet had been unfortunately permitted to escape Lord Keith.

Brenton, in his Life of Lord St. Vincent, thus alludes to the delay in my promotion: "Lord St. Vincent *was so much pressed* on the subject of Lord Cochrane's promotion for taking the *Gamo*, that it became almost a point of etiquette with the earl *not to make him a captain!* An illustrious person is reported to have said, 'My Lord, we must make Lord Cochrane "post,"' to which Lord St. Vincent replied, 'The First Lord of the Admiralty knows *no must.*'"

There is no doubt that Captain Brenton received this account from Lord St. Vincent himself, and as the object of his book was to shield his lordship in questionable matters, we may receive this version as it was given to his biographer.

The only direct application that I was at the time aware of having been made was a letter from my father to Lord St. Vincent, *after* the post rank had been reluctantly conceded by placing me *at the bottom of the list,* below others previously my juniors in the service! My father's letter and Lord St. Vincent's reply are subjoined.

"No. 14, Mortimer Street, Sept. 23, 1801.

"MY LORD,—I beg leave, in behalf of my son, Lord Cochrane, who is now in Scotland, to bring under your Lordship's view, for your consideration, some facts and circumstances which may not hitherto *officially* have come to your Lordship's knowledge, from the perusal of which I flatter myself it will appear to your Lordship that there are few instances of as much being performed by one individual in the like space of time, and with a force so inferior.

"When I first heard of Lord Cochrane's engagement with the *Gamo,* I reckoned it as a matter not admitting of a doubt that your Lordship would reward him by immediately appointing him to a post ship, and I was the more confirmed in this belief from the circumstance that the *Gamo was not taken by surprise,* but at noonday, after an action of an hour and ten minutes; during all of which time the *Gamo's* yards were locked with the *Speedy's* rigging. The determination of the two vessels to engage was mutual; Lord Cochrane turned up his ship's company at five in the morning, and informed them of his intention to engage the Spanish frigate.

"The anxiety I must naturally feel for whatever concerns the honour and rank of my son, led me, on Wednesday last, to inquire at the Admiralty how his name stood on the post captains' list. And I must be allowed to state the surprise and disappointment I felt on finding several masters and commanders on the Mediterranean station—his juniors long before, and for several months after, the taking of the *Gamo* —now placed before him on that list.

"I beg leave to call your Lordship's attention to what Lord Cochrane's feelings must be, and what the situation he will be placed in on service from this supersession; and whether his being thus postponed in rank will not have a tendency to detract from the merit of one of the most gallant actions during this or any other war? And whether it may not induce the public at large, or the Navy in particular, to believe that your Lordships have had cause to disapprove of some part of Lord Cochrane's conduct?

"If all the circumstances of the engagement had come to your Lordship's knowledge in due time, I am persuaded you would have shown an additional mark of your approbation of Lord Cochrane, by making him post from the date of the capture of the *Gamo*, or, at least, that you would not have put over him a number of masters and commanders on the Mediterranean station, who, perhaps equally capable as he of distinguishing themselves, have not been equally fortunate in similar opportunities. I am likewise convinced, my Lord, that those individual officers, who have thus been preferred to him, would not think it any matter of injustice that Lord Cochrane should retain, as post captain, the same seniority he held over them, both before and after his engagement, as master and commander.

"Allow me therefore to request that your Lordship will be pleased to give Lord Cochrane that rank in the navy which it is presumed he would have held if the circumstantial accounts of his engagements had reached your Lordship at an earlier date, or that he had not been so unfortunate as to have been taken by three French line-of-battle ships. I cannot suppose any censure is intended to attach to his conduct on that point; for, in the narrative of his capture, your Lordship will see that during a chase of several hours upon a wind, he received the broadside and bow-chasers of a seventy-four gun ship, and did not strike until, at the distance of musket shot, he received a full broadside of round and grape from the *Dessaix.*

" I do not, however, my Lord, rest my son's claim for seniority in promotion solely upon the capture of the *Gamo.**
Although these particulars, from their being stated in Lord Cochrane's letters to Captain Dixon of the *Généreux,* are known to your Lordship, yet I cannot help here repeating them as *from their not being published in the Gazette,* a very erroneous opinion generally prevails that the *Gamo was taken* by surprise, and not after so long and close an engagement as was really the case.

" But perhaps, my Lord, I may in the whole of this letter have been impelled by the ardour and anxiety of my own feelings, to urge that which your Lordship's good intentions may have wholly anticipated towards Lord Cochrane. If so, my Lord, I have only to entreat your excuse for a zeal on my part for the honour and character of my son, for which I hope parental-sensations will plead a forcible apology.

"I have the honour, &c. &c.

"DUNDONALD.

" The Right Hon. Lord St. Vincent."

To this letter Lord St. Vincent next day replied as follows : —

"Admiralty, Sept. 24, 1801.

"MY LORD,—I can have no difficulty in acknowledging that the capture of the *Gamo* reflects the highest degree of credit on Lord Cochrane and the officers and crew of the *Speedy.*

"The first account of that brilliant action reached the Admiralty *very early in the month of August* (it was fought on the 6th of May), previously to which intelligence had been received of the capture of the *Speedy,* by which Lord Cochrane was made prisoner.

* " He has," &c. &c., [Here follows a recapitulation of particulars, with which the reader is already acquainted.]

" Until his exchange could be effected, and the necessary inquiry into the cause and circumstances of the loss of that sloop had taken place, it was impossible for the Board, consistently with its usual forms, to mark its approbation of his Lordship's conduct. Lord Cochrane was promoted to the rank of post captain on the 8th of August, the day on which the sentence of acquittal for the loss of the *Speedy was received*—which was all that could under existing circumstances be done.

" Having entered into this explanation with your Lordship, it remains for me only to add that, however disposed the Board might be to pay attention to the merits of his Lordship, it could not, consistent with its public duty, give him rank from the time of the capture of the *Gamo*—a measure quite unprecedented — without doing an act of injustice to other deserving officers.

"I have the honour, &c. &c.

" St. Vincent.

"The Earl of Dundonald."

I shall not shrink from canvassing this matter, the less because Lord St. Vincent has been represented as considering himself bored on the subject. An account of the capture of the *Gamo* did reach the Admiralty, though later than it ought to have done, and was unjustifiably laid aside. Little that I effected was allowed to find its way into the *Gazette!* Even the log extracts given in the two last chapters, though relating to matters which occurred sixty years ago, are, for the most part, news to the public of the present generation.

But supposing that information relative to the capture of the *Gamo* had not reached the Admiralty, before the news of my being made prisoner, even then it clearly entitled me to post rank from *the date of my acquittal.* Lord St. Vincent asserted that it entitled me to promotion only from the date on which news of my acquittal *was received!* Reference to the Navy List at the time will show that the postponement of my rank was rather owing to the bane of the Admiralty — family influence, and that some of my former juniors were put over my head because it was politically imperative on the Board to promote others before me.

That my promotion to post rank for a previous action, was impossible, because I had some time afterwards the misfortune, whilst in a trumpery sloop, to be captured by three French ships of the line; and therefore could not be promoted " *until my exchange could be effected,*" was a subterfuge unworthy of Lord St. Vincent. Had this been the rule of the Admiralty, officers taken prisoners by the French could neither have been tried nor promoted, for *there was no system of exchange,* so that the reward of their services would not depend upon the discretion of the Admiralty or the generosity of their country, but on the will of the enemy's Minister of Marine, who might detain them prisoners till the close of the war.

By Lord St. Vincent's interpretation of the Admiralty rule, I should not have been promoted *at all,* or even tried for the loss of the *Speedy,* if, as Lord St. Vincent asserted, no promotion could be given till " my exchange was effected." The fact is, that I never was exchanged, in the Admiralty sense of the term; for at that period, as has been said, there was no exchange of prisoners with France, nor had any previously taken place for many years. The *Hannibal* and *Speedy's* prisoners owed their liberation to the fact that the French did not know what to do with them; and I owed mine to the fact of Captain Keats having, a few days after I had been liberated on parole, taken a ship of the line, the *San Antonio;* for whose second captain, by courtesy of Admiral Linois towards that officer, my liberation was effected.

Still it was not so much the neglect to promote me, of which proper complaint was made, as the injustice of placing over my head especially, a younger man and a junior officer, gazetted on the same day for a subsequent service, to the success of which he in no degree contributed.* Further discussion is unnecessary, my object being to show the principle, or rather want of it, which prevailed at the Admiralty where influence was concerned.

It must, however, be explained, that these remarks in no way apply to the officer promoted, but to the act of promotion. That officer was my former messmate Lieutenant — afterwards Admiral — Dundas, a truly honourable man, whom, in later years, I was proud to call my friend. Strangely enough, the Admiralty which had placed him before me on the list, killed him in the end through grief at his inability to reform abuses; he having been called to the Board, where he worked so assiduously in the vain endeavour to purge the corruption around him, that his health

---

* The action in the Straits of Gibraltar, alluded to at page 128, when Captain Keats destroyed two line-of-battle ships, and captured a third, the remainder of the squadron being witnesses only.

became undermined, and he was one day found dead in a retiring room of the Augean establishment at Whitehall.

Before quitting the Mediterranean, a letter was addressed by me to Lord St. Vincent, requesting him to promote my gallant First Lieutenant Parker, who, as stated in my despatch, was severely wounded in boarding the *Gamo*. No answer being returned to this application, up to the period of my arrival in England, another letter was forwarded to his lordship, which met with the same reception, and afterwards a third, which produced from Lord St. Vincent the reply that my application could not be entertained, for that " it was unusual to promote two officers for such a service, — besides which the small number of men killed on board the *Speedy* did not warrant the application."

It was impossible not to feel nettled at a reply so unexpected : that because few men had been killed on board the *Speedy*, her first lieutenant was considered unworthy of promotion, though terribly cut up.  To argue with a First Lord is no doubt an imprudent thing for a naval officer to attempt, and my remonstrance in this instance had such an effect as to get my name placed on the black list of the Admiralty, never again to be erased.

In my letter to Lord St. Vincent, the following incautious observations were made, viz. that " his reasons for not promoting Lieutenant Parker, because there were only three men killed on board the *Speedy*, were in opposition *to his lordship's own promotion to an earldom*, as well as that of his flag-captain to knighthood, and

his other officers to increased rank and honours: for
that in the battle from which his lordship derived his
title there was only *one man* killed on board his own
flagship, so that there were more casualties in my sloop
than in his line-of-battle ship."

From the receipt of that letter Lord St. Vincent became my bitter enemy, and not he only, but his suc-
cessors thought it incumbent on them to perpetuate
his lordship's displeasure. My reply was no doubt
keenly felt at the time, when it was a common remark
in the Navy that the battle of St. Vincent was gained
by the inshore squadron, under Nelson, the commander-in-chief being merely a spectator, at a distance
which involved only the loss of one man in his own
ship.

Notwithstanding this refusal of the First Lord to
promote my lieutenant, my determination was to persevere with the Board collectively, and accordingly I
addressed an official letter to the Secretary of the Admiralty, Mr. Nepean, embodying Lord St. Vincent's
reply, and concluding, that "if their Lordships judge
by the small number killed, I have only to say that it
was fortunate the enemy did not point their guns
better": indeed, had I not taken care to place the
*Speedy* in a position where the Spanish guns went over
her, many would have swelled the list whom it was my
happiness to have saved."

This letter was dated May 12th, 1802, and, receiving
no reply, the annexed official letter was addressed to
their Lordships on the same subject: —

"14 Old Cavendish street, May 17, 1802.

"My Lords, — The anxiety I feel for the promotion of a meritorious officer, Lieutenant Parker, late of the *Speedy*, whose name I have not seen in the recent list of commanders, even though a very extensive promotion has taken place, induces me to address your Lordships.

"Lieutenant Parker served as sole lieutenant of the *Speedy* at the capture of the *Gamo*, of 32 guns and 319 men, carried by boarding, after an action of upwards of an hour; during the greatest part of which time the yards and rigging of the vessels were locked together.    In boarding and carrying the Spanish vessel he was severely wounded by a sword, run through his thigh, and a musket ball lodged in his chest.

"I have always understood it to be an invariable rule with the Board of Admiralty, to promote officers of unimpeachable character who have distinguished themselves in action, or who have been first lieutenants of His Majesty's ships of war at the capture of vessels of superior force — especially of a force so very superior as that of the *Gamo* to the *Speedy*; the latter, as your Lordships know, mounting 14 4-pounders, having on board only 54 men, whilst the force of the *Gamo* was 32 guns, with a complement of men six times greater than that of the *Speedy*.

"When these circumstances are brought to your Lordships' recollection, I am fully convinced that you will see proper to reward Lieutenant Parker by appointing him to the rank of commander in His Majesty's service, which will tend to cherish and promote that spirit of exertion among the lieutenants, subordinate officers, and crew, without whose zealous cooperation the endeavours of the captain alone would prove of small avail.

"I have the honour to be, &c. &c.
(Signed)        "COCHRANE.

"To the Right Hon. the Lords Commissioners
of the Admiralty."

On the 26th of May the following reply was received from the Secretary :—

"Admiralty Office, 26th May, 1802.

" My Lord,—I have received and read to my Lords Commissioners of the Admiralty your Lordship's letter to me of the 17th inst., and the representation which accompanied it, and am commanded by their Lordships to acquaint you that your application to me is perfectly regular, *but that it is not so for officers to correspond with the Board.*

"I am, &c. &c.

" E. Nepean.

" Captain Lord Cochrane."

Determined not to be foiled in what I conceived to be the right of Lieutenant Parker, I replied to the Secretary as follows :—

"Old Cavendish street, May 27th, 1802.

" Sir, — I have been favoured with your letter acknowledging that you had received and read to the Lords Commissioners of the Admiralty my letter of the 17th inst., and that you are commanded by their Lordships to acquaint me that my application to you was perfectly regular, but that it is not so for officers to correspond with the Board.

" I have, therefore, to request that you will inform the Lords Commissioners of the Admiralty, that, although I have received your letter, still I wait in expectation to be favoured with an answer to the representation which, through you, I had the honour to transmit to their Lordships.

" I am, &c. &c.

" Cochrane.

" E. Nepean, Esq., Sec. to the Admiralty."

The reply to this necessarily cut short all further correspondence.

"Admiralty Office, 29th May, 1802.

"My Lord,— I have received and read to my Lord Commissioners of the Admiralty your letter of the 27th inst., and have nothing in command from their Lordships to communicate to you.

"I am, &c. &c.

"Evan Nepean.

"Captain Lord Cochrane."

In spite of this rebuff I nevertheless continued to persevere, but it was not till some years afterwards that the promotion of Lieutenant Parker was obtained, with a result to that able and gallant officer which proved his ruin, and eventually caused his death.

The circumstances under which this took place were positively diabolical. Despairing of promotion, Lieutenant Parker had retired to a little farm near Kinsale, by the cultivation of which, in addition to his half-pay, he was realising an existence for his family. From my determined perseverance on his behalf, he was at length made commander, and ordered to join the *Rainbow* sloop, represented to be stationed in the West Indies. Selling off everything, even to his household furniture, he proceeded to Barbadoes, and reported himself to Sir Alexander Cochrane; but, as the vessel could not be found, Sir Alexander furnished him with a passage to look for her at the Bermudas, where he supposed she might be fitting for sea. Not finding her there, Lieutenant Parker returned to Barbadoes, when *it became evident that no such vessel was on the North American station!*

On ascertaining this, poor Parker returned to England

a ruined man.  Lord Melville, who had succeeded as
First Lord, expressed his surprise and regret that such
a circumstance should have occurred, and promised the
unhappy man that he should not only be amply com-
pensated for the loss and expense attending his outfit
and fruitless voyage to the West Indies, but that he
should have another command on the first opportunity.
This generous intention was however counteracted, for
*he never received either the one or the other.*

Lieutenant Parker's loss, consequent to the sale of
his property, the expense attendant on settling his family,
together with his outfit and voyage, amounted to upwards of 1000*l*.  His prospects ruined, his domestic
arrangements destroyed, and his pride wounded, his
spirit and constitution gradually gave way, and at
length overwhelmed with sorrow he sank into a premature grave, leaving a wife and four daughters to
deplore the loss of their only protector.

I never could find out who had thus imposed on one
of the most gallant officers in the Navy this infamous
deception, concocted, doubtless, out of pure malevolence
to myself.  Be he whom he may, I am very sorry that
it is not in my power to hold up his name to the exe-
cration of posterity.  It is even at the present day
the duty of the Admiralty to remedy the injury inflicted on his destitute family — for he had left four
daughters unprovided for, who had no opportunity to
escape from indigence.

# CHAP. VIII.

## NAVAL ADMINISTRATION SIXTY YEARS AGO.

POLITICAL FAVOURITISM.—REFUSAL OF FURTHER EMPLOYMENT.—NAVAL
CORRUPTION. — DOCKYARD PRACTICES. — SHAMEFUL TREATMENT OF
PRISONERS OF WAR.—ECONOMY THE REMEDY.—RESULTS OF MEDICAL
ECONOMY. — EMPTY PHYSIC BOTTLES. — SEAMEN'S AVERSION TO THE
SERVICE. — A POST CAPTAIN AT COLLEGE.

IT will be evident on a perusal of the previous chapter,
that there was no fixed principle for the promotion of
officers who had distinguished themselves, but that
however desirous the Board might be to reward their
services, it was in the power of persons holding inferior
offices to thwart the intentions of the Board itself.

Were such a principle admitted, nothing could be
more detrimental to the service. Let every officer
know the regulated reward for a national service, with
the certainty that he cannot be deprived of it, and rely
upon it, that whenever opportunity presents itself, the
service will be performed. There is nothing mercenary,
or even selfish about this; but, on the contrary, an
ambition which should be carefully fostered..

In my own case, I can conscientiously avow my
leading motive to have been that of exerting myself to
the utmost in the hope of thereby attaining promotion
in my profession, to which promotion the capture of

an enemy's frigate, as well as of a large number of privateers and other vessels, had entitled me, according to a judicious rule for the encouragement of efforts useful to the nation— to a place on the list, from which I conceived myself unjustly excluded by the promotion of a younger man, a junior commander too, for no great apparent reason than that of his father being a personal and political friend of the First Lord of the Admiralty.

To those who may think my conduct towards the First Lord and the Board disrespectful, I can only say, that were my life to begin anew, with my present experience of consequences, I would again pursue the same course. I cannot imagine anything more detrimental to the interests of the Navy and the nation, than political favouritism on the part of the Admiralty— of itself sufficient to damp that ardour which should form one of the first requisites for future command. I would rather say to the young officer — " If you have, in the exercise of your profession, acquired a right which is wrongfully withheld— demand it, stick to it with unshaken pertinacity ; — none but a corrupt body can possibly think the worse of you for it ; even though you may be treated like myself — you are doing your country good service by exposing favouritism, which is only another term for corruption."

Favouritism on the part of the Admiralty must ever be the bane of the Navy, and may prove its ruin. Either let it be understood that the institution is a parliamentary vote market, or that it is what it ought to be—an institution for the promotion of zeal by the reward of merit. Only let it not sustain both characters, or between the two stools the country may one day go to the ground.

Such was the offence taken by the authorities at my persistence in my own right, and in that of the officers under my command, that an application to the Board for another ship met with refusal ; and as it was clear that Lord St. Vincent's administration did not again intend to employ me, the time on my hands was devoted to an investigation of those abuses which were paralysing the Navy ; not that this was entered upon from any spirit of retaliation on the Admiralty, but as preparatory to the more ambitious aim of getting into Parliament, and exposing them.

One of the most crying evils of our then naval administration had fallen heavily upon me, though so young in command — viz. the Admiralty Courts ; but for the peculations consequent on which, the cruise of the *Speedy* ought to have sent home myself, officers, and crew, with competence. As it was, we got all the fighting, whilst the Admiralty Court and its hungry parasites monopolised the greater portion of our hard won prize-money. In many cases they took the whole ! and in one case brought me in debt, though the prize was worth several thousand pounds !

Hitherto no naval officer had ventured to expose, in Parliament or out of it, this or indeed any other gross abuse of the naval service ; and having nothing better to do, want of employment appeared to offer a fitting opportunity for constituting myself the Quixote of the profession ; sparing no pains to qualify for the task, though well aware of its arduous, if not hopeless nature

— as directed against a mass of corruption, such as
— it is to be hoped — may never again strike at the
noblest arm of our national safety a blow worse than
any enemy can inflict.

After what has been stated with regard to my unpleasant relations with Lord St. Vincent and his Board
of Admiralty, it will perhaps be better not personally
to enter on the subject of then existing naval abuses,
lest I might be suspected of exaggerating their extent.
Some such explanation is necessary in justification of
the course which I subsequently thought it my duty to
pursue, but it will answer every purpose to have recourse
to the experience of a contemporary officer — Captain
Brenton, the biographer of Lord St. Vincent — in justification of my self-imposed task.

"In the first edition of the Naval History, I have com-
mented on the profligate system of hired vessels and transports.    In this — borough influence reigned paramount, and
the most solid information was disregarded when the perpe-
trator of the greatest frauds was a supporter of Government."
—(BRENTON's *Life of Lord St. Vincent,* p. 167.)

"A ship purchased by a man of influence was a certain
fortune to him.    He cleared his money in the first year at
the rate of 400*l*. per month, and if the ship were coppered at
7500*l*. per annum.    About twenty copper-bottomed transports were lying for three years in the harbour of Messina,
without being employed in any duty."—(p. 169.)

The expense of these alone, no doubt all owned by
" men of influence " as Captain Brenton terms them,
was for the three years 270,000*l*.    As these transports
formed only a trifling illustration of the system, there

is little wonder at the enormous accumulation of the national debt, for results so inadequate.

Captain Brenton might have gone farther, and stated with great truth, that not only were transports hired from men of influence, but that vessels utterly worthless were purchased by the Government from their political supporters, and then patched up into ships of war! It was my misfortune to be subsequently appointed to *a collier* so converted—with what result will appear in the sequel.

From the ships let us follow Captain Brenton into the dockyards.

"When Mr. Colquhoun, in his celebrated police reports, stated that the Government was plundered from the dock-yards at the rate of *a million a year,* he was supposed to have exceeded all probability. I am satisfied he was under the mark, and if the *consequences* of these frauds are added to the amount of peculation, the aggregate will be frightful. The manner in which the villany was carried on was dreadful indeed. *Whole ships' crews were destroyed at one fell swoop.* Every ship was supposed to have a certain number of bolts driven to secure her fabric. The tops and points of the bolts only were driven, and the rest was carried away. It is probable that the loss of the *York* of 64 guns, and the *Blenheim* of 74 guns, was the consequence. The *Albion,* 74, we know to have been nearly lost by this hellish fraud."— (BRENTON, pp. 159, 160.)

"I can remember what our slop clothing was, for which the poor seamen were charged an extravagant price; the contract being *always given as a matter of favour for elec- tioneering purposes.*"—(p. 156.)

"Not only were the grossest impositions practised in the supply of the most important stores, by sending in damaged goods, but even the raw materials were *again sold* before they reached their destination."—(p. 157.)

" At the cooperage of Deptford, 1020*l*. 10*s*. 5*d*. was charged for work proved to be worth only 37*l*. 2*s*. 3*d*. At the cooperage at Plymouth, the king's casks were stolen, and sixty-four of them were found in one brewery."—(p. 183.)

"It was a common expression with the receiving clerks that they ' *had not been hampered*—' when they refused to receive articles into store. The ' hampering' meant a bribe in the shape of wine or other articles, as the price of their certificates.'—(p. 155.)

" It would scarcely be believed to what extent peculation was carried on in every department."—(p. 155.)

" Hampers of wine and ale were liberally supplied to the inspectors of timber, and I conclude that the same treatment was applied to the measuring clerks of the dockyard."—(p. 179.)

" From the foregoing it may be inferred that the dockyards were the most fruitful sources of plunder and national ruin." —(p. 180.)

" Report No. 6 relates to the dockyards, wherein a shameful system of plunder had long existed."

" Reports 10 and 11 state other abuses to an enormous extent, so that Lord St. Vincent used the elegant expression that ' *our dockyards stank of corruption*.' "—(p. 190.)

From this disgraceful picture let us pass on to another still more revolting.

" The victualling establishment at home was not less corrupt. The charge for the supply of prisoners of war was ample, but three-fourths of the amount was pilfered. The same nefarious system pursued in the hospitals abroad was followed at home in a more guarded manner, and *fortunes were made* by cheating the sick and wounded seamen out of the comforts and necessaries allowed them by a grateful country. Lord Cochrane endeavoured to procure better rations and treatment for the French prisoners, but the charge of sick and wounded prisoners of war fell in its administration into the hands of a set of villains whose seared consciences were proof against the silent but eloquent pleadings of their fellow-creatures."—(p. 165.)

" Report No. 7 relates to the hospitals, beginning with Stonehouse at Devonport. Here was discovered waste, corruption, fraud, extravagance, and villany to a disgusting extent. Four thousand gallons of porter were consumed in six months, being more than four times the proportion used in Haslar. On board the *Calne* hulk, appropriated to sick prisoners of war, the surgeon's chief assistant kept a table for the officers at the cost of 1500*l*. or 2000*l*. a year. He could afford the purser a large salary, in lieu of his share of the profit of the concern. The worst and most scandalous feature was, that when the wretches in the wardroom were rioting in luxury they were consuming the necessaries which the Government had liberally supplied for the use of the sick prisoners of war.

" I hope there is sufficient virtue in Parliament to punish *great delinquents*, if not the country will not stagger long under the practice of these blood-sucking leeches."—(*Letter of Lord St. Vincent, quoted by Brenton.*)

Abroad the condition of affairs was infinitely worse, both as regarded the navy and army. The following extract from the " Annual Register," at a period when the press hardly dared to speak truth, will serve as a sample of the practices prevailing wherever an official staff was to be found : —

" The abuses committed in the West Indies are said to exceed everything that was ever stated in romance. The commissioners are stated to have discovered that forged bills and receipts, for articles never purchased, and bills drawn on government indorsed under forged and fictitious names, were common and notorious. They found a most base collusion between the officers of government, and the merchants and contractors, by which the latter were allowed to charge stores at a much higher rate than they might have been obtained for in the market. In one instance it was discovered, that to conceal this iniquity, a bribe of 87,000*l.* had been given: in another a bribe of 35,000*l.* Vessels, houses, stores, &c. were usually hired at most extravagant rates, in consequence of fraudulent contracts, where others might have been obtained much cheaper. But worse than either of these iniquities was the diabolical fraud of suffering the merchants and contractors to furnish his Majesty's troops with inferior and bad rum, and other articles, at an extravagant rate, by which the lives of the troops were endangered, as well as the country defrauded. And, for the purpose of committing these practices, all free competition for the supply of articles was prevented; and every obstacle was put in the way, even of the purchase of bills on the treasury. They were dated in one island and negotiated in another; and they were sold at a much more advantageous exchange than that at which the officers debited themselves in their accounts."

There is no doubt but that Lord St. Vincent was desirous of putting a stop to this national plunder, and the wholesale destruction of sick, wounded, and prisoners, which was its direct consequence; but the means he took were inadequate. His lordship's remedy was "*economy!*" leaving the influential delinquents in quiet possession of their places. The most extravagant contracts and profuse expenditure of the public money were thus to be cured by no expenditure at all on necessary objects.

One of Lord St. Vincent's agents in this notable scheme, was a Dr. Beard, who possessed his lordship's highest confidence. To this person was confided the

task of regenerating the hospitals. As may be supposed, from his profession, economy in medicine was
the first step.    An order was issued that blue ointment
and pills, requisite only for complaints that migh t be
avoided, were doled out in *minimum* quantity.   The
consequence was, that the captains and surgeons of
ships of war had to purchase these essential medicines
out of their own pockets! more especially as a subsequent order was issued that no such complaints should
be treated in the hospitals!

A more barbarous regulation was enforced, viz. that
from the expense of *lint* in dressing wounds, *sponge*
should be substituted, as it might be used over again !
The result was that even slight cases, became infected
by the application of sponges which had been used on
putrescent sores, and this shameful practice cost the
lives or limbs of many.   I was myself on a survey at
the Devonport hospital, where seven persons had lost
limbs from this cause.! and proposed to the other
surveying captains to draw up a representation to the
Admiralty on the consequences of applying infected
sponge ; but the advice was not followed for fear of
giving offence.

One of the unfortunate sufferers, amongst others, was
a son of the boatswain or gunner of the then flagship,
the *Salvador del Mundo*.   The poor boy had bruised
his shin, to which an infected sponge was applied,
and he lost his leg !  Persons so mutilated had no
claim on the service for pension or reward.    It was
this very hospital to which Captain Brenton, in the
preceding extracts, applied the terms " waste, corrup-

tion, fraud, extravagance, and villany to a disgusting extent." The remedy was the application of infected sponge!!

Dr. Beard had the oddest possible notions of the mission with which he was entrusted. As to striking at the root of an evil he had not the most remote conception, otherwise than by saving. He one day said to me: "The extravagance of this place is incredible. I have to-day found what will save one thousand pounds." "Ah, Doctor," said I, "what is that?" "Why," replied he, "would you believe it, in the cellars under the hospital I have found tens of thousands of empty physic bottles! Did you ever hear of such waste!" And the doctor set busily to work to dispose of the empty bottles in order to pay for his medicines,—this being his idea of correcting the most crying evil of the hospital.

A still more absurd instance of the doctor's economy gave rise at the time to considerable amusement. Everybody knows that a sailor requires as much looking after as a child. It was Jack's practice when sick in hospital, to get out and scale a wall for the purpose of smuggling in spirits, these of course undoing the little that medical treatment could effect. To put an end to the practice, the authorities had ordered the wall to be raised, but Dr. Beard stopped the work, because a coating of broken glass-bottles on the top of the old wall would be more economical to the nation and equally effectual! A *chevaux de frise* of broken glass was accordingly put on, but, to the doctor's annoyance, Jack, with a brick-bat, pounded up the broken glass, and got to the

spirit shop as before.   Whereupon the doctor declared
his belief that " sailors were as far gone in wickedness
as the hospital authorities themselves."

These were the kinds of reform adopted, the ultimate
result being that Lord St. Vincent was more blamed
than had been any of his predecessors, and was, on
quitting the Admiralty, driven to the undignified alternative of *filing a string of affidavits in the King's Bench
in defence of his character!* *

Much has been said about the difficulty of manning
the Navy, by persons who had not a knowledge of the
arbitrary and cruel practices above mentioned, and of
many others on which it would be tedious to dilate, but
which, under pretence of zeal for the promotion of the
service, rendered the service at that time almost in-
tolerable.   No man acquainted with the facts can
wonder that interminable cruises, prohibition to land
in port, constant confinement without salutary change
of food, and consequent disease engendering total de-
bility, should have excited disgust, and even terror of a
sailor's life; to which may be added, the condemnation
of invalids to harbour-duty, far more severe than duty
afloat, with no chance of escape but by a return to
actual service, where, strange to say, though unfit, such
men were again received!

The instance of abuses just given form but a brief
outline of the state of the Navy at that period.   From
these the reader may imagine the rest.   Suffice it to
say, that I used all diligence to store both my memory

* See Brenton, vol. ii. p. 356.

and note-book with facts, to be used when I might be able to expose them with effect.

No opportunity, however, immediately occurring, I betook myself to the College of Edinburgh, then distinguished by possessing some of the most eminent professors in the kingdom. In the early part of this volume the desultory and imperfect education which fell to my lot has been noticed. It had, nevertheless, sufficed to convince me of the truth of the axiom that " knowledge is power," and also to decide that in my case power if proportioned to knowledge could be of no very high order. It was therefore my determination to increase both to the best of my ability.

It was, perhaps, an unusual spectacle for a post-captain fresh from the quarter-deck, to enter himself as a student among boys. For my self-imposed position I cared nothing, and was only anxious to employ myself to the best advantage. With what success may be judged from the fact of my never being but once absent from lectures, and that to attend the funeral of a near relative.

Whilst at Edinburgh, I made few acquaintances, preferring secluded lodgings and study without interruption to the gaiety of my contemporaries. Besides which, if my object of getting into Parliament were to be accomplished, it was necessary to be economical, since all that the Admiralty Court had been pleased to leave me of my prize-money would not more than suffice to satisfy the yearnings of a small borough, for which the only hope of election was by outbribing my antagonists.

Amongst my contemporaries at the Edinburgh College was Lord Palmerston, who resided with the most eminent of the then Scotch professors, Dugald Stewart, and attended the classes at the same time with myself.

I might also mention others, of whose society in after life I should have been proud, had not the shameful treatment which it was afterwards my lot to experience from a corrupt faction, driven me from society at a time when it ought to have afforded me a welcome relaxation from hard and unintermitting exertions in the service of my country.

# CHAP. IX.

## EMPLOYMENT IN THE *ARAB*.

APPOINTMENT TO THE ARAB. — PROJECTED INVASION BY NAPOLEON. —
THE ARAB ORDERED TO WATCH THE FRENCH COAST. — THEN TO
CRUISE IN THE NORTH SEA. — RETIREMENT OF LORD ST. VINCENT.

ON the renewal of war with France in 1803, application
was made by me to the Admiralty for a ship, first taking
the precaution to visit the various dockyards to see what
vessels were ready, or in preparation.   My object was
to obtain a suitable vessel, which should enable me to
operate inshore and harass the French coast in the
Atlantic, as the *Speedy* had done the Spanish coast in the
Mediterranean.   My success there formed sufficient
warrant for such an application, as previous to the Peace
of Amiens, the enemy's coasting trade from Bayonne
to Boulogne had been carried on almost with impunity.

My application was made to Lord St. Vincent, who
informed me that at present there was no vessel available.   Having ascertained beforehand what vessels
were in preparation for sea, I began to enumerate
several, all of which his lordship assured me were promised to others.   On mentioning the names of some in
a less forward state, an objection was raised by his
lordship that they were too large.   This was met by a

fresh list, but these his lordship said were not in progress.    In short, it became clear that the British Navy
contained no ship of war for me.

I frankly told his lordship as much, remarking that
as " the Board was evidently of opinion that my services were not required, it would be better for me to go
back to the College of Edinburgh and pursue my studies,
with a view of occupying myself in some other employment." His lordship eyed me keenly, to see whether
I really meant what I said, and observing no signs of
flinching, — for beyond doubt my countenance showed
signs of disgust at such unmerited treatment,—he said,
" Well, you shall have a ship.   Go down to Plymouth,
and there await the orders of the Admiralty."

Thanking his lordship, I left him, and repairing to
Plymouth, found myself appointed to the *Arab*.    There
was some difficulty in finding her, for my sanguine
imagination had depicted a rakish craft, ready to run
over to the French coast, and return with a goodly
batch of well-laden coasters.    In place of this, a dockyard attendant showed me the bare ribs of a collier,
which had been purchased into the service in the
manner described by Captain Brenton, as quoted in
the last chapter.    I would not have cared for this,
but a single glance at the naked timbers showed me
that, to use a seaman's phrase, " she would sail like a
haystack."    It was not my wish however to complain,
but rather to make the best of the wretched craft provided for me; and therefore there was nothing to be
done but to wait patiently whilst she was completed,—

for the most part with old timber from broken-up vessels.

As soon as the *Arab* was ready for sea, instead of being permitted to make a foray on the French coast — for which, however, she was ill-adapted — orders were given to take a cruise round the Land's End, into St. George's Channel, and return to Plymouth.

This experimental service being accomplished, without result of any kind, although we sighted several suspicious vessels, which from our bad sailing qualities we could not examine ; on our return, the *Arab* was ordered to join the force then lying in the Downs, quietly watching the movements of the enemy on the opposite coast.

Though Napoleon had not a marine capable of competing with ours, he had, during the last war, become aware that any number of French gun-boats could sail along their own coasts under the protection of the numerous batteries, and hence he conceived the project of uniting these with others at Boulogne, so as to form collectively a flotilla capable of effecting an invasion of England, whose attention was to be diverted by an attempt on Ireland, for which purpose an army and fleet were assembled at Brest.

The means by which this invasion of the Kentish or Sussex coast was to be effected is worth adverting to. The various towns of France were invited to construct flat-bottomed boats, to be distinguished by the names of the towns and departments which furnished them. They were divided into three classes, and transported to the nearest port-town, thence coastwise to Boulogne, there to be filled with troops, and convoyed to the English shores by ships of war. It has been the custom to deride this armament, but had it not been for Nelson's subsequent victory at Trafalgar, I see no cause to doubt that sooner or later it might have been successful. In our day of steam-ships the way to prevent the success of a similar project is by the maintenance of a navy more efficiently manned than modern governments appear to think necessary for national safety.

I do not mean efficiency as to the *number* of vessels of war — for in my early day the number was very great, but their efficiency, from causes already mentioned, very trifling. I mean rather, that every care should be taken to keep a sufficient number in a high state of discipline, but above all, that the stimulus of reward for merit should be so applied, as that parliamentary influence should not interfere with officers, nor a paltry hankering after saving with the crews.

The *Arab* was sent to watch the enemy in Boulogne. To those acquainted with the collier build, even as they appear in the Thames to this day, it is scarcely necessary to say that she would not work to windward. With a fair wind it was not difficult to get off Boulogne, but to get back with the same wind was — in such a craft — all but impossible. Our only way of effecting this was by watching the tide, to drift off as well as we could. A gale of wind anywhere from N. E. to N. W. would infallibly have driven us on shore on the French coast.

Under such circumstances, the idea of effectively watching the port, as understood by me, viz. — to look out for troop-boats inshore — was out of the question, our whole attention being necessarily directed to the vessel's safety. Considering this compromised, I wrote to the admiral commanding, that the *Arab* was of no use for the service required, as she would not work to windward, and that her employment in such a service could only result in our loss by shipwreck on the French coast.

My letter was no doubt forwarded to the Admiralty, for shortly afterwards an order arrived for the *Arab* to convoy the Greenland ships from Shetland, and then to cruise in the North Sea, to *protect the fisheries*. The order was, in fact, to cruise to the N. E. of the Orkneys, *where no vessel fished, and where consequently there were no fisheries to protect ! ! !* Not so much as a single whaler was seen from the mast-head during the whole of that lonely cruise, though it was as light by night as by day.

The Board had fairly caught me, but a more cruel order could not have been devised by official malevolence. It was literally naval exile in a tub, regardless of expense to the nation. To me it was literally a period of despair, from the useless inactivity into which I was forced, without object or purpose, beyond that of visiting me with the weight of official displeasure.

I will not trouble the reader with any reminiscences of this degrading command, or rather dreary punishment, for such it was no doubt intended to be, as depriving me of the opportunity of exerting or distinguishing myself; and this for no better reason, than my having most truly, though perhaps inconsiderately, urged, in justification of the promotion of the gallant lieutenant of the *Speedy*, that all Lord St. Vincent's chief officers had been promoted for an action in which fewer men fell in a three-decker than in my brig.

Of this protracted cruise it is sufficient to state that my appointment to the *Arab* was dated October 5th, 1803, and that she returned to England on the 1st of December 1804, a period which formed a blank in my life.

On my arrival, Lord St. Vincent, fortunately for me, had quitted, or rather had been compelled to retire from the Admiralty. The late Duke of Hamilton, the premier peer of Scotland, and my excellent friend, was so indignant at my ignominious expulsion from active service, where alone it would be beneficial to the country, that, unsolicited by any one, he strongly impressed upon Lord Melville, the successor of Lord St. Vincent, the necessity of relieving me from that penal hulk, the *Arab*, and repairing the injustice which had been inflicted on me, by employing me on more important service. Lord Melville admitted the injustice, and promptly responded to the appeal, by transferring me from the wretched craft in which I had been for fifteen months in exile — to the *Pallas*, a new fir-built frigate of 32 guns.

# CHAP. X.

## CRUISE OF THE *PALLAS*.

ORDERS OF THE PALLAS EMBARGOED. — CAPTURE OF THE CAROLINA. — ARRIVAL OF THE PRIZES. — CAPTURE OF PAPAL BULLS. — A CHASE. — ADMIRAL YOUNG. — ELECTION FOR PORTSMOUTH. — NOVEL ELECTION TACTICS. — BECOME A REFORMER. — PAINFUL RESULTS.

ON my appointment to the *Pallas*, Lord Melville considerately gave me permission to cruise for a month off the Azores under Admiralty orders. The favour — the object of which was to give me an opportunity of trying my luck against the enemy, independent of superior command — was no doubt granted in consideration of the lengthened, not to say malevolent, punishment to which I had been condemned in the *Arab*.

My orders were to join my ship at Plymouth, with a promise that my instructions should be forwarded. In place of this, and in disregard of Lord Melville's intention, the Admiralty orders were embargoed by the Port Admiral, Sir W. Young, who had taken upon himself to recopy them, and thus to convert them into orders *issued under his authority*. The effect was, to enable him to lay claim to the admiral's share of any prize-money that we might make, even though captured out of his jurisdiction, which extended no further than the Sound.

The mention of this circumstance requires brief comment, in order to account for the result which followed. Perhaps the most lucid explanation that can be given will be an extract from a letter of Lord St. Vincent to the Admiralty when in command of the Channel fleet. " I do not know," says Lord St. Vincent, " what I shall do if you feel a difficulty to give orders to despatch such ships as you may judge necessary to place under my command.   I have a notion that he (Admiral Young) *wishes to have the power of issuing orders for their sailing, in order to entitle him to share prize-money ! !* " (BRENTON, vol. ii. p. 249.)   From this extract from Lord St. Vincent, it is evident that if Admiral Young, according to the system then prevailing, had the power — as on his Lordship's authority unquestionably appears — of paralysing the operations of a whole fleet, on the question of sharing prize-money, remonstrance on my part against the violation of Admiralty promises, made by Lord Melville himself, would have been disregarded.   Nothing was therefore left but to submit.

The first object was to equip the *Pallas* with all speed; and for this we were obliged to resort to impressment, so much had my do-nothing cruise in the *Arab* operated against me in the minds of the seamen. Having, however, succeeded in impressing some good men, to whom the matter was explained, they turned to with great alacrity to impress others; so that in a short time we had an excellent crew.   This was the only time I ever found it necessary to impress men.

As the cruise off the Western Islands—when arrived

there — was restricted to a month, it was matter of consideration how to turn such orders to the best account, without infringing on the letter of my instructions. We therefore crossed the Bay of Biscay, and having run to the westward of Cape Finisterre, *worked up* towards the Azores, so as to fall in with any vessels which might be bound from the Spanish West Indies to Cadiz.

Scarcely had we altered our course, when, on the 6th of February, we fell in with and captured a large ship, the *Carolina*, bound from the Havannah to Cadiz, and laden with a valuable cargo. After taking out the crew, we despatched her to Plymouth.

Having learned from the prisoners that the captured ship was part of a convoy bound from the Havannah to Spain, we proceeded on our course, and on the 13th captured a second vessel, which was still more valuable, containing, in addition to the usual cargo, some diamonds, and ingots of gold and silver. This vessel was sent to Plymouth as before.

On the 15th, we fell in with another, *La Fortuna*, which proved the richest of all, as, besides her cargo, she had on board a large quantity of dollars, which we shifted into the *Pallas*, and sent the ship to England.

On the 16th we captured a fine Spanish letter-of-marque, with more dollars on board; but as a heavy sea then running prevented us from taking them on board the *Pallas*, these were therefore despatched with her to Plymouth.

Whilst securing the latter vessel, we observed at sunset an English privateer take possession of a large ship. On seeing us—evidently knowing that we were an English man-of-war, and therefore entitled to share in her capture—the privateer crowded all sail and made off with her prize in company. Unluckily for this calculation, the prize was subsequently taken by a French squadron, when it turned out that the captured vessel —the *Preciosa* — was the richest of the whole Spanish convoy, having, in addition to her cargo, no less than a million dollars on board. Singularly enough, the privateer belonged to my agent Mr. Tied, from whom I afterwards learned the value of the vessel which his captain's mistaken greed had sacrificed.

The sensation created on the arrival of the prizes at Plymouth was immense, as the following curious extracts from a local paper will show.

"*February* 24. — Came in the *Caroline* from Havanah with sugar and logwood. Captured off the coast of Spain by the *Pallas*, Captain Lord Cochrane. The *Pallas* was in pursuit of another with a very valuable cargo when the *Caroline* left. His lordship sent word to Plymouth, that if ever it was in his power, he would fulfil his public advertisement (stuck up here) for entering seamen, of filling their pockets with Spanish ' pewter ' and ' cobs,' nicknames given by seamen to ingots and dollars.

"*March* 7. — Came in a rich Spanish prize, with jewels, gold, silver, ingots, and a valuable cargo, taken by the *Pallas*, Captain Lord Cochrane. Another Spanish ship, the *Fortuna*, from Vera Cruz, had been taken by the *Pallas*, laden with mahogany and logwood. She had 432,000 dollars on board, but has not yet arrived.

"*March* 23. — Came in a most beautiful Spanish letter-of-marque of fourteen guns, said to be a very rich and valuable prize to the *Pallas*, Captain Lord Cochrane."

A still greater sensation was excited by the arrival of the *Pallas* herself, with three large golden candlesticks, each about five feet high, placed upon the mast heads. The history of these is not a little curious. They had been presented by the good people of Mexico, together with other valuable plate, to some celebrated church in Spain, the name of whose patron saint I forget, and had been shipped on board one of the most seaworthy vessels.

Their ultimate destination was, however, less propitious. It was my wish to possess them, and with this view an arrangement had been made with the officers and crew of the *Pallas*. On presenting the candlesticks at the Custom-house, the authorities refused to permit them to pass without paying the full duty, which amounted to a heavier sum than I was willing to disburse. Consequently, although of exquisite workmanship, they were broken in pieces, and thus suffered to pass as old gold.

The following incident relating to the capture of one of the vessels had escaped my recollection, till pointed out in the *Naval Chronicle* for 1805. It is substantially correct.

" Lord Cochrane, in his late cruise off the coasts of Spain and Portugal, fell in with, and took, *La Fortuna*, a Spanish ship bound to Corunna, and richly laden with gold and silver to the amount of 450,000 dollars (132,000*l*.), and about the same sum in valuable goods and merchandise. When the Spanish captain and his supercargo came on board the *Pallas*, they appeared much dejected, as their private property on board amounted to the value of 30,000 dollars each. The captain said he had lost, in the war of 1779, a similar fortune, having then been taken by a British cruiser, so that now, as then, he had to begin the world again.    Lord Cochrane, feeling for the dejected condition of the Spaniards, consulted his officers as to their willingness to give them back 5,000 dollars each in specie.    This being immediately agreed to, his lordship ordered the boatswain to pipe all hands, and addressing the men to the like purpose, the gallant fellows sung out, 'Aye, aye, my lord, with all our hearts,' and gave the unfortunate Spaniards three cheers."

Another curious circumstance must not be passed over.    In one of the captured vessels was a number of bales, marked " *invendebles*."    Making sure of some rich prize, we opened the bales, which to our chagrin consisted of pope's bulls, dispensations for eating meat on Fridays, and indulgences for peccadilloes of all kinds, with the price affixed.    They had evidently formed a venture from Spain to the Mexican sin market, but the supply exceeding the demand, had been reconsigned to the manufacturers.    We consigned them to the waves.

On our way home we were very near losing our suddenly acquired wealth and the frigate too.    Whilst between the Azores and Portugal, one of those hazes common in semi-tropical climates, had for some time prevailed on the surface of the sea, the mast-heads of the ship being above the haze, with a clear sky.    One day the look-out reported three large ships steering for us, and on going aloft I made them out to be line-of-battle ships in chase of the *Pallas*.    As they did not show any colours, it was impossible to ascertain their national character, but from the equality of the force and maintopgallantmasts, there was little doubt they were French.

The course of the frigate was immediately altered, and the weather changing, it began to blow hard, with a heavy sea.

The *Pallas* was crank to such a degree, that the lee main-deck guns, though housed, were under water, and even the lee-quarter-deck carronades were at times immerged.

As the strange ships were coming up with us hand over hand, the necessity of carrying more sail became indispensable, notwithstanding the immersion of the hull.

To do this with safety was the question. However, I ordered all the hawsers in the ship to be got up to the mast-heads and hove taut. The masts being thus secured, every possible stitch of sail was set, the frigate plunging forecastle under, as was also the case with our pursuers, which could not fire a gun—though as the haze cleared away we saw them repeatedly flashing the priming. After some time the line-of-battle ships came up with us, one keeping on our lee beam, another to windward, each within half a mile, whilst the third was a little more distant.

Seeing it impossible to escape by superior sailing, it appeared practicable to try a manœuvre, which might be successful if the masts would stand. Having, as stated, secured these by every available rope in the frigate, the order was given to prepare to clew up and haul down every sail at the same instant. The manœuvre being executed with great precision,—and the helm being put hard a-weather, so as to wear the ship as speedily as possible,—the *Pallas*, thus suddenly brought up, shook from stem to stern, in crossing the trough of the sea. As our pursuers were unprepared for this manœuvre, still less to counteract it, they shot past at full speed, and ran on several miles before they could shorten sail, or trim on the opposite tack. Indeed, under the heavy gale that was now blowing, even this was no easy matter, without endangering their own masts.

There was no time for consideration on our part, so having rapidly sheeted home, we spread all sail on the opposite tack. The hawsers being still fast to the masts, we went away from our pursuers at the rate of thirteen knots and upwards; so that a considerable distance was soon interposed between us and them; and this was greatly increased ere they were in a condition to follow. Before they had fairly renewed the chase night was rapidly setting in, and when quite dark, we lowered a ballasted cask overboard with a lantern, to induce them to believe that we had altered our course, though we held on in the same direction during the whole night. The trick was successful, for, as had been calculated, the next morning, to our great satisfaction, we saw nothing of them, and were all much relieved on finding our dollars and his Majesty's ship once more in safety. The expedient was a desperate one, but so was the condition which induced us to resort to it.

Of the proceeds of the above-mentioned captures — all made within ten days — Sir William Young, on the strength of having recopied my orders from the Admiralty, *claimed and received* half my share of the captures. No wonder that Lord St. Vincent said of him, that he wished to "*have the power of giving orders, and so share prize-money.*"

Being then young and ardent, my portion appeared inexhaustible. What could I want with more? The sum claimed and received by Admiral Young was not worth notice.

On our return to Plymouth the country was on the eve of a general election, and the time appeared a fitting one to carry out my long cherished scheme of getting into Parliament. The nearest borough in which there was a chance was Honiton, and accordingly I applied to the port admiral for leave of absence to contest that "independent" constituency. The prize-money procured it without scruple.

My opponent was a Mr. Bradshaw, who had the advantage of a previous canvass. From the amount of prize money which was known to have fallen to my share, that gentleman's popularity was for a moment in danger, it being anticipated that I should spend my money sailor fashion, so that it became unmistakeably manifest that the seat in Parliament would be at my service, if my opponent were outbid! To use the words of "an independent elector" during my canvass: "You need not ask me, my lord, who I votes for, I always votes for Mister Most."

To the intense disgust of the majority of the electors, I refused to bribe at all, announcing my determination to "stand on patriotic principles," which, in the electioneering *parlance* of those days, meant "no bribery." To my astonishment, however, a considerable number of the respectable inhabitants voted in my favour, and my agent assured me that a judicious application of no very considerable sum, would beat my opponent out of the market. This, however, being resolutely refused, the majority voted in favour of his five pound notes, and saved my friends of the Admiralty Court and other naval departments from an exhibition of misplaced zeal, which, as subsequently proved, could only have ended in my parliamentary discomfiture.

To be beaten, even at an election, is one thing; to turn a beating to account is another. Having had decisive proof as to the nature of Honiton politics, I made up my mind that the next time there was a vacancy in the borough, the seat should be mine without bribery. Accordingly, immediately after my defeat, I sent the bellman round the town, having first primed him with an appropriate speech, intimating that " all who had voted for me, might repair to my agent, J. Townsend, Esq., and *receive ten pounds ten!* "

The novelty of a defeated candidate paying double the current price expended by the successful one — or, indeed, paying anything — made a great sensation. Even my agent assured me that he could have secured my return for less money, for that the popular voice being in my favour, a trifling judicious expenditure would have turned the scale.

I told Mr. Townsend that such payment would have been bribery, which would not accord with my character as a reformer of abuses — a declaration which seemed highly to amuse him. Notwithstanding the explanation that the ten guineas was paid as a reward for having withstood the influence of bribery, the impression produced on the electoral mind by such unlooked-for liberality, was simply this — that if I gave ten guineas for being beaten, my opponent had not paid half enough for being elected; a conclusion which, by a similar process of reasoning, was magnified into the conviction that each of his voters had been cheated out of five pounds ten.

The result was what had been foreseen. My opponent, though successful, was regarded with anything but a favourable eye; I, though defeated, had suddenly become most popular. The effect at the next election, must be reserved for its place in a future chapter.

It was this election that first induced me to become a parliamentary Reformer, or as any one holding popular opinions was called in those days, a "Radical," *i. e.* a member of a political class holding views not half so extreme as those which form the parliamentary capital of reformers in the present day, and even less democratic than were the measures brought in during the last session of parliament by a Tory Government, whose predecessors consigned to gaol all who, fifty years ago, ventured to express opinions conferring political rights on the people.

It is strange that, after having suffered more for my political faith than any man now living, I should have survived to see former Radical yearnings become modern Tory doctrines. Stranger still, they should now form stepping-stones to place and power, instead of to the bar of a criminal court, where even the counsel defending those who were prosecuted for holding them became marked men.

Still it is something worth living for—even with the remembrance of my own bitter sufferings, for no greater offence than the advocacy of popular rights, and the abolition of naval abuses.

# CHAP. XI.

## SERVICES IN THE *PALLAS* CONTINUED.

On the 28th of May 1805, the *Pallas* again sailed from Portsmouth in charge of a convoy for Quebec. On this voyage little occurred worthy of note, beyond the fact that when we made the American coast we were, from a cause presently to be mentioned, no less than thirteen degrees and a half out in our *dead reckoning!* The reader must not imagine that we were 800 miles out of our course, for that was corrected whenever observations of the sun or stars could be obtained; but as these might at any time be rendered uncertain from the fogs prevalent on the banks, the most vigilant care was necessary to prevent the ship and convoy from being wrecked.

In my former voyage in the *Thetis* we had the advantage of a very clever man on board — a Mr. Garrard — who not being able to subsist on his salary as assistant astronomer and calculator at Greenwich, was glad to accept the berth of schoolmaster on board my uncle's frigate. From the instructions of this gentlemen, I had formerly profited considerably, and was not a little pleased when he applied to me for a similar berth on board the *Pallas*. With so skilful an observer, there could be no mistake about the error just mentioned; which arose from this circumstance, that for the sake of economy, the Navy Board or the dockyard authorities had surrounded the binnacle of the *Pallas* with iron instead of copper bolts; so that the compass was not to be depended upon. Fortunately the atmosphere was tolerably clear, so that no danger was incurred.

As, however, I had no inclination to risk either the ship or my own reputation amongst the fogs of Canada for the sake of false economy, the course of the *Pallas* and her convoy were directed to Halifax, there to free the compass from the attraction of iron. On demanding copper bolts from the dockyard officers, they were refused, on the ground that permission must be first obtained from the authorities in London! To this I replied, that if such were the case, the *Pallas* should wait with the convoy at Halifax whilst they communicated with the Admiralty in England! for that on no account should she enter the Gulf of St. Lawrence till our compass was right. The absurdity of detaining a convoy for six months, on account of a hundred weight of copper bolts was too much even for dockyard routine, and the demand was with some difficulty conceded.

It would be wearisome to detail the uninteresting routine of attending the convoy to Quebec, or of my taking charge of another for the homeward voyage; further than to state, that from the defect of having no proper lights for the guidance of the convoy by night, the whole lost sight of us before reaching the Lizard ; where we arrived with only one vessel, and that in tow.

The carelessness of merchant captains when following a convoy can only be estimated by those who have to deal with them. Not only was this manifested by day, but at night their stern cabins glittered with lights, equally intense with the convoy light, which therefore was not distinguishable. The separation of the convoy on the following day was thus rather a matter of course than of surprise.

This want of proper distinguishing lights, and the consequent dispersion of convoys, were thus frequent causes of the capture of our merchantmen, and to remedy this I constructed a lamp powerful enough to serve as a guide in following the protecting frigate by night. The Admiralty, however, neglected its application, or even to inspect my plan.

Some few years afterwards, the clamour of shipowners compelled the Board to direct its attention to the subject, and, passing over my communications, they offered a reward of fifty pounds to the inventor of the most suitable lamp for the purpose. On this I directed my agent, Mr. Brooks, to offer my lamp *in his own name*, feeling convinced that my connection with it would, if known, ensure its rejection. He did so, and after repeated trials against others at Sheerness, Spithead, and St. Helens, the fifty pound prize was adjudged to Mr. Brooks *for my lamp ! !* The fact afterwards becoming known, *not a lamp was ever ordered*, and the merchantmen were left to the mercy of privateers as

before.   I do not relate this anecdote as telling against
the *directing* powers of the Admiralty, but with the *administrative* powers, it was then and afterwards clearly
a fixed rule that no invention of mine should be carried
into effect.

On our way home, we one day made an experiment
which even now I believe might occasionally be turned
to account; viz. the construction of gigantic kites to
give additional impetus to ships.   With this view a
studdingsailboom was lashed across a spare flying
jibboom to form the framework, and over this a large
spread of canvas was sewn in the usual boy's fashion.
My spars were, however, of unequal dimensions throughout, and this and our launching the kite caused it to
roll greatly.   Possibly too I might not have been sufficiently experienced in the mysteries of " wings and
tail," for though the kite pulled with a will, it made
such occasional lurches as gave reason to fear for the
too sudden expenditure of his Majesty's stores.   The
power of such machines, properly constructed, would be
very great; and in the case of a constant wind, might
be useful.   The experiment, however, showed that
kites of smaller dimensions would have answered better.

On our return to England in December, the *Pallas*
was ordered to join the squadron of Admiral Thornborough, appointed to operate on the French and
Spanish coasts.   Instructions were, however, given to
cruise for a few days off Boulogne before finally proceeding to Plymouth.

We sailed from the Downs on the 23rd of January
1806, and on the 31st seeing a French merchant ves-

sel at anchor near the mouth of the river Somme, the boats were sent inshore to cut her out. On nearing her, a battery opened fire on them, when we wore and engaged the battery, whilst the boats brought off the vessel, with which we anchored in Dover roads on the following morning.

On the 8th of February, the *Pallas* sailed from Dover, and stood over towards the French coast, where we captured a fast sailing lugger, having on board a number of letters addressed to various persons in London. Shortly after this we were ordered to join the Admiral.

On the 22nd the *Pallas* sailed with Vice Admiral Thornborough's squadron from Plymouth, and remained in company till the 24th of March, when seeing some vessels off Isle Dieu, the boats went in chase, and returned with seven French fishing smacks; to the surprise of whose crews we bought their fish, and let them go.

From information communicated by the fishing boats, the *Pallas* ran off shore, and in the night following, returned and captured a vessel freighted with wine, which was taken on board the frigate. The next night the boats again went in, and brought off another vessel similarly laden. On the following morning we made sail with our two prizes, but observing a brig at anchor off Sable d'Olonne, ran in again after dark, and sent the boats to cut her out. A fire being opened on the boats from the town, we discharged several broadsides, on which the townspeople desisted, and the brig was brought off. Whilst engaged in this operation, another brig was seen to run ashore for safety. On the morning of the 28th, the boats were again despatched to get her off, when, the people mustering along shore to attack them, we fired several shotted guns to warn them from interfering, and the brig was safely brought out.

This propensity of French crews thus to run their vessels ashore—on being chased by boats—was principally caused by a galley which had been constructed at my own expense by the Deal boatbuilders, and shipped on board the *Pallas*. She rowed double banked, and required eighteen hands at the oars, and this together with her beautiful build rendered her perhaps the fastest boat afloat. Escape from such a craft being hopeless, she became so notorious, that the enemy's coasters ran their vessels ashore, and jumping into their boats, thus saved themselves from being made prisoners.

On the 29th, we manned the largest prize, the *Pomone*, and sent her to England in charge of the others. On the same day we fell in with the admiral, and supplied the squadron with prize wine, of which a large quantity had been taken, most of the vessels captured being laden with wine of fine quality, on its way to Havre for the Parisian market.

On quitting the squadron, we proceeded to the southward in chase of a convoy, one of which we captured, and on the 5th of April ran for the Garonne, having received intelligence that some French corvettes were lurking in the river and its vicinity, one of which vessels was reported to be lying some miles up the river as a guardship. Keeping out of sight for the remainder of the day, I determined on making an attempt to cut her out on the following night.

After dark the *Pallas* came to an anchor off the Cordovan lighthouse, and the boats, manned with the whole crew of the frigate, except about forty men, pulled for the corvette, under the command of their gallant First Lieutenant Haswell, who found her at 3 A.M. on the morning of the 6th, anchored near two batteries. As the weather was thick when the attack was made, the boats came upon the enemy unawares, and after a short but gallant resistance, the corvette was carried, proving to be the *Tapageuse* of 14 guns.

No sooner was this effected, than two others, whose presence was unexpected, came to her rescue. Lieutenant Haswell, however, promptly manned the guns of the captured vessel, and beat off his assailants, the tide rendering it imprudent for the prize or the boats to follow in pursuit.

Whilst this was going on, the *Pallas* remained at single anchor waiting for the boats, and soon after daylight three strange sail appeared to windward, making for the river. As the private signal was unanswered, there could be no doubt but that they were enemies to oppose whom we had only forty hands on board, the remainder of the crew, as previously stated, being in the prize brig.

There was no time to be lost, and as it was of the first importance to make a show of strength, though we possessed none, I immediately set the few hands we had to fasten the furled sails with rope yarns; the object being to cut the yarns all at once, let fall the sails, and thus impress the enemy with an idea that from such celerity in making sail we had a numerous and highly disciplined crew.

The manœuvre succeeded to a marvel. No sooner was our cloud of canvas thus suddenly let fall than the approaching vessels hauled the wind, and ran off along shore, with the *Pallas* in chase, our handful of men straining every nerve to sheet home, though it is surprising that the French officers did not observe the necessary slowness of the operation.

By superior sailing we were soon well up with one of them, and commenced firing our bow guns—the only guns, in fact, we were able to man. Scarcely had we fired half a dozen shots, when the French captain deliberately ran his ship ashore as the only way of saving himself and crew. The corvette was dismasted by the shock and immediately abandoned by the crew, who got ashore in their boats; though had they pulled on board the *Pallas* instead, we were literally incapable of resistance.

After the crew had abandoned the wreck, we ran nearly close, and fired several broadsides into her hull, to prevent her floating again with the tide. Whilst thus engaged, the other corvettes, which had previously run out of sight, again made their appearance to the S. S. W. under a press of sail, evidently coming up fast to the assistance of their consort.

As it was necessary once more to take the initiative, we quitted the wreck, ran up our colours, and gave chase, firing our bow guns at the nearest, which soon afterwards followed the example of the first, and ran ashore too,—with the same result of being dismasted—the crew escaping as in the case of the other.

Of the remaining corvette we for a time took no notice, and made sail towards the mouth of the Garonne to pick up our crew, which had necessarily been left on board the vessel captured on the river. As the *Pallas* neared the Cordovan lighthouse, we observed the third corvette making for the river. Finding herself intercepted she also ran on shore, and was abandoned in like manner.

The chase of these corvettes forms one of my most singular recollections, all three being deliberately abandoned and wrecked in presence of a British frigate with only forty men on board! Had any one of the three known our real condition, or had we not put a bold face on the matter, we might have been taken. The mere semblance of strength saved us, and the panic thereby inspired destroyed the enemy.

Having joined our prize—the *Tapageuse*—the prisoners were shifted on board the *Pallas*, which made sail in quest of the squadron, rejoining it on the 10th, when, by order of Admiral Thornborough, the prisoners were distributed among different ships.

The subjoined despatches will afford further explanation of the events just narrated.

"*Pallas*, off Chasseron, 8th April, 1806.

"Sir,—Having received information—which proved correct—of the situation of the corvettes in the river of Bordeaux, a little after dark on the evening of the 5th, the *Pallas* was anchored close to the shoal of Cordovan, and it gives me satisfaction to state that about 3 o'clock on the following

morning the French national corvette, *La Tapageuse*, of
14 long 12-pounders and 95 men, who had the guard, was
boarded, carried, and cut out, about twenty miles above the
shoal, and within two heavy batteries, in spite of all resistance, by the first lieutenant of the *Pallas*, Mr. Haswell,
the master, Mr. Sutherland, Messrs. Perkyns, Crawford, and
Thompson, together with the quartermasters and such of the
seamen and crew as were fortunate enough to find places in
the boats.

"The tide of flood ran strong at daylight. *La Tapageuse*
made sail. A general alarm was given. A sloop-of-war
followed, and an action continued — often within hail — till
by the same bravery by which the *Tapageuse* was carried,
the sloop-of-war, which before had been saved by the rapidity
of the current alone, was compelled to sheer off, having
suffered as much in the hull as the *Tapageuse* in the rigging.

"The conduct of the officers and men will be justly appreciated. With confidence I shall now beg leave to recommend them to the notice of the Lord Commissioner of the
Admiralty.

"It is necessary to add, that the same morning, when at
anchor waiting for the boats (which, by the by, did not
return till this morning), three ships were observed bearing
down towards the *Pallas*, making many signals, and were
soon perceived to be enemies. In a few minutes the anchor
of the *Pallas* was weighed, and with the remainder of the
officers and crew we chased, drove on shore, and wrecked one
national 24-gun ship, one of 22 guns, and the *Malicieuse*, a
beautiful corvette of 18 guns. Their masts went by the
board, and they were involved in a sheet of spray.

"All in this ship showed great zeal for his Majesty's service.
The warrant officers and Mr. Tattnall, midshipman, supplied the place of commissioned officers. The absence of
Lieutenant Mapleton is much to be regretted. He would
have gloried in the expedition with the boats. The assistance rendered by Mr. Drummond of the Royal Marines was
such as might have been expected. Subjoined is the list of

wounded, together with that of vessels captured and destroyed since the 26th ult.

"I am, &c. &c.

"COCHRANE.

"To Vice-Admiral Thornborough."

"*Prince of Wales*, off Rochefort,
9th April, 1806.

"MY LORD, — I have the honour to transmit to your lordship a copy of a letter I have this day received from Captain Lord Cochrane of H. M. S. *Pallas*, under my orders.  It will not be necessary for me, my Lord, to comment on the intrepidity and good conduct displayed by Lord Cochrane, his officers and men, in the execution of a very hazardous enterprise in the Garonne, a river, the most difficult, perhaps, in its navigation, of any on the coast.  The complete success that attended the enterprise, as well as the destruction of the vessels of war mentioned in the said letter on the coast of Arcasson, speaks their merits more fully than is in my power to do.  To which may be fairly added, that nothing can show more clearly the high state of discipline of the crew of the *Pallas* than the humanity shown by them in the conflict.

"I have the honour, &c. &c.

"EDWARD THORNBOROUGH.

"The Right Hon. the Earl St. Vincent."

"*Hibernia*, off Ushant, April 14th, 1806.

"SIR, — I yesterday received from Admiral Thornborough a letter with its enclosure from Captain Lord Cochrane, of which copies are herewith transmitted for the information of my Lord Commissioner of the Admiralty.

"The gallant and successful exertions of the *Pallas* therein detailed, reflect very high honour on her captain, officers and crew, and call for my warmest approbation.

"I am, &c. &c.

"ST. VINCENT.

"W. Marsden, Esq."

The cold, reluctant praise bestowed by this letter, was no doubt intended by Lord St. Vincent as a wet blanket on the whole affair, and contrasts strongly with the warm-hearted sailor-like frankness of Admiral Thornborough. It had its full effect; not a word of approbation did I receive from the Admiralty. The *Tapageuse* was not bought into the navy, though a similar vessel, subsequently captured by another officer at the same place, was purchased. My First Lieutenant, Haswell, was not promoted. In short, if we had done something worthy of disapprobation, it could scarcely have been more marked. On this subject further comment will presently become necessary.

To return to our cruise. On the 14th of April we again quitted the squadron, and made for the corvettes run on shore on the 7th. The French had erected a battery for the protection of one of them which was still sound in the hull; but we silenced the battery and set fire to the corvette. After this the *Pallas* proceeded towards the wreck of the northernmost vessel stranded, but as strong breezes came on, and she was evidently breaking up in the surf, we deemed it prudent to work off shore, and in so doing captured another vessel, which turned out to be a French packet.

On the 20th the *Pallas* ran down abreast of the remaining corvette, and out boats for the purpose of burning her, but these being exposed to the fire of another battery which had been thrown up to protect the wreck, and the *Pallas* not being able, on account of the shoaliness of the water, to get near enough to fire with effect, we desisted from the attempt, and again made sail.

On the 23rd we came to an anchor off the Malmaison passage, and on the following day reconnoitred the French squadron inside Isle Rhe. Whilst thus engaged, the British squadron appeared to windward, and shortly afterwards came to an anchor.

On the 24th we worked up to windward to join the admiral, and on the following day stood into Basque Roads to reconnoitre the enemy's squadron. On approaching within gunshot, a frigate and three brigs got under weigh, and we made sail to meet them, endeavouring to bring them to action by firing several broadsides at them. On this they tacked after returning the fire, and stood in under their batteries. Having completed our reconnoissance, we beat out again and rejoined the admiral, to whom I made the annexed report.

> "H.M.S. *Pallas*, off Isle d'Aix,
> "April 25th, 1806.

"Sir, — Having stood within gunshot of the French squadron this morning, I find it to consist of the following vessels.

"One of three decks, 16 ports below; one of 80 guns, 15 ports; three of 74, 14 ports; two heavy frigates, of 40 guns; three light frigates, 13 ports on main-deck, and three brigs of from 14 to 16 guns.

"The *Calcutta* * is not among them. Neither are there any corvettes, unless a very clumsy 20-gun ship can be called one. The ships of the line have all their topmasts struck and topgallant yards across. They are all very deep, more so than vessels are in general for common voyages.

"They may be easily burned, or they may be taken by sending here eight or ten thousand men, as if intended for the

---

* An Indiaman, recently captured by the French off St. Helena.

Mediterranean. If people at home would hold their tongues about it *, possession might thus be gained of the Isle d'Oleron, upon which all the enemy's vessels may be driven by sending fire vessels to the eastward of Isle d'Aix.

"A frigate and the three brigs were ordered to get under weigh. These stood towards the *Pallas* and exchanged a few broadsides. After waiting from ten o'clock till past two, close to Isle d'Aix, we were obliged to come out no better than we went in. They could not be persuaded to stand from under their batteries.

"I have the honour, &c. &c.

" COCHRANE.

"Edw. Thornborough, Esq.,
    " Vice-Admiral of the Blue."

Having found by experience, that the French had organised a system of signal-houses, by means of which they were able to indicate the exact position of an enemy, so as to warn their coasters from impending danger, I resolved on destroying one of their principal stations on Isle Rhe, at the town of St. Martin. The result will be gathered from the subjoined despatch to Admiral Thornborough.

"Pallas, St. Martin's Road, Isle Rhe,

"May 10th, 1806.

" Sir, — The French trade having been kept in port of late, in a great measure by their knowledge of the exact position of his Majesty's cruisers, constantly announced at the signal posts; it appeared to me to be some object, as there was nothing better to do, to endeavour to stop this practice.

"Accordingly, the two posts at Point Delaroche were

---

* It is a curious fact, that there being no such thing as confidence or secrecy in official quarters in England, the French were as well advised as to our movements as were our own commanders, and were consequently prepared at all points.

demolished, next that of Caliola.    Then two in L'Anse de
Repos, one of which Lieutenant Haswell and Mr. Hillier
the gunner took in a neat style from upwards of 100 militia.
The marines and boats' crews behaved exceedingly well.    All
the flags have been brought off, and the houses built by
government burnt to the ground.

"Yesterday too the zeal of Lieutenant Norton of the
*Frisk* cutter, and Lieutenant Gregory of the *Contest* gun
brig, induced them to volunteer to flank the battery on
Point d'Equillon, whilst we should attack in the rear by
land; but it was carried at once, and one of fifty men who
were stationed to three 36-pounders was made prisoner —
the rest escaped.    The battery is laid in ruins — guns spiked
— carriages burnt — barrack and magazine blown up, and
all the shells thrown into the sea.    The convoy got into a
river beyond our reach.    Lieutenant Mapleton, Mr. Sutherland, master, and Mr. Hillier were with me, and as they do
on all occasions so they did at this time whatever was in their
power for his Majesty's service.    The petty officers, seamen,
and marines failed not to justify the opinion that there was
before reason to form; yet it would be inexcusable were not
the names of the quartermasters Barden and Casey particularly mentioned, as men highly deserving any favour that can
be shown in the line to which they aspire.

" I have the honour, &c. &c.<br>
" COCHRANE.

" Edw. Thornborough, Esq.,
    " Vice-Admiral of the Blue."

Early in the morning on the 14th of May, the *Pallas*
again stood in close to the Isle of Aix, to renew her
reconnoissance of the French squadron under Admiral
Allemand, then anchored at the entrance of the Antioche passage, and also in the hope of once more
getting within range of the vessels which we had failed
to bring to an action on the 25th ultimo.    In order to

prevent their again taking shelter under the batteries
on Isle d'Aix, we cleared for action and ran within
range of the latter; the frigate shortly afterwards
getting under weigh to meet us.

Scarcely had she done so, than the three brigs also
got under weigh to support her, making a formidable
addition to the force to be encountered, the frigate alone
showing a broadside superior to ours. We however
remained under our topsails by the wind to await them,
and when the brigs came within point-blank shot, a
broadside from the *Pallas* dismantled one of them. We
then veered, and engaged the frigate and the other brig
— the batteries on Isle d'Aix meanwhile firing at us.

After an hour's fighting, we observed that considerable damage had been done by the fire of the *Pallas* to
the frigate and another of the brigs, the maintopsail yard
of the latter being cut through, and the aftersails of the
frigate shot away, though the action was not continuous,
owing to the frequent necessity on our part of tacking
to avoid shoals.

About one o'clock we managed to gain the wind of
the frigate, and running between her and the batteries,
gave her two or three smart broadsides, on which her
fire slackened, and she showed signs of meditating a
retreat. Perceiving this, I directed Mr. Sutherland, the
master, to lay us aboard, which at 1.40 P.M. was gallantly,
but rather too eagerly effected.

Just at this moment, unobserved by us, the French
frigate grounded on a shoal, so that on coming in contact,
the spars and rigging of both vessels were dismantled.
The concussion drove our guns back into the ports, in

which position the broadside was again discharged, and the shot tore through her sides with crushing effect, her men taking refuge below, so that the only return to this broadside was three pistol shots fired at random. The French captain was the only man who gallantly remained on deck.

To clear away our own wreck was one object; to board the frigate the next; but two more frigates were observed to quit the enemy's squadron, and crowd all sail to her assistance. This, in our crippled condition, was too much; there was, therefore, nothing for it but to quit the grounded ship and save ourselves. Accordingly we bore up, and made what sail was possible, cutting away and repairing the wreck as we best could; the two frigates following in chase.

About 5.40 P.M. we were joined by the *Kingfisher* sloop, commanded by Captain, now Admiral, Seymour; who promptly took us in tow, and the enemy desisted from the pursuit, turning their attention to their disabled consort. The subjoined report to Admiral Thornborough details a few other particulars of the action, though at that time we neither knew the names nor the strength of our opponents.

" His Majesty's Ship *Pallas*, 14th May,<br>
" Off the Island of Oleron, May 15th, 1806.

"SIR,— This morning when close to Isle d'Aix, reconnoitring the French squadron, it gave me great joy to find our late opponent, the black frigate, and her companions the three brigs, getting under sail; we formed high expectations that the long wished for opportunity was at last arrived.

" The *Pallas* remained under topsails by the wind to await them; at half past eleven a smart point blank firing com-

o 4

menced on both sides, which was severely felt by the enemy.
The maintopsailyard of one of the brigs was cut through,
and the frigate lost her aftersails. The batteries on l'Isle
d'Aix opened on the *Pallas*, and a cannonade continued,
interrupted on our part only by the necessity we were under
to make various tacks to avoid the shoals, till one o'clock,
when our endeavour to gain the wind of the enemy and get
between him and the batteries proved successful; an effectual
distance was now chosen, a few broadsides were poured in,
the enemy's fire slackened. I ordered ours to cease, and
directed Mr. Sutherland, the master, to run the frigate on
board, with intention effectually to prevent her retreat.

" The enemy's side thrust our guns back into the ports, the
whole were then discharged, the effect and crash were
dreadful; their decks were deserted; three pistol shots were
the unequal return.

" With confidence I say that the frigate was lost to France
had not the unequal collision tore away our foretopmast,
jibboom, fore and maintopsailyards, spritsailyards, bumpkin,
cathead, chain plates, forerigging, foresail, and bower anchor,
with which last I intended to hook on, but all proved in-
sufficient. She was yet lost to France had not the French
admiral, seeing his frigate's foreyard gone, her rigging
ruined, and the danger she was in, sent two others to her
assistance.

" The *Pallas* being a wreck, we came out with what sail
could be set, and his Majesty's sloop the *Kingfisher* afterwards took us in tow.

" The officers and ship's company behaved as usual; to the
names of Lieutenants Haswell and Mapleton, whom I have
mentioned on other occasions, I have to add that of Lieutenant
Robins, who had just joined.

"I have the honour to be, &c. &c.

"COCHRANE."

" *Killed.* — David Thompson, marine.

" *Wounded.* — Mr. Andrews, midshipman, very badly;
John Coger, and three other seamen, slightly.

" Edw. Thornborough, Esq., Vice-Admiral of the Blue."

On the 17th, being still ignorant of the name of the frigate we had engaged, we landed some French prisoners under a flag of truce, and thus learned that she was the 40-gun frigate *La Minerve*. The brigs were ascertained to be the *Lynx*, *Sylphe*, and *Palinure*, each carrying 16 guns.

On the 18th, the *Pallas* was ordered to Plymouth in charge of a convoy of transports, and arrived on the 27th without any other occurrence worthy of notice.

A device practised by us when, at various times, running close in to the French shore, must not be omitted. A number of printed proclamations, addressed to the French people, had been put on board, with instructions to embrace every opportunity of getting them distributed. The opportunities for this were, of course, few, being chiefly confined to the crews of boats or small fishing craft, who would scarcely have ventured on their distribution, had the proclamation been entrusted to them.

The device resorted to was the construction of small kites, to which a number of proclamations were attached. To the string which held the kite, a match was appended in such a way, that when the kite was flown over the land, the retaining string became burned through, and dispersed the proclamations, which, to the great annoyance of the French government, thus became widely distributed over the country.

# CHAP. XII.

## MY ENTRANCE INTO PARLIAMENT.

MY ENTRANCE INTO PARLIAMENT.—ENTHUSIASTIC RECEPTION. — SEEK
PROMOTION FOR HASWELL.—CUTTING OUT LE CÆSAR.—GROSS INSTANCE
OF PARTIALITY.—CLARET AGAINST SMALL BEER.—STORY OF MR. CROKER.
—MR. CROKER'S REVENGE. — COMMAND THE IMPERIEUSE.—DRIFT
TOWARDS USHANT. — JOIN THE SQUADRON IN THE BASQUE ROADS.—
ANCHOR OFF CORDOVAN.—SUPPLY THE ATALANTE.

On the termination of the cruise, the *Pallas* was
thoroughly refitted, the interval thus occupied affording
me time for relaxation, but nothing occurred worthy
of record till, in the July following, the electors of
Honiton chose me as their representative in parliament.

The story of this election is worth relating. My
former discomfiture at Honiton, and the ten guineas
a head paid to those who had voted for me on the
previous occasion, will be fresh in the recollection of
the reader. A general election being at hand, no time
was lost in proceeding to Honiton, where considerable
sensation was created by my entrance into the town in
a *vis-à-vis* and six, followed by several carriages and
four filled with officers and seamen of the *Pallas*, who
volunteered to accompany me on the occasion.

Our reception by the townspeople was enthusiastic,
the more so, perhaps, from the general belief that my

capture of the Spanish galleons—as they were termed
—had endowed me with untold wealth; whilst an
equally fabulous amount was believed to have resulted
from our recent cruise, during which my supporters
would have been not a little surprised to learn that
neither myself, officers, nor crew, had gained anything
but a quantity of wine, which nobody would buy;
whilst for the destruction of three French corvettes
we never received a shilling!

Aware of my previous objection to bribery, not a
word was asked by my partisans, as to the price expected in exchange for their suffrages. It was enough
that my former friends had received ten guineas each
after my defeat, and it was judged best to leave the
cost of success to my discretion.

My return was triumphant, and this effected, it was
then plainly asked, what *ex post facto* consideration was
to be expected by those who had supported me in so
delicate a manner.

" Not one farthing!" was the reply.

"But, my Lord, you gave ten guineas a head to the
minority at the last election, and the majority have
been calculating on something handsome on the present occasion."

" No doubt. The former gift was for their disinterested conduct in not taking the bribe of five pounds
from the agents of my opponent. For me now to pay
them would be a violation of my own previously
expressed principles."

Finding nothing could be got from me in the way
of money payment for their support, it was put to my

generosity whether I would not, at least, give my constituents a public supper.

"By all means," was my reply, "and it will give me great satisfaction to know that so rational a display of patriotism has superseded a system of bribery, which reflects even less credit on the donor than the recipients."

Alas! for the vanity of good intentions. The permission thus given was converted into a public treat; not only for my partisans, but for my opponents, their wives, children, and friends; in short, for the whole town! The result showed itself in a bill *for some twelve hundred pounds!* which I refused to pay, but was eventually compelled to liquidate, in a way which will form a very curious episode hereafter.

One of my first steps, subsequent to the election, was to apply to the Admiralty for the promotion of my first lieutenant, Haswell, who had so gallantly cut out the *Tapageuse* from the Bordeaux river; and also for that of poor Parker, whose case has been notified in connection with the *Speedy*, though it was not till after my becoming a member of the House of Commons that he was promoted after the fashion previously narrated.

It is unnecessary to recapitulate the services of these gallant officers, further than to state briefly, that on the 6th of April, 1806, Lieutenant Haswell, with the boats of the *Pallas* alone, acting under my orders, cut out the French guardship, *La Tapageuse*, from the river Garonne, and brought off his prize, in the face of heavy batteries, and despite the endeavours of two vessels of war — each of equal force to the captured corvette.

For this service Lieutenant Haswell remained unpromoted!

On the 15th of July, in the same year, the boats of Sir Samuel Hood's squadron, under the orders of Lieutenant Sibley, performed the somewhat similar, though certainly not superior exploit of cutting out *Le Cæsar*, of 16 guns and 86 men, from the same anchorage. Within three weeks after the performance of this service, Lieutenant Sibley was *promoted to the rank of commander*, and so palpable an instance of favouritism determined me to urge afresh the neglected claims of both Parker and Haswell.

My renewed application being met with evasion in the case of both officers, I plainly intimated to the Admiralty authorities that it would be my duty to bring before the House of Commons a partiality so detrimental to the interests of the navy. The threat produced what justice refused to concede, and these deserving officers were both made Commanders on the 15th of August, 1806; Parker, for a service performed upwards of five years before, and Haswell for one four months previously. Notwithstanding this lapse of time, Haswell's promotion was dated *eleven days after* that of Lieutenant Sibley! though the former officer had effected with the boats of a small frigate, and against *three* ships of war, as much as Lieutenant Sibley had accomplished against *only one*, though with the boats of a whole squadron! viz., the boats of the *Centaur, Conqueror, Revenge, Achilles, Prince of Wales, Polyphemus, Monarch, Iris,* and *Indefatigable.* Lieut. Sibley's exploit with this overwhelming force had a medal awarded, and appears. in the Navy List to this day; Lieut. Has-well's capture of the *Tapageuse* under my directions was unnoticed in any way.

The fact is, that neither of my highly meritorious officers would have been promoted, but that, after Lieutenant Sibley's promotion for a less distinguished service, it was impossible to evade their claims if brought under the notice of the legislature; and it was only by this threatened exposure of such palpable injus-tice, that the promotion of either officer was obtained.

Another gross instance of partiality in the course pursued by the Admiralty towards my officers and crews, consisted in the refusal to purchase the *Tapa-geuse* into the navy; though the *Cæsar* — prize to Sir Samuel Hood's squadron — was so purchased. For the four vessels of war, viz. the *Tapageuse*, 14 guns; the *Malicieuse*, 18 guns; the *Garonne*, 22; and the *Gloire*, 24,—total, 78 guns, driven on shore by the *Pallas*, in one day, no remuneration was awarded; the pretence for withholding it being, that as there were no proceeds there could be no reward; whilst, as the enemy's crews escaped, head money was denied, though the Act of Parliament conferring it, was expressly framed to meet such cases, the nonpayment practically deciding, that it was not worth a commander's while to expose himself and ship in destroying enemy's vessels! Supposing it to have been necessary to adhere stringently to the Admiralty regulation, the rule itself rendered it the more incumbent on the Board to give remuneration for the *Tapageuse*, by purchasing that vessel into the service, as was done to Lieutenant Sibley and his men in the case of the *Cæsar*. Such remuneration was, however, wholly withheld.*

Another curious circumstance connected with the *Pallas* may be here mentioned. As the reader is aware, that ship — on her last cruise — had taken a number of chasse-marées, some of which were laden with the finest vintages of the south of France. Independently of the wine gratuitously supplied by the *Pallas* to the squadron of Admiral Thornborough, a large quantity of the finest had been reserved to be sold for the benefit of the captors ; so much, in fact, that in an easily glutted market, like that of Plymouth, it was not saleable for anything beyond the duty.

An offer was made to the Victualling Board to accept, for our claret, the price of the villanous small beer then served out to ships' companies, so that Jack might have a treat without additional expense to the nation. The offer was unwisely refused, despite the benefit to the health of the men.

As customs officers were placed on board the prize-vessels containing the wine, considerable expense was incurred. We therefore found it imperative that something should be done with it, and as the Victualling

---

* If a vessel were captured and destroyed, head money was awarded, as in the case of the *Calcutta*, which surrendered to the *Impérieuse* in the subsequent affair of Basque Roads. It was sworn to by others that she surrendered to the squadron ; but that this was not the case is proved by the French government having shot her captain for surrendering *to me alone;* a sentence which was not likely to have been passed had he surrendered to eight or ten ships. In this case head money was awarded to Lord Gambier's fleet, on which account I declined to touch a shilling of it.

Board refused to take it, there was no alternative but to knock out the bungs of the casks, and empty the wine overboard.

My agent had, however, orders to pay duty on two pipes, and to forward them, on my account, to my uncle the Honourable Basil Cochrane, who had kindly offered to stow them in his cellars in Portman Square. Knowing the quality of the wine, the agent took upon himself to forward seven pipes instead of two, and on these duty was paid. As it was impossible to consume such a quantity, the whole was bottled, in order to await opportunity for its disposal.

On this wine hangs a curious story. My residence in town was in Old Palace Yard, and one of my constant visitors was the late Mr. Croker, of the Admiralty, then on the look-out for political employment. This gentleman had an invitation to my table as often as he might think proper, and of this — from a similarity of taste and habit, as I was willing to believe — he so far availed himself as to become my daily guest; receiving a cordial reception, from friendship towards a person of ardent mind, who had to struggle as I had done to gain a position.

Croker was one day dining with me, when some of the *Pallas* wine was placed on the table. Expressing his admiration of my "superb claret," for such it really was, notwithstanding that the Victualling Board had rejected wine of a similar quality for the use of seamen, though offered at the price of small beer, he asked me to let him have some of it. The reply was, that he should have as much as he pleased, at the cost of duty and bottling, taking the wine as I had done from the French, for nothing: jocosely remarking, that the claret would be all the better for coming from a friend instead of an enemy, he stated his intention to avail himself of my offer.

Shortly after this incident, Croker, who had previously been in parliament, was appointed secretary to the Admiralty, and from that day forward he never presented himself at my apartments; nor did I, by any chance, meet him till some time afterwards, we encountered each other, by accident, near Whitehall.

Recognising me in a way meant to convey the idea, that as he was now my master, our relations were slightly altered, I asked him why he had not sent for his wine? His reply was, " Why, really I have no use for it, my friends having supplied me more liberally than I have occasion for!" Well knowing the meaning of this, I made him a reply expressive of my appreciation of his conduct towards me personally, as well as of the wine sources from which he had been so liberally supplied. This, of course, was conclusive as to any future acquaintance, and we parted without one additional word.

This incident converted into a foe one who had been regarded by me in the spirit of sincere and disinterested friendship. He was, moreover, in a position to make his enmity felt, and when I was hunted down by that infamous trial which blasted at a blow my hopes and reputation, the weight of official vengeance was all the more keenly felt, as being the return of former hospitality.

In my previous attempts to call the attention of the House to naval abuses, Croker was my constant opponent; and as, in our days of friendship, I had unreservedly unbosomed to him my views and plans of action, he was in a condition to fight me with my own weapons, which thus became employed in continuance of the corrupt system at which they were aimed. If, at that period, there were any naval abuses requiring reformation, Mr. Croker was certainly the greatest stumbling-block to their removal, for no better reason than that plans for their remedy emanated from me, though in the days of our friendship, he had not only approved those plans, but even suggested others.

On the 23rd of August, 1806, I was appointed to the command of the *Impérieuse* frigate, which was commissioned on the 2nd of September following, the crew of the *Pallas* being turned over to her.

We left Plymouth on the 17th of November, but in a very unfit condition for sea.

The alacrity of the port authorities to obtain praise for despatching vessels to sea before they were in fit condition, was reprehensible. It was a point in those days for port admirals to hurry off ships, regardless of consequences, immediately after orders for their sailing were received; this " *despatch*," as it was incorrectly termed, securing the commendation of the Admiralty, whom no officer dared to inform of the danger to which both ships and crews were thereby exposed.

The case of the *Impérieuse* was very near proving the fallacy of the system. She was ordered to put to sea, the moment the rudder — which was being hung —

would steer the ship. The order was of necessity obeyed, but her crank condition, from being built of fir, compelled me to request some tons of iron ballast. Time was not, however, given to stow this away. We were therefore compelled to leave port with a lighter full of provisions on one side, a second with ordnance stores on the other, and a third filled with gunpowder towing astern. We had not even opportunity to secure the guns; the quarter deck cannonades were not shipped on their slides; and all was in the utmost confusion.

The result of this precipitation was — for it had no object — that as soon as the land was out of sight, we were obliged to heave to, in mid-channel, to unstow the after hold, get down the ballast, and clear the decks. Worse still — the rigging had not been effectually set up, so that had a gale of wind come on, the safety of the frigate might have been compromised; or had we been attacked by an enemy— even a gunboat—we could not have fired a shot in return, as, from the powder coming on board last, we had not a cartridge filled.

The weather becoming thick on the following day, no observation could be taken. The consequence was, that from the current and unknown drift of the frigate whilst hove-to, to set up the new rigging, secure the masts, and stow the hold, we drifted toward Ushant, and in the night struck heavily three or four times on a shelf, but fortunately forged over into a deep pool, in which, as it was blowing hard, we had to let go three anchors to hold the ship till the following morning.

As soon as it became daylight, it was found that the

*Impérieuse* was inside of Ushant, instead of outside, to the manifest peril of the frigate. As it was, we sounded our way out with difficulty, and happily without material injury.

I afterwards demanded a court-martial on my conduct in this affair, but it was not granted; because it was known that the blame would have fallen on others, not on me. This unwise and arbitrary conduct, in hastily and prematurely forcing vessels to sea, was mistaken by the public as a manifestation of official zeal in carrying on the service!

It would be easy to mention numerous instances of the like nature, but this being my own case, I can vouch for its authenticity.

In a future chapter it will be necessary again to advert to these and other evils to which men and ships were not only exposed but actually sacrificed, by hurry or neglect of equipment.

On the 29th we joined the blockading squadron in Basque Roads, and were ordered by the admiral to cruise off shore in the vicinity, but without effect, till the 19th of December, when we captured two vessels off Sable d'Olonne, and on the 31st a third at the entrance of the Garonne.

On the 4th of January we gave chase to several vessels which ran in the direction of Arcassan. On the following day the boats were sent in chase of a galliot and another vessel in shore, but the cutter being swamped in the surf, both escaped into the creek or basin, and ran ashore. We then anchored about three miles from the entrance.

On the 6th we again hoisted out boats and sent them with the stream anchors to warp off the vessels, in which operation they were successfully obstructed by a battery on an island at the entrance of the creek. As the water was too shoal for the frigate to approach with safety, the boats were manned, and before daylight on the 7th we carried the battery by assault, spiking or otherwise destroying the guns, which consisted of four 36-pounders, two field pieces, and a 13-inch mortar; this done, we collected their carriages, and what wood we could find, with which we set fire to the fort. Several gunboats being at anchor in the rear of the island, we burned them, as well as the vessels previously chased, not thinking it prudent to remain and get them off, as a general alarm had been excited along the coast.

Having destroyed this battery, we again sailed for the Garonne, and on the 9th anchored off Cordovan, in the hope of intercepting any vessels entering or quitting the river; but notwithstanding we remained here till the 19th, none showed themselves, nor was any attempt made by the enemy to dislodge us from our position. Our anchorage was, however, exposed, and heavy gales coming on, we were compelled to make sail on the 19th.

Shortly after this the *Impérieuse* was ordered home, arriving at Plymouth on the 11th of February, without further incident. Indeed the cruise would not be worthy of record, except to preserve the order of time in this narrative of my services unbroken.

On the 26th we chased some vessels off Isle Dieu, but they ran under the protection of a battery with which we exchanged some shots, and then made sail in the direction of Sable d'Olonne. On the 29th joined the squadron, and were ordered to supply the *Atalante* with provisions and water. A further notice respecting this operation will be found in the parliamentary debate in the next chapter.

# CHAP. XIII.

## DISSOLUTION OF PARLIAMENT.

ON the 27th of April, 1807, the short but busy parliament was dissolved, "his Majesty being anxious to
recur to the sense of his people." In other words, it
was dissolved for political reasons not within the scope
of the present work to enter.

In the following month of May writs were issued for
a general election, and as my Honiton constituents,
even during the short period I had been ashore, had
heartily sickened me of further connection with them,
by the incessant cry for places with which they had
assailed me, I made up my mind to become a candidate
for Westminster, with the object of adding the weight
of an important constituency to my own representations
on naval or other abuses whenever opportunity might
occur. Or, as I told the electors of Westminster at a
meeting convened at the St. Alban's Tavern, my motive
for soliciting their suffrages was, that " a man representing a rotten borough could not feel himself of equal

consequence in the House with one representing such a city as Westminster—that disclaiming all attachment to parties or factions, it was not only my wish to be independent, but to be placed in a position where I could become so with effect, and that as this was impossible with no more efficient backers than my late constituents, my connection with them had ceased, and I had taken the liberty of soliciting the suffrages of the electors for Westminster."

The candidates for Westminster were, the Right Hon. Brinsley Sheridan, Mr. Elliot, Mr. Paul, and myself. It was not till the poll had commenced, that Sir Francis Burdett—at that time confined to his bed by a dangerous wound received in a duel with Mr. Paul — was put in nomination, without his knowledge, the nature of his wound not permitting any person to communicate with him, except his medical attendant.

I was regarded as the opponent of Mr. Sheridan, and for want of better argument that gentleman's partisans in the press sought to depreciate me in the estimation of the electors by representations of the most unjust character, a far more reprehensible act than that of pointing out to them the advantage of retaining an eminent and tried man in preference to one of whose political tendencies they could practically know nothing.

In electioneering all devices are considered fair, so in place of resenting or retaliating, they were met by my declaration, that —

"Whatever gentlemen might say of their long political services — to the electors belonged the privilege of judging for themselves, and that in looking for security for the performance of pledges, they should also consider the character of those who gave them. I was not a mere professed reformer, but the zealous friend of reform, earnestly desiring to see it thoroughly carried out as regarded many abuses which had crept into our constitution. Much had been said of profligacy and profusion of public money. But what was to be said of a Commander-in-chief of the Navy, who would give away those commissions which formed the stimulus, and should be the reward of honourable merit, in exchange for borough interests? If I had the honour of being returned for Westminster, I should feel confident in rising to arraign such abuses. But in representing a rotten borough, I was under restriction."

This explanation was favourably received, and the result was, that on the 10th of May I was at the head of the poll, whilst my detractors were at the bottom; Sir Francis Burdett being third, and Mr. Sheridan fourth, — a circumstance which called forth from the latter gentleman one of those diatribes for which he had become famous.

To this I replied as follows : —

"I perfectly approved of the sentiments professed by the right honourable gentleman, that 'with respect to his own principles, he would prefer the approbation of his country before the favour of any administration, or other set of men.' It had, however, been said, that naval officers were unfit for representatives of the people in parliament. But how were abuses in the Navy to be pointed out or redressed by parliament, without the presence of men competent to point them out, give accurate information, and suggest remedies?

"For six years past, such abuses had prevailed as were paralysing the Navy. It was not the place to enter into details, but a few of the more prominent points might be mentioned.   Under what was called the system of economy, adopted in the fleet, ships were kept at sea month after month, and in such a crazy state of repair, as scarcely to be in a condition to float.   The system was, that when such vessels came into harbour for repair, the Admiralty artificers were sent on board to examine them.   These men were afraid to tell the truth, if they considered it unpalatable to their employers, lest they should lose their places.   They therefore reported, that such ships would do awhile longer, with some slight repairs.

"The vessels received those repairs, without coming into dock, and were sent to sea, where they were wrecked or foundered!   This was the case with the *Atalante*, ship of war, which was four months off Rochefort last winter.   I was ordered to victual that ship for a long voyage, and re-monstrated — declaring my opinion that she was unfit to go to sea, and that, if she were sent, the first intelligence from her would be, that she had foundered.   The result was ex-actly as I had foretold.   In spite of remonstrance, she was sent to sea, and ship, crew, and all went to the bottom (loud laughter).   It was no laughing matter.   Like the fable of the frogs, it might be fun to some, though anything but fun for brave men, whose lives were so valuable to their families and their country.   A similar fate attended the *Felix* schooner, which was compelled to proceed to sea in a like condition, and went down with officers and crew, of whom one man only was saved.

"Another point might be mentioned.   What could be said of a man at the head of the Navy, who would lavishly grant away, in exchange for rotten borough interests, naval commissions which ought to be the reward of those brave officers who had for years devoted their lives at every hazard in the service of their country?   Yet it was notorious such things were done.

" It had been asserted, that naval and military officers were ineligible to seats in parliament, because they might at any time be called away by their professional duty.   But such men might — and often did — effect more for their country in a few days — sometimes in a few hours — than half those gentlemen who continued for seven years, sitting on their cushions in the House of Commons, without speaking a word for the public good, — nay, very often voting against it (laughter and applause).

"With regard to reform, it would be my wish to bring back the constitution to its ancient purity — to exclude altogether from parliament those placemen and pensioners who, by ancient laws, were excluded from it, but whom modern practice had deemed it expedient to place in the Legislature. What had the Committee of Reform done — of whose labours and intentions so much had been said? When the dissolution came, they were found sitting where they began their task, without having effected anything whatever."

At the final close of the poll, Sir Francis Burdett and myself, being at the head, were declared elected, and I had the honour of representing a body of constituents whose subsequent support, under the most trying events of my life, forms one of my most gratifying recollections. I must also record it, to the honour of my Westminster friends, that during my long connection with them, no elector ever asked me to procure for himself or relatives a place under Government, whilst the multitude of applications for place from my late constituents formed, as has been said, a source of intolerable annoyance.

This election was remarkable as being the first in which public opinion firmly opposed itself to party faction. It had become unmistakeably manifest that the two great factions into which politicians were divided had no other object than to share in the general

plunder, and, as a first step to this, to embarrass the
government of the "*ins*" by the factious opposition of
the "*outs*." Indeed, so obvious had this become, that
the appellations of Whig and Tory were laid aside by
common consent, and the more descriptive names of
"*outs*" and "*ins*" substituted in their stead. My
election had no doubt been secured by the emphatic
declaration, that I would belong to neither party, supporting or opposing either as in my judgment might
seem conducive to the national good.

The animosity of these respective parties against each
other was favourable to such a course. Each accused
the other of grasping at offices for the sake of personal
or dependent advantage, and averred that the aim of
their opponents was neither the administration of government — which, as has been seen, was left to administer
itself in its own way — nor the good of the country,
but the possession and distribution of the public money.
So virulent did these mutual recriminations become, that
it cannot be wondered at if people took the disputants
at their word ; the more so as the moment either party
was in power they threw aside the principles which
had gained momentary ascendency, and devoted their
sole attention to their former practices, knowing that,
as their possession of office might be short, a tenure so
uncertain must be made the most of. Statesmanship
amongst such people was out of the question. Neither
party could even foresee that the very disgust which
their scramble for office was exciting in the public mind,
must one day overthrow both factions.

It was at this very Westminster election that the patriotism of the electors made itself felt throughout the length and breadth of the land, and laid the foundation of that reform which has been obtained by the present generation. To the error which had been committed both factions became speedily alive, and each in turn persecuted the expression of public opinion whenever opportunity offered. The press, as far as possible, was gagged; public writers and speakers heavily fined, and sentenced to lengthened imprisonment; and, where the rank or position of the offender rendered this impracticable, both parties joined in the most uncompromising hostility to him, as afterwards I had but too much reason to know to my cost.

On the 24th of June, the electors of Westminster insisted on carrying Sir Francis Burdett from his house in Piccadilly to a magnificent entertainment at the Crown and Anchor Tavern in the Strand. A triumphal car was provided, which on its passage through immense crowds of spectators was enthusiastically greeted, the illustrious occupant reclining with his wounded leg on a cushion, whilst the other was placed on a figure, inscribed with the words " VENALITY AND CORRUPTION," which were thus emblematically trampled under foot.

On the 26th the House was formally opened by the delivery of his Majesty's speech, through the instrumentality of commissioners, viz. Lord Chancellor Eldon, and the Earls of Aylesford and Dartmouth. In the course of the debate on the address, during which much party recrimination took place, I excited great animosity by expressing a hope that, " as each party charged the other with making jobs in order to influence the elections, the conduct of both might in this respect be inquired into, and that hence, some third party would arise, which would stand aloof from selfish interests, and sinecure places, for that, as parties were at present constituted, I would not support either unless they were prepared to act on other principles than those by which their present course appeared to be guided."

On the 7th of July, pursuant to notice, I brought forward a motion to the following effect : —

"That a committee be appointed to inquire into, and report upon, to this House, an account of all offices, posts, places, sinecures, pensions, situations, fees, perquisites, and emoluments of every description, paid out of or arising from the public revenues, or fees of any courts of law, equity, admiralty, ecclesiastical, or other courts, held or enjoyed by, or in trust for, any member of this House, his wife, or any of his descendants for him, or either of them, in reversion of any present interest ; with an account of the annual amount of such, distinguishing whether the same arises from a certain salary or from an average amount; that this inquiry extend to the whole of his Majesty's dominions, and that the said committee be empowered to send for persons, papers, and records."

My argument was, " that if this motion were granted, the result would prove whether there was any possibility of making those *who had lived on, and enriched themselves by the public money*, feel for the extraordinary burthens under which the people laboured. The late plan of finance proved that as much as could be exacted had been drawn from the people, and that it was not possible to extract more — ingenuity having exhausted itself in devising new sources of taxation ; so that it was necessary to satisfy the greed of dependents on the public purse by the expedient of profligate advertisements, offering for sale the public patronage, and even seats in a certain assembly. It was proper to show the public that there was nothing in the character or habits of those composing that House'which they desired to conceal."

There was nothing factious in this, but the fear of the Government was, that were such a motion agreed to, the country would perceive that the vast accumulation of the national debt did not arise so much from warlike expenditure, defensive or aggressive, as from political profligacy. The motion was, therefore, opposed by one of the leading members of the House, on the ground that it was invidious and improper *to convey to the public an insinuation that members of parliament were influenced by considerations of private advantage for themselves or their dependents ; and that it was most essential, at this critical period, the character of the House of Commons should not be degraded or depreciated.*

In this view both factions joined *con amore*, for the question as to which it was aimed at was only that of being *in or out of office.* That there was any chance of such a motion being passed was not expected by any one, and least of all by myself; but the predicament in which it had placed the House was that of either assenting to the correctness of its principle, or of asserting boldly that there were no grounds for the inquiry. The latter course was too high to be taken with safety.

Mr. Whitbread, a most excellent man, and a great peacemaker when practicable, came to the rescue, by stating that though he concurred in principle with my motion, yet it might be sufficient to refer it to a committee of finance, with instructions to inquire into and report upon the matters therein contained. Such a course would be useful without being invidious, and a report based upon such alteration would probably be attended with beneficial results.

Mr. Perceval caught at the alternative thus presented, and immediately proposed that the motion should be thus altered : —

"That there should be an instruction to the committee of public expenditure, to procure a list of all places, pensions, &c., specifying by whom they were held, with the exception of those belonging to the Army *and Navy,* and officers *below* 200*l. a year in the revenue,* and that they should cause this list to be laid on the table."

To this compromise I demurred, stating that " my motive had not been made in expectation of pecuniary saving, but because a general feeling existed in the country regarding *the corruption of the House of Commons! It was notorious that commissions in the Army and Navy had been given for votes in that House,* and to such an extent was the system carried, that the best way to preferment was considered to be by the purchase of a house or two in usually contested boroughs. I could not accept as a substitute for my motion an alphabetical list of pensions and places, though it would be an object of great curiosity, and though many might be ashamed of holding such offices if their names were exposed to public view. On these grounds I would press my motion to a division,"—which was carried against me by a majority of 29.

Mr. Perceval then moved his amendment, which elicited from Mr. Whitbread a declaration, that " it was unquestionably Lord Cochrane's meaning that there should be exhibited, during the present session of parliament, a list of *all* the members of that House holding sinecure offices, places, &c., under Government, and *in that way liable to have their conduct influenced. If such a return were not made, the House would disgrace itself.* Those who at present respected the House would suspect that all was not right ; whilst those who already suspected it would have their suspicions confirmed."

Mr. Sheridan also pronounced Mr. Perceval's amendment " to be nothing but an evasion of my motion, intended to overwhelm the enquiry, and thus to suffocate the object Lord Cochrane had in view." The House, however, was not inclined to publish its own shame, and Mr. Perceval's amendment was carried by a large majority. So far as the production of the general pension list was concerned, my first essay in the House was thus a success.

The ill-feeling, however, engendered towards myself amongst men of both parties, the greater portion of whom were either implicated in, or recipients of, the corruption denounced by a few servants of the crown,

cannot at the present day be conveyed to the imagination
of the reader.  To appreciate it he must have been
conversant with such matters fifty years ago, and have
witnessed the first onslaught made upon them from a
quarter so unexpected.

On the 10th of July, I brought forward a motion on
naval abuses.  As in the present day any discussion of
a matter so remote would be tedious, it will suffice for
the continuation of the narrative to transcribe from the
pages of Hansard all that need be said on the subject.

"LORD COCHRANE rose and said, — ' Sir, — A wish to avert
part of the impending dangers of my country has made me resolve to move for certain papers relative to the Naval Service,
not with a retrospective view to blame individuals, but that
unnecessary hardships may cease to exist.  I am willing to
believe that members of this House, whose talents are capable
to do justice to the cause, are ignorant of circumstances which
for years have embittered the lives of seamen employed in
His Majesty's Service; and that as to the gentlemen of the
naval profession who have seats here, I suppose that the
diffidence occasioned by the awe which this House at first
inspires, has prevented them from performing this important
duty.

"'I shall be as brief as possible, but as the nature of some
of the papers for which I am about to move is unknown to
many members of this House, it will be necessary that I
should give some explanation.  The first motion is, "That
there be laid before this House copies of all letters or representations made by Commanders of H. M.'s sloop *Atalante*
and schooner *Felix*, addressed to Captain Keats (commanding
off Rochefort) respecting the state and condition of those
vessels, and the sick therein."

"'The object of this motion is to prove that vessels under
the present system, are kept at sea in a dangerous state, and

that the lives of many officers and men are in constant peril. Lieutenant Cameron, who commanded the *Felix*, and since lost in that vessel, was one of the best and ablest officers I ever knew. He found it incumbent on him to report that the *Felix* ought to be sent into port to repair. I shall read part of two letters from the surgeon, dated three months before they all perished, and previous to Lieutenant Cameron's being appointed to command that vessel. The other dated eight days before that melancholy event. On the 14th of November, he says,—"Our noble commander has been very active in his endeavours to get confirmed to this vessel, much more than I should be; she sails worse and worse, and I think the chances are against our ever bringing her into an English port." On the 14th of January, 1807, the surgeon says,—"Every endeavour has been put in force by Cameron and myself to get her into port, but without success. He attacked the commodore with most miserable epistles of distress throughout, and I attacked him with a very formidable sick list, but all, my friend, would not do."

"'I may be told that there is danger in agitating such subjects; but there can be none at any time in bringing to the knowledge of the Legislature, for redress, that which is notorious to those who have a right to claim it. No, Sir, let grievances be redressed in time, and complaints will cease. When the *Impérieuse*, the ship I command, was about to leave Rochefort, I was ordered to revictual the *Atalante* for six weeks, though she had then been out eight months—a period sufficient to ruin the health, break the energy, and weary the spirit of all employed in such a vessel. The *Atalante* was hauled alongside, the commander and several officers came on board, and informed me of the bad condition of their sloop. They said she was wholly unfit to keep the sea, and that a gale of wind would cause her inevitable loss. I think they said the foremast, and bowsprit, and fore-yard, were all sprung; besides, the vessel made twenty inches of water per hour. I thought it well to mention the circumstances, thus reported, to the commanding officer off Rochefort — for I well knew that the minds of subordinate officers ordered to survey, were impressed with terror, lest any vessel surveyed should not be found, on arriving in port quite so bad as represented. Their usual plan therefore is, to say such a vessel can keep the sea a while longer — knowing that if any accident occurs it will be ascribed to zeal for the good of His Majesty's service! So much impressed was I with the bad state of this vessel, that I said to the builder of Plymouth-yard, in the presence of Admiral Sutton, on my arrival there, that the first news we should have from Rochefort, if there should happen to be a gale of wind, would be the loss of the *Atalante*. Under the harassing system of eight or nine months' cruises, men get tired of their lives, and even indifferent as to the choice between a French prison and their present misery.

" ' The next document I propose to move for is — " An abstract of the weekly accounts of H. M.'s ships and frigates employed off Brest and Rochefort, from the 1st of March, 1806, until the 1st of March, 1807." From this the number of men employed, the number of sick, the time the ships have been kept at sea, and the time they have been allowed in harbour to refit the vessels and recruit the crews will appear. The *Plantagenet*, for instance, was eight months within four hours' sail of England. She was then forced, by stress of weather, into Falmouth, where she remained twelve days wind-bound; but an order existed (which I shall presently make the subject of a motion,) by which neither officer nor man could stretch his legs on the gravel beach within fifty yards of the ship! In order to show how little benefit has been derived from supplies at sea, as a substitute for refreshment and recreation which the crews were formerly suffered to enjoy, I shall next move — " That there be laid before this House an account of the quantity of fresh provisions, expressed in day's allowance, received at sea by each of H. M.'s ships off Rochefort and Brest, from the 1st of March, 1806, to the 1st of March, 1807." Formerly, when the four months' provisions were expended, the return of a ship to port was a matter of course; but now they are victualled and revictualled at sea; so that an East India voyage is performed with more refreshment than a Channel cruise. Lime-juice is the substitute for fresh provisions, a debilitating antidote to the scurvy — unfit to re-establish the strength of the body impaired by the constant use of salt provisions.

" ' The next motion (which I shall propose) is — " That there be laid before this House all orders issued and acted on between the 1st of March, 1806, and March, 1807, respecting leave to be granted or withheld from officers or men, distinguishing who was Commander-in-chief at the times of issuing such orders." It is a hard case that in harbour neither officer nor men shall be permitted to go on shore; these orders I do not hesitate to condemn; and the injustice appears the more striking, when it is remembered that the Commander-in-chief resided in London, enjoying not only the salary of his office, but claiming the emolument of prize-money gained by the toil of those in active service. I shall not be surprised to find the office of Commander-in-chief bestowed on some favourite as a sinecure by some future minister.

" ' With respect to the sick, I feel it necessary to say a few words, but I shall first read my motion on that subject — " That there be laid before this House all orders issued and acted on between the 1st of March, 1805, and the 1st of March, 1807, by, or by the authority of the Commander-in-chief of H. M.'s ships and vessels in the Channel, allowing or restraining commanding officers from sending men to the naval hospitals, or restricting their admission to such hospitals." In consequence of regulations established in these institutions, men are frequently refused admittance. No man, whatever may be his state of health, can be sent to an hospital from any of the ships in the Channel fleet, unless previously examined by the surgeon of the Commander-in-chief. Deaths, amputations, and total loss of health, were the consequences of the impossibility of this officer going

from ship to ship, in bad weather, when opportunity offered
to convey the sick to port. So pertinaciously were such regulations adhered to, that although I sent a sick lieutenant
and a man ruptured to the hospital, they were not admitted.
The disease of the one (who was under salivation) was declared to be contrary to the order regulating admission, and
he was returned through sleet and rain: the other was refused because everything *possible* had not been done to
reduce the rupture, as he had not been hung up by the
heels, in a rolling sea, which might have proved his death!

"'The system of naval hospitals is thoroughly bad. Mistaken economy has even reduced the quantity of lint for the
purpose of dressing wounds. To the ships there is not half
enough allowed. Unworthy savings have been unworthily
made, endangering the lives of officers and seamen. Indeed
the grievances of the Navy have been, and are so severe,
through rigour and mistaken economy, that I can see nothing
more meritorious than the patience with which these grievances have been endured.'

"Sir Samuel Hood, Admiral Harvey, Admiral Markham,
the Chancellor of the Exchequer, Mr. Windham, and others,
spoke against the motion.

"Lord Cochrane rose *in reply*, and said, 'I disclaim, Sir,
any motive whatever, except a regard for the real interests of
my country, though I confess that I cannot help feeling in
common with others the treatment received. Improper motives have been imputed to me, and I might reply to one of
those gentlemen who has denied facts which I can prove,
that he was one of those who established this abominable
system. What his abilities may be, in matters not connected
with the naval service, I know not; but it is a known fact
that his noble patron, the Earl of St. Vincent, sent the master
of the *Ville de Paris*, to put his ship in some tolerable order.
(Here there was a cry of order, order, from Admiral Harvey
and others.)

"'With respect to the assertion made by the same gentleman, that the health of the men is increased by long cruises

at sea, and that of the Commander-in-chief is improved by
being on shore, he may reconcile that if he can. I shall not
follow the example of imputing improper motives (looking
at Captain Sir Samuel Hood); but another complaint is, that
under this obnoxious system of favouritism, captains have
been appointed to large commands of six and seven sail of
the line, as many frigates and as many sloops of war, the
right of admirals who have served, and can serve their country,
and who have bled in its cause. But perhaps, for such times,
their ranks did not afford a prospect of their being sufficiently
subservient.

" 'This House, I believe, need not be told that from this
cause there are admirals of ability who have lingered in
neglect. (A cry of order, order, from Admiral Harvey and
others.) Sir, two parts of the statement of the Honourable
Knight are especially worthy of notice, so far as they were
meant as a reply to my statement. He said he had an hundred men killed and wounded in his ship, and no complaint,
no inconvenience arose from want of lint, or anything else.
First, this occurred when surgeons supplied their own necessaries, and next, the wounded men were sent on the day
following to Gibraltar Hospital.

" ' Now, Sir, with respect to the blame said to be attributed
by me to Lord St. Vincent for the loss of the *Felix* and
*Atalante* — I have to say, that it is of the general system
and its consequences of which I complain — of endless cruises,
rendering surveys at sea a substitute for a proper examination of the state of ships in port. The Honourable Knight
is a little unfortunate in the comparison he has made —
saying, that Lord St. Vincent was no more to blame in the
case of these vessels, than for my getting the *Impérieuse* on
shore on the coast of France. Now since this subject has
been touched on, I must state, that I made application for a
court-martial on my conduct; but it was not granted, because the blame would have fallen where it ought — on the
person whose repeated positive commands sent the ship to
sea in an unfit condition. The people of the yard had not

finished the work, all was in confusion. The quarter-deck guns lay unfitted, forty tons of ballast, besides provisions of all kinds, remained on deck. The powder (allowed to be taken on board only when the ship is out of harbour) was received when the ship was in that condition, and the *Impérieuse* was hurried to sea without a cartridge filled or a gun loaded! The order issued was, to quit the port the instant the ship would steer, regardless of every other material circumstance. (Another cry of order, order, from the same gentlemen. The Speaker said the Noble Lord must confine himself to the motion before the House.)

" ' Well, Sir, it is asserted that a profusion of oranges is supplied to the fleet at Lisbon, in reply to my statement, that none are allowed in the hospitals at home. I have not heard from any of those who have so zealously spoken on the other side, a defence of the obnoxious order to keep all officers and men on board. All such grievances may seem slight and matter of indifference to those who are here at their ease; but I view them in another light, and if no one better qualified will represent subjects of great complaint, I will do so, independent of every personal consideration.

" ' In the course of the debate it has been asserted, that I said lime-juice was a bad cure for the scurvy — no, it is a cure, and almost a certain cure, but debilitating — it destroys the disease, but ruins the constitution. An Hon. member (Mr. Sheridan) has said, that all this should have been represented to the Admiralty, that this House is an improper place for such discussions, and he has threatened to call for all letters from me to the Board. To the first I answer, that Boards pay no attention to the representations of individuals whom ' they consider under their command; next, that if the Right Honourable gentleman calls for my letters, he will find some that will not suit his purpose.

" ' Sir, besides the public abuses, the oppression and scandalous persecution of individuals, often on anonymous information, has been, and is matter of great complaint. Sir, if the present Admiralty shall increase the sum allowed for the refreshment of crews in port, instead of corrupting their bodies by salt provisions, and then drenching them with lime-juice, they will deserve the gratitude and thanks of all employed. In the Navy, we have had to lament the system that makes the Admiralty an appendage of the minister of the day, and that just as a Board begin to see, and perhaps, to plan reform, they are removed from office. I trust, Sir, that I shall not be denied the papers moved for, and that my motion will not be got rid of by a blind vote of confidence, or the subterfuge of the previous question.'

" The motion was negatived without a division." *

From the preceding extract it will have been seen that my motion produced no effect upon the House. It however produced a *cessation of my legislative functions!* for immediately afterwards I was ordered to join Lord Collingwood's fleet in the Mediterranean; it being perhaps anticipated that I should vacate my seat in consequence; but this the electors of Westminster prevented, by giving me unlimited leave of absence from my parliamentary duties.

* Hansard's Parliamentary Debates, vol. ix.

# CHAP. XIV.

## CRUISE OF THE *IMPÉRIEUSE*.

ON the 12th of September, 1807, the *Impérieuse*
sailed from Portsmouth to join Lord Collingwood's fleet
in the Mediterranean, having in charge a convoy of
thirty-eight sail of merchantmen, destined for Gibraltar
and Malta. We reached Malta on the 31st of October,
and finding that Lord Collingwood was cruising off
Palermo, sailed on the 5th of November to join his
fleet.

On the 14th, under the land of Corsica, two strange
sail were discovered, and it being calm, the boats were
manned, and gave chase, the larger of the vessels showing English colours. Finding that this *ruse* did not
check the progress of the boats, she hove to, and when
they had advanced within musket-shot, hauled in her
colours and commenced firing with musketry and long
guns; the boats however dashed alongside, and in five
minutes, after considerable slaughter, were in possession.

She proved to be a Maltese privateer of 10 guns; her crew, however, consisting of Russians, Italians, and Sclavonians, the captain only being a Maltese.   In this affair we lost one man killed and two officers and thirteen men wounded.   The loss of the privateer was far more considerable, her treachery being severely punished.

I was much vexed at this affair, for the vessel, though hailing from Malta, was in reality a pirate, and ought to have been treated as such.   After despatching her to Malta, I addressed the following letter on the subject to Lord Collingwood : —

" H. M. S. *Impérieuse*, off Corsica,<br>
14th Nov. 1807.

" My Lord, — I am sorry to inform your lordship of a circumstance which has already been fatal to two of our best men, and I fear of thirteen others wounded two will not survive.   These wounds they received in an engagement with a set of desperate savages collected in a privateer, said to be the *King George*, of Malta, wherein the only subjects of his Britannic Majesty were three Maltese boys, one Gibraltar man, and a naturalised captain ; the others being renegadoes from all countries, and great part of them belonging to nations at war with Great Britain.

" This vessel, my lord, was close to the Corsican shore. On the near approach of our boats a union-jack was hung over her gunwale.   One boat of the three, which had no gun, went within hail, and told them that we were English. The boats then approached, but when close alongside, the colours of the stranger were taken in, and a volley of grape and musketry discharged in the most barbarous and savage manner, their muskets and blunderbusses being pointed from beneath the netting close to the people's breasts.

" The rest of the men and officers then boarded and

carried the vessel in the most gallant manner.  The bravery
shown and exertion used on this occasion were worthy of a
better cause.

> " I have the honour, &c.
> " COCHRANE.
" The Right Hon. Lord Collingwood."

This pirate, for the capture of which, as was subsequently learned, 500*l.* had been offered, was after much
trouble condemned as a *droit of Admiralty !* it being
evidently hoped that by this course such influence might
be brought to bear as would eventually procure her
restoration : for it was currently reported at Malta that
certain persons connected with the Admiralty Court
had a share in her !  Be this as it may, we never obtained the premium for her capture, but in place thereof
were *condemned by the Court of Admiralty to pay five
hundred double sequins !*  After this, the Maltese court
always threw every obstacle in the way of condemning
our prizes, and, when this was effected, with such costs
as to render the term " prize " almost a misnomer ; a
subject on which some strange stories will have to be
told in another place.

On the 19th, we joined Lord Collingwood's fleet off
Toulon, consisting of the *Ocean, Malta, Montague,
Tiger, Repulse, Canopus,* and *Espoir.*  The *Impérieuse*
was forthwith ordered to Malta, to land the wounded,
after which we were directed by Lord Collingwood to
proceed to the Archipelago, his lordship giving me an
order to supersede the officer in command of the
blockading squadron there.

On the 26th we again fell in with the fleet off Sardinia,

and on the 29th anchored in Valetta, our pirate prize
having arrived on the preceding evening.    On the 6th
of December, the *Impérieuse* sailed for the Archipelago,
and on the 8th passed between Zante and Cephalonia.
On the 11th we joined the blockading squadron in the
Adriatic, consisting of the *Unité*, *Thames*, *Porcupine*,
and *Weasel*, which were then watching some French
frigates in Corfu.    On the 12th, the *Impérieuse* overhauled three Russian vessels, one of which threw overboard three bundles of letters.    By prompt exertion
we were lucky enough to rescue these, and found them
to contain important intelligence.

On arriving off Corfu, and pending the necessary
arrangements for transferring the command of the
blockading squadron to myself, I asked leave of the
senior officer still in command to take a run to the
north end of the island.    This being granted, we sailed
forthwith, and to our surprise soon afterwards fell in
with thirteen merchantmen, as leisurely proceeding
along the blockaded coast as though we had belonged
to their own nation!    Singling out the three nearest to
us, we took possession of them, and to our astonishment found that each had a pass from the officer I was
ordered to supersede!

Despite this unlooked-for protection, I sent them to
Malta for adjudication, and they were, I believe, condemned.    The immediate result to myself, however —
as Lord Collingwood long afterwards told me—was *the
withdrawal of my appointment to the command of the
blockading squadron!*    The commanding officer, whose
passes I had intercepted, promptly took the initiative,

and without apprising me, despatched one of his vessels to Lord Collingwood, with a letter stating generally that, *"from my want of discretion I was unfit to be entrusted with a single ship, much less with the command of a squadron!"* Lord Collingwood acted on the representation without making enquiry into its cause, and the consequence was my recall to receive further orders from his lordship, this amounting to my deposition from the only command of a squadron that was ever offered to me.

I was, of course, ignorant of Lord Collingwood's reasons for recalling me, though greatly disappointed at such a result. It was not till some time afterwards, when too late to remedy the injury, that I ventured to ask his lordship the reason of such a proceeding. He frankly told me, when I as frankly informed him of the intercepted passes, and that my senior officer had traduced me to his Lordship, by way of first blow in a serious scrape. Lord Collingwood was very indignant, but from the lapse of time, and probably from having neglected to investigate the matter at the time, he thought it better not to reopen it,, and thus my traducer continued his pass trade with impunity.

I give the above incident as it occurred. Those to whom such a statement may appear incredible, will find on consulting the pages of Captain Brenton, that it was not an isolated instance.

I shall add, that on my return from the Mediterranean, in 1809, an officer, who shall be nameless, waited on me at Portsmouth, and begged me not to make official or public mention of the preceding circumstance, or it would be his ruin. I made him no promise, but having then the preparation for the Basque Roads attack on my hands, there was no time to attend to the matter, and as the circumstance had not been officially reported by me at the time—as indeed it did not come within my province to report it—I never afterwards troubled myself about it, though this shameless proceeding had deprived me of the only chance I ever had to command more than a single ship! *·

On the 17th we fell in with a brig bound from Trieste to Lord Collingwood with despatches, announcing that Russia had declared hostilities against England. This intelligence was fortunate, as there were several Russian ships of war in the Gulf, with one of which— a line-of-battle ship — we had fallen in only two days previous.

The professed origin of the declaration of Russia against England was our questionable conduct at Copenhagen. But, notwithstanding the assumption by Russia, that she had endeavoured to serve our cause at Tilsit, there is no doubt but that she was secretly leagued with Napoleon against us. I never knew what was in the letters we rescued, as they were sent to Lord Collingwood ; but no doubt they contained important intelligence for the French squadron then in the Archipelago, and, coming from a Russian source, there was little question as to the nature of their contents,

---

* The excuse offered to me was, that the purser had been making use of the captain's name, for his own purposes ! A very improbable story, as in such a case it would not have been difficult to convict the purser and exonerate himself. The disgraceful letter to Lord Collingwood, however, clearly pointed out the delinquent.

which appeared to be conclusive in the estimation of the British authorities.

On the 22nd the *Impérieuse* stood into the Gulf of Valona under French colours, and saw some vessels close in under the batteries. As soon as it became dark, we manned the boats and brought out a Turkish vessel under the fire of a battery. On the 30th again joined the squadron, and learned that the Russian fleet, consisting of five sail of the line and three frigates, had left Corfu and gone up the Adriatic.

On the 2nd of January, 1808, we joined Lord Collingwood, the fleet then bearing up in the direction of Syracuse. On the 8th gave chase to some vessels off the south point of Cephalonia, sending the boats after them into the bay; but the enemy being on the alert, and the vessels being run on shore, it became necessary to recall the boats. On the 12th, when off Otranto, we captured a vessel from Corfu to that place, laden with clothing and iron.

On the 23rd we again joined Lord Collingwood off Corfu, and were despatched to Malta with sealed orders, arriving there on the 28th. Having filled up our water and provisions, the *Impérieuse* was then ordered to Gibraltar, for which port we sailed on the 31st, my expectations of increased command, thanks to the adroit turn given to my seizure of the intercepted passes, being thus at an end.

The instructions now given me by Lord Collingwood were to harass the Spanish and French coast as opportunity served. These instructions, though forming a poor equivalent for the command of a squadron, were

nevertheless considered by me complimentary, as acknowledging the good effected by my former cruises in
the *Speedy*. Consequently, I determined to make
every exertion to merit his lordship's approbation in
the present instance.

On the 9th of February we made the high land of
Spain to the eastward of Barcelona, and at daylight on
the following morning fell in with two vessels bound
from Carthagena to Marseilles, both of which were
captured and sent to Malta with the prisoners.

On the 11th looked into Barcelona, where a considerable number of vessels lay at anchor, but knowing the
fortifications to be too strong to warrant success in an
attempt to cut any of them out, the *Impérieuse* again
made sail. On the 18th we ran in close to Valencia,
and having on the previous day perceived some vessels
anchored within a mile of the town, the boats were
sent off after dark to capture them, but as they unfortunately proved to be American our labour was abortive.

On the 15th we arrived off Alicant, and at daylight
stood close to the town under American colours. Two
boats came out, but finding their mistake when within
gunshot they immediately made for the shore, and the
batteries opened fire upon us. As there was no purpose
to be answered in returning this, we passed by Cape
Palos where four gunboats showing Russian colours
were observed at anchor under the protection of one
of the numerous batteries with which the Spanish coast
was studded.

On the 17th entered a bay about eight miles to the
westward of Carthagena to intercept some vessels ob-

served running along shore. After a long chase with the boats we succeeded in capturing two. As I had made up my mind to get possession of the gunboats seen two days previously, we stood off out of sight of land in order to lull suspicion, and at sunset on the 19th again steered for the bay in which they were at anchor. At 9 P.M. we distinctly saw them quit their anchorage, on which we cleared for action, remaining undiscovered till they had passed the point which forms one extremity of the bay. They now attempted to return, but too late. Running in amongst them, we opened both our broadsides with effect, and dashing at them with the boats, took one, armed with a 32-pounder, a brass howitzer, and too smaller guns. Another sank with all hands, just as the boats were alongside, and a third sank shortly afterwards. A fourth escaped by running for Carthagena, where we did not think it politic to follow her, lest we might bring upon us the Spanish fleet at anchor there. A brig with a valuable cargo also fell into our hands.

Having received information from the prisoners taken in the gunboats that a large French ship, laden with lead and other munitions of war, was at anchor in the Bay of Almeria, I determined on cutting her out, and the night being dark, it became necessary to bring to. At daylight on the 21st, we found ourselves within a few miles of the town, and having hoisted American colours, had the satisfaction to perceive that no alarm was excited on shore.

The boats having been previously got in readiness, were forthwith hoisted out, and the large pinnace, under the command of Lieutenant Caulfield, dashed at the French ship, which, as the pinnace approached, commenced a heavy fire, in the midst of which the ship was gallantly boarded, but with the loss of poor Caulfield, who was shot on entering the vessel. The other pinnace coming up almost at the same moment completed the capture, and the cable being cut, sail was made on the prize.

Some smaller vessels were also secured, but before we could get clear, the wind died away; and the *Impérieuse* and her prizes were becalmed, — the batteries of the town and citadel opening upon us a heavy fire, which lasted till 11 A.M., when a light breeze carried us out of gun-shot.

Of these batteries our most formidable opponent was a four-gun tower, situated on an eminence above us; but by exercising great care in laying our guns, we contrived to keep this battery from doing mischief, except that now and then they managed to hull the prize, which had been placed between the battery and the frigate. By midday however we were clear of the batteries, with the prize safe. It was fortunate for us that a breeze sprang up, for had it continued calm, we could not have brought a vessel out in the face of such batteries, not more than half a mile distant.

Neither, perhaps, should we ourselves have so easily escaped, on another account, — for about four o'clock in the afternoon a Spanish ship of the line suddenly appeared in the offing, no doubt with the intention of ascertaining the cause of the firing. We, however, kept close to the wind, and got clear off with the French ship, mounting 10 guns, and two brigs laden with cordage. The scene must have been an interesting one to the people of Almeria, great numbers of the inhabitants lining the shore, though at some risk, as from our position many shots from the *Impérieuse* must have passed over them.

On the 23rd the frigate arrived at Gibraltar, with the prizes in company, and on the following day we attended the remains of Lieutenant Caulfield to the grave.

On the 2nd of March, we received orders again to proceed up the Mediterranean together with the *Hydra*, with which vessel we sailed in company on the 4th. Heavy weather setting.in, prevented our return to Almeria, as had been intended ; but on the 12th we stood close into the entrance of Carthagena, where only the guardship and a sloop of war were at anchor under strong fortifications. As nothing could be done here, we anchored about two miles to the eastward of the port, in the hope of catching vessels running along shore. At daylight the next morning we gave chase to a ship rounding Cape Negretti, but she escaped into a bay in the vicinity, under the protection of a powerful battery and several gunboats. As we knew nothing of the anchorage we did not attempt to molest them.

On the 13th the *Impérieuse* steered in the direction of Majorca, near which, on the 19th, we captured a vessel bound to Port Mahon. At daylight on the 21st went in close to the entrance of Mahon, where we found the Spanish fleet at anchor, and captured a brig within three miles of the shore, sending her on the following

day to Gibraltar, with some prisoners taken out of
another brig on the previous evening by the *Hydra*.

On the 23rd fell in with the *Renommé*, to which we
reported that the Spanish fleet was in Mahon harbour.
After supplying us with water, she parted company for
Gibraltar.    On the 26th we again made Port Mahon,
where six sail of the Spanish fleet appeared to be in
readiness for sea.    Seeing a sloop to leeward, we made
sail in chase, and captured her in the evening ; she was
bound from port Mahon to Sardinia.

On the 28th at daylight, having observed some vessels
in Alcudia Bay, we sent in the boats ; these soon afterwards returning with a tartan laden with wine, which
we sent to Gibraltar ; soon afterwards we captured
another partly laden with wine, which we took out and
set her adrift.    On the 29th gave chase to two vessels
rounding an island ; one succeeded in getting in safe,
the other, under Moorish colours, we took, notwithstanding the fire of the forts, and sent her to Malta ;
she had several male and female passengers on board,
who were highly delighted when, two days afterwards,
we put them on shore.

On the 2nd of April the *Impérieuse* was again close
to Minorca, when reconnoitring a small bay we observed
a strong tower, apparently just built.    Landed, and
blew it up without molestation from the inhabitants.
Though ready for an armament, none had been placed
upon it.

On the 5th at daylight, passed close to Cittadella in
chase of a vessel which escaped ; made sail after a
brig coming from the direction of Majorca ; at 3 P.M.

she ran in shore, and anchored under a small fort, which opened a smart fire upon us, but was soon silenced. The crew then abandoned the brig, which was brought off and sent to Gibraltar.

On the 6th, again reconnoitred Port Mahon, and saw three sail of the line at the entrance of the harbour, ready for sea. On the 8th captured a French brig, laden with 163 pipes of wine for the use of the Spanish fleet at Port Mahon; sent her to Gibraltar, and put the prisoners on shore.

On the 11th, off Cittadella, we captured another vessel, sailing under Moorish colours, but laden with Spanish wine; took out the wine, and as she belonged to the unfortunate Moors who manned her, to their great gratification we gave them back the vessel.

On the 13th it blew so hard, that we were compelled to anchor within range of a pile of barracks placed upon a high cliff—a position certainly not taken by choice. The troops commenced firing, which we returned, and by 4 P.M. had pretty well demolished the barracks. I then despatched an officer in the gig with a barrel of powder to complete the work, but just as they had got up, a large reinforcement of troops came upon them and compelled them to make a retreat, leaving the powder behind them. After this we got underweigh.

On the 18th fell in with the *Leonidas*, which on the previous day had left Lord Collingwood with 16 sail of the line. Parted company in quest of the fleet, but did not fall in with it.

On the 22nd we re-entered Alcudia Bay, and sent the

pinnace ashore, when she captured some sheep. On the following day another boat's crew managed to procure some bullocks and pigs, which were very acceptable, but all their efforts to obtain water failed.

A few days previous to this, when close to Majorca, we had been fired upon from the small battery of Jacemal, and having subsequently reconnoitred it more closely, it appeared practicable to destroy it by a night attack. Accordingly, we again ran in, and soon reaching the tower, blew it up, dismounting three guns. A guard-house near the battery was set on fire, after which we returned to the frigate without loss. At daylight on the following morning we had the gratification to perceive that our work had been effectual, the whole being in ruins. As the place stood on an eminence very difficult of access, and commanding two bays, its demolition was desirable.

On the 26th fell in with the *Leonidas*, which had been in quest of, but had not succeeded in falling in with, Lord Collingwood's fleet. From her we learnt that the French fleet was at anchor in Corfu. On ascertaining this, I determined on paying another visit to the Spanish coast, and accordingly parted company with the *Leonidas*.

At daylight on the 27th, observing a brig and a smaller vessel in shore, made sail in chase. The brig got safe into Palamos Bay, where there were several other vessels deeply laden, but well protected by ports and gun-boats. The smaller vessel was boarded by Mr. Harrison in the gig, before she had time to get under the ports, but perceiving a large galley full of

men in pursuit of him, he was obliged to relinquish
the prize, and make for the frigate; the galley pressed
him hard, but on perceiving the *Impérieuse* bringing
to for her reception, she gave up the chase, and the gig
returned in safety.

We were now in great distress from want of water,
and as it could only be obtained from the enemy's
coast, we sent a boat on shore to the westward of
Blanco, but she returned without success, having been
fired upon from a fortification on an eminence in the
vicinity. As a supply of this essential fluid had become
essentially necessary, even if it had to be fought for, we
made every preparation for a second attempt on a
sandy beach, between Blanco and Cabella, where a
large river was found, on which the frigate was brought
to an anchor about a quarter of a mile from the place,
and, thanks to our bold front, we obtained an abundant
supply without molestation; though, as we came off,
a considerable body of troops showed themselves, and
a fire of musketry was opened upon us, but the frigate
promptly replying with round shot, our assailants retreated into the woods, as hastily as they had emerged
from them, and we again made sail.

On the 5th of May observing a vessel under Moorish
colours to leeward, we made all sail in chase, and by ten
o'clock she was in our possession, proving to be a
xebec from Marseilles to Tripoli, laden with lead.
Her crew were Genoese, and having given us information that on the preceding evening they were in
company with a large French ship also laden with lead,
and other munitions of war, destined for the use of

the French fleet, we despatched the prize to Gibraltar, and made sail for the mainland, in order to intercept the Frenchman.

On nearing the coast, we observed several vessels running along shore, and singling out the one which most nearly answered the description given us by the Genoese, she struck after a few shots; the information thus proving correct. She was bound from Almeria to Marseilles, laden with lead and barilla. Despatched her after the other to Gibraltar.

At daylight on the 6th, gave chase to three ships, running under the land. On observing us they parted company, one going round a shoal near Oliva, and another running into a small harbour. The third, a fine vessel, we chased into Valencia, but she escaped, as we did not venture after her. Retracing our course, we saw on the following morning one of the others anchored close in shore, and sent the boats to bring her off. On nearing her she opened a smart fire, which being steadily returned by our men, her crew abandoned her, and we took possession without loss. As soon as she was boarded it was found that she had just touched the ground, but the boats promptly taking her in tow, succeeded in getting her afloat, and brought her safely off despite the fire of two towers close to the town of Cullera, in the neighbourhood of Valencia. A considerable number of people assembled to witness the attack from the neighbouring hills.

On the 8th, perceived a vessel rounding Cape St. Antonio. On seeing us, she made sail, as we also did in chase. At sunset lost sight of her, and despatching

our prize to Gibraltar, altered our course so as to cut
her off from Marseilles, whither we suspected she was
bound.   At daylight we again caught sight of her,
and by ten o'clock had gained upon her considerably,
when to our disappointment she sent a boat on board,
proving to be a Gibraltar privateer instead of a Spaniard.

At daylight the following morning, we ran close to
Tarragona, and captured a large xebec under Moorish
colours.   At twelve o'clock observed a fine vessel coming
round the shoals of Fangalo, and knowing that she
could not have witnessed the capture of the xebec we
immediately furled all sail in order to escape observation.   An alarm was, however, promptly raised along
the coast, and this causing her to alter her course, we
immediately started in pursuit.   At sunset it fell calm,
the ship being then distant about twelve miles.   At
3 A. M. she was discovered close in shore, when we
hoisted out boats and pulled smartly for her, but on
arriving almost within gun-shot, she caught a breeze,
and went away from us, endeavouring to get into a
creek; but the boats being in a position to cut her off,
and making every effort to head her, she bore up, and
at 7 A. M. anchored under a two-gun battery, which
kept up a constant fire on the boats.

The *Impérieuse* now rapidly approaching, gave the
tower a gun and recalled the boats, in order to send
other crews, those engaged in the chase being necessarily much fatigued.   About 3 P. M. we were joined
by the Gibraltar privateer, which bore up to engage
the tower, keeping up a smart fire, as did also the ship.
The *Impérieuse* now came to an anchor, and opened

her broadside on the tower, which was soon silenced. The boats were once more manned, as were also those of the privateer, and the prize towed out, proving to be a large Spanish ship — the same as we had chased into Valencia — bound from Alicant to Marseilles. We learned from her the unpleasant news of one of our lieutenants, Mr. Harrison, having been captured by some gunboats, and taken into Denia; this intelligence being subsequently confirmed by a fishing-boat boarded off Denia on the 17th.

On the 20th passed close to Cape Palos, the forts on which fired several shots at us, but without damage. At 9 o'clock on the 21st, observed twelve vessels coming round the Cape, four of which were evidently gunboats. We at once made all sail in chase, and as we tacked, the gunboats opened a smart fire upon us, continuing this till we again tacked and stood towards them, when they made off, with the exception of one which stood towards the Cape; the other three running aground on the beach. As we were now very close to the gunboats, the *Impérieuse*, whilst in stays, also took the ground, but luckily got off again, and opened a fire of musketry upon them, which, in about twenty minutes, obliged two crews to quit the vessels, the third keeping her colours flying till her captain was mortally wounded.

It now came on to blow hard, and as there was no probability of saving the prizes, we set fire to the two gunboats and a large vessel laden with barilla, the crews having all escaped on shore. The other gunboat, which had gallantly kept her colours flying to the last, we got off, bringing her wounded captain and two other officers on board the frigate. About 6 P. M. both gunboats blew up with great explosion.

Our own situation was at this time critical, as we were in only four fathom water, and it was blowing a gale of wind. By nine o'clock the wind fortunately came off the land, which enabled us to run out a couple of miles and anchor for the night. We learned from the officers, that the convoy was bound from Carthagena to Barcelona, and that each gunboat had a long gun in the bow, and two aft, with a complement of 50 men.

Two other vessels having run on shore on the morning of the 22nd, we again despatched the boats to bring them off if possible, as well as to recover our anchor and cable, which had been slipped when getting the *Impérieuse* afloat. They succeeded in bringing off one of the vessels which was laden with barilla, but the other vessel, being immovable, was set fire to. This done we put to sea with our prizes in tow.

In the course of the night the Spanish captain died, his wounds having been from the first hopeless. Every attention possible was paid to the poor fellow, from admiration of his gallantry, but anything beyond this was out of our power. On the following morning we committed his remains to the deep, with the honours of war.

We now made sail for Gibraltar with our prizes, one of which was with difficulty kept afloat. On the 25th passed Malaga, and on the 31st arrived at Gibraltar with all the prizes except one, which had been placed in charge of the Hon. Mr. Napier (the late Lord Napier), then a midshipman.*

On the 1st of June, the *Trident* arrived from England with convoy, and the intelligence of a revolution in Spain, which, being shortly afterwards confirmed by proclamation, a friendly communication was opened between the garrison and the Spaniards, and on the 8th, Lord Collingwood arrived at Gibraltar in the *Ocean*, to be in readiness to act as circumstances might require.

A few words on our altered relations with Spain, though coming rather within the province of the historian than the biographer, may here be necessary, in order to account for so sudden a change in my own personal operations.

On the 6th of June, 1808, Napoleon issued a decree, notifying that, as it had been represented to him by the Spanish authorities that the well-being of Spain required a speedy stop to be put to the provisional government, he had proclaimed his brother Joseph, King of Spain and the Indies!

To this extraordinary proclamation the Supreme Junta, *on the same day*, replied by another, accusing Napoleon of violating the most sacred compacts, forcing the Spanish monarch to abdication, occupying the country with troops, everywhere committing the most horrible excesses, exhibiting the most enormous ingratitude for services rendered by the Spanish nation to France, and generally treating the Spanish people with perfidy and treachery, such as was never before

---

* Afterwards ambassador to China, where his lordship died.

committed by any nation or monarch against the most barbarous people.

On these and other accounts the Junta declared war against France by land and sea, at the same time proclaiming durable and lasting peace with England, and commanding that no further molestation be offered to English ships or property, whilst, by the same proclamation, an embargo was laid on all French ships and property.

Another proclamation, more immediately concerning the ensuing chapters, is an order of the Junta, forming the Spaniards generally into an organised national militia for the defence of the country. The French, pretending to consider this militia in the light of non-combatants, having no right to engage in war, committed amongst them the most barbarous atrocities, in retaliation for which many of the succeeding operations of the *Impérieuse* were undertaken, in pursuance of orders from Lord Collingwood to assist the Spaniards by every means in my power.

# CHAP. XV.

### CRUISE OF THE *IMPÉRIEUSE* CONTINUED.

SHORTLY after Lord Collingwood's arrival at Gibraltar, his lordship ran down to Cadiz, to watch events, and wait instructions from the government. On the 18th of June the *Impérieuse* sailed from Gibraltar to join Lord Collingwood's fleet before Cadiz, and on the 21st was ordered by his lordship to cruise in the Mediterranean, and render every possible assistance to the Spaniards against the French. On the 22nd we returned to Gibraltar for our prize tender, which had been fitted as a gunboat, and manned with twenty men, under the command of a lieutenant.

At daylight on the 23rd we passed close to Almeria, with English and Spanish colours flying at the main, and on the evening of the 25th came to an anchor in the outer road of Carthagena. On the following morning a number of Spanish officers came off to bid us welcome, and at noon we paid a visit to the Governor, by whom, as well as by the populace, we were received with every mark of friendship, notwithstanding our recent hostile visits in the vicinity. Indeed our whole passage along the coast was one continued expression of good feeling.

On the 2nd of July the *Impérieuse* arrived off Majorca. The inhabitants were at first shy, apparently fearing some deception, but as we were bearers of the good news that the English and Spaniards were now friends, confidence was soon restored, and presents of all kinds were sent off to the ship, payment being resolutely refused. We had also the satisfaction of here recovering our lost midshipmen, Harrison, and the late Lord Napier, who, whilst in charge of prizes, had been taken and carried into Port Mahon.

On the 5th the *Impérieuse* passed close to Barcelona, and hoisting English and Spanish colours at the main, fired a salute of 21 guns! The French, who were in possession of the place*, to our great amusement resented the affront by firing at us from all their batteries,

---

* Barcelona had been seized by General Duhesme just before Buonaparte announced his intention of placing his brother on the throne of Spain. Having arrived in the vicinity of the city on the 15th of February, he requested permission to halt and refresh his troops for a few days, before going on to Valencia. The gates were forthwith opened, and the French treated as friends and allies. On the 16th, the *generale* was beat, as though they were about to proceed on their march, and the townspeople came out to bid them farewell. To the surprise of the latter, the French general ordered one part of his force to the citadel, and the other to Fort Monjui, possessing himself of both. Pampeluna was occupied on the same day by similar treachery.

but their shot fell short. We could distinctly see the inhabitants crowding the house-tops and public places of the city by thousands, and the French cavalry and infantry meanwhile patrolling the streets. Knowing that the French held their own with difficulty, especially in the adjacent towns, we again hove to and displayed English colours over French, and then Spanish over French, firing an additional salute, which increased the cannonade from the batteries, but to no purpose.

We then bore up along the coast, and when clear of the enemy's lines, a number of boats came off complaining bitterly of the French troops who were burning their towns on the least resistance, or even pretended resistance, and were permitted by their officers to plunder and kill the inhabitants with impunity. Perhaps it would be more in accordance with military justice to say, that with the ideas of equality and fraternity then prevalent amongst the soldiers, their officers had no control over them.

On the 6th the *Impérieuse* came to an anchor between the towns of Blanco and Mataro, in nearly the same position as that taken up on the last cruise. Great numbers of people came off, and the frigate was speedily filled with visitors of both sexes, bringing with them all kinds of presents; being most politely oblivious of all the mischief we had been effecting in their vicinity for months past. On the 7th, after paying a visit to Blanco, we got under weigh, the Spaniards having sent us word that the French had entered the town of Mataro, at the same time requesting our co-operation against them.

On the 8th we were becalmed close to several villages, one of which had been nearly destroyed by the French on pretence of some trifling resistance. A deputation from the inhabitants of one village came off, and informed us that their church had been plundered of everything, and that forty-five houses had been burned to the ground. A wretched policy truly, and one which did the French great harm by the animosity thus created amongst the people, who were treated as rebels, rather than in the light of honourable adversaries.

The *Impérieuse* could effect nothing against the French in Mataro, from its unassailable position, but having received intelligence that a considerable force under General Duhesme was advancing towards Barcelona, it occurred to me that their progress might be checked. Landing accordingly with a party of seamen, we blew down the overhanging rocks and destroyed the bridges so effectually as to prevent the passage either of cavalry or artillery, at the same time pointing out to the Spaniards how they might impede the enemy's movements elsewhere along the coast by cutting up the roads,—an operation on which they entered with great alacrity, after being shown how to set about their work.

The nature of these operations will be readily comprehended by the statement that a considerable portion of the main road ran along the face of the precipitous rocks nearest the sea. By blowing up the roads themselves in some places, and the overhanging rocks in others, so as to bury the road beneath the *débris*, it was rendered impassable for cavalry or artillery, whilst removal of the obstructions within reasonable time was out of the question—indeed, so long as the frigate remained in the vicinity, impossible, as any operation of the kind would have been within reach of our guns.

Having effected all the damage possible, and there being no beneficial end to be answered by longer stay in the vicinity of Mataro, we again made sail, and on the 17th the *Impérieuse* arrived at Port Mahon, where we found a squadron embarking Spanish troops for Catalonia, the crews of the six ships of the line in harbour taking their places in manning the batteries. On the 19th the troops sailed under convoy of some English frigates, as did others destined for Tortosa.

Having filled up with provisions and water, we quitted Port Mahon for another cruise on the Spanish coast, and on the 22nd were close to St. Philou, when the whole of the convoy entered the harbour to the great delight of the inhabitants, who reported that, despite the obstacles created, the French had, in the absence of the *Impérieuse*, forced the pass from Mataro, and marched for Gerona, to which place the Spanish troops, just disembarked, were next day despatched, together with 1200 militia, raised from amongst the peasantry in the neighbourhood. Heavy firing was heard shortly afterwards in the interior, and at night it was ascertained that the French had made an attack on Hostalrich and were beaten back. This place was about nine miles from St. Philou.

On the 24th we again anchored about four miles from Mataro, and there learned the mode in which the French had surmounted the obstacles interposed by the

Spaniards in cutting up the roads, viz. by compelling
the inhabitants to fill up the gaps with everything
moveable, even to their agricultural implements, furniture and clothes.   After this, the French, by way of
deterring the Spaniards from again interfering with
the highways, sacked and burned all the dwelling-houses
in the neighbourhood.

Taking a party of marines on shore, we again blew
up additional portions of the road to the eastward, and
as the gaps made on our last visit had been chiefly
filled up with wood, and other inflammable articles
just mentioned, we set fire to them, and thus not
only renewed the obstacles, but created fresh ones, in
the assurance that as everything moveable was now
destroyed, the obstruction must become permanent.
Whilst this was going on the seamen and marines of
the *Impérieuse* destroyed a battery completed by the
French, and threw over the cliff the four brass twenty-
four-pounders.   These were next day recovered.

On the 26th we dropped down to the town of Cañette,
and embarked some more brass guns which the enemy
had placed in position on the top of a high cliff.   These
guns were got on board by means of hawsers carried
from the frigate to the cliff, one end being made fast to
the masthead.   By the application of the capstan and
tackles, the guns were thus hopped on board.   After
these had been secured, I again took a party of seamen
and marines on shore, and broke down or blew up the
road in six different places.   On paying a visit to the
town, there was scarcely a house which the French
had not sacked, carrying off everything that was

valuable, and wantonly destroying the remainder. The inhabitants were in a miserable condition.

The two next days were employed in blowing down rocks, and otherwise destroying roads in every direction which the French were likely to take, the people aiding heart and soul, anxiously listening to every suggestion for retarding the enemy's movements, and evincing the greatest alacrity to put them in practice. In short, I had taken on myself the duties of an engineer officer, though occupation of this kind was, perhaps, out of my sphere as commander of a frigate; and there is no doubt that I might have better consulted my personal interests by looking after prizes at sea, for, except from Lord Collingwood, not so much as an acknowledgment of my persevering exertions was vouchsafed. I was, however, indignant at seeing the wanton devastation committed by a military power, pretending to high notions of civilisation, and on that account spared no pains to instruct the persecuted inhabitants how to turn the tables on their spoilers; making—as throughout life I have ever done — common cause with the oppressed.

Having effected all the mischief possible, we weighed for Mongat, ten miles from Barcelona, and anchored off the place at sunset. I had previously received intelligence that General Duhesme was approaching Barcelona with a strong force to relieve the French garrison in possession, and my object was to destroy the fort at Mongat before Duhesme's force came up. For this, however, we were too late, the advanced guard having occupied the fort before our arrival. The people, however, came off with an assurance that, if we would attack the French, 800 Spaniards were ready to assist us. As the destruction of the fort was my principal object, I at once assented, and we commenced blowing up the road between Barcelona and Mongat, so that the communication on that side was effectively cut off, whilst the guns of General Duhesme's force were rendered immoveable on the other; these he afterwards abandoned.

On the 30th it fell calm, and having weighed anchor we drifted down as far as Mataro, but too distant from the shore to attempt anything. Having received intelligence of the continued advance of General Duhesme, we again returned, and anchored within five miles of Mongat, the inhabitants coming off to beg for assistance, as the French in the fort were keeping up a constant fire on their party in the woods, though without venturing to dislodge them.

It is, perhaps, here necessary to explain that General Duhesme had on the 16th of August been compelled by a well-executed movement on the part of the Count de Caldagues, to raise the siege of Gerona, in which he had been employed for upwards of a fortnight, his force being driven to Sarvia, where they were protected by their cavalry. During the night they separated into two divisions, one retreating towards Figueras, and the other in the direction of Barcelona.

It was to the latter division that my attention was directed. To reach Barcelona with heavy guns, the enemy must of necessity proceed by way of Mongat, the castle or fort of which place commanded a pass on their way. By breaking up the roads, the passage of the guns was impeded, as has been described; but, as the French had possession of the castle, it was essential that they should be dislodged as speedily as possible. The Spanish militia, being eager to second our efforts, I determined to make the attack forthwith.

At 8 A.M. on the 31st the *Impérieuse* got under weigh, and stood towards the castle, whilst I landed in the gig, and mounted the hills overhanging the position, for the purpose of reconnoitring; finding an attack practicable, I returned on board, and we cleared for action.

The Spaniards, seeing the *Impérieuse* stand in, and being eager for the onset, gallantly dashed up a hill where the French had established an outpost, and either killed or took the whole prisoners; upon which the garrison in the fort opened a heavy fire to dislodge the victorious Spaniards, but without effect. By this time I had got the *Impérieuse* well in, and had given the castle a couple of well-directed broadsides when the enemy hung out flags of truce.

On this I landed with a party of marines, but the exasperated Spaniards, elated by their recent victory, paid no attention to the flags of truce, and were advancing up the hill to storm the place, the French still firing to keep them in check. I was immediately conducted to the castle, where the French troops were drawn up on each side of the gate. On entering, the commandant requested me not to allow the peasantry to follow, as they would only surrender to me, and not to the Spaniards, of whose vengeance they were evidently afraid.

After giving the commandant a lecture on the barbarities that had been committed on the coast, and pointing out the folly of such a course, inasmuch as, had his troops fallen into the hands of the Spanish peasantry, not a man would have escaped with life, I acceded to the request to surrender to us alone, and promised the escort of our marines to the frigate.

The commandant then gave me his sword, and his troops forthwith laid down their arms. We had, however, even after this surrender, some trouble in keeping out the irritated Spaniards, who were actuated rather by the excitement of vengeance than by the rules of war; and it was not without a few blows, and forcing some of the assailants over the parapet, that we succeeded in keeping them off.

The Spaniards were with some difficulty made to understand that, however exasperated they might be at the conduct of the French, the latter were British prisoners, and not a hair of their heads should be hurt. When we were somewhat assured of their safety, the prisoners were marched down to the boats; and glad enough they were to get there, for the Spaniards accompanied them with volleys of abuse, declaring that they might thank the English for their lives, which, had the Spanish party succeeded in storming the fort, should have been sacrificed.

What became of the men forming the captured outpost I never knew, and was not anxious to enquire. Having placed the troops on board, we took off four brass field-pieces with their appendages, and threw the iron guns over the parapet; after which the Spaniards were allowed to ransack the fort. At 6 P.M. we laid a train to the French ammunition, and soon after the whole blew up. Spanish colours were then hoisted on the ruins, amidst the hearty cheers of thousands with arms in their hands, who had by this time flocked to the spot, though when we landed not a single inhabitant was to be seen. Soon after we gained possession, men, women, and children came from their hiding-places in abundance, expressing grateful satisfaction at the capture of the enemy.

It would have been well if the leaders of the French army in other parts of Spain could have seen the exasperation produced by the barbarous propensities of these detachments of troops, who appeared to be under no moral discipline. Except, perhaps, in actual fight, their officers had no control over them, so that their path was marked by excesses of every kind. This is a fatal mistake in armies, as the French afterwards found elsewhere—it degrades war into extermination. Our prisoners did not even deny that the Spaniards would only have exercised a just retaliation by immolating them, but contented themselves by saying that they would never have given in to the Spaniards whilst a man remained alive.

After we had blown up the castle, the *Cambrian* arrived, and to her, by permission of her captain, we transferred half our prisoners. On the following morning we sailed from Mongat, having first presented the chief commanding the Spaniards with two of the field-pieces taken the day before, together with a sufficient supply of powder and ammunition.

General Duhesme reached Barcelona by making a *détour* into the interior, after an absence of about a month, during which the destruction of the roads had been going on.  He was highly exasperated with the unfortunate inhabitants, though for no better reason than that all his plans had been thwarted, and, pointing the guns of the citadel on the town, he threatened it with destruction, unless his force was supplied with 12,000 rations daily, with wine and brandy in proportion ; following up this injustice by seizing the most respectable inhabitants for the purpose of extorting ransoms for their liberation.

Great credit is due to the Catalans for the spirit thus manifested at a time when all the more important strongholds of Catalonia were in the hands of the enemy.  I say Catalonia, as being concerned with that province only, though there was reason to know that the like patriotism was manifested in the western provinces, though, from the preponderance of the enemy, with less effect.

Even when Duhesme had reached Barcelona, he had great difficulty in maintaining himself, as the activity of the patriots in cutting off his supplies by land was worthy of their cause, and the *Impérieuse* and other English vessels of war took care that he got no supplies by sea.

On the 31st of July I addressed the subjoined despatch to Lord Collingwood : —

"H. M. S. *Impérieuse*, off Mongat, Catalonia,
"31 July, 1808.

"My Lord, — The castle of Mongat, an important post, completely commanding a pass on the road from Gerona to Barcelona, which the French are now besieging, and the only post between these towns occupied by the enemy, surrendered this morning to His Majesty's ship under my command.

"The Spanish militia behaved admirably in carrying an outpost on a neighbouring hill. Lieutenant Hore of the marines took possession of the castle, which, by means of powder, is now levelled with the ground, and the pending rocks are blown down into the road, which in many other places is also rendered impassable to artillery, without a very heavy loss of men if the French resolve to repair them.

"I inclose to your Lordship a list of the prisoners, and of the material part of the military stores, all of which that could be useful to the Spaniards have been delivered to them.

"I have the honour, &c.
"COCHRANE.

"The Rt. Hon. Lord Collingwood."


Having effected everything possible at Mongat, we made sail on the 4th of August, and anchored off St. Philou, where,—whilst the ship was employed in filling up water—I rode five miles into the country to inspect a battery which the Spaniards had erected to prevent the French from marching on the town. It was situated on an eminence, commanding the road to Gerona and Mataro, and was completely surrounded by high trees, so as not to be visible from the road. If properly defended, it would have presented a formidable obstacle, but as it was, the French infantry would have taken it in a few minutes. I gave the Spaniards instructions how to strengthen the position, but as they told me they could in a short time collect 3000 armed peasantry, I bid them rather rely on these by maintaining a guerilla warfare, which, if conducted with their usual judgment and activity, would harass the enemy more than the battery.

The Catalans made capital guerilla troops, possessing considerable skill in the use of their weapons, though previously untrained. A character for turbulence was often attributed to them ; but, in a country groaning under priestcraft and bad government, the sturdy spirit of independence, which prompted them to set the example of heroic defence of their country, might be, either mistakenly or purposely — the latter the more probable — set down for discontent and sedition. At any rate the descendants of men who, in a former age, formed the outposts of the Christian world against Mahomedism, in no way disgraced their ancestors, and became in the end the terror of their enemies. One quality they preeminently possess, viz. patience and endurance under privation ; and this, added to their hardy habits and adventurous disposition, contributed to form an enemy not to be despised — the less so that they were in every way disposed to repay the barbarities of the French with interest.

At 8 A.M. on the 6th, the *Impérieuse* got under sail from St. Philou, and passing close to Palamos, arrived in the afternoon at Rosas, where we found the *Montague* and *Hind*, to the latter of which we transferred the prisoners. The *Hind* was bound for Port Mahon with the Governor of Figueras and his family, who had to be escorted to the ship by the marines of the

*Montague*, in order to protect him from popular vengeance, so exasperated were the Spaniards on account of the governor's cowardice or treachery in allowing the French to enter the fortress he had commanded, though from its position and strength he could easily have held out.

The fortress of Figueras was about twelve miles from Rosas, and was a place of amazing strength, having been constructed for the defence of one of the principal passes on the borders of Spain, and being well garrisoned and provisioned, it ought certainly to have withstood a considerable force. The Rosas people had a right to be indignant at its pusillanimous surrender, for not only did this expose their town, but it formed a marked contrast to one of their own exploits, when, being attacked by a large French force, they drove them back with the loss of 300 men.

On the 7th we filled up with water at a wretched place on the opposite side of the Bay of Rosas, and on the 8th sailed for Philou, where we arrived on the 9th. On the 10th we were again off Barcelona, when a flag of truce was sent by the French to ask what had become of the troops we had taken at Mongat. On the 11th, we bore up for St. Philou and were joined by our gun-boat, after which we proceeded to see what was being done on the French coast, and bore up for Marseilles.

My object in proceeding in this direction was, that as the French troops kept out of our reach, there was no beneficial object to be gained by remaining on the Spanish coast; and it occurred to me, that by giving the French, in the neighbourhood of Marseilles, a taste of the evils they were inflicting on their Spanish neighbours, it would be possible to create an amount of alarm, which would have the effect of diverting troops intended for Catalonia, by the necessity of remaining to guard their own seaboard. It is wonderful what an amount of terrorism a small frigate is able to inspire on an enemy's coast. Actions between line-of-battle ships are, no doubt, very imposing; but for real effect, I would prefer a score or two of small vessels, well handled, to any fleet of line-of-battle ships.

On the 15th we stood into the Bay of Marseilles, and anchored off the mouth of the Rhone, which was distant about eight miles. Sent the gunboat in chase of a small vessel, but the crew ran her on shore, and escaped. The gunboat burned her, and joined us again on the following morning, when we anchored abreast of a telegraph employed in signalising our appearance on the coast. Here was a hint, the beneficial nature of which could not be doubted, and at once I decided on destroying the enemy's communications along shore. As a commencement, this telegraph was demolished without opposition.

On the 16th sent the gunboat in chase of two vessels, close to Cette. They escaped, but she brought back a boat with four men, who gave such information as induced me to send her on a cruise.

On the 17th, there being nothing in sight, we made preparations for destroying the signal-station on the island of Boni, which commands the entrance to the Rhone. Landing ninety men in the boats, we were just in time to see the troops in charge of the station abandon it; and having possessed ourselves of the signals, we blew up the place and returned to the ship.

We then got under weigh, and by 4 o'clock were close to Montpelier, firing on a fort as we passed. Perceiving another signal-station in the vicinity, we again out boats, and proceeded to destroy it, but found this not so easy a matter as on the last occasion, for we had two rivers to ford, each midleg in mud, and had moreover to encounter a fire of musketry, but at a distance which did no harm, so that with some difficulty we accomplished our object. This station was called Frontignan, the one last blown up being named La Pinede. At 8 P.M. we returned to the *Impérieuse*, with no other damage than being thoroughly encased in mud.

In the night we ran out about ten miles, having no confidence in the anchorage, and at daylight on the 19th again went in shore, carefully feeling our way by the lead, which showed us that the soundings were highly dangerous. We, nevertheless, came to an anchor off a place called Dumet, when we again out boats and destroyed another signal-tower, together with four houses connected with it. At 2 P.M. we got under sail and bore up, joining the gunboat to leeward. Supplying her with a new yard and bowsprit, her former spars being carried away, we sent her in shore.

On the 21st it fell so calm, that the *Impérieuse* had to be brought to an anchor in Gulf Dumet. At 3 A.M. the boats were manned to destroy a building which we had been informed was a custom-house. This having been set fire to, they returned on board, and were

shortly afterwards despatched to destroy another signal-
station; but as troops were now perceived on the look-
out, it was not worth while to risk the men, and the
boats were recalled. We then got under sail, passing
once more close to Montpelier and Cette, where we
again joined the gunboat, and stood into the Bay of
Perpignan—forming the west portion of Marseilles Bay
—where we destroyed another signal-station called
Cañet.

At 3 A.M., on the 24th, the morning being still dark,
we manned three boats to destroy another signal-station
called St. Maguire, about three miles distant, and at
about half-past four, when within ten yards of the beach,
were saluted by two heavy guns with grape, which
passing over the boats luckily did no damage. Fearing
an ambuscade, we pulled out of reach of musketry,
but calculating that the French would not venture
far in the dark—my favourite time for attacks of any
kind — instead of returning to the ship, we made
straight for the signal-station, and blew it up amidst a
dropping fire of musketry, which, as we could not be
distinguished, failed in its direction, and consequently
did no harm. Having completed our work, we next
marched along the beach in line towards a battery,
observed on the previous evening, skirmishing as we
proceeded, our boats meanwhile covering us with their
nine-pounders; the French also keeping up a constant
fire with their guns, but in a wrong direction.

On storming the battery, with the usual British cheer,
the enemy rushed out in an opposite direction, firing as
they went, but without effect. We then took possession

of two brass 24-pounders, but whilst making preparations to get them off were alarmed by recall guns from the
frigate, from the masthead of which, as day was now
beginning to break, a force of cavalry had been seen
making for us over the crest of a hill.

We had already had one narrow escape, for on taking
possession of the battery it was found that the magazine
was prepared for blowing us up, but fortunately, in the
hurry of its late occupants to escape, the match had
not caught fire. There was, however, now no time to be
lost, so placing a barrel of powder under each gun and
setting fire to the matches, both were blown up, as was
also the battery itself by lighting the match attached to
the magazine.

This somewhat staggered the cavalry in pursuit, but
they soon recovered, and some smart skirmishing took
place on our retreat to the boats, which all the time
maintained a well directed fire on the enemy, keeping
them in check, so that we got clear off with the loss of
one seaman only—a gallant fellow named Hogan—who
was blown up and terribly shattered, in consequence
of a cartouch box buckled round his waist having exploded while setting fire to the trains. We otherwise
arrived safe on board about 7 A.M., somewhat fatigued
by the night's adventure.

We now got under sail, passing close to Perpignan,
and were fired upon from Point Vendré, where a French
brig of war lay at anchor under the fortification, and
therefore was too well protected to be safely interfered
with.

In this cruise against the French signal stations, the

precaution of obtaining their signal books before destroying the semaphores was adopted; and in order to
make the enemy believe that the books also were destroyed, all the papers found were scattered about in
a half burnt condition. The trick was successful, and
the French authorities, considering that the signal
books had been destroyed also, did not deem it necessary to alter their signals, which were forwarded
by me to Lord Collingwood, who was thus informed
by the French semaphores when re-established of all
the movements of their own ships, as well as of the
British ships from the promontory of Italy northward!

# CHAP. XVI.

## CRUISE OF THE *IMPÉRIEUSE*—CONTINUED.

THE FRENCH FLEET.—THE MOLE OF CIOTAT.—THE GULF OF FOZ.—TAKE
POSSESSION OF THE BATTERY.—SILENCE THE BATTERIES.—ANCHOR
OFF CETTE.—DESPATCH THE PRIZES.—HOW WE OBTAINED FRESH
WATER.—DEMOLISH A TELEGRAPH.—FRIGATE TO LEEWARD.—ORDERED
TO GIBRALTAR.—INGRATITUDE OF GOVERNMENT.—LETTER OF LORD
COLLINGWOOD.—LETTER OF LORD COCHRANE.

ON the 2nd of September the *Impérieuse* rejoined
the fleet off Toulon, and received orders from Lord
Collingwood to renew operations on the enemy's coasts.
As the French, though by our previous operations, and
by the spirit thereby inspired amongst the inhabitants,
were disinclined to advance into Catalonia, they were
nevertheless in considerable force in the neighbourhood of Figueras and Rosas, we therefore leisurely
sailed in the direction of the latter port.

Keeping well in with the French coast, some gun-
boats were observed at 8 A.M. on the following morning
close in with the town of Ciotat, between Toulon and
Marseilles.   One of these being somewhat detached, we
hoisted out all boats in chase, but on the remaining gun-
boats and a battery on shore opening a heavy fire on
them, they were recalled, and we cleared for action.
At 10 A. M. six sail of French line of battle ships were

observed to quit Toulon, but as they were far to
leeward, there was nothing to apprehend from their
interference; indeed after manœuvring for a short
time, they returned to port, no doubt satisfied that the
firing which had taken place was of little importance.

At 11 A.M. we anchored under an island, within range
of our main deck guns, but in such a position as to
shelter us from the fire of the battery, which, finding
that their guns could not be brought to bear, commenced a constant discharge of shells; but as no accurate
aim could be taken, these inflicted no damage, though
occasionally dropping near us. Taking no notice of
these, we out boats, and sending them to a point
out of sight of the battery, commenced throwing
rockets into the town, which was twice set on fire; but
as the houses were for the most part built of stone, the
conflagration was confined to the spot where it had
broken out. Our reason for molesting the town was
that the inhabitants everywhere showed themselves in
arms to oppose us.

Finding the place impervious to rockets, and the
ship being too far out for a successful cannonade, we
got under weigh, and took up a position within range
of the fort, on which we continued firing till 8 P.M.,
almost every shot falling in the place. As it now came
on to blow hard from the N.W. we were obliged to
anchor.

During the night the enemy had got up a large gun
close to the lighthouse, and by 10 o'clock on the following morning, a squadron consisting of four line of
battle ships and three frigates left Toulon and com-

menced beating up towards us. We therefore did not again open fire, being unwilling to excite the squadron to pursue us.

However, at 3 P.M., as a large settee was running into the mole of Ciotat, we discharged two shots at her, which went over and fell in the town. Upon this the mortar battery, seeing their squadron approaching, again opened fire, but, as before, without effect. We took no notice of this, but seeing the enemy manning the gun at the lighthouse, we beat to quarters, and prepared everything in case they should fire upon us, which was done at 4 P.M.

We again opened a heavy fire upon the town, every shot telling upon the houses, from which the inhabitants fled, no person being anywhere visible. At the expiration of an hour the lighthouse people left off firing, and the gun was pointed eastward to show that they did not intend to renew the conflict, upon which we ceased also, my object being not to batter the town, but to get possession of some of the numerous vessels anchored within the mole.

This purpose was, however, defeated by the perseverance of the Toulon squadron, the headmost ship of which—a fine frigate—was now within six miles of us, and coming up fast, supported by the others. We therefore thought best to get under weigh, and did so under the fire of batteries and mortars, none of which touched us. As soon as the enemy's fleet saw us under sail, they bore up and again ran into Toulon.

On the 6th at midday, we anchored in the Bay of

Marseilles, within half a mile from the shore, just out
of range of the strongly fortified islands in the bay.
Our appearance created the greatest alarm on the
coast, from which people were hurrying with their
movables beyond the reach of shot. We had, however, no intention to molest them.

The *Impérieuse* was now becalmed till midday on
the 7th, when a breeze springing up, we again got
under sail, and exchanged signals with the *Spartan*,
which shortly afterwards joined company. Having
discovered three vessels lying in a small cove, we out
boats, and brought out two of them, setting fire to the
other. As the enemy had numerous troops ashore,
they opened a brisk fire on the boats, and would probably have defeated our intention, had not the ships
kept up a fire upon them whenever they approached.
Thus aided, the boats lost only one man, with another
wounded.

On the 8th the *Spartan* and *Impérieuse* stood towards the Gulf of Foz, where, seeing a number of
troops placed for the defence of a signal telegraph, both
ships manned boats, and in addition to the seamen,
the marines of the *Impérieuse* were sent with a nine-
pounder field piece—one of our prizes from Duhesme's
army. On effecting a landing, the enemy's troops retired to the interior, when firing two volleys after
them, the telegraph named Tignes was taken and
blown up, the signals being secured as before.

On the 9th we passed close to Port Vendre, *Spartan* in company, and anchored about a mile from
the shore; but an alarm having been raised, and the

troops on shore having got our range, we were at 3 A. M. on the 10th, compelled to shift our position.

Before daylight the boats of both ships were manned, and pulled on shore, a battery firing at us, but as the shot went over, no mischief was done. Our seamen and marines having landed to the right of the battery, the enemy's troops fled, and we took possession, spiking the guns, destroying their carriages, and blowing up the barracks. These operations were scarcely completed, when a considerable body of troops made their appearance in the distance, and by the time we returned on board, a number of cavalry and artillery had assembled on the site of their demolished battery.

We now passed close to a small fishing town, where other guns were observed in position, both on the right and on the left, these being manned by regular troops and backed by hundreds of armed peasantry, who showed a bolder front than had the garrison of the battery recently destroyed. By way of feint, to draw off the attention of the cavalry, both *Spartan* and *Impérieuse* manned their small boats and the rocket boats with the ships' boys, dressed in marines' scarlet jackets, despatching these at some distance towards the right, as though an attack were there intended. The device was successful, and a body of cavalry, as we anticipated, promptly set off to receive them.

Meanwhile the ships stood towards the town, under a smart fire from the batteries, the shot from which several times took effect. When close in, the *Impérieuse* opened her broadside, and the *Spartan* following, an incessant fire was kept up for an hour, at the expiration of which the marines of both ships were landed. As soon as the boats touched the shore, the enemy fled from the battery, the guns of which were immediately spiked.

The cavalry, which had gone off to repel the sham attack to the right, having found out the trick which had been played upon them, were now seen galloping back to save the battery, which had just been rendered useless, and from which our marines were now re-embarking. So intent were they on rescuing their guns, that they did not appear to have noticed the altered position of the ships, which, as soon as the horsemen approached within musket shot, opened upon them with grape so effectually, that all who were not knocked out of their saddles rode off as fast as they could, and the marines leisurely returned to their respective ships.

As the French troops had now taken shelter in the town, and the people were everywhere armed, I returned to the *Impérieuse* for the large boats, in each of which a gun was mounted, with the object of clearing the beach and silencing the other battery. By 6 o'clock this was accomplished, not only the battery, but many of the houses and vessels being destroyed. As our boats neared the town, a numerous body of troops again began a brisk fire with musketry; and by the time one of the largest vessels, which yet remained un-demolished, could be blown up, the fire became so warm that it was advisable to cease from further operations, and we returned to the frigate.

'In this affair a considerable number of people must

have been killed ashore during the five hours and a half continued firing; the cavalry and infantry engaged amounting to several hundreds, whilst the armed inhabitants mustered in equal, if not superior numbers. Neither *Spartan* nor *Impérieuse* had any killed, and only a few wounded, though, from their proximity to the shore, the rigging of both ships was a good deal cut up, and several shots passed through their hulls. Besides the seamen, we had only fifty marines engaged, thirty from the *Impérieuse*, and twenty from the *Spartan*.

On the 11th at 8 P.M. we anchored off the town of Cette, just out of gunshot, the batteries on shore however maintaining a brisk fire, which was consequently thrown away.

At midnight two boats were despatched from the *Impérieuse* and one from the *Spartan*, to throw rockets into the town, the batteries continuing their fire in all directions till daylight, but doing no damage.

At 4 A.M. on the 12th we got under weigh, and when within a mile of the shore, between Cette and Montpellier, sent the boats to burn two large pontoons, close to the signal station, which the *Impérieuse* had attempted to destroy on the 18th *ultimo*. One of the pontoons was burned, and the other blown up without opposition, together with the signal station and other public buildings which we had not been able to destroy on the former occasion. A number of troops showed themselves, but were contented with firing at a harmless distance. As nothing more remained to be done, we again made sail.

On the morning of the 13th a convoy was discovered
in shore. As soon as they saw us, the vessels composing it altered their course, and by 12 o'clock had
taken refuge in a deep bay in the vicinity, it being,
no doubt, calculated that we should not venture to pass
over an extensive shoal, which almost closed up the
entrance of the bay. By careful sounding we, however,
managed to effect a passage, and three of the smaller
vessels perceiving that we should attain our object,
passed over the opposite end of the shoal and got
away.

About midday it blew a hurricane, and both ships
were rapidly driving towards shore, but by letting go
another anchor they were brought up. In about a
couple of hours the wind abated, when we weighed
and anchored close to the remaining vessels, taking
possession of the whole that remained, viz., a ship,
two brigs, a bombard, a xebec, and a settee, but all
aground. We, however, succeeded in getting off the
ship, one brig, the bombard, and settee. The remainder were burned. During these operations a
body of French troops lined the beach; we did not,
however, attempt to molest them, as it was still
blowing so hard that the prizes were with difficulty
got off.

On the 16th we despatched some of the prizes to
Gibraltar, and the remainder to Rosas. The *Spartan*
now parted company with us to rejoin the Toulon
fleet, and the *Impérieuse* held on her course for Rosas
with the prize brig in tow, she having been so much
damaged by beating on the shoals before she was

captured, as to require the greatest exertion to keep her afloat.

On the 18th we came to an anchor off Rosas, and on the 23rd, having patched up our prize, she was sent to Gibraltar in charge of Lieutenant Mapleton.

On the 24th the *Impérieuse* again sailed for the French coast, and passing Cette, stood into the Gulf of Foz.

In these cruises our greatest difficulty was to procure fresh water, which was only to be obtained on the enemy's coast, so that the men had frequently to be placed on short allowance. As we were now destitute of this necessary, I determined to run for the entrance of the Rhone, and fill up with water by a novel expedient. Our foretopmast studding-sails were sewn up and converted into huge bags nearly water-tight; these — as the water at the river's mouth was brackish — were sent in the boats higher up the stream where it was pure. The bags being there filled, were towed alongside the ship, and the water pumped as quickly as possible into the hold by means of the fire engine, the operation being repeated till we had obtained a sufficient supply.

Having thus replenished our water, we made an attempt to obtain fresh meat also at the enemy's expense. Whilst engaged in watering, a number of cattle had been observed grazing on the banks of the river, and a party was taken on shore to secure some. But this time circumstances were against us. The lowlands on the banks of the river having been flooded, we found on landing a complete morass; the men never-

theless gave chase to the cattle, but they were so
wild, that after a run of three miles, often up to the
middle in water, nothing was caught but the herds-
man, a poor wretch, who no doubt believing, according
to current report in France, that the English killed
all their prisoners, began to prepare for death in the
most exemplary manner, scarcely crediting the evidence of his senses on being liberated.

In this excursion we had perceived a new telegraph
station, about three miles from Foz, the building being
complete with the exception of the machine   We set
fire to the building, but the destruction not being
fully accomplished, the boats were again sent on shore
to blow it up, which was done in the presence of about
a hundred troops assembled for its protection.  A
shot from the ship was so well aimed that it fell right
amongst the party, killing one man and wounding
several.  A few more shots completely dispersed them
in such haste as to compel them to relinquish their
dead comrade.

On inspecting the abandoned body through a glass,
it evidently appeared to be that of an officer, and hence
it occurred to me that he might have papers about him
which would prove useful.  In order to secure them, if
there were any, the frigate's barge was again despatched
on shore, but before the men could land, a horse was
brought from the interior, and the body being laid
across him, a shot was fired from the ship over the
heads of the party in charge of the horse, which becoming restive, the body was again abandoned.  The
boat's crew having by this time landed, found it to be

that of an officer, as I had conjectured, the poor fellow been nearly cut in two by a round shot. As no papers of any consequence were found, our men wrapped him in a sheet which the troops had brought with the horse, and again returned on board.

The *Impérieuse* continued her course along the coast, and on the 30th, seeing some small vessels at anchor near Boni, the boats were sent to destroy them. This being effected in the face of a detachment of troops and the armed population of a small fishing town, the latter also shared the same fate. Passing close to Boni, we saw several vessels at anchor, and made preparations to attack them, but it coming on to blow hard from the westward, we held on our course towards Marseilles, off which a large polacca-rigged ship passed astern of the *Impérieuse*, out of gunshot. The boats were lowered, but the wind increasing, they had to be taken on board again, and the polacca got into Marseilles, which was then distant about eight miles.

On the 1st of October we again passed close to Ciotat, but saw nothing to attract our attention. On the 2nd some French ships were discovered at anchor near the land to the westward of Toulon, and several guns were fired at us from four batteries on the coast, but without damage, as we were not within reach of shot.

Seeing a frigate to leeward, we exchanged numbers, and found her to be our former consort the *Spartan*, which had been engaged in reconnoitring the enemy's port. Shortly afterwards she bore up and made all sail, the French line of battle ships quitting port in pursuit. When within about four miles of these we came to the wind, and the *Spartan* signalled that, since the previous evening, five of the enemy's frigates and a storeship had sailed from Toulon.

As the *Spartan* again signalled for us to pass within hail, I went on board, and from the information communicated, bore up in search of the admiral. Not finding him where we expected to fall in with him, we ran with a fair wind for Minorca, arriving off Port Mahon on the 5th.

As there was only a Spanish ship of the line in harbour, we again proceeded in quest of the flagship, and soon after midday fell in with her on her way to Minorca. On communicating to Lord Collingwood intelligence of the escape of the five frigates from Toulon, his lordship ordered the *Impérieuse* to Gibraltar with despatches. We therefore wore ship and made sail for that port, where we arrived without further incident.

For these operations on the coast of France I never received the slightest acknowledgment from the Admiralty, though, regardless of prize-money, I had completely disorganised the telegraphic communication of the enemy from the seat of war in Catalonia, to one of the principal naval arsenals of France; and had created an amount of terrorism on the French coast, which, from inculcating the belief that it was intended to be followed up, prevented the French Government from further attempts at throwing a military force on the Mediterranean coast of Spain. This as has been said was my object, as the Spaniards were now in alliance with us. For the panic thus created on the French coast, and its consequences, French writers have given me credit, but the British Government none!

By people of narrow views it has been said that such operations formed no business of mine, and that my zeal exceeded my discretion, which I deny. The commander-in-chief, Lord Collingwood,— confiding in my discretion —had sent me to do what I could to assist the Spaniards and annoy the French—and I am proud to say that both objects were effected to his lordship's satisfaction, as will appear from his letters. What damage can I do to the enemy? was my guiding principle, and the excitement of accomplishing the mischief was my only reward,— for I got no other.

To the disgrace of the then corrupt British administration, which withheld not only reward, but praise, because I had connected myself with a radical constituency, and had set up as a reformer of naval abuses, nothing was manifested in return for these services but hatred. I am proud, however, to make known the subjoined testimony of Lord Collingwood, who gave me the credit of paralysing the enemy's operations by the panic which the *Impérieuse* created on the coast of France; thus neutralising military expeditions intended to act against Catalonia, or, in other words, preventing, by means of a single frigate, the march of an army into the Mediterranean provinces of Spain, where it could at the time have operated with complete effect. Posterity may not believe the effect of these exertions as narrated by myself. To Lord Collingwood they *must* give credit.

"Admiralty Office, Jan. 7th, 1809.

" *Copy of a Letter from* Vice-Admiral LORD COLLINGWOOD, *Commander-in-Chief of His Majesty's ships and vessels in the Mediterranéan, to the* Hon. WELLESLEY POLE, *dated on board the* Ocean, *off Toulon, the 19th of October*, 1808.

" SIR,—I enclose a letter which I have just received from the Right Honourable Lord Cochrane, captain of the *Impérieuse*, stating the services in which he has been employed on the coast of Languedoc. Nothing can exceed the zeal and activity with which his lordship pursues the enemy. The success which attends his enterprises clearly indicates with what skill and ability they are conducted, besides keeping the coast in constant alarm — causing a general suspension of the trade, and harassing a body of troops employed in opposing him. He has probably prevented *these troops which were intended for Figueras from advancing into Spain, by giving them employment in the defence of their own coasts.*

*   *   *   *   *

"I have the honour to be, &c.<br>" COLLINGWOOD."

(Enclosure.)

" *Impérieuse*, Gulf of Lyons, 28th Sept. 1808.

" My LORD, — With varying opposition, but with unvaried success, the newly constructed semaphoric telegraphs — which are of the utmost consequence to the safety of the numerous convoys that pass along the coast of France — at Bourdique, La Pinede, St. Maguire, Frontignan, Canet, and Fay, have been blown up and completely demolished, together with their telegraph houses, fourteen barracks of *gens* d'armes, one battery, and the strong tower on the lake of Frontignan.

"Mr. Mapleton, first lieutenant, had command of these expeditions. Lieutenant Johnson had charge of the field pieces, and Lieutenant Hore of the Royal Marines. To them, and to Mr. Gilbert, assistant-surgeon, Mr. Burney, gunner, Messrs. Houston Stewart * and Stoven, midshipmen, is due whatever credit may arise from such mischief, and for having, with so small a force, drawn about 2000 troops from the important fortress of Figueras in Spain, for the defence of their own coasts.

"The conduct of Lieutenants Mapleton, Johnson, and Hore, deserves my praise, as well as that of the other officers, Royal Marines, and seamen.

"I have the honour to be, my Lord,
"Your obedient servant, &c.
"COCHRANE.

" Vice-Admiral Lord Collingwood."

*Impérieuse.* — None killed, none wounded, one singed in blowing up the battery.

*French.* — One commanding officer of troops killed. How many others unknown.

* The present gallant Admiral Sir Houston Stewart, commanding Her Britannic Majesty's squadron on the North American station.

# CHAP. XVII.

## CRUISE OF THE *IMPÉRIEUSE* CONTINUED.

CAPTURE A SETTEE. — GET UNDER SAIL. — FIGHT BETWEEN THE PATRIOTS
AND FRENCH. — MAKE SAIL FOR ROSAS. — FORT TRINIDAD. — GALLANTRY
OF CAPTAIN WEST. — BRAVERY OF THE CATALAN. — REPULSE OF THE
FRENCH. — ATTACK OF THE IMPÉRIEUSE. — THE FRENCH REDOUBLE THEIR
EFFORTS. — OCCUPATION OF CATALONIA. — THE CASTLE OF TRINIDAD. —
NATURE OF OUR POSITION. — NATURE OF OUR OPERATIONS. — MANU-
FACTURE OF A MAN-TRAP. — LOSE MY NOSE. — THE FRENCH ASSAULT
ROSAS. — PRACTICE OF THE FRENCH. — PRESENTIMENT. — THE FRENCH
ATTACK. — THE ATTACK REPULSED. — BRAVERY OF A FRENCH SOLDIER.
— HEAVY GALE OF WIND. — UNFORTUNATE ACCIDENT. — EVACUATE THE
FORTRESS. — STAND TOWARDS SCALLA. — LETTER FROM LORD COLLING-
WOOD. — DESPATCH TO LORD COLLINGWOOD. — LETTER TO THE ADMI-
RALTY. — TESTIMONY OF THE SPANIARDS. — SIR WALTER SCOTT. —
OFFICIAL GRATITUDE.

On the 19th of October we again quitted Gibraltar for
the eastward, having learned that the French frigates
which had succeeded in getting out of Toulon were at
anchor in St. Fiorenzo bay, in the island of Corsica.
After leaving Gibraltar, we stood over towards the
Spanish possessions on the Barbary coast, and finding
everything right there, passed on to the Zaffarine Islands, inside of which we anchored for the purpose of
painting and refitting the ship, which stood much in
need of renovation.

This being accomplished, we again sailed on the
29th, and on the 31st arrived in the harbour of Car-

thagena, where we found the Russian ambassador to
Austria on his way to Trieste. No English man-of-war
having been here since our former visit, we were
received with great hospitality and attention by the
authorities and inhabitants, who unanimously expressed
their delight at being at peace with England; though,
as a Spanish fleet lay dismantled in the harbour, it
struck me that they might aid England to better purpose by looking after the enemy. Even their convoys
had to be protected by English ships, for whilst we lay
at Carthagena, the *Myrtle* arrived from Tarragona, with
twelve sail of transports which she had convoyed thither
with Spanish troops from Lisbon, and again returned
for more.

The *Impérieuse* left Carthagena on the 10th of
November, and rounding Cape Palos, passed between
Majorca and the mainland, where, on the 11th, we
captured a settee. On the 12th we anchored off Bar-
celona, which place was still in possession of the French.
The *Cambrian* was at anchor in the roads.

At night we sent the boats of the *Impérieuse* to
throw rockets into the fort, and at daylight on the following morning got under weigh, but perceiving two
boats full of men in chase of some Spanish settees,
we lowered ours, and pulled for the boats, which on
seeing our intention, abandoned their prey, and ran in
under the forts for protection.

On our arrival at Barcelona the *Cambrian* went out
for a run, leaving the *Impérieuse* to watch the enemy.
On her return we again out boats, and proceeded to
blow up a fort close to the entrance of Llogrebat

river, and succeeded in so far shattering its foundations, as to render it useless. On the 14th the *Impérieuse* anchored near the mouth of this river for the purpose of watering, sending at the same time a boat to throw rockets into the barracks, in order to divert the attention of the Barcelona garrison.

Having completed watering on the 15th, we again got under sail, and resumed our position before the town, shortly after which we observed about 2000 of the French army march out and ascend the hills, where they soon became engaged with a large body of Spanish peasantry. The ships followed, keeping as far as practicable in shore; but still at too great a distance to render any material assistance to the patriots, who were at last forced from their position. As soon as this action was over, the batteries commenced firing shells at us. In place of replying to this, both ships opened a heavy fire on the portion of the town occupied by French troops, amongst whom, as we afterwards learned from the Spaniards, our shot told with great effect.

Irritated by this unexpected movement, the whole of the batteries ashore began to ply us with shot and shell, the latter of which were thrown with excellent precision as regarded their direction, but fell either over or short of us, two only bursting near the *Impérieuse*, but without doing us any harm. The *Cambrian*, lying a little farther out, escaped with similar impunity. With round shot the batteries were in our case more lucky, one of these passing through the barge and galley, and another striking the muzzle of a brass 32-pounder on the forecastle, in such a way as to render it useless, though without injury to the men who were at the time working the guns.

The circumstances under which the destruction of this gun was effected, are too curious to be passed over.

By an extraordinary coincidence the enemy's shot entered the muzzle at the moment our men were firing it, so that the two shots met in the bore! The consequence was, that the gun was blown up nearly in the middle, the exterior being forced into a globular form —to our great annoyance, for this gun was one of our most useful weapons.

On the 17th another action took place between the mountaineers and a French force on the hills, the object of the patriots being to get possession of the heights, where the French had established a battery, but which on every side annoyed the *cordon* of irregular troops employed in intercepting provisions, from which the Spaniards could not dislodge them, though they appeared to make their attacks with so much judgment and vigour as to compel the enemy to remain on the defensive. In the present case the attack was unsuccessful, the patriots being compelled to retire without accomplishing their object.

After this affair was concluded, several Spanish officers came on board the *Impérieuse*, and spoke confidently of being able to drive in the French advanced spot as soon as General Reding's force joined. They informed me that the presence of the *Impérieuse* and *Cambrian* had been of great use, by compelling the

French to keep a considerable portion of their troops in the town, and to employ others in manning the coast batteries, so that few were available for operations elsewhere; but beyond this we had no opportunity of assisting the patriots, as the heights to which the enemy clung so tenaciously were beyond the reach of shot or shell from the ships.

On the 19th I received information of the French having invested Rosas, and knowing that Lord Collingwood attached considerable importance to this place, I considered it my duty, in accordance with his lordship's instructions, to proceed in that direction, hoping that the *Impérieuse* might there render substantial service; we therefore left the *Cambrian* before Barcelona, and made sail for Rosas, where we arrived on the following day. As it fell calm, the ship was compelled to anchor ten miles from the fortress.

On our arrival a heavy cannonade was going on between the ships and a French battery thrown upon the cliff above Fort Trinidad. The *Impérieuse*, as has been said, being out of range, I took the gig and landed in the town, to ascertain how we might best employ ourselves. Having satisfied myself on this point, I sent back the gig with orders for the frigate to make every effort to get within range of the French troops surrounding the town, so as to enfilade them. As the calm continued, she was, however, unable to approach till the following day, I meanwhile remaining in Rosas, to encourage the Spanish troops, whose spirit was beginning to give way.

Previous to our arrival the marines of the *Excellent*,

together with some Spanish troops, had occupied the
citadel. Many of these having been wounded, the *Excellent* took upwards of forty on board and sailed,
leaving the *Fame* to watch the place, and her commander withdrew some thirty marines, who, with sixty
or seventy Spaniards, occupied Fort Trinidad. The
departure of the *Excellent* in the first place, and the
withdrawal of the marines in the second, greatly dis-
pirited the Spaniards, who on the evening of the 21st
began to quit the town in boats.

A brief outline of what had occurred previous to my
arrival in the *Impérieuse*, will here be requisite, in order
to comprehend the events which followed. On the
6th of November a body of 6000 French, or rather
Italians, coming from Rigueras, had taken possession of
the town and the heights commanding the bay. The
inhabitants forthwith fled; but the *Excellent* and *Meteor*,
then lying in the harbour, speedily drove out the in-
vaders.

On the assault of the town some of the inhabitants
had fled to the citadel, which was in a wretched condition, one of its bastions having been blown down
during the last war; and such had been the negligence
of the Spanish military authorities, that it had received
no better repair than a few planks and loose stones;
whilst the stores were even in a more wretched condition than the works. It was, however, necessary to
put it, as far as possible, in a defensible condition, and
to this Captain West, of the *Excellent*, energetically
applied himself.

To the eastward of the town, on an eminence commanding the harbour, stood Fort Trinidad, of which a description will presently be given. In this fortress Captain West placed five-and-twenty of the *Excellent's* marines, in addition to the Spaniards who manned the fort; and, at the same time, sent fifty seamen into the citadel to support the garrison.

The Spanish governor, O'Daly, now sent a request to the Junta of Gerona for reinforcements; but the French, managing to intercept his despatches, caused it to be reported to the Junta that the English had taken forcible possession of the fortress, and deposed the governor; whereupon, in place of sending reinforcements, the Junta wrote to Captain West, demanding an explanation of conduct so extraordinary, and, till this explanation revealed the trick, it remained undiscovered.

On the 9th the citadel was attacked by General Reille, and a breach effected; but Captain West, placing the *Meteor* in a position to flank the breach, and sending some boats to enfilade the shore, prevented the assault, and despatching more seamen to the citadel, the next day it was again in a tolerably defensive state, so much so that Captain West had sallied out with the seamen and effected the rescue of a party of Catalonian militia.

The French commander, thus foiled by the gallantry and judgment of Captain West, now deemed it necessary to proceed against Rosas by regular siege, but first made an attempt to storm Fort Trinidad, in which he was repulsed with considerable loss; but the fort was so much in danger that, in order to prevent surprise, Captain West reinforced it with thirty additional marines, who entered by means of rope ladders.

The French now, despite opposition from the ships, began to erect batteries on the heights for the demolition of Fort Trinidad, and threw up an entrenchment 300 yards from the citadel, for the purpose of breaching that also. A 3-gun battery also opened against the town walls, and the joint effect of these being occasionally directed against the ships compelled them to retire out of range.

Captain West was now superseded by Captain Bennett of the *Fame*, and, as a breach had nearly been effected in the lower bomb proof of Fort Trinidad, Captain Bennett withdrew the marines. At this juncture I arrived at Rosas in the *Impérieuse*, having, indeed, come there to render what assistance I could to the Spaniards, and, knowing the endurance, as well as indomitable bravery of the Catalan or *Michuelet** character; feeling, moreover, assured that the Junta of Gerona would supply early assistance; I determined to replace the marines which Captain Bennett had withdrawn, with others from my own frigate. As it was generally known amongst vessels on the Mediterranean station that I was acting under discretionary orders from Lord Collingwood, Captain Bennett, though he had withdrawn his own men, and notwithstanding that he was my senior officer, did not attempt to thwart my resolution,

* A name given at this period to the irregular Catalonian troops, as well as to other Spaniards embodied with them, from one of their old leaders, Michelot de Prato, the companion of Cæsar Borgia, and the principal agent in many of his atrocities. In the old wars of Arragon, they were called Almogavares, and at the period of which I write had lost little of their traditional daring, or that ready ingenuity in difficulties, which supplied the want of a more efficient warlike equipment.

probably because he considered that by so doing he
might be interfering with the instructions given me by
Lord Collingwood.

On the 22nd, after having given further instructions
on board the *Impérieuse* for annoying the enemy
during my absence, I again went on shore to the
citadel, into which the French were incessantly throwing shells, but without much effect; for although every
shell fell within the place, the shelter was excellent,
and no great damage was done.

Having ascertained the position of the enemy's en-
trenchments, I returned on board, and despatched a
party from the frigate to fire upon them at the distance
of about 600 yards, as well as to harass the batteries
in course of construction. The work was so well performed by our men as to embarrass the troops in the
batteries, and thus lessen their fire on the citadel, the
preservation of which, ·till further assistance should
arrive, was my principal object. A battery of 24-
pounders on the top of a cliff, and therefore inacces-
sible to our fire, kept up, however, an unremitting fire
on Fort Trinidad, every shot striking; but the fort
being bomb-proof, without injury to the little garrison,
which, like that of the citadel, was well sheltered, but
had no means of returning the fire except occasionally
by musketry.

After pounding away at the fort for several days, the
French made up their minds to storm, but on coming
within range of musket-shot, they got such a reception
from the garrison as to render a hasty retreat imperative. As their discomfiture was visible from the

ship, we fired a salute of twenty-one guns by way of sarcastic compliment, but the enemy had not the politeness to return the courtesy.

The *Impérieuse* now got under weigh, and cleared for action, taking up a position to the left of the citadel, and within musket-shot of the French lines, into which we poured such a storm of shot as to drive out the enemy. Satisfied with the success, I went on shore at Rosas, and got 700 Spaniards to embark in the boats, afterwards putting them on board a light vessel, with the intention of landing them at the back of Fort Trinidad, so as to dislodge the troops from the battery on the cliff, and threw the guns over. The movement was, however, detected by the French commander, and a force which had just been engaged at a distance was hastily recalled, and rushed on, driving the Spaniards and some Germans before them. Manning the batteries, the French instantly turned their attention to the *Impérieuse*, against which they directed such a well aimed shower of shells as rendered it imperative to get under sail and anchor out of range.

The firing between the batteries and the citadel was kept up during the night without intermission, and at daylight the Spaniards we had landed for the attack on the cliff battery appeared in such confusion, that it became necessary to despatch the boats to bring off a party of marines, who had been put on shore with them. Our men reported that the Spaniards had unaccountably refused to follow them to the attack, and, as is usual in such cases, had suffered far more severely than they would have done had they per-

severed in the attempt to capture the battery. On
sending boats to bring off the Spaniards we only got
300 out of the 700, the remainder being either killed
or made prisoners.

On the 23rd we again ran in under Fort Trinidad,
but this time on the opposite side to the battery on
the cliff, where we could effect considerable mischief,
without receiving much in return. It now fell dead
calm, so that it was lucky we had not taken up our
former position, where we might have been terribly
annoyed.

The French, without paying much attention to us,
now appeared to redouble their efforts against both
castle and citadel, whilst their troops mustered strongly
on the hills, with the evident intention of an attack on
both, the moment a breach became practicable.

Finding this to be the case, the *Fame* withdrew her
marines from Fort Trinidad, upon which I went ashore,
and after careful inspection of the breach in course of
formation, considering it still capable of prolonged defence, begged the commandant to hold out till next
day, when he should be reinforced with marines from
the *Impérieuse*, promising at the same time to remain
myself in the fortress with the men. With some difficulty he was induced to consent to this arrangement,
after telling me that it had been his intention to capitulate on the same evening.

Nor was the Spanish governor at all to blame for his
intention to surrender the fortress. Captain Bennett
had withdrawn his men, thinking, no doubt, that it
was untenable, and that therefore nothing was to be

gained by their exposure; so that the Spanish governor might fairly plead that further resistance had
been deemed unavailing by the English themselves.

Lord Collingwood had, however, entrusted me with
discretionary orders to assist the Spaniards, and it appeared to me that the present was an instance where
those orders might be carried into effect, for I had no
doubt, if assistance arrived promptly, that the French
would be compelled to raise the siege of Rosas, as
they had done that of Gerona. In which case they
would find themselves isolated at Barcelona; and being
cut off, as they already were by land, and exposed to
bombardment by sea, must surrender. The occupation
of Catalonia, in short, turned on two points; 1st,
whether the Junta of Gerona supplied an adequate reinforcement; and, 2ndly, whether I could hold Fort
Trinidad till it arrived. Neither do I blame Captain
Bennett for withdrawing his men. It was simply
matter of opinion, his being that neither fort not
citadel would long hold out — mine, formed on actual
inspection of the fort, that it was still in a condition to
maintain itself, and being so; that its retention was essential for the preservation of the town and citadel. And
had there been a little more alacrity on the part of the
Gerona Junta in supplying reinforcements, that opinion
would have been justified. Captain Bennett perhaps
knew the dilatory habits of the Spaniards better than
I did; but although my senior officer, he was disinterested enough not in any way to interfere with my
plans.

Before daylight on the 24th we landed fifty men,

ordering all the marines to follow after sunset. Our first object was to effect such repairs as would put the fort in a better state of defence, and this was accomplished without any great difficulty, as the French were confining their attention to one particular spot, where, by a constant succession of quick firing, they hoped to make a practicable breach. This we could not prevent, having no artillery to reply to theirs.

My principal ground for a belief in the practicability of holding the fort arose from the peculiar form and thickness of the walls, to penetrate which was no easy matter, if resolutely defended. Even if eventually successful, it would not be difficult to evacuate the fort by the lower portion, before the enemy could establish themselves in the upper, whilst a well constructed mine would involve both them and the castle in one common ruin.

The Castle of Trinidad stood on the side of a hill, having by no means a difficult descent to the sea, but this hill was again commanded by a higher and more precipitous cliff, which would have enabled an enemy to drive out the occupants with ease, but for the peculiar construction of the fortress.

Next to the sea was a fort constructed with strong walls some 50 feet high. Behind this and joined to it, rose another fort to the height of 30 or 40 feet more, and behind this again was a tower rising some 20 or 30 feet still higher, the whole presenting the appearance of a large church with a tower 110 feet high, a nave 90 feet high, and a chancel 50 feet. The tower, having its back to the cliff, as a matter of course shel-

tered the middle and lower portions of the fortress
from a fire of the battery above it. Nothing, in short,
for a fortress commanded by adjacent heights could
have been better adapted for holding out against
offensive operations, or worse adapted for replying to
them; this on our part being out of the question, as
the French battery was too much elevated on the cliff
for artillery to reach, whilst the tower which prevented
their shot from annoying us, would also have prevented
our firing at them, even had we possessed artillery.

It was to this tower therefore that the French chiefly
directed their attention, as a practicable breach therein,
followed by a successful assault, would in their estimation place the fortress at their mercy, so that we must
either be driven out or forced to surrender. In consequence of the elevated position of the enemy's battery on the cliff, they could however only breach the
central portion of the tower, the lowest part of the
breach being nearly sixty feet above its base, so that
when practicable, it could only be reached by long
scaling ladders.

A pretty correct idea of our relative positions may
be formed if the unnautical reader will imagine our
small force to be placed in the nave of Westminster
Abbey, with the enemy attacking the great western
tower from the summit of a cliff 100 feet higher than
the tower, so that the breach in course of formation
nearly corresponded to the great west window of the
abbey. It will hence be clear that, in the face of a
determined opposition, it would be no easy matter to
scale the external wall of the tower up to the great

west window, and more difficult still to overcome impediments presently to be mentioned, so as to get down into the body of the church. These were the points I had to provide against, for we could neither prevent the French from breaching nor storming.

It so happened, that just at the spot where the breach was in process of formation, there was a lofty bomb proof interior arch, upwards of fifty feet in height. This arch, reaching from the lower part of the breach to the interior base of the tower, was without much difficulty converted into an obstacle, of which the French little dreamed; viz., into a chasm, down which they must have plunged headlong had they attempted to penetrate an inch beyond the outer wall, even after they had gained it.

The only operation necessary was to break in the crown of the arch, so that all who on an assault ventured on penetrating farther than the outer wall of the breach, must of necessity be hurled to the bottom. But as the fall of a portion of the enemy might not deter the rest from holding possession of the outer wall till they were provided with the means of overcoming the obstacle, I got together all the timber at hand, and constructed a huge wooden case, exactly resembling the hopper of a mill — the upper part being kept well greased with cooks' slush from the *Impérieuse*, so that to retain a hold upon it was impossible. Down this, with the slightest pressure from behind, the storming party must have fallen to a depth of fifty feet, and all they could have done, if not killed, would have been to remain prisoners at the bottom of the bomb proof.

The mantrap being thus completed,—and to do the Spaniards justice, they entered with ardour into the work,—the next object was to prepare trains for the explosion of the magazines, in case evacuation of the fort became compulsory. This was done in two places; the first deposit of powder being placed underneath the breach, with the port-fire so arranged, as to go off in about ten minutes; the other beneath the remaining part of the fortress, with a port-fire calculated to burn until we ourselves were safe on board the frigate.

The French were highly exasperated on finding that the castle had been reinforced from the *Impérieuse*, of which ship they had by this time not a few unpleasant reminiscences; they therefore adopted additional measures to put a stop to our cooperation.

In addition to the previously mentioned battery, another was erected on the cliff commanding the fortress; and on the 25th, upwards of 300 shots were directed at the tower, the result being a hole, which speedily widened into a tolerable breach. Our men were now engaged in blocking it up as fast as it was made, and working as they did under cover, no loss was sustained, though every shot brought down large masses of stone within the fortress; the French thus supplying us with materials for repair, though rendering a sharp look-out against splinters necessary.

On this day I received a wound, which caused me intolerable agony. Being anxious, during an ominous pause, to see what the enemy were about, I incautiously looked round an angle of the tower towards the battery overhead, and was struck by a stone splinter in the face ; the splinter literally forcing back my nose into the cavity of my mouth.   By the skill of our excellent doctor, Mr. Guthrie, my nose was after a time rendered serviceable.

Whilst the enemy were breaching the tower, the boats of the *Impérieuse* inflicted on them such severe chastisement, that detachments of infantry were stationed on the hills to drive off the boats with musketry; but our people managed to keep out of harm's way, whilst directing a destructive fire upon the nearer portion of our opponents.

On the 26th the French renewed their fire ; but as during the previous night we had filled up the breach with loose rubble, their progress was by no means rapid, the rubble forming almost as great an obstacle as did the wall itself.   It was, however, evident that the breach must sooner or later become practicable, so that we turned our attention to the erection of interior barricades, in case of a sudden attempt to storm.   In addition to these barricades festoons of top chains were brought from the ship, and suspended over the hopper and elsewhere ; the chains being moreover armed with large fishhooks, so securely fastened, that there was little danger of those who were caught, getting away before they were shot.

The barricades constituted what may be termed a rampart within the breach, constructed of palisades, barrels, bags of earth, &c., these supplying the place of walls, whilst the descent from the crown of the bomb-proof to the bottom, constituted a formidable substitute for a ditch.

We got to-day a trifling though welcome reinforcement of sixty regular Spanish, or rather Irish troops in the Spanish service, and sent an equal number of peasants to Rosas; for though these men were brave, as are all Catalans, and ready enough, yet their want of military skill rendered them ill adapted to the work in hand. As soon as the Irish comprehended our means of defence, and the reception prepared for the enemy, their delight at the prospective mischief was highly characteristic, and could not have been exceeded had they been preparing for a "scrimmage" in their native country.

At midnight the French made a general assault on the town of Rosas, and after several hours' hard fighting obtained possession. The *Impérieuse* and *Fame* now approached, and commenced a fire which must have caused great loss to the besiegers, but which failed to dispossess them. Towards morning — when too late — a detachment of 2000 Spanish troops arrived from Gerona! Six hours earlier would have saved the town, the preservation of which was the only object in retaining the fortress.

The practice of the French when breaching the walls of Rosas, was beautiful. So skilfully was their artillery conducted, that, to use a schoolboy similitude, every discharge "ruled a straight line" along the lower part of the walls; this being repeated till the upper portion was without support, as a matter of course, the whole fell in the ditch, forming a breach of easy ascent.

This operation constituted an object of great interest to us in the fortress, from which the whole proceedings were clearly visible.

Having secured the town, the French redoubled their efforts against the castle, and had they continued with the same vigour, we must have been driven out. Two of our marines were killed by shot, as was a third by a stone splinter, so that with all my desire to hold out, I began to doubt the propriety of sacrificing men to the preservation of a place which could not be long tenable.

The French being also heartily tired of the loss they were sustaining from the fire of the ships and boats, sent us a flag of truce, with the offer of honourable capitulation. This being declined on our part, the firing recommenced more heavily than before.

On the 28th the fire of the enemy slackened, their troops being engaged in throwing up intrenchments and constructing batteries in the town, a second detachment of Spanish troops being on its way now that the place had fallen. Soon after midday they sent a small party with another flag of truce. As it was, however, evident that their object was this time to spy out the state of our defences, we threw some hand grenades towards them, to show that we would not hold any parley, on which they retired, and the firing was again renewed.

On the 29th the French opened upon the castle from five different batteries on the hills, but without damage to life, as our men were now kept close. The ships and bombs, however, directed upon them a destructive fire with shot and shell, which considerably damped their ardour. To-day all access to the citadel was cut off, the French having succeeded in erecting batteries on both sides the sea gates, so that all communication with the boats was rendered impossible.

The dawn of the 30th might have been our last, but from the interposition of what some persons may call presentiment. Long before daylight I was awoke with an impression that the enemy were in possession of the castle, though the stillness which prevailed showed this to be a delusion. Still I could not recompose myself to sleep, and after lying for some time tossing about, I left my couch, and hastily went on the esplanade of the fortress. All was perfectly still, and I felt half ashamed of having given way to such fancies.

A loaded mortar, however, stood before me, pointed, during the day, in such a direction that the shell should fall on the path over the hill which the French must necessarily take whenever they might make an attempt to storm. Without other object than that of diverting my mind from the unpleasant feeling which had taken possession of it, I fired the mortar. Before the echo had died away, a volley of musketry from the advancing column of the enemy showed that the shell had fallen amongst them, just as they were on the point of storming.

Rushing on, their bullets pattered like hail on the walls of the fort. To man these was the work of a moment; for, as may be supposed, our fellows did not wait for another summons, and the first things barely discernible amidst the darkness were the French scaling ladders ready to be placed at the foot of the breach, with an attendant body of troops waiting to ascend, but hesitating, as though the unexpected shell from our mortar rendered them uncertain as to our preparations . for defence.   To the purposeless discharge of that piece of ordnance we owed our safety, for otherwise they would have been upon us before we even suspected their presence; and so exasperated were they at our obstinate defence, that very little attention would have been paid to any demand for quarter.   The French deserved great credit for a silence in their movements which had not even attracted the attention of the sentries on the tower.

Whilst the enemy were hesitating, we became better prepared, our men being ready at every point which commanded the breach.   It was not in the nature of the French to slink off on being detected.   In a few minutes on they came up the ladders, to the certainty of getting either into the mantrap, or of being hurled from the walls as fast as they came up, retreat being for a short time impossible, on account of the pressure from behind.   There was now just light enough for them to see the chasm before them, and the wall was crowded with hesitating men.   About forty had gained the summit of the breach, all of whom were swept off with our fire; whilst a crowd was waiting below for the chance of sharing the same fate.   Giving them no time for deliberation, several shells which had been suspended by ropes half-way down the wall, were ignited, our hand grenades were got to work, and these, together with the musketry, told

fearfully on the mass — which wavered for a few moments, and then retreated amidst the loud huzzas of
our fellows. The French, however, gallantly carried off
their wounded, though they were compelled to leave
the dead, who, till the following morning, lay in a heap
close to the foot of the tower.

Scarcely had we got rid of our assailants, when a
numerous body of troops came down from the hills
with muskets firing and drums beating, nothing doubting that their comrades were in possession of the
fortress. Our lads, having their hands now free,
returned their fire with excellent effect, dropping some
at every discharge; when at length, finding that the
assault had failed, and that we were able to offer
effectual resistance, the detachment retreated up the
hills as fast as they could, amidst the derisive cheer-
ing of our men.

The force which formed the storming party, consisted, as we afterwards learned from our prisoners,
of one company of grenadiers, two of carabineers, and
four of the voltigeurs of the 1st Light Regiment of
Italy, in all about 1200 men. They were gallantly led,
two of the officers attracting my especial attention.
The first was dropped by a shot, which precipitated
him from the walls, but whether he was killed or only
wounded, I do not know, probably wounded only, as his
body was not seen by us amongst the dead. The other
was the last man to quit the walls, and before he could
do so, I had covered him with my musket. Finding
escape impossible, he stood like a hero to receive the
bullet, without condescending to lower his sword in

token of surrender. I never saw a braver or a prouder man. Lowering my musket, I paid him the compliment of remarking, that so fine a fellow was not born to be shot down like a dog, and that, so far as I was concerned, he was at liberty to make the best of his way down the ladder; upon which intimation he bowed as politely as though on parade, and retired just as leisurely.

In this affair we had only three men killed — one of the marines and two Spaniards, another Spaniard being shot through the thigh and the Spanish governor of the fortress through the hand; there were, however, a few minor casualties. The total loss of the enemy, judging from the dead left behind — upwards of fifty — must have been severe. My determination not to quit the fortress was therefore increased, as there was every reason to be satisfied with the efficacy of my hopper trap and fish-hook chains. In short, it was impossible for any one to get over the one or through the other. Not a Frenchman had advanced beyond the outer wall.

After this the enemy did not molest us much, except with musketry, which did no damage, as our men were well under cover. They, however, turned their attention to the citadel, the Spanish garrison replying smartly to their fire. The Spaniards with us in the castle likewise behaved with great gallantry, as did the soldiers of the Irish brigades in the Spanish service, by whom the peasants before mentioned had been supplanted. Had the latter remained, the repulse of our assailants might have been more difficult, though equally certain.

On the 1st of December we passed a tolerably quiet day, the French being engaged in erecting a new battery, to annoy our boats when coming on shore, with which they appeared to content themselves.

The 2nd passed over in the same quiet way.

On the 3rd the troops in the citadel made a sortie apparently in the hope of dislodging the French from their intrenchments, and an obstinate engagement ensued, with considerable loss on both sides. By the time this was over, our friends on the hill had nearly completed another new battery, and were trying its effect on us somewhat unpleasantly, every shot knocking down great quantities of stone. A still more unpleasant circumstance was, that a heavy gale of wind had arisen, before which the *Impérieuse* was visibly dragging her anchors, and might be compelled to go to sea, leaving us to defend ourselves till her return.

On the 4th, the French opened all their batteries on the citadel, eleven of their guns being brought to bear upon the old breach elsewhere mentioned as never having been properly repaired. At this point an immense number of shot and shell were directed, and towards night a breach was nearly practicable. This operation against the citadel seeming decisive, the new battery on the hill began upon us in the castle with redoubled vengeance, and every shot told with effect ; the object no doubt being to storm both fortresses simultaneously on the following day.

An unfortunate accident occurred in the castle to-day. Five of our men were loading a gun, intended for employment against a body of French troops, who

were throwing up an intrenchment below us, with
the evident object of cutting us off from retreat or communication with the frigate; by some mischance the
gun exploded, blowing off the arms of a marine, who
died soon after, and knocking a seaman over the castle
wall, a depth of fifty feet. The poor fellow was taken
up by the boat's crew, and carried on board in a
dreadfully shattered condition.

At daylight on the 5th, the French again opened
their batteries on the citadel, and by 8 A.M. the breach
was quite practicable. A large body of troops had
assembled for the assault, but the firing suddenly ceased
on both sides, and from the number of men lounging
about the breach, it was clear that a capitulation was in
progress. Under these circumstances it became my
duty not to sacrifice our marines and seamen to the
mere excitement of fighting a whole army which could
now pay us undivided attention. We therefore began
to think of taking our departure, and getting our
baggage collected, we made signals to the *Impérieuse*
for all boats to be in readiness to take us off, if the
garrison in the citadel should capitulate. The battery
however, continued firing upon us as usual, and with
decisive effect on the tower. Without taking any notice
of this we laid trains ready for blowing up the fort.

Soon after our signals were made, the *Fame* and
*Magnificent* — the latter of which had recently come into
the anchorage — got under weigh and beat towards the
landing-place. Our signals having been also understood
by the French, the batteries overhead ceased firing,
and a number of troops approached to take possession.

At 11 A.M. we made the signal for the boats — the *Impérieuse* attending them close in shore.

We now commenced evacuating the fortress, sending down the troops of the Bourbon regiment first; the Irish brigade next, and our marines and seamen last. On the boats pulling in, the ships opened fire with shot and shell upon the French. We did not, however, receive any molestation from the latter, whilst our men went down the rope ladders out of the fort, and by one o'clock all were out of the castle except the gunner and myself, we having remained to light the portfires attached to the trains.

After this we got into the boats also unopposed, but the moment they pulled off from the shore the French opened upon us with musketry and round shot, fortunately without injury to any one. A stiff breeze now blowing, enabled the *Impérieuse* to get close in, so that we were soon on board.

The French having become practically acquainted with some of our devices were on their guard and did not take possession of the castle immediately on our quitting it, and it was lucky for them that they did not, for shortly after we got on board the first explosion took place, blowing up the portion of the fortress which they had been breaching; but the second train failed, owing, no doubt, to the first shock disarranging the portfire. Had not this been the case, scarcely one stone of the castle would have remained on another.

In the evening I directed the *Impérieuse* to get under weigh and stand towards Scalla, where we landed the Spanish troops. On the following morning the

*Fame* parted company for Lord Collingwood's fleet; and leaving the *Magnificent* at anchor with the bombs, we stood towards St. Philon, having the mortification of seeing the French flag flying over what remained of the Castle of Trinidad, which we had so pertinaciously endeavoured to defend, and failing in this, should have wholly destroyed but for the accident of the second port fire becoming out of order.

In the defence of this fortress, we lost only three killed and seven wounded; the loss of the Spaniards amounting to two killed and five wounded. Next to the thorough accomplishment of the work in hand my care was for the lives of the men. Indeed, it is matter of congratulation to me that no commander having gone through such service ever had fewer men killed. Lord St. Vincent on a former occasion gave this as a reason for not promoting my officers, but even a rebuff so unworthy failed to induce me to depart from my system of taking care of the men, the death of one of whom would have affected me more than the death of a hundred enemies, because it would, in my estimation, have been attributable to my own want of foresight.

The destruction of the French must have been very great. We who were cooped up in the fortress had only one collision with them, but in that they suffered fearfully, whilst we escaped scot free. But the fire of the ships must have told upon them to a great extent.

The subjoined letters from Lord Collingwood to the Secretary of the Admiralty constitute the only commendations I received for the services detailed in the preceding chapters.

*Extract of a letter from* Vice-Admiral Lord Collingwood *to the* Hon. W. W. Pole, *dated on board the* Ocean, *Dec.* 14, 1808.

" My letter of the 1st instant would inform you of the enemy having laid siege to the castle of Rosas, and of the measures taken by the British ships in that bay in aid of the Spaniards for its defence.   The *Scout* joined the squadron off Toulon on the 7th, and by her I received further accounts from Captain Bennett, of the *Fame,* of the progress the enemy was making against that important fortress.

" Captain Lord Cochrane has maintained himself in the possession of Trinity castle with great ability and heroism. Although the fort is laid open by the breach in its works, he has sustained and repelled several assaults, having formed a sort of rampart within the breach with his ship's hammock cloths, awnings, &c., filled with sand and rubbish.   *The zeal and energy with which he has maintained that fortress excites the highest admiration.   His resources for every exigency have no end.*   The Spanish governor of the castle is wounded and on board the *Meteor.*

" COLLINGWOOD."

This expression of opinion on the part of Lord Collingwood should have procured me some commendation from the Naval authorities at home ; the more so as it was spontaneous on his lordship's part, no official despatch from me on the subject having at that time reached him.   I was, however, a black sheep at the Admiralty, and, had it been my good fortune to have been instrumental in raising the siege of Rosas, the only care taken by the Tory Government at home would, in all probability, have been how to conceal a knowledge

of the fact from the public.    After the evacuation and
destruction of the fortress I addressed to Lord Collingwood the subjoined despatch.

"H. M. Ship *Impérieuse*, Bay of Rosas,
5th Dec. 1808.

" My Lord, — The fortress of Rosas being attacked by an
army of Italians in the service of France (in pursuance of discretionary orders which your lordship gave me, to assist the
Spaniards whenever it could be done with most effect), I
hastened here.  The citadel on the 22nd instant was already half
invested, and the enemy was making his approaches towards
the south-west bastion, which your lordship knows was blown
down last war by the explosion of a magazine and tumbled
into the ditch ; a few thin planks and dry stones had been
put up by the Spanish engineers, perhaps to hide the defect ;
all things were in the most deplorable state without and
within ; even measures for their powder and saws for their
fuses were not to be had, and mats and axes supplied their
place.    The castle of Trinity, situated on an eminence, but
commanded by heights, was also invested.    Three 24-pounders
battered in breach, to which a fourth was afterwards added,
and a passage through the wall to the lower bomb-proof
being nearly effected on the 23rd, the marines of the *Fame*
were withdrawn.  I went to examine the state of the castle,
and, as the senior officer in the bay had not officially altered
the orders I received from your lordship, I thought this a
good opportunity, by occupying a post on which the acknowledged safety of the citadel depended, to render them an
effectual service.    The remaining garrison consisted of about
eighty Spaniards, who were on the point of surrendering ;
accordingly, I threw myself into the fort with fifty seamen
and thirty marines of the *Impérieuse*.    The arrangements I
made need not be detailed to your lordship ; suffice it to say,
that about a thousand bags (made of old sails), besides barrels
and palisades, supplied the place of walls and ditches, and

that the enemy, who assaulted the castle on the 30th with full 1000 picked men, were repulsed with the loss of their commanding officer, storming equipage, and all who had attempted to mount the breach. The Spanish garrison having been changed, gave good assistance. As to the officers, seamen, and marines of this ship, the fatigues they underwent, and the gallant manner in which they behaved, deserve every praise. I must, however, particularly mention Lieutenant Johnson, of the navy, Lieutenant Hore, of the marines, Mr. Burney, the gunner, Mr. Lodowick, the carpenter, and Messrs. Stewart, Sloven, and Marryat, midshipmen.

" Captain Hall, of the *Lucifer*, at all times and in every way gave his zealous assistance. I feel also indebted to Captain Collens, of the *Meteor*, for his aid.

" The citadel of Rosas capitulated at twelve o'clock this day. Seeing, my lord, farther resistance in the castle of Trinity useless, and impracticable against the whole army, the attention of which had naturally turned to its reduction ; after firing the trains for exploding the magazines, we embarked in the boats of the *Magnificent, Impérieuse,* and *Fame.*

" I have the honour to be, &c.<br>(Signed)     " COCHRANE.

" The Rt. Hon. Lord Collingwood."

LORD COLLINGWOOD's *Letter to the Admiralty.*

" H. M. Ship *Ocean*, Jan. 7. 1809.

" SIR, — The *Impérieuse* having with other ships been employed in the Bay of Rosas, to assist the Spaniards in defending that fortress, and Captain Lord Cochrane having taken on himself the defence of Trinity Castle, an outwork of that garrison, I have received from him a letter, dated the 5th of December, a copy of which is enclosed, stating the surrender of Rosas by the Spaniards on that day, and of his having embarked the garrison of Trinity Castle on board his ship from the castle destroyed.

"The heroic spirit and ability which have been evinced by Lord Cochrane in defending this castle, although so shattered in its works, against the repeated attacks of the enemy, is an admirable instance of his lordship's zeal; and the distinguished conduct of Lieutenants Johnson and Hoare, of the Royal Marines, and the officers and men employed in this affair under his lordship, will, doubtless, be very gratifying to my Lords Commissioners of the Admiralty.

(Signed, &c.)     "COLLINGWOOD.

"To the Secretary of the Admiralty."

To these despatches I may be pardoned for appending the following extract from the *Gerona Gazette*, as it appeared in the Naval Chronicle of 1809.

### LORD COCHRANE.

The Spanish *Gerona Gazette*, when inserting a letter from Lord Cochrane, January 1, 1809, subjoins the following liberal testimony to his noble conduct:—

"This gallant Englishman has been entitled to the admiration and gratitude of this country from the first moment of its political resurrection. His generosity in co-operating with our earliest efforts, the encouragement we received from the interest he took with the commanders of the Balearic islands, to induce them to succour us with troops and ammunition, can never be erased from our recollection. The extraordinary services which we owe to his indefatigable activity, particularly this city and the adjacent coast, in protecting us from the attempts of the enemy, are too well known to be repeated here. It is a sufficient eulogium upon his character to mention, that in the defence of the castle of Trinidad, when the Spanish flag, hoisted on the wall, fell into the ditch, under a most dreadful fire from the enemy, his lordship was the only person who, regardless of the shower of balls flying about him, descended into the ditch, returned with the flag, and happily succeeded in placing it where it was."

Without any degree of egotism, I may — considering that no praise beyond Lord Collingwood's was ever awarded to me for my defence of Trinidad — be excused from adducing the following remarks, known to be from the pen of Sir Walter Scott.

"Thus, in consequence of our cooperation, were the French detained a whole month before a neglected and ill provided fortress, which, without that cooperation, could not have resisted the first attack.   The event might have been different had there been a floating army off the coast — the whole of the besieging force might then have been cut off.   Of the errors which the English Government committed in the conduct of the Spanish war, the neglect of this obvious and most important means of annoying the enemy, and advantaging our allies, is the most extraordinary.   Five thousand men, at the disposal of Lord Cochrane or Sir Sidney Smith, or any of those numerous officers in the British Navy who have given undoubted proofs of their genius as well as courage, would have rendered more service to the common cause *than five times that number on shore*, because they could at all times choose their points of attack, and the enemy, never knowing where to expect them, would everywhere be in fear, and everywhere in reach of the shore in danger.

"Lord Cochrane, during the month of September 1808, with his single ship the *Impérieuse*, kept the whole coast of Languedoc in alarm, — destroyed the numerous semaphoric telegraphs, which were of the utmost consequence to the numerous coasting convoys of the French, and not only prevented any troops from being sent from that province into Spain, but even excited such dismay that 2000 men were withdrawn from Figueras to oppose him, when they would otherwise have been marching farther into the peninsula. The coasting trade was entirely suspended during this alarm;

yet with such consummate prudence were all Lord Cochrane's enterprises planned and executed, that *not one of his men were either killed or hurt*, except one, who was singed in blowing up a battery."

For none of the services detailed in the last two chapters did I ever receive praise or reward from the Admiralty authorities! though from the nature of the services they were necessarily accompanied by the deprivation of all chance of prize money, either to myself, officers, or crew. The check opposed to the advance of the French in Catalonia — as testified by Lord Collingwood—was therefore made at *my expense*, without costing a farthing to the nation beyond the expenditure of ammunition ; a strange contrast to some of the costly expeditions of the period for less results, and one which ought to have secured for me anything but the political animosity with which all my services were regarded.

# CHAP. XVIII.

## CRUISE OF THE *IMPÉRIEUSE* CONTINUED.

DEFEAT OF THE SPANIARDS.—ATTACK SOME FRENCH VESSELS.—FRENCH
OPERATIONS.—LETTER OF LORD COCHRANE.—LORD COLLINGWOOD.—
OPERATIONS OF THE ENEMY.—FALL IN WITH THE CYRENE.—SAIL
FOR MINORCA.—APPLY FOR LEAVE.—MOTIVES FOR LEAVING.—
APATHY OF THE GOVERNMENT.—REPROACHED FOR SERVICE.—NEG-
LECT OF THE ADMIRALTY.

WHEN in the roads of St. Philou, on the 7th of January,
a boat came off with a request from the Spanish commandant that I would reconnoitre the enemy's position in the direction of Gerona. I had, at first, considerable doubts whether compliance with a request to
act in a military capacity came within the sphere of a
naval officer's duty; but considering that Lord Collingwood's instructions were to aid the Spaniards by
any means within my power, I resolved for once to
forego my reluctance to leave the frigate, and accordingly accompanied the commandant and his staff in the
direction of the enemy, whom we found assembled in
such numbers as to render successful opposition out of
the question.

Being unable to advise the Spaniards in this locality
to adopt any beneficial course, or indeed how to act in

any effective way against the enemy, we again sailed
in the direction of Barcelona, where a Spanish force of
40,000 men, under General Vives, was closely invest-
ing the town, so as to cut off supplies from the French
garrison.  As the consequent scarcity of provisions
affected the inhabitants also, all who could afford to
hire boats were quitting the place with their families;
the garrison offering no obstacle.

On the 17th, a body of French—or rather Italian
troops embodied in the French army—made their
appearance for the purpose of relieving the garrison.
As they numbered only about 10,000, and the Spaniards
fully 40,000, posted on the top of a hill, with every
advantage in their favour, the defeat of the Franco-
Italians appeared so much a matter of course as to
induce me to go on shore to witness the engagement.

To my surprise, Vives allowed his flank to be turned,
and the French attacking in front and rear at the same
time the Spaniards became panic-struck, and fairly ran
away.  The rout was complete; and it was with difficulty that I managed to get on board the frigate.

Shortly after gaining the ship, a boat full of officers
was seen to put off from the shore and make for the
*Impérieuse.*  On coming alongside, it was reported to
me that General Vives was amongst their number, on
which I returned a message expressive of disbelief;
adding that it could not be the general, for that to my
certain knowledge he was on shore, driving back the
French who were attempting to relieve Barcelona.
After some hesitation, General Vives personally avowed
himself, and demanded a conveyance for himself,

officers, and 1000 men to Tarragona; which demand
being flatly refused, they left for the *Cambrian*, which
lay at anchor not far off.

On the 19th we got under weigh, and soon after
fell in with a vessel bound for Palamos, and crowded
with families escaping from Barcelona, all of whom
bitterly complained of the shameful treatment they had
experienced at the hands of the French soldiery. On
the 21st we came to off St. Philou, which had just been
plundered of everything.

Nothing material occurred till the 30th, when, beating up towards Caldagues Bay, we received intelligence
that several French vessels, bound to Barcelona with
provisions for the relief of the French army, were at
anchor there. To attack these, as we had reason to
believe that there was a considerable body of the enemy
at Caldagues, and as the harbour was not more than
half a mile broad, was a dangerous affair, on account
of the necessity of anchoring within point-blank range
of musketry. It was, however, of great importance
that the provisions should not reach their destination,
and, in place of waiting for them to proceed on their
voyage, I decided on attacking them as the convoy lay
at anchor.

At mid-day we were close to the entrance of the
harbour, and made out the convoy and two vessels of
war in charge of them, the whole being protected by
a battery and a number of French troops on the
hills. Bringing the *Impérieuse* to an anchor we commenced firing on the vessels of war, one of which
shortly afterwards sank; when directing our attack on

her consort, she also sank and fell on her broadside, the crew escaping on shore.

The protecting vessels being thus disposed of, we warped closer in shore for the purpose of silencing some guns which whilst engaged in sinking them had repeatedly struck us. In order to divide the enemy's attention, a party of marines was despatched to make a feint of landing near the town, whilst with the other marines and the blue jackets we dashed on shore between the former and the French who were still firing on us from the battery. The latter, seeing the double attack and afraid of being cut off from their comrades in the town, ran off to the hills, abandoning their guns, which, on landing, we threw over the cliff, with the exception of four brass 18-pounders and one 24-pounder, which were taken on board the *Impérieuse*. We then blew up the magazine.

The coast being now clear, all boats were sent in to bring out eleven vessels laden with provisions, and by dark they were all close alongside, with our marines safely on board. They had, indeed, met with no opposition, the French troops in the town having run away and joined their comrades on the hills, the whole shortly afterwards marching in the direction of Rosas. During this affair the inhabitants remained quiet spectators on the hills—afraid to assist us, lest the French, who were certain to return on our departure, should retaliate after their usual fashion.

On the 31st we made an effort to raise the vessels of war which had sunk in shallow water near the shore, and after some time, succeeded in stopping the leak of the one which had fallen over on her broadside, and was full of water, which being pumped out she floated and was towed alongside the frigate.

By this time a number of Spanish boats from the neighbouring coast came in, and without ceremony set to work plundering our prizes! It was not till after some rough treatment from a party of marines sent for the protection of the captured vessels, that the Spaniards were made to comprehend that the prizes belonged to us and not to them!

Towards midnight the Spaniards gave us information that the French, with reinforcements from Rosas, were on the point of re-entering the town. We therefore sent a party of marines on board the brig-of-war to protect her from recapture.

Early in the morning of the 1st of January 1809, the enemy opened upon the brig with a smart fire of musketry, which the marines as smartly returned, — the frigate and a gun in the pinnace meanwhile plying the assailants with grape so effectually that they immediately abandoned their position, and marching round a hill, commenced firing from the other side, where, as the movement was anticipated by the frigate, they met with a similar reception immediately on showing themselves. Finding us fully prepared at all points, they followed the example of their predecessors, and retreated to the hills, offering no further opposition, whilst we were engaged in weighing the other vessel of war, in which we succeeded also. As soon as the French saw that they could not save either of these vessels, they abandoned the victuallers, and again marched off in the direction of Rosas.

The 2nd was employed in repairing our prizes, and in getting off other brass guns found on shore. On the 3rd we blew up the barrack and another magazine close to the town, without any further interference on the part of the enemy. Our operations being now completed, the smallest vessel of war was despatched to Lord Collingwood, off Toulon, with the following account of our success.

" His Majesty's Ship *Impérieuse*, Caldagues,
2nd January, 1809.

" My LORD, — Having received information of two French vessels of war, and a convoy of victuallers for Barcelona being in this port, I have the honour to inform your lordship, that they are all — amounting to thirteen sail — in our possession.

" The French have been driven from the tower of Caldagues with the loss of nine cannon, which they had mounted or were mounting on the batteries.

" I have the honour, &c.
" COCHRANE.

" The Right Hon. Lord Collingwood."

" *La Gauloise*, cutter, 7 guns and 46 men, commanded by Mr. Avanet, Member of the Legion of Honour.
" *La Julie*, lugger, 5 guns, 4 swivels, 44 men, commanded by Mr. Chassereau.
" And eleven victuallers."

In consequence of which his lordship was pleased to write to the Admiralty as follows : —

" *Copy of a Letter from* Vice-Admiral Lord Collingwood, *Commander-in-Chief of His Majesty's ships and vessels in the Mediterranean, to the* Hon. W. W. Pole, *dated on board the* Ocean, *at sea, the 6th of May* 1809.

" Sir, — I inclose — to be laid before their Lordships — a letter I have received from Lord Cochrane, captain of his Majesty's ship *Impérieuse*, who has been for some time past employed on the coast of Catalonia, and where the good services of his lordship in aid of the Spaniards and in annoyance of the enemy could not be exceeded.

" I have, &c.

" Collingwood."

Having put to sea with our prizes, except the smallest, which we gave to the Spaniards,— the *Impérieuse* stood, on the 9th of January, towards Silva, anchoring in that port at 4 P.M.  Observing a battery of ten guns mounted ashore, we landed, rolled them into the sea, and afterwards demolished the battery without opposition.

On the 10th, the Spaniards gave us intelligence of a large detachment of French troops being on their march from Rosas.  Anticipating much the same kind of opposition as we had experienced at Caldagues, the marines were directed to take possession of the hill on which the demolished battery had been placed, and soon afterwards the enemy was seen advancing in three divisions.  Shortly before reaching the hill, they halted and reconnoitred, after which they filed off towards the opposite mountain, and piled their arms in sight of the ship.

About noon they were reinforced by great numbers, and the whole advanced down the hill, their skirmishers keeping up a brisk fire upon our marines. As it was impossible for these to hold their position against such numbers, and as there was no particular object in so doing, it became necessary to embark them, for which purpose the boats had been placed in readiness. On the first appearance of the reinforcement, the French reentered their battery, but only to find the iron guns thrown in the sea and the brass ones in our possession. Exasperated at this, they opened upon us so heavy a fire of musketry that we were glad to get off as fast as we could, with the loss of three men.

Scarcely had we pushed off, when they manned a lower battery, which we had not had time to destroy—but though they fired very smartly, we had only two men wounded. It was fortunate we took precautions to reembark the marines in time—five minutes later would have lost us half their number, and we might have been compelled to leave some of the wounded. It was no less fortunate that, from the entrance being high and narrow, I had, before anchoring in a passage so exposed, taken the precaution of laying out a kedge to seaward, with something like a mile of coir rope attached, to be used in case of emergency. Hauling on this, we were quickly out of reach of the battery, but again anchored just within our own range of the enemy, when the frigate reopened her fire with shot and shell, keeping up an intermitting cannonade till after nightfall.

We learned in a curious way that the principal portion of the troops who attacked us were Swiss! About midnight a boat was reported alongside with a letter from the commandant of the troops with which we had been engaged. Wondering what he could want with me, I opened the letter, and found it to contain a rigmarole account of himself and the extraordinary achievements of his regiment, which belonged to some canton whose name I forget ; the letter concluding with a request for a few *bottles of rum ! !* I sent him the rum, together with a reply not very complimentary to his country or present occupation.

On the 11th some of our missing men got on board, and reported that the French had received still larger reinforcements, with heavy artillery, of which, indeed, we had ample proof, they having this morning got their guns to bear so accurately, that almost every shot struck us, so that it became necessary to display the better part of valour, and be off. The wind, unluckily for us, had died away, but a southerly air at length springing up, we put our prisoners ashore, and stood out of the bay, anchoring on the following day at Caldagues.

It would be tedious to narrate the remainder of our cruise, which chiefly consisted in sailing along the Spanish coast, and firing upon French troops wherever they came within reach, this being principally in the vicinity of Barcelona.

On one occasion only did we make much havock amongst them, viz. on the 22nd. On the previous day we had been reconnoitring Barcelona, and fell in with the *Cyrene*. Whilst rounding a small promontory in company, we observed a foraging expedition of at least 5000 troops, with immense numbers of mules laden with provisions, — the spoil of the surrounding

country,—coming along a road close to the sea.    Both
ships immediately beat to quarters, and running well
within shot and shell range, commenced a heavy fire,
which told admirably on the troops and convoy, as was
evident from the disorder into which they were thrown.
After about two hours persevering,—though not continuous fire,—as from the strong breeze blowing, we
were occasionally carried past the enemy, and lost time
in regaining our position; the French abandoned their
line of march, and filed off into the interior, the ships
harassing their retreat with shells till they were out of
range.    The loss of the enemy on this occasion must
necessarily have been very severe.

On the 30th we joined Admiral Thornborough's
squadron of thirteen sail at Minorca.    On the following
day we received the unwelcome intelligence of Lieutenant Harrison's having been taken prisoner by the
French.    I had placed this excellent officer in command
of the man-of-war cutter taken with the French convoy
at Caldagues, and when off Tarragona he imprudently
went on shore with only two hands, to gain information
about us.    On landing he was immediately surrounded
by French troops, a body of whom was embarked in
boats to regain possession of his cutter, but by promptly
making sail she escaped.

Some time previous to this period I had applied to
the Admiralty for permission to return to England.
My reasons for the application were various, the osten-
sible ground being the state of my health, which had
in reality suffered severely from the incessant wear
and tear of body and mind to which for nearly two

years I had been exposed. A more urgent reason was
to get back to my place in the House of Commons,
in order to expose the robberies of the Admiralty
Courts in the Mediterranean, the officials of which
were reaping colossal fortunes at the expense of naval
officers and seamen, who were wasting their lives and
blood for official gain! The barefaced peculations of
these courts would be almost incredible, especially as
regarded the Maltese Court, were there not some living
at the present time who can testify to their enor-
mity. To such an extent was this now carried, that a
ship captured without cargo never yielded a penny to
the captors, the whole proceeds being swallowed up by
the Admiralty Court. With cargo, some trifling surplus
might remain, but what between pilfering and official
fees, the award was hardly worth the trouble of
capture

The effect of this upon the Navy generally was most
disastrous, and not upon the Navy only, but upon the
nation also, which had upwards of 1000 ships in commission without any result at all commensurable with
the expenditure. Captains were naturally disinclined
to harass themselves and crews for nothing, and avoided
making prizes certain to yield nothing but the risk
and trouble of capture, and which, in addition, might
bring them in debt, as was the result in my own case.

It will now be evident why I preferred harassing
the French army in Spain to making prizes for the
enrichment of the officials of the Maltese and other
Admiralty courts. It was always my aim to serve my
country before my own interests, and in this case I

judged it better to do so where the service could be
most effectual.    Prizes, of which the proceeds were
monopolised by a body of corrupt officials, neither
under the eye nor control of the government, were not
worth troubling ourselves about; so I determined on
a course of service where there were no prizes to take,
but abundance of highly interesting operations to be
undertaken.    The frigate's officers and crew willingly
seconding my views, I now — more on their account
than my own — put on record that *none* of the services previously narrated, though lauded by the admirals commanding them, and by historians subsequently, were ever rewarded, either as regarded myself, or any one under my command, even promotion
to the officers being shamefully withheld; their fault,
or rather misfortune, consisting in having served under
my command.

My chief motive, however, for wishing to return to
England was, that during our operations against the
French on the Spanish coast, I had seen so much of
them as to convince me, that if with a single frigate I
could paralyse the movements of their armies in the
Mediterranean—with three or four ships it would not
be difficult so to spread terror on their Atlantic shores,
as to render it impossible for them to send an army
into Western Spain.    My object then was—as from
long and unceasing experience I considered myself entitled to the command of more than one ship — to
propose to the Government to take possession of the
French islands in the Bay of Biscay, and to let me
with a small squadron operate against the enemy's sea-

board there, as I had previously done with the *Speedy* and *Impérieuse*, from Montpellier to Barcelona.

Had this permission been granted, I do not hesitate to stake my professional reputation that *neither the Peninsular war, nor its enormous cost to the nation, from* 1809 *onwards, would ever have been heard of.* It would have been easy — *as it will always be easy in case of future wars* — that is, provided those who have the direction of national affairs have the sagacity to foresee disaster, and, *foreseeing it, to take the initiative,* so to harass the French coast as to find full employment for their troops at home, and thus to render any operations in Western Spain, or even in foreign countries, next to impossible.

By members not aware of this power of harassing an enemy's coast by means of a few frigates, the ministry was greatly blamed for not having sent a military force to Catalonia, instead of despatching the very inadequate force under Sir John Moore to the western shores of the Peninsula. That the latter step was a great mistake, likely only to end in disaster, is now admitted. But what I contend for is, that no military force was at all needed in Spain, had the government seized and held, by a comparatively small military force, the isles on the coast of France, viz., Isles Dieu, Rhe, Olerôn, and a few others ; following up or preceding this seizure by a limited number of active frigates harassing the whole western coast of France, which, in consequence, would not have been able to send a single regiment into Spain, and hence, as has been said, we should have had no Peninsular war with its hundreds of millions of

national debt. Had the French been thus employed in
the defence of their own coasts, the Spaniards on the
west coast would have been a match for their enemies,
as, with the assistance of a few small British frigates,
they were rendered a match for them on the east coast.
This was the work I was prepared to recommend to
the British Government; considering, moreover, that
from the part the *Impérieuse* had taken in harassing
the enemy on the east coast of Spain, I was fairly entitled to ask that any small squadron of frigates, appointed for the purpose of operating on the west coast
of France, should be placed under my command.

How my plans for this end, and together with them,
my own career as a naval officer, were sacrificed by an
occurrence which forms the subject of the next chapters,
will there be seen.

The reader will by this time have gathered some
idea of what the *Impérieuse* had effected, as testified
by the warmly expressed satisfaction of Lord Collingwood; yet it will scarcely be believed that, in place of
approbation, I was reproached for the expenditure of
more sails, stores, gunpowder, and shot than had been
used by any other captain in the service!

Attention to saving ropes and sails, though without
other results, was praised. Expending them, though
in energetic service, remarked with displeasure. Nothing that I had done was deemed worthy of notice
at home, whilst officers who brought back their ships
in as good condition as they left port, were honoured
with praise and substantially rewarded; but no mark
of approbation or reward was ever conferred on me till

twenty years afterwards, on my restoration to the rank of which I had infamously been deprived, Sir James Graham generously remedied the injustice by conferring upon me the ordinary good service pension. A comparison of my services with the services of those who were rewarded with pensions of 1000*l.* and 1200*l.* a year, will show the actuating principle of the Admiralty of that day, which bestowed on me nothing but marked neglect.

# CHAP. XIX.

## APPOINTMENT TO COMMAND FIRE-SHIPS IN BASQUE ROADS.

UNDERTAKING AGAINST ROCHEFORT.—HOPES EXCITED.—PRESENT MYSELF AT THE ADMIRALTY. — AM CONSULTED BY LORD MULGRAVE.—LORD GAMBIER'S STATEMENT. — ANXIETY OF GOVERNMENT. — MY PLAN OF ACTION. — DECLINE THE COMMAND. — THE COMMAND PRESSED UPON ME. — RETURN TO THE IMPÉRIEUSE. — PREPARATIONS FOR ATTACK. — LORD GAMBIER OBTAINS THE LAURELS,—BUT DISSUADES THE ATTACK. — THE ISLE D'AIX. — LORD GAMBIER'S STATEMENT.

ALMOST immediately after arrival of the *Impérieuse* at Plymouth, I received the subjoined letter from the Hon. Johnstone Hope, Second Lord of the Board of Admiralty :—

"Admiralty, March 21, 1809.

"MY DEAR LORD, — I congratulate you on your safe arrival after the fatigues you underwent at Trinity. Be assured your exertions there were highly applauded by the Board, and were done most ample justice to by Lord Collingwood in all his despatches.

"There is an undertaking of great moment in agitation against Rochefort, and the Board thinks that your local knowledge and services on the occasion might be of the utmost consequence, and, I believe, it is intended to send you there with all expedition; I have ventured to say, that if you are in health, you will readily give your aid on this business.

"Before you can answer this I shall be out of office, and

on my way to Scotland, as I found I could not continue here and keep my health. But if you will write to Sir R. Brotherton in reply, and state your sentiments on the getting at the enemy at Rochefort, I am sure it will be kindly taken.

<blockquote>
"I am, my dear Lord, your's faithfully,

"W. Johnstone Hope.

"Captain Lord Cochrane."
</blockquote>

On the receipt of this letter hope appeared to dawn. The St. Vincent or any other official *animus* against me had evidently been satisfied with the punishments with which I had in one shape or other been visited. I was now to be consulted and employed on matters in which my experience and services were to be fully recognised, and my ambition of being ranked amongst those brave defenders of my country, to whose example I had looked up, was about to be fulfilled! Alas, for the simplicity of my ideas! Nothing could be further from the intention of those who wanted to consult me!

Scarcely had the letter reached me, when a telegraphic message was transmitted from the Admiralty, requiring my immediate presence at Whitehall. A brief narrative of recent events will show the reason for the summons.

Early in the year Lord Gambier had been appointed to blockade the French fleet at Brest. Towards the end of February they, however, contrived to elude his vigilance, and got out without leaving a trace as to the direction taken. Despatching Admiral Duckworth in pursuit, his lordship returned to Plymouth. Admiral Duckworth meanwhile reached Cadiz, where he ascertained that the Brest fleet had not entered the

Mediterranean.   He then ran for Madeira, in the hope of obtaining intelligence of them, should they, as was feared in England, have made for the West Indies.

The fact was that the French squadron, consisting of eight sail of the line and two frigates, had gone to L'Orient, and liberated the ships there blockaded.  They next made for Isle d'Aix, intending further to reinforce themselves with the ships at that anchorage, and thence proceed to harass our West India colonies.  By the vigilance of Admiral Stopford they were, however, disco-vered and thwarted as to their ultimate purpose, though successful in forming a junction with the Rochefort squadron.   On finding Admiral Stopford in their vicinity, though with four ships of the line only, they put into Basque Roads, subsequently withdrawing into Aix Roads, where Admiral Stopford having been reinforced, blockaded them with seven ships of the line. On the 7th of March Lord Gambier arrived in Basque Roads with an additional five sail, several frigates and small vessels, the British squadron being now numeri-cally superior to that of the enemy.

On presenting myself at the Admiralty, the First Lord (Mulgrave) did me the honour to consult me confidentially as to the practicability of destroying or disabling the French squadron as it lay at anchor under the protection of the batteries of Isle d'Aix, where, as his lordship told me, the commander-in-chief did not consider it prudent to attack them.   Lord Mulgrave further stated that the Board of Admiralty, fearing that " the French fleet might again slip out, as it had done at Brest, were extremely desirous that it should forthwith be destroyed.  With that view they had already consulted various naval officers on the practicability of accomplishing the object by means of fire-ships ; but that their opinions were discouraging."

" Now," added his lordship, " you were some years ago employed on the Rochefort station, and must, to a great extent, be practically acquainted with the difficulties to be surmounted.  Besides which, I am told that you then pointed out to Admiral Thornborough some plan of attack, which in your estimation would be successful.  Will you be good enough again to detail that or any other plan, which your further experience may suggest.  But first let me tell you what Lord Gambier has written to the Admiralty on the subject."

Lord Mulgrave then read me an extract from Lord Gambier's letter, to the following effect, that " an attack by means of fire-ships was hazardous, if not desperate;" but that "if the Board of Admiralty wished to order such an attack, it should be done secretly and quickly."

I respectfully reminded his lordship that he was asking me to suggest means for an attack which the admiral commanding considered " hazardous, if not desperate ; " and which other naval officers, no doubt my seniors in the service, had pronounced impracticable. On both these accounts there was reason to fear that if means suggested by me were adopted, the consequence would be an amount of ill-feeling on the part of those officers, which any naval officer in my position should feel reluctant to provoke.

Lord Mulgrave replied that " the present was no

time for professional etiquette.   The Board was, if possible, bent on striking some decisive blow before the French squadron had an opportunity of slipping out ; for if their sailing were not prevented they might get off to the West Indies, and do our commerce an immense amount of mischief.   However," added his lordship, " there is Lord Gambier's letter.   Give me your opinion on it."

As this letter was afterwards made public, there can be no reason for withholding it.

" *Caledonia*, off the Nertuis d'Antioche,
" 11th March, 1809.

" MY DEAR LORD, — The advanced work between the Isles of Aix and Oleron, which I mentioned in my last letter, I find was injured in its foundation, and is in no state of progress ; it is, therefore, no obstacle to our bombarding the enemy's fleet, if you should be disposed to attempt to destroy it.

" A trial was made six years ago, when a Spanish squadron lay at the same anchorage, but without effect.   The report of it you will find in the Admiralty.   It was made by Sir C. Pole.

" The enemy's ships lie much exposed to the operation of fire-ships, *it is a horrible mode of warfare, and the attempt hazardous, if not desperate;* but we should have plenty of volunteers for the service.   If you mean to do anything of the kind, it should be with secrecy and quickly, and the ships used should not be less than those built for the purpose — at least a dozen, and some smaller ones.

" Yours, my dear Lord, most faithfully,
" GAMBIER.

" The Right Hon. Lord Mulgrave."

" You see," said Lord Mulgrave, " that Lord Gambier will not take upon himself the responsibility of attack, and the Admiralty is not disposed to bear the *onus* of failure by means of an attack by fire-ships, however desirous they may be that such attack should be made."

It was now clear to me why I had been sent for to the Admiralty, where not a word of approbation of my previous services was uttered. The Channel fleet had been doing worse than nothing. The nation was dissatisfied, and even the existence of the ministry was at stake. They wanted a victory, and the admiral commanding plainly told them he would not willingly risk a defeat. Other naval officers had been consulted, who had disapproved of the use of fireships, and, as a last resource, I had been sent for, in the hope that I would undertake the enterprise. If this were successful, the fleet would get the credit, which would be thus reflected on the ministry; and if it failed, the consequence would be the loss of my individual reputation, as both ministry and commander-in-chief would lay the blame on me.

I had, however, no fear of failure in the plans at that moment uppermost in my mind, but from the way in which my co-operation was asked, I determined to have nothing to do with the execution of the plans, believing that I should have to deal with some who would rather rejoice at their failure than their success.

My reply to Lord Mulgrave, therefore, was, that " the opinion of Lord Gambier, and the naval officers consulted by the Admiralty, as to the use of fire-ships, coincided with my own; for if any such attempt were made upon the enemy's squadron, the result would in all probability be, that the fire-ships would be boarded

by the numerous row-boats on guard,—the crews murdered,—and the vessels turned in a harmless direction.
But that if, together with the fire-ships, a plan were
combined which I would propose for his lordship's
consideration, it would not be difficult to sink or scatter
the guard-boats, and afterwards destroy the enemy's
squadron, despite any amount of opposition that might
be offered.  I further told Lord Mulgrave that my
opinion agreed with the expression of Lord Gambier,
that the fortifications on Isle d'Aix were " no obstacle;"
though this opinion on my part was expressed for
different reasons to the one assigned by his lordship,
my own previous knowledge of the anchorage satisfying
me that the channel was of sufficient breadth to enable
an attacking force to interpose the enemy's fleet
between itself and Isle d'Aix, as well as to keep out of
reach of the fortifications on Aix, even though those
fortifications might be in a state of efficiency, in place
of being "no obstacle," from their dilapidated condition, as Lord Gambier had, no doubt, correctly described them.

I then briefly recapitulated to his lordship the outline
of my plan, which, if seconded by the fleet, must certainly result in the total destruction of the French
squadron.  His lordship appeared very much gratified
by the communication, and after praising its novelty and
completeness, frankly expressed his entire confidence in
the result, requesting me to put the substance of my
suggestion in writing, so that he might at once lay it
before the Board of Admiralty, which was then sitting.

The request was immediately complied with, and the

letter placed in the hands of Lord Mulgrave, who shortly afterwards personally communicated to me his own satisfaction, and the entire concurrence of the Board in my plan. His lordship at the same time asked me " if I would undertake to put it in execution ? "

I told him that " for reasons before assigned I would rather not do so, as being a junior officer, it would excite against me a great amount of jealousy. Besides which, Lord Gambier might consider it presumptuous on my part to undertake what he had not hesitated to describe as ' hazardous, if not desperate.' It was, moreover, by no means certain that Lord Gambier would be satisfied to put my plans in execution, as it was not impossible that he might deem them still more ' desperate' and 'horrible' than those to which he had already objected. I, however, assured his lordship that the plans were at the service of the Admiralty, and Lord Gambier also, irrespective of any share in their execution to which I might be considered entitled."

" But," objected his lordship, " all the officers who have been consulted deem an attack with fire-ships impracticable, and after such an expression of opinion, it is not likely they would be offended by the conduct of fire-ships being given to another officer who approved of their use."

My answer was, " that the plan submitted to his lordship was not an attack with fire-ships alone, and when its details became known to the service, it would be seen that there was no risk of failure whatever, if made with a fair wind and flowing tide.

On the contrary, its success on inspection must be evident to any experienced officer, who would see that as the enemy's squadron could not escape up the Charente, their destruction would not only be certain, but, in fact, easy. The batteries on Isle d'Aix were scarcely worth notice, not so much from their dilapidated condition, though that was rightly estimated in Lord Gambier's letter, as from there being plenty of room to steer clear of them, as well as from the ease with which the enemy's ships might be brought between the fortifications and the ships attacking; the channel being sufficient for this purpose, as well as for their passage without any exposure to shot likely to be detrimental. As all this would be apparent to the officers of the fleet whenever the plan submitted should be communicated to them, I must emphatically repeat my objection to undertake its execution, not only on this ground, but for the additional reason that my health had been so much shattered by recent exertions as to require repose.

Lord Mulgrave did not deny the reasonableness of my objections, admitting that " although he did not believe Lord Gambier would feel hurt at my undertaking to put my own plan in execution, other officers might not be well pleased that its superintendence should be committed to a junior officer. On this ground he would reconsider the matter, and endeavour to find some one else to put it in execution."

I then took leave of Lord Mulgrave, who, next day, again sent for me, when he said, " My lord, you must go. The Board cannot listen to further refusal or delay. Rejoin your frigate at once. I will make you all right with Lord Gambier. Your own confidence in the result has, I must confess, taken me by surprise, but it has increased my belief that all you anticipate will be accomplished. Make yourself easy about the jealous feeling of senior officers, I will so manage it with Lord Gambier, that the *amour propre* of the fleet shall be satisfied."

On this I requested a short time for final consideration, and before its expiration sent a letter to his lordship again declining the command; but at the same time informing him that it had ever been a maxim with me not to shrink from duty to my country under any circumstances, however disadvantageous to myself, and that if officers my seniors could not be found to put the project in execution, I would then waive further objection.

The immediate result was the following letter from Lord Mulgrave, who, contrary to the tenour of mine, had construed it into an unqualified acceptance of the command.

[Private.]

" Admiralty, March 25, 1809.

" My dear Lord, — The letter I have just received from your lordship is truly characteristic of the whole tenour of your professional life. If your health will admit of your undertaking the important service referred to, I am fully persuaded that I cannot so well commit it to any other hands.

"I have the honour to be, with the highest esteem,
" Your lordship's most faithful servant,
" Mulgrave.

" The Lord Cochrane."

" P. S. I think the sooner you go to Plymouth the better. You will there receive an order to join Lord Gambier, to whom a secret letter will be written, directing him to employ your lordship on the service which we have settled against the Rochefort fleet."

I have been thus minute in detailing the circumstances connected with my acceptance of a command so unusual, because it has been said, and for anything that has appeared to the contrary, may still be considered, that I thrust myself into the position, which, as my own foresight had anticipated, became eventually a very serious one for me, as bringing upon my head an amount of enmity, such as even my own misgivings had not considered possible.

Having made the requisite suggestions to Lord Mulgrave relative to the contents and mode of fitting up the explosion vessels, the fire-ships to be employed being of the usual description, I returned on board the *Impérieuse* at Plymouth, there to await further orders from the Admiralty.

Such was the despatch used, that by the 19th of March the Board was in a position to apprise Lord Gambier of the steps taken, by the following letter addressed to his lordship by the Board of Admiralty.

" Admiralty Office, March 19th, 1809.

" MY LORD, — I am commanded by my Lords Commissioners of the Admiralty to acquaint you lordship, that they have ordered twelve transports to be fitted as fire-ships, and to proceed and join you off Rochefort; and that Mr. Congreve (afterwards Sir W. Congreve) is under orders to proceed to your lordship in a coppered transport (the *Cleveland*), containing a large assortment of rockets, and supplied with a detachment of marine artillery, instructed in the use of them, and placed under Mr. Congreve's orders.

" That the vessels named in the margin (*Etna*, *Thunder*, *Vesuvius*, *Hound*, and *Fury*), are likewise under orders to fit for sea with all possible expedition, and to join you as soon as they may be ready. That all preparations are making with a view to enable your lordship to make an attack upon the French fleet at their anchorage off Isle d'Aix, if practicable; and I am further commanded to signify their Lordships' directions to you, to take into your consideration the possibility of making an attack upon the enemy, either conjointly with your line-of-battle ships, frigates, and small craft, fire-ships, bombs, and rockets — or separately by any of the above-named means.

" It is their Lordships' further direction, that you state to me for their information, whether any further augmentation of force of any description is in your opinion necessary to enable you to perform this service with full effect, that it may be prepared and forwarded to you without a moment's delay — their Lordships having come to a determination to leave no means untried to destroy the enemy's squadron.

(signed)        " W. W. POLE.

" The Right Hon. Lord Gambier."

Lord Gambier's reply to this intimation, that on the receipt of the above-mentioned appliances he would be expected to attack the French squadron, was, that " *if the Board* deemed an attack practicable, he would obey any orders with which they might honour him, however great might be the loss of men and ships." A plain declaration that he *still declined to take upon himself the responsibility of attack.*

It will be necessary to bear this fact in mind, as after

the attack was made, Lord Gambier, in his first despatch to the Admiralty, gave me credit for everything
but the success of my plan, and in his second despatch
*omitted my name altogether as having had anything
to do with either planning or executing it!!!* and in
the vote of thanks subsequently given to his lordship in parliament, the officers under my orders were
thanked, but no mention whatever was made of me,
either as having conducted, or even taken any part
in the attack, the whole merit of which was ascribed
to Lord Gambier, who was never nearer than nine miles
to the scene of action, as will subsequently appear.

Lord Gambier's answer to the previous letter from
the Board is, however, so material to the right understanding of the events which followed, that it will be
better to subjoin the whole of it.

> " *Caledonia*, in Basque Roads,
> " March 26th, 1809.

"Sir, — In obedience to their Lordships' directions to me,
contained in your letter of the 19th instant, I beg leave to
state that it is advisable that I should be furnished with six
gun-brigs in addition to those I may be able to collect of
such as are under my command; at present there are only
two at this anchorage. I shall, however, order the *Insolent*
and *Contest* to join me from Quiberon Bay; and I should
hope that the *Martial* and *Fervent* will shortly return from
Plymouth.

"It is proper I should state for their Lordships' information,
the position in which the French fleet is at present anchored
under the Isle d'Aix, that their Lordships may be able to
form a judgment of the success that may be expected to
attend an attack upon the enemy's fleet, in either of the
modes directed by their Lordships in your letter above-
mentioned.

" The enemy's ships are anchored in two lines, very near each other, in a direction due south from the Isle d'Aix, and the ships in each line not farther apart than their own length ; by which it appears, as I imagined, that the space for their anchorage is so confined by the shoalness of the water, as not to admit of ships to run in and anchor clear of each other. The most distant ships of their two lines are within point-blank shot of the works on the Isle d'Aix; such ships, therefore, *as might attack the enemy would be exposed to be raked by red-hot shot, &c. from the island, and should the ships be disabled in their masts, they must remain within range of the enemy's fire until they are destroyed* — there not being sufficient depth of water to allow them to move to the southward out of distance.

"The enemy having taken up their position apparently with the view not only to be protected by *the strong works on the Isle d'Aix*, but also to have the entrance of the Charente open· to them, that in case of being attacked by fire-ships and other engines of the kind, they can run up the river beyond the reach of them. The tide and wind that are favourable to convey this kind of annoyance to the enemy, serve equally to carry them up the river.

" With respect to the attempt that may be made to destroy the enemy's ships with shells, &c., I am not competent to give an opinion until it is ascertained whether the bombs can be placed within the reach of their mortars from the enemy's ships, without being exposed to the fire of the Isle d'Aix.

"I beg leave to add that, *if their Lordships* are of opinion that an attack on the enemy's ships by those of the fleet under my command is practicable, I am ready to obey any orders they may be pleased to honour me with, *however great the risk may be of the loss of men and ships.*

" I have the honour, &c.<br>" GAMBIER.

" The Hon. W. W. Pole."

I have marked some passages of this singular letter

in italics, for the purpose of showing their important bearing on subsequent events. On the 11th Lord Gambier had informed the Board of Admiralty—as to my own personal knowledge was the fact—that, " the advanced work on the Isle d'Aix was *no obstacle to bombardment.*" " Now," says his lordship, " *the ships attacking would, from the fire of this fort, be exposed to be raked by red-hot shot, and if disabled in their masts, must be destroyed.* In the former letter his lordship stated that the fort was *"injured in its foundations,* and in no state of progress." It is now characterised as " *the strong works* " on *the* Isle d'Aix.

That there was really little damage to be feared from these fortifications, either to ships or bombs, was afterwards corroborated by the fact, that when a partial attack only was reluctantly made, neither suffered from their fire, the result proving that these works had from the first been rightly characterised by Lord Gambier as " *forming no obstacle,*" though magnified into " strong works."

In my interview with Lord Mulgrave, I had stated to his lordship, that the works on the Isle d'Aix were no impediment, because of the facility with which the enemy's ships could be brought between the attacking British force and the fortifications, so as completely to interpose between the fire of the latter. Lord Gambier does not appear to have taken this view, but he completely proved its soundness by stating that the enemy's ships lay within point-blank shot of their own works, so as to expose them to the fire of their own forts on Aix, if these fired at all, whilst my previous knowledge of the anchorage made it a matter of certainty to me, that it was not difficult for the British fleet to place the enemy in such a position. Lord Gambier's assertion was one of the main points relied on in the subsequent court-martial, and his lordship's own letter just quoted is in direct contradiction to the evidence upon which he relied for acquittal.

A more singular declaration is made by his lordship, that if the enemy were attacked " by fire-ships and other engines of the kind, they could run up the river beyond their reach." In place of this the result, as will presently be seen, proved that the attempt to do so only ended in all runing ashore, with the exception of two, and they ultimately escaped up the river because they were not attacked at all! But we must not anticipate.

Had Lord Gambier been, as I was, from having previously blockaded Rochefort in the *Pallas*, practically acquainted with the soundings, he must have taken the same views that I had laid before Lord Mulgrave, and in place of writing to the Admiralty all sorts of evil forebodings to " men and ships," he would have seen that the attack, with the means indicated, was certain in effect, and easy of accomplishment.

# CHAP. XX.

WITHOUT waiting to convoy the fire-ships and explosion vessels, the *Impérieuse* sailed forthwith for Basque Roads in order to expedite the necessary arrangements, so that on their arrival, no time might be lost in putting the project in execution; a point on which the Board of Admiralty was most urgent, not more in a belligerent than a political point of view, for as has been stated, the public was dissatisfied that the enemy had been permitted to escape from Brest; whilst our West Indian merchants were in a state of panic lest the French squadron, which had escaped the vigilance of the blockading force before Brest, might again slip out, and inflict irretrievable disaster on their colonial interests, then the most important branch of our maritime commerce.

The *Impérieuse* arrived in Basque Roads on the 3rd of April, when I was received with great urbanity

by the commander-in-chief; his lordship without reserve communicating to me the following order from
the Admiralty:—

"Admiralty Office, 25th March, 1809.

"MY LORD, — My Lords Commissioners of the Admiralty
having thought fit to select Captain Lord Cochrane for the
purpose of conducting, under your lordship's direction, the
fire-ships to be employed in the projected attack on the
enemy's squadron off Isle d'Aix, I have their Lordships' commands to signify their direction to you to employ Lord
Cochrane in the above-mentioned service accordingly, whenever the attack shall take place; and I am to acquaint you
that the twelve fire-ships, of which you already had notice,
are now in the Downs in readiness, and detained only by contrary winds, and that Mr. Congreve is also at that anchorage,
with an assortment of rockets, ready to proceed with the
fire-ships.

"I am also to acquaint you that the composition for the
six transports, sent to your lordship by Admiral Young, and
1000 carcasses for 18-pounders, will sail in the course of
three or four days from Woolwich, to join you off Rochefort.

"I have, &c. &c.
"W. W. POLE.

"Admiral Lord Gambier."


Whatever might have been the good feeling manifested by Lord Gambier, it did not, however, extend
to the officers of the fleet, whose *amour propre* Lord
Mulgrave had either not attempted, or had failed to
satisfy. Every captain was my senior, and the moment
my plans were made known, all regarded me as an
interloper, sent to take the credit from those to whom it
was now considered legitimately to belong. "Why

could we not have done this as well as Lord Cochrane?" was the general cry of the fleet, and the question was reasonable; for the means once devised, there could be no difficulty in effectually carrying them out. Others asked, "Why did not Lord Gambier permit us to do this before?" the second query taking much of the sting from the first, as regarded myself, by laying the blame on the commander-in-chief.

The ill-humour of the fleet found an exponent in the person of Admiral Harvey, a brave Trafalgar officer, whose abuse of Lord Gambier to his face was such as I had never before witnessed from a subordinate. I should even now hesitate to record it as incredible, were it not officially known by the minutes of the court-martial in which it some time afterwards resulted. *

On ascertaining the nature of my mission, and that the conduct of the attack had been committed to me by the Board of Admiralty, Admiral Harvey came on board the flag-ship with a list of officers and men who volunteered, under his direction, to perform the service which had been thrust upon me. On Lord Gambier informing him that the Board had fixed upon me for the purpose, he said, " he did nót care ; if he were passed by, and Lord Cochrane or any other junior officer was appointed in preference, he would immediately strike his flag, and resign his commission ! "

Lord Gambier said he " should be sorry to see him resort to such an extremity, but that the Lords of the

---

* Minutes of a court-martial on Admiral Harvey, on board H.M.S. *Gladiator*, at Portsmouth, May 22nd, 1809.

Admiralty having fixed on Lord Cochrane to conduct the service, he could not deviate from their Lordships' orders."

On this explanation being good-naturedly made by Lord Gambier, Admiral Harvey broke out into invectives of a most extraordinary kind, openly avowing that "he never saw a man so unfit for the command of the fleet as Lord Gambier, who instead of sending boats to sound the channels, which he (Admiral Harvey) considered the best preparation for an attack on the enemy, he had been employing, or rather amusing himself with mustering the ships' companies, and had not even taken the pains to ascertain whether the enemy had placed any mortars in front of their lines; concluding by saying, that had Lord Nelson been there, he would not have anchored in Basque Roads at all, but would have dashed at the enemy at once."

Admiral Harvey then came into Sir Harry Neale's cabin, and shook hands with me, assuring me that " he should have been very happy to see me on any other occasion than the present. He begged me to consider that nothing personal to myself was intended, for he had a high opinion of me ; but that my having been ordered to execute such a service, could only be regarded as an insult to the fleet, and that on this account he would strike his flag so soon as the service was executed." Admiral Harvey further assured me, that " he had volunteered his services, which had been refused."

To these remarks I replied : " Admiral Harvey, the

service on which the Admiralty has sent me was none of my seeking. I went to Whitehall in obedience to a summons from Lord Mulgrave, and at his lordship's request gave the Board a plan of attack, the execution of which has been thrust upon me, contrary to my inclination, as well knowing the invidious position in which I should be placed."

" Well," said Admiral Harvey, " this is not the first time I have been lightly treated, and that my services have not been attended to in the way they deserved ; because I am no canting methodist, no hypocrite, no psalm-singer, and do not cheat old women out of their estates by hypocrisy and canting! I have volunteered to perform the service you came on, and should have been happy to see you on any other occasion, but am very sorry to have a junior officer placed over my head."

" You must not blame me for that," replied I ; " but permit me to remark that you are using very strong expressions relative to the commander-in-chief."

" I can assure you, Lord Cochrane," replied Admiral Harvey, " that I have spoken to Lord Gambier with the same degree of prudence, as I have now done to you in the presence of Captain Sir H. Neale."

" Well, admiral," replied I, " considering that I have been an unwilling listener to what you really did say to his lordship, I can only remark that you have a strange notion of prudence."

We then went on the quarter-deck, where Admiral Harvey again commenced a running commentary on Lord Gambier's conduct, in so loud a tone as to attract the attention of every officer within hearing, his observations being to the effect that "Lord Gambier had received him coldly after the battle of Trafalgar, that he had used him ill, and that his having forwarded the master of the *Tonnant's* letter for a court-martial on him, was a proof of his methodistical, jesuitical conduct, and of his vindictive disposition; that Lord Gambier's conduct, since he took the command of the fleet, was deserving of reprobation, and that his employing officers in mustering the ships' companies, instead of in gaining information about the soundings, showed himself to be unequal to the command of the fleet." Then turning to Captain Bedford, he said, "you know you are of the same opinion."

Admiral Harvey then left the ship, first asking Captain Bedford "whether he had made his offer of service *on any duty* known to the commander-in-chief?" To which Captain Bedford replied in the affirmative.

My reason for detailing this extraordinary scene, the whole of which, and much more to the same effect, will be found in the minutes of the court-martial previously referred to—is to show into what a hornets' nest my plans had involuntarily brought me. It may readily be imagined that I bitterly regretted not having persisted in my refusal to have anything to do with carrying them into execution, for now they were known, all believed,—and, being my senior officers, had no doubt a right to believe—that they could execute them better than myself.

So far as regarded the neglect to take soundings of even the approaches to the channel leading to the enemy's fleet, Admiral Harvey was quite right in his statement. Nothing of the kind had been attempted beyond some soundings on that part of the Boyart shoal, *farthest from the French fleet!* Had not my previous knowledge of the anchorage, as ascertained in the *Pallas* a few years before, supplied all the information necessary for my conduct of the plans proposed, this neglect would in all probability have been fatal to their execution. Unlike Admiral Harvey, I am not, however, prepared to blame Lord Gambier for the neglect, as a slight acquaintance with the masters, whose duty it was to have made the examination, showed me that they were quite capable of misleading the commander-in-chief, by substituting their own surmises for realities. Certain it was, that although no soundings whatever of the approaches to the enemy's fleet had been taken, those whose duty it was to have made them, as far as practicable, pretended to know more of the anchorage than I did!* and had, no doubt, impressed the commander-in-chief that their reports were founded on actual observations.

How far Admiral Harvey was justified in his intemperate allusions to the "*musters*" and *quasi* religious practices on board the fleet, is a point upon which I do not care to enter, further than to state that these "musters" were found to relate to catechetical exami-

---

* In the subsequent court-martial, one of these men constructed a chart of the soundings, as from his own personal knowledge, and in his verbal evidence said that he had never sounded at all ! His chart was, nevertheless, made the basis of the trial, to the exclusion of the official charts !

nations of the men, and that I had not been many days in the fleet before the commander-in-chief sent a number of tracts on board the *Impérieuse*, with an injunction for their distribution amongst the crew.

Having by this time ascertained that, rightly or wrongly, the fleet was in a state of great disorganisation on account of the orders given to various officers for the distribution of tracts, and being naturally desirous of learning the kind of instruction thereby imparted, I found some of them a most silly and injudicious character, and therefore declined to distribute them, but imprudently selected some, and sent them to my friend Cobbett, together with a description of the state of the fleet, in consequence of the tract controversy. It was a false step, though I did not at the time contemplate the virulent animosity which might be excited at home from Cobbett's hard-hitting comments, nor the consequent amount of enmity to myself, which only ceased with my eventual removal from the Navy!

The fact was, that the fleet was divided into two factions, as bitter against each other as were the Cavaliers and Roundheads in the days of Charles I. The above-mentioned imprudent step incurred the ill will of both parties. The tractarian faction, consisting for the most part of officers appointed by Tory influence or favour of the Admiral, and knowing my connection with Burdett and Cobbett, avoided me; whilst the opposite faction, believing that from the affair of the tracts I should incur the irreconcilable displeasure of Lord Gambier, lost no opportunity of denouncing me as a concocter of novel devices to advance my own interests at the expense of my seniors in the service.

Strange as it may appear, almost the only persons who treated me with consideration, were Lord Gambier, his second in command, Admiral Stopford, and his flag-captain, Sir H. Neale.

For this urbanity Lord Gambier had to incur the bitter sarcasm of the fleet — that when the Admiralty wanted to attack the enemy with fire-ships, he had denounced the operation as a " horrible and anti-Christian mode of warfare;" but that now he saw my plan of explosion vessels, in addition to fire-ships, was likely to be crowned with success, he no longer regarded it in the same light.

It was evident that amidst these contending factions, so fatal in a fleet where all ought to be zeal and unity of action—I should have to depend on myself. Disregarding, therefore, the disunion prevalent, and, indeed, increased four-fold by the further division of opinion with respect to Admiral Harvey's disrespectful expressions to the commander-in-chief, I determined to reconnoitre for myself the position of the French ships, especially as regarded their protection by the batteries on Isle d'Aix, and for this purpose made as minute a *reconnaissance* as was practicable.

Perhaps it ought to have been previously mentioned, that on the evening of our arrival, I had gone close in to the island, and had embodied the result of my observations in the following letter to Lord Mulgrave, to whom I considered myself more immediately responsible.

*" Impérieuse*, Basque Roads, 3rd April.

"My Lord, — Having been very close to the Isle d'Aix, I find that the western sea wall has been pulled down to build a better. At present the fort is quite open, and may be taken, as soon as the French fleet is driven on shore or burned, which will be as soon as the fire-ships arrive. The wind continues favourable for the attack. If your lordship can prevail on the ministry to send a military force here, you will do great and lasting good to our country.

"Could ministers see things with their own eyes, how differently would they act; but they cannot be everywhere present, and on their opinion of the judgment of others must depend the success of war — possibly the fate of England and all Europe.

"No diversion which the whole force of Great Britain is capable of making in Portugal or Spain, would so much shake the French government as the capture of the islands on this coast. A few men would take Oleron; but to render the capture effective, send twenty thousand men, who, without risk, would find occupation for a French army of a hundred thousand.

"The batteries on Oleron are all open, except two of no importance. Isle Gros would also be of infinite use to our cruisers in the destruction of the French trade.

"The commerce on this coast — and indeed on all the French coasts — is not inferior to that of England in number of vessels and men employed, though not in size of coasting craft.

The coasting trade is the great nursery of English seamen, and yet we strangely affect to despise the French coasting trade. Must not the corn of the French northern provinces give food to the south? Are the oil and wine of the south of no consequence to those who grow none for themselves? I do not state these matters to your lordship but as an answer to the opinions generally current in England, and, indeed, too much entertained in the naval service also.

"Ships filled with stones would ruin for ever the anchorage

of Aix, and some old vessels of the line well loaded would be excellent for the purpose.

"I hope your lordship will excuse the way in which I have jumbled these thoughts together. My intentions are good, and if they can be of any use, I shall feel happy.

"I have the honour to be, my Lord,

"Your most obedient servant,

"COCHRANE.

"The Right Hon. Lord Mulgrave."

In this hurried letter the reader will readily recognise the principles laid down by me in a former chapter, for the most advantageous mode of warfare, viz., by harassing the enemy on his own coast, and by a perpetual threat of a descent thereon at any moment, to prevent his employing his forces elsewhere.

In place of the advice being even taken in good part, I had afterwards reason to know, that the views briefly expressed in this letter, were regarded by the government as an act of impertinence. Yet nothing could be more sound. The French islands captured, and occupied by an adequate force, protected by a few ships, would have kept the enemy's coasts in a constant state of alarm, so that it would have been impossible for the enemy to detach armies to the Spanish peninsula; had this policy been pursued, the Peninsular war, as has been stated in a former chapter, and its millions of National Debt, would never have been heard of. So much does the useful or useless expenditure of war depend on the decision of a cabinet, which can practically know little of the matter.

As it was — the French laughed at the clouds of cruisers intent on watching their coasting trade, which was carried on almost without interruption ; our vessels going in shore in the day time, when the French coasters kept close under their batteries, and going off shore in the night, when they pursued their course unmolested. Provisions and stores were thus moved as wanted from one part of the enemy's coast to another, with absolute safety. The great number of prizes which had fallen to the lot of the *Speedy*, *Pallas*, and *Impérieuse* was almost solely owing to our working in shore at night, when the enemy's coasters were on the move. In the day time we are usually out of sight of land, with the men fast asleep in their hammocks.

The constant readiness at sea for an enemy who never willingly left port, was, in those days, a great evil, though it was the one point inculcated by the Admiralty. It would have been far more to the purpose to have inculcated the necessity of damaging and alarming the limited seaboard of France, by means of small frigates capable of running in-shore, and to have left the French fleets, whenever they ventured out, to the supervision of squadrons composed of large ships, and specially appointed for the purpose. From the hundreds of ships then in commission, traversing the seas with no advantage to themselves or the country, such an arrangement would have annihilated the commerce, and with it the naval power of France. In place of this, attention to the condition of ships was the most certain way to reward. As the men could not always be employed in exercising guns and furling sails, a system of cleaning and polishing was enforced, till it became positive cruelty to the crews.

If the reader will refer to a previous letter of Lord
Collingwood to the Board of Admiralty, he will fully
comprehend my meaning.   His lordship states that
Lord Cochrane's services on the coast of Languedoc
in the *Impérieuse* "kept the French coast in constant alarm, causing a total suspension of trade, and
harassing a body of troops employed to oppose him ;
he has probably prevented those troops, which were
intended for Figueras, from advancing into Spain, by
giving them employment in the defence of their own
coasts."  For "Figueras" read "Corunna," and it will be
evident, that had the same course been generally pursued on the Atlantic coasts of France, by order, or even
under the countenance of the Admiralty, Sir John
Moore would neither have retreated nor fallen ; because, from the occupation which the French army
would have found on its own coasts, he could not have
encountered one on the Spanish soil.

One of my principal objects in returning to England,
as has been said in a former chapter, was to impress
upon the government the efficiency of this mode of
proceeding on the Atlantic coasts of France, so as to
prevent reinforcements from being sent to their army
in the Peninsula.  The success of the *Impérieuse*, I
again repeat, warranted such an application on my part
to the Board of Admiralty, in the expectation of being
appointed to the command of an expedition to be carried into effect on this principle.

To return from this digression to the *reconnaissance*
of the enemy's works on Isle d'Aix.

The opinion which I had expressed to Lord Mulgrave respecting the trifling importance of these works, was strengthened on actual inspection; indeed any opposition which they could have offered was too insignificant for notice, as was afterwards proved when a partial attack took place.

I could not say as much to Lord Gambier, after the opinion he had expressed in his letter to the Admiralty, for this would have amounted to a flat contradiction of his judgment, even though, as was afterwards known, such opinion had been formed on the reports of others, who gave his lordship their surmises as ascertained facts, an assertion which will be hereafter fully demonstrated.

In place, therefore, of officially reporting the result of my *reconnaissance*, I urged upon his lordship not to wait the arrival of the fire-ships from England, but as the fleet had abundance of materials, rather to fit up, as fire-ships and explosion vessels, some transports which happened to be present.

With this request Lord Gambier promptly complied, manifesting his anxious desire that my project should be put in execution without delay. Several vessels were, therefore, chosen for the purpose; the fire-ships being prepared by the fleet, whilst I worked hard at the explosion vessels, two, at least, of which I determined to conduct personally; not because I deemed myself more competent to conduct them than others, but because, being novel engines of warfare, other officers could not have given that attention to their effect which long deliberation on my part had led me to anticipate, if directed according to the method on

which their efficacy depended; it being certain, even
from the novelty of such a mode of attack, that the
officers and crews of the line of battle ships would be
impressed with the idea that every fire-ship was an
explosion vessel, and that in place of offering opposition,
they would, in all probability, be driven ashore in their
attempt to escape from such diabolical engines of warfare, and thus become an easy prey.  The creation of
this terrorism amongst the enemy's ships, was indeed a
main feature of the plan, the destruction or intimida-
tion of the guard-boats being secondary, or rather
preparatory.

The nature of the explosion vessels will be best
understood from the subjoined description of the
manner in which one was prepared under my own
directions.  The floor of the vessel was rendered as
firm as possible, by means of logs placed in close contact, into every crevice of which other substances were
firmly wedged, so as to afford the greatest amount of
resistance to the explosion.  On this foundation were
placed a large number of spirit and water casks, into
which 1500 barrels of powder were emptied.  These
casks were set on end, and the whole bound round
with hempen cables, so as to resemble a gigantic mortar,
thus causing the explosion to take an upward course.
In addition to the powder casks were placed several
hundred shells, and over these again nearly three
thousand hand grenades; the whole, by means of
wedges and sand, being compressed as nearly as possible into a solid mass.

This was the vessel in which I subsequently led on

the attack. A more striking comment on the " red-hot shot," &c., of which Lord Gambier made so much in one of his letters to the Admiralty, could scarcely be found. Of course, had a red-hot shot from the batteries on Aix reached us — and they were not half a mile distant *— nothing could have prevented our being " hoist with our own petard." I can, however, safely say, that such a catastrophe never entered into my calculations, for the simple reason, that from previous employment on the spot, on several occasions, I well knew there was plenty of room in the channel to keep out of the way of red-hot shot from the Aix batteries, even if, by means of blue lights or other devices, they had discovered us.

The explosion vessels were simply naval mines, the effect of which depended quite as much on their novelty as engines of war, as upon their destructiveness. It was calculated that, independently of any mischief they might do, they would cause such an amount of terror, as to induce the enemy to run their ships ashore as the only way to avoid them and save the crews. This expectation was fully answered, but no adequate attack on the part of the British force following up the effect of the explosion vessels, the stranded ships were permitted to heave off, and thus escaped, for the most part, as will be detailed in the succeeding chapter.

* Admiral Allemand had given instructions to the commandant on the Isle d'Aix to use every precaution in case of the anticipated attack.

# CHAP. XXI.

ON the 10th of April, the *Beagle*, having arrived from England with the fireships in company, I pressed Lord Gambier to permit an attack to be made on the same night; but, notwithstanding that the weather was favourable, his lordship saw fit to refuse. My reason for pressing an immediate attack was, that as the enemy could not remain in ignorance of the character of the newly arrived vessels, they might have less time to make additional preparations for their reception.

Notwithstanding the importance of prompt action in this respect, argument was unavailing. His lordship urged that the fireships might be boarded, and the crews murdered, though there was more danger of this from delay, than from attacking unawares. There was in reality no danger; but I urged in vain that it was an essential part of my plan personally to embark in an explosion-vessel, *preceding* the fireships, so that in conducting and firing her all risk would fall on myself and the volunteer crew which would accompany me; it not being probable that after the explosion the enemy's guard boats would board the fireships which might follow, as every one would certainly be taken for a mine similarly charged. Under that impression, however gallant the enemy, there was little chance of the fireships being boarded.

His lordship replied, that "if I chose to rush on self-destruction that was my own affair, but that it was his duty to take care of the lives of others, and he would not place the crews of the fireships in palpable danger."

To this I rejoined, that there could not be any danger, for the use of explosion-vessels being new to naval warfare, it was unlikely that, after witnessing the effect of the first explosion, the enemy's officers and men would board a single fireship. I further told his lordship that my brother, the Hon. Basil Cochrane, and Lieut. Bissel were on board the *Impérieuse* as my guests, and so well satisfied were both of the little danger to be apprehended that they had volunteered to accompany me. Lord Gambier, however, remained firm, and further remonstrance being useless, I had no alternative but to delay, whilst the French, who quickly

became aware of the character of the newly arrived
vessels, adopted all necessary precautions.*

A most favourable opportunity was thus thrown
away. The French admiral, however, lost no time in
turning the delay to account, by altering the positions
of his fleet, so as to expose it to the smallest possible
amount of danger.

The enemy's ships of the line struck their topmasts,
got their topgallant yards on deck, and unbent sails, so
as to expose as little inflammable matter aloft as possible ; the frigates only being left in sailing trim, ready
to act as occasion might require ; whilst the boats and
launches of the fleet, to the number of seventy-three,
were armed and stationed in five divisions for the purpose of boarding and towing off the fireships.†

The French admiral, Allemand, disposed his force in
the following manner :—The ten sail of the line, which
before the arrival of the fireships had been moored in
two lines overlapping each other, were formed afresh

---

* " Le 10 il arriva 16 batimens, qui me parurent des transports
ou brulôts. Je fis dégréer le mats de perroquets, et caler ceux de
hune," &c. — Vice-Admiral Allemand's Despatch, of the 12th of
April.

† The subjoined was the French force at anchor in Aix roads:—
SHIPS OF THE LINE : L'Océan, 120, bearing the flag of Vice-
Admiral Allemand; Foudroyant, 80, bearing the flag of Rear-
Admiral Gourdon; Cassard, 74; Tourville, 74; Regulus, 74;
Patriote, 74 ; Jemappes, 74 ; Tonnerre, 74 ; Aquilon, 74 ; Ville de
Varsovie, 74. Total, 10.
FRIGATES : Indienne, Elbe, Pallas, and Hortense. Total, 4.
STORESHIP : Calcutta, 56, armed en flûte. This vessel had been a
British East Indiaman, captured some time before off St. Helena.
Total, 15.

in a double line, nearly north and south ; the outer line comprising five, and the inner six ships, including the *Calcutta;* the inner line being so anchored as to face the openings between the ships of the outer line, the extremity of which was somewhat more than a mile from the batteries on the Isle of Aix.    About half a mile in advance of the whole lay the four frigates, and immediately in front of these was a boom of extraordinary dimensions.    As this boom will form an important feature in the narrative, I subjoin the French admiral's description, first premising that, although there was reason to expect that an obstacle of the kind would have to be encountered, its exact nature was not known till the attack was made * : —

" Notre armée étoit sur deux lignes de bataille, endentées, très-serrées, gisant au nord, un quart nord-ouest et sud, un quart sud-est du monde, afin de présenter moins de surface à l'envoi des brûlots.

"Elle étoit flanquée *d'une estacade à quatre cents toises au large, qui avoit huit cents toises de long,* le bout nord étoit à une encablure et demie des roches de l'île.

" Au coucher du soleil il ventoit encore très-gros frais. *Je laissai chaque capitan libre de sa manœuvre pour la sûreté de son vaisseau.*

" J'envoyai un officier prévenir le général Bronard, commandant à l'île d'Aix, que l'ennemi, par sa manœuvre, annonçoit vouloir profiter du gros vent et de la marée pour

---

* A better proof of the subsequent untruths uttered by the masters of the fleet and the flagship, as to their pretended knowledge of the soundings in the vicinity of the enemy, could not be afforded, than their ignorance of the existence of this boom, which must from its magnitude have occupied a considerable time in its construction, and laying down the necessary moorings.

entreprendre un *coup de main.* Il me fit dire qu'il l'atten-
doit de pied ferme, et qu'il répondoit de la terre."—*Vice-
Admiral Allemand's Despatch of the* 12*th of April.*

The French, no doubt, considered their position
secure against fireships, having no expectation of other
means of attack ; and so it undoubtedly was, from the
protection afforded by the boom, which, from its peculiar
construction, could neither be destroyed nor burned by
fireships—as well as further defended by the guard-
boats, which were judged sufficient to divert the course
of such fireships as might drift past the boom.   Their
fleet was anchored so as to expose the smallest possible
front ; and what added no little to their sense of security
was the delay which had taken place on the part of
the British admiral without attack of any kind.   On
such grounds, therefore, they not unreasonably felt confident that, if the fireships failed, as from the judicious
preparations made, Admiral Allemand had every reason
to anticipate, no attack on the part of the British fleet
would follow.   In this belief, on altering their position,
the French dressed their fleet with flags, and, by way of
contempt for their assailants, hung out the English ensign
of the *Calcutta*—which, as has been said, was a captured English vessel—under her quarter gallery !   The
peculiar nature of the insult needs not to be explained
—to naval men it is the most atrocious imaginable.

The fortifications on Isle d'Aix, alluded to by Admiral Allemand, were, as Lord Gambier had reported to
the Admiralty in his letter of the 11th of March, insignificant, or, as his lordship at first expressed it, " no
obstacle ;" a dozen guns being the utmost number

mounted on the batteries commanding the roads, though these were afterwards characterised by his Lordship as the " strong works on the Isle of Aix." * The nearest of the batteries on *Oleron* was out of gun-shot, and therefore of no account.

As narratives of the attack on the French fleet in Basque Roads have been often, though in some of the main points incorrectly, written from the contradictory, and in many instances incomprehensible, evidence on the subsequent court-martial, as compared with the no less contradictory despatches of Lord Gambier, I shall in the following account strictly confine myself to what took place under my own personal conduct and observation.†

On the 11th of April, it blew hard with a high sea. As all preparations were complete, I did not consider the state of the weather a justifiable impediment to the attack, to which Lord Gambier had now consented ;

---

* Two ships of the line would have been quite sufficient to silence " the batteries on Aix."—*Captain Broughton's Evidence on the Court Martial.*

† The British force present in Basque Roads was as follows : —

SHIPS OF THE LINE: *Caledonia*, 120, bearing the flag of Lord Gambier; *Cæsar*, 80, bearing the flag of Rear-Admiral Stopford ; *Gibraltar*, 80; *Revenge*, 74 ; *Donegal*, 74; *Heron*, 74; *Illustrious*, 74; *Valiant*, 74 ; *Bellona*, 74 ; *Resolution*, 74 ; *Theseus*, 74. Total, 11.

FRIGATES : *Indefatigable, Impérieuse, Aigle, Emerald, Unicorn, Pallas*, and *Mediator*. Total, 7.

GUNBRIG SLOOPS : *Beagle, Dotterel, Foxhound, Lyra, Redpole.* Total 5.

GUN-BRIGS: *Insolent, Conflict, Contest, Encounter, Fervent,* and *Growler.* Total, 6.

OTHER VESSELS : *Whiting, Nimrod, King George,* and 23 fire-ships and explosion-vessels. Total, 55.

so that after nightfall, the officers who volunteered to command the fireships were assembled on board the *Caledonia*, and supplied with instructions according to the plan previously laid down by myself.

The *Impérieuse* had proceeded to the edge of the Boyart shoal, close to which she anchored with an explosion vessel made fast to her stern, it being my intention, after firing the one of which I was about to take charge, to return to her for the other, to be employed as circumstances might require. At a short distance from the *Impérieuse* were anchored the frigates *Aigle*, *Unicorn*, and *Pallas*, for the purpose of receiving the crews of the fireships on their return, as well as to support the boats of the fleet assembled alongside the *Cæsar*, to assist the fireships. The boats of the fleet were not, however, for some reason or other, made use of at all.

The enemy had calculated on the impending attack, and, as was afterwards ascertained, by way of precaution against fireships, sent two divisions of their guard boats, with orders to lie under the boom till two in the morning; but wind and tide being against them, they were compelled to put back, without effecting their orders. Both wind and tide, however, though dead against the French boats, were favourable for the boats of the British fleet, had they been employed as arranged; and they would have been of great use to the less efficient boats of the fireships, some of which, in returning, were nearly swamped. For want of such assistance, as will presently be seen, most of the fireships were kindled too soon, no doubt to save the men the terrible pull back, against a gale of wind and a high sea.

Having myself embarked on board the largest explosion vessel, accompanied by Lieut. Bissel and a volunteer crew of four men only, we led the way to the attack; the *Impérieuse* afterwards, in accordance with my instructions, signalising the fireships to " proceed on service."

The night was dark, and as the wind was fair, though blowing hard, we soon neared the estimated position of the advanced French ships, for it was too dark to discern them. Judging our distance, therefore, as well as we could, with regard to the time the fuse was calculated to burn, the crew of four men entered the gig, under the direction of Lieut. Bissel, whilst I kindled the port fires; and then, descending into the boat, urged the men to pull for their lives, which they did with a will, though, as wind and sea were strong against us, without making the progress calculated.

To our consternation, the fuses, which had been constructed to burn fifteen minutes, lasted little more than half that time, when the vessel blew up, filling the air with shells, grenades, and rockets ; whilst the downward and lateral force of the explosion raised a solitary mountain of water, from the breaking of which in all directions our little boat narrowly escaped being swamped. In one respect it was, perhaps, fortunate for us that the fuses did not burn the time calculated, as, from the little way we had made against the strong head wind and tide, the rockets and shells from the exploded vessel went over us. Had we been in the line of their descent, at the moment of explosion, our destruction, from the shower of broken shells and other missiles, would have been inevitable.

.The explosion vessel did her work well, the effect constituting one of the grandest artificial spectacles imaginable. For a moment, the sky was red with the lurid glare arising from the simultaneous ignition of 1500 barrels of powder. On this gigantic flash sub-siding, the air seemed alive with shells, grenades, rockets, and masses of timber, the wreck of the shattered vessel; whilst the water was strewn with spars, shaken out of the enormous boom, on which, according to the subsequent testimony of Captain Proteau, whose frigate lay just within the boom, the vessel had brought up, before she exploded. The sea was convulsed as by an earthquake, rising, as has been said, in a huge wave, on whose crest our boat was lifted like a cork, and as suddenly dropped into a vast trough, out of which, as it closed upon us with a rush of a whirlpool, none expected to emerge. The skill of the boat's crew, however, overcame the threatened danger, which passed away as suddenly as it had arisen, and in a few minutes nothing but a heavy rolling sea had to be encountered, all having again become silence and darkness.

This danger surmounted, we pulled in the direction of the *Impérieuse*, whose lights could be distinguished at about three miles' distance. On our way we had the satisfaction of seeing two fireships pass over the spot where the boom had been moored. Shortly afterwards we met the *Mediator* steering in the direction of the enemy, whose ships of the line were now firing towards the spot where the explosion had taken place, and consequently on their own advanced frigates! which, as was afterwards learned, cut their cables, and shifted their berths to a position in the rear of the larger ships.

On reaching the *Impérieuse*, I found, to my great mortification, that the second explosion vessel, which, by my orders, had been made fast to the frigate's stern, had been cut away, and thus set adrift; a fireship in flames having come down on her instead of the enemy! The *Impérieuse* herself had a narrow escape of being burned, and was only saved by veering cable; the fireship which caused the disaster drifting harmlessly away on the Boyart Shoal. This clumsy occurrence completely frustrated the intention with which I had reserved her, viz. for further personal operations amongst the enemy's fleet, now that the first explosion vessel had cleared the way.

Of all the fireships, upwards of twenty in number, *four only reached the enemy's position, and not one did any damage!* The way in which they were managed was grievous. The *Impérieuse*, as has been said, lay three miles from the enemy, so that the one which was near, setting fire to her, became useless at the outset; whilst several others were kindled a mile and a half to windward of this, or four miles and a half from the enemy. Of the remainder, many were at once rendered harmless, from being brought to on the wrong tack. Six passed a mile to windward of the French fleet, and one grounded on Oleron. · I could scarcely credit my own vision when I saw the way in which they were handled ; most of them being fired and abandoned before they were abreast of the vessels anchored as guides.

The fear of the fireships operated strongly enough, but, notwithstanding the actual effect attributed to them by naval historians, they did no damage whatever. A matter of little consequence, had the British fleet, or even a portion thereof, subsequently taken advantage of the panic created amongst the enemy.

As the fireships began to light up the roads, we could observe the enemy's fleet in great confusion. Without doubt, taking every fireship for an explosion vessel, and being deceived as to their distance, not only did the French make no attempt to divert them from their course, but some of their ships cut their cables and were seen drifting away broadside on to the wind and tide, — whilst others made sail, as the only alternative to escape from what they evidently considered certain. destruction from explosive missiles !

Had the commander-in-chief witnessed this scene, he would never again have deemed such extraordinary precaution on his part requisite to guard against fireships being boarded when preceded by explosion vessels. In place of becoming the aggressors, as his Lordship had anticipated, the only care of the enemy was how to get out of the way, even at the risk of running their ships ashore. Unfortunately the commander-in-chief was with the fleet, fourteen miles distant.

At daylight on the morning of the 12th not a spar of the boom was anywhere visible, and with the exception of the *Foudroyant* and *Cassard*, *the whole of the enemy's vessels were helplessly aground.* The former of these ships lying out of the sweep of the tide, and being therefore out of danger from the fireships, appeared not to have cut her cable, and the *Cassard*, which had at first done so, again brought up about two cables' length form the *Foudroyant*.

With these exceptions, every vessel of the enemy's fleet was ashore. The flag-ship of Admiral Allemand, *L'Océan*, three-decker, drawing the most water, lay outermost on the north-west edge of the Palles Shoal, nearest the deep water, where she was most exposed to attack; whilst all, by the fall of the tide, were lying on their bilge, with their bottoms completely exposed to shot, and therefore beyond the possibility of resistance.

The account given by the captain of the *Indienne*, French frigate, Captain Proteau, of the position of the grounded ships, will not be called in question. It is as follows :—" The *Indienne* aground on Port Aiguille, near the fort; the *Pallas* off Barques; the *Elbe* and *Hortense* on the Fontenelles; the *Tourville, Patriote,* and *Tonnerre*, as seen from the *Indienne*, in a line on the Palles Shoal; the *Calcutta, Regulus, Jemappes* on the extremity of that shoal; the *Varsovie* and *Aquilon* aground on Charenton; and the *Océan*, three-decker, close to the edge of the Palles."

We did not reach the *Impérieuse* till after midnight. At daylight observing seven of the nearest enemy's ships ashore, amongst which was the admiral's ship *L'Océan*, and a group of four others lying near her, in a most favourable position for attack, without the possibility of returning it, at 6 A.M. we signalised the admiral to that effect. As the *Impérieuse* at this time lay just within range of the batteries on Aix, which had commenced to fire upon us, we weighed, and stood in the direction of the fleet, letting go our anchor as soon as the ship was out of range. At 7 A.M. we signalised again, "*All the enemy's ships, except two, are on shore;*" this signal, as well as the former one, being merely acknowledged by the answering pennant; but, to our surprise, no movement was visible in any part of the fleet indicating an intention to take advantage of the success gained.

Reflecting that, from the distance of the British force from the stranded enemy's ships, viz. from twelve to fourteen miles, the commander-in-chief could not clearly be acquainted with their helpless condition, I directed the signal to be run up, "*The enemy's ships can be destroyed;*" this also meeting with the same cool acknowledgment of the answering pennant.

Not knowing what to make of such a reply, another signal was hoisted, "*Half the fleet can destroy the enemy.*" This signal was again acknowledged by the answering pennant, the whole fleet still remaining motionless as before. On this I made several telegraph signals, one of which was probably regarded as impertinent, viz. "*The frigates alone can destroy the enemy,*" though it was true enough, their ships aground being perfectly helpless. To my astonishment the answering pennant was still the only reply vouchsafed!

Eight and nine o'clock passed without any indica-
tion of movement on the part of the fleet, though the
tide was now fast rising, so that any ships sent to the
attack of the stranded vessels would have had the
flood-tide to go in and the ebb to return, after having
accomplished their destruction; whilst it was evident
that if not attacked, the same flood-tide would enable
the French ships aground to float and escape, with which
view some were heaving their guns and stores overboard. On ascertaining this, I again signalized, "*The
enemy is preparing to heave off;*" and entertaining no
doubt that the Commander-in-chief would not permit
such a catastrophe, the *Impérieuse* dropped her anchor
close to the Boyart Shoal, in readiness for any service
that might be required.

As much has been said respecting the alleged nar-
rowness of the channel leading to Aix Roads, by way
of excuse for the British fleet not having followed up
the advantage gained by the panic created on the previous night, from terror of the explosion vessels, I may
here mention, that on our coming to an anchor, a fort on
Isle d'Oleron commenced firing shells at us. As not
one of these reached us, the French gunners adopted the
expedient of loading their mortars to the muzzle, this
being evident from the fact that they now discharged
them by means of portfires, the men gaining a place of
security before the mortars exploded. Not a shell,
even thus fired, reached our position, a clear proof that
had the British fleet come to the attack, it could have
been in no danger from Oleron, though even these
distant batteries were afterwards brought forward as a
source of danger.

At 11 A.M. the British fleet weighed, and stood towards Aix Roads. By this time the *Océan*, three-decker, and nearest ships aground were busily employed in heaving off, with a view of making sail for the Charente!! The advance of our fleet had been too long delayed; nevertheless, as the bulk of the enemy's ships were still aground, good service might have been rendered. To our amazement, the British fleet, after approaching within seven or eight miles of the grounded ships, *again came to anchor about three and a half miles distant from Aix*, i.e. just out of range.

There was no mistaking the admiral's intention in again bringing the fleet to an anchor. Notwithstanding that the enemy had been four hours at our mercy, and to a considerable extent was still so, it was now evident that *no attack was intended* *, and that every enemy's ship would be permitted to float away unmolested and unassailed! I frankly admit that this was too much to be endured. The words of Lord Mulgrave rang in my ears, " *The Admiralty is bent on destroying that fleet before it can get out to the West Indies.*"

The motive of Lord Gambier in bringing the ships to an anchor being beyond doubt, I made up my mind, if possible, to force him into action by attacking the enemy with the *Impérieuse*, whatever might be the consequence. It was, however, a step not to be taken without consideration, and for some time I hesitated to carry out this resolution, in the hope that a

---

* Lord Gambier afterwards admitted, that as the object of their destruction seemed to be attained, there was no occasion to risk any part of the fleet!!!

portion, at least, of the British fleet would again weigh and stand in.

Noon passed. The *Océan*, three-decker, had now got afloat, and the group of four others on shore near her, seeing the British fleet anchor, proceeded with additional energy to heave off. From her position the three-decker, lying as she did on the edge of the shoal, nearest the deep water, ought to have been the easiest prize of the whole; for whilst she lay on her bilge, close to the most accessible part of the channel, even a single gunboat might have so riddled her bottom as to have prevented her from floating off with the rising tide !

The surprise of the enemy at seeing the fleet anchor was probably greater than my own. Before that, they had been making great exertions to lighten and heave off, but no sooner had the fleet brought up, than, seeing the possibility of escape, they strained every nerve to hasten the operation.

In place of the fleet, or even the frigates, a single bomb, which, being armed with a 13-inch mortar, could project her shells to a great distance, without being exposed to danger from shot, was ordered in to shell the ships aground. On my asking her commander, *"what attack was going to be made on the enemy by the fleet?"* he replied, that " he knew nothing further than that he was ordered to bombard the ships ashore." This was proof enough that no intention of attacking with the fleet, or any part of it, existed.

In despair, lest the ships still aground should also effect their escape, at 1 P.M. I ordered the anchor of the *Impérieuse* to be hove atrip, and thus we drifted stern foremost towards the enemy. I say "*drifted*," for I did not venture to make sail, lest the movement might be seen from the flagship, and a signal of recall should defeat my purpose of making an attack with the *Impérieuse ;* the object of this being to *compel* the commander-in-chief to send vessels to our assistance, in which case I knew their captains would at once attack the ships which had not been allowed to heave off and escape.

Had this means not been resorted to, *not a single enemy's ship would have been destroyed*, for all could have hove off almost without damage, and that, to all appearance, without the slightest attempt at molestation on the part of the British fleet. It was better to risk the frigate, or even my commission, than to suffer such a disgraceful termination to the expectations of the Admiralty, after having driven ashore the enemy's fleet ; and therefore we drifted by the wind and tide slowly past the fortifications on Isle d'Aix, about which the commander-in-chief had expressed so many fears in his last letter to the Board; but though they fired at us with every gun that could be brought to bear, the distance was too great to inflict damage.

Proceeding thus till 1.30 P.M., and then suddenly making sail after the nearest of the enemy's vessels escaping, at 1.40 P.M. the signal was run up to the peak of the *Impérieuse*, "*Enemy superior to chasing ship, but inferior to the fleet.*" No attention being paid to this signal, at 1.45 P.M. I again signaled, "*In want of assistance,*" which was true enough, being in a single frigate, close to several enemy's ships of the line.

As this signal, according to the code then in use, was coupled with the one signifying " *In distress,*" the signal officer on board the flagship thus interpreted it to the commander-in-chief; a circumstance which will require brief explanation.

In order to divert our attention from the vessels we were pursuing, these having thrown their guns overboard, the *Calcutta*, which was still aground, broadside on, began firing at us. Before proceeding further, it became, therefore, necessary to attack her, and at 1.50 we shortened sail, and returned the fire. At 2 the *Impérieuse* came to an anchor in five fathoms; and veering to half a cable, kept fast the spring, firing upon the *Calcutta* with our broadside, and at the same time upon the *Aquilon* and *Ville de Varsovie* with our forecastle and bow guns, both these ships being aground, stern on, in an opposite direction.

This proceeding — though there could be no doubt of our being " *In want of assistance,*" seeing that our single frigate, unaided, was engaging three line-of-battle ships — did not look much like being " *In distress,*" as the signal officer of the *Caledonia* had interpreted the signal; the nature of which could not, however, have deceived the commander-in-chief, who must have witnessed the circumstances under which the signal had been made by the *Impérieuse.*

After engaging the *Calcutta* for some time, and simultaneously firing into the sterns of the two

grounded line-of-battle ships, we had at length the
satisfaction of observing several ships sent to our assistance, viz. *Emerald, Unicorn, Indefatigable, Valiant,
Revenge, Pallas,* and *Aigle.* On seeing this, the captain
and crew of the *Calcutta* abandoned their vessel, of
which the boats of the *Impérieuse* took possession before the vessels sent to our " assistance " came down.

   On the subsequent court-martial, it was declared
that the *Calcutta* did not strike to the *Impérieuse,*
but to the ships sent to her assistance. This was
deliberately untrue; as proved beyond question by
the fact that the French government ordered a court-
martial on the captain of the *Calcutta,* Lafon, and
condemned him to be shot, clearly *for having abandoned his ship to inferior force.* The French did not
shoot any of the other captains for abandoning their
ships, and would not have shot Captain Lafon for
fighting his vessel as long as he could, and then
abandoning her to two line-of-battle ships and five
frigates. On the contrary, they would have highly
rewarded him, for saving his crew against such odds.
There cannot be a stronger proof, if proof in addition
to my word be wanted, that Captain Lafon abandoned
the *Calcutta* to the *Impérieuse,* and not to the line-of-
battle ships which came up afterwards, as was disgrace-
fully asserted.

   On the arrival of the two line-of-battle ships and the
frigates, the *Impérieuse* hailed them to anchor, or they
would run aground on the Palles Shoal, on the very
edge of which the *Impérieuse* had taken up her berth.
They anchored immediately, and commenced firing on

the *Calcutta*, *Aquilon*, and *Ville de Varsovie*. On this I signaled the *Revenge* and others to desist from firing, as the *Calcutta* had already struck to the *Impérieuse*, and we had at that time a boat's crew on board her.

On this they desisted, and turned their fire wholly on the other two vessels. At 3.30 P.M. the *Impérieuse* ceased firing, the crew being thoroughly exhausted by fatigue; whilst I was so much so, as to be almost unable to stand. My reason, however, for ordering the *Impérieuse* to cease firing was, that the ships sent to our assistance were more than sufficient to destroy the enemy which remained, and had they been sent in time—not to our "*assistance*," but for the more legitimate object of attacking the grounded ships — they were abundantly sufficient to have destroyed all those that got away.

At 5.30 P.M. the *Aquilon* and *Ville de Varsovie* struck.

Shortly afterwards, the *Calcutta* was set on fire, and in half an hour was burning furiously. At 6.0 P.M. the crew of the *Tonnerre*, which was not attacked, set fire to her, escaping in their boats. At 7.0 the *Tonnerre* blew up, and at 9.0 the *Calcutta* also, with an effect, from the large quantity of ammunition on board, almost equalling that of the explosion-vessels the night before. The *Calcutta* was the storeship of the French fleet.

It has been said, that my having rushed single-handed amongst the enemy's ships, and then hoisted the signal, "*In want of assistance*," was unjustifiable, as forcing the commander-in-chief to attack against his judgment. My answer to this is, that the expectations entertained by the Admiralty of destroying the enemy's fleet would not have been in any way carried out, had not this means been adopted; because, as has been said, not a ship belonging to the enemy would have sustained even the slightest damage from the measures of the commander-in-chief.

The fire-ships entrusted to my command had failed, not from any fault of mine, but of those who were entrusted with them. It was, then, a question with me, whether I should disappoint the expectations of my country; be set down as a *charlatan* by the Admiralty, whose hopes had been raised by my plan; have my future prospects destroyed; or force on an action which some had induced an easy commander-in-chief to believe impracticable.

Some proof has been given of the jealousy of a portion of the fleet towards me. Another instance of this occurred even after the two line-of-battle ships and the frigates came down. Perceiving that the shot from two sloops, or rather brigs, ordered to protect the *Etna* bomb, did not reach the enemy, from the long range at which she had anchored, I made the signal for them to close. As no signal was at hand to express brigs only, to the exclusion of frigates or larger vessels, I endeavoured to explain my meaning, that the signal was intended for the brigs, by firing towards them from the main-deck of the *Impérieuse*, the object of this being to *avoid giving offence* to my senior officers in command of the frigates and line-of-battle ships now present,

The signal " *to close* " in the same defective code expressing also " *to close the Admiral*," it was construed by my seniors into an insult to them, as arrogating to myself the position of chief-in-command, which was simply absurd; as, being my seniors, I had no power to order them, nor was I so ignorant of my duty as wantonly to usurp the functions of the commander-in-chief. Yet this at the time gave great offence, though afterwards satisfactorily explained to Lord Gambier.

I may here mention a singular incident which occurred some time after the *Aquilon* and *Ville de Varsovie* had struck, and after their officers and crews had been removed on board the British ships. The captain of the *Aquilon* having informed me that he had left his personal effects behind, I volunteered to take him on board in my boat and procure them. As we left the *Aquilon* a shot from a heated gun on board one of the vessels to which the French had set fire—the *Tonnerre*, if I recollect rightly—struck the stern sheets of the boat on which both he and I were sitting, and lacerated the lower part of the gallant officer's body so severely that he shortly afterwards expired.

Before daybreak on the following morning the officer of the watch called me, and reported that three lights were hoisted in the squadron outside. This proved to be a signal, afterwards reported to have been made by Admiral Stopford, for the recall of the ships that had been sent in on the previous evening! In obedience to this signal, they, at 4 A.M., got under weigh, having previously kindled the French line-of-battle ships *Aquilon* and *Ville de Varsovie;* an act for which there was not the slightest necessity, as they could easily have been got off. Fatigued, and mentally harassed as I was, I had neither time nor opportunity to protest against this wanton destruction; besides which, not knowing that the magazines of the burning ships had been drowned, my attention was directed to the preservation of the *Impérieuse*, which was in close proximity.

The two ships, *Foudroyant* and *Cassard*, had cut their cables and made sail, when on the previous evening the British fleet stood towards Aix Roads, but afterwards so unaccountably came to an anchor. On seeing this they shortened sail, but ran aground in the middle of the channel leading to the Charente.

It being clear to me that these ships were not in a fighting condition, I determined, notwithstanding the recall of the British vessels, to remain and attack them; considering the signal of recall to be addressed only to the ships sent to our assistance, which, in obedience to that signal, were working out of the inner anchorage without any attempt to destroy other ships which were clearly at their mercy. As they were passing out I hailed the *Indefatigable*, and asked the captain if he would go on one quarter of the three-decker (*l'Océan*), whilst the *Impérieuse* engaged the other? The reply was that " he would not, and that they *were going out to join the fleet.*"

To his infinite credit, Captain Seymour, of the *Pallas* (the present distinguished admiral, Sir George Seymour), hailed us to know " if he should remain with the *Impérieuse* ?" he being evidently as reluctant as myself to give up advantages so manifest. I replied, that if no orders had been given him to the contrary, I should be obliged to him so to do; whereupon the *Pallas* anchored, and four brigs, the *Beagle*, *Growler*, *Conflict*, and *Encounter*, followed her example.

We now commenced clearing the decks for further action, throwing overboard a boat which had been shot to pieces. The carpenters were then set to stop shot holes in the sides and decks, and the seamen to repair the rigging, and shift the fore-topmast which had been shot through. The brave, but unfortunate, captain of the *Calcutta* had, in our short action, inflicted on us an amount of damage which the forts on Aix and Oleron had in vain attempted to effect; neither the one nor the other having once touched us.

Whilst the refitting of the frigate was going on, I ordered our only bomb, the *Etna*, protected by the brigs, to fire on the enemy's Vice- and Rear-Admiral's ships, as well as on the *Foudroyant* and *Cassard*, which, having thrown all overboard, were now pressing sail to get up the Charente, thus taking on myself to commence the action anew, *after the auxiliary line-of-battle ships and frigates had retired!*

To my regret, a signal of recall was immediately hoisted on board the *Caledonia!* To this I replied by another, " *The enemy can be destroyed;*" of which no notice was taken. Shortly afterwards a boat brought me the following letter from Lord Gambier :—

" *Caledonia*, 13th of April.

" MY DEAR LORD,— *You have done your part so admirably that I will not suffer you to tarnish it by attempting impossibilities\**, which I think, as well as those captains who have come from you, any further effort to destroy those ships would be. You must, therefore, join as soon as you can, with the bombs, &c., as I wish for some information, which you allude to, before I close my despatches.

" Yours, my dear Lord, most sincerely,

" GAMBIER.

" Capt. Lord Cochrane."

" *P. S.*—I have ordered *three brigs and two rocket-vessels to join you*, with which, and the bomb, you may make an attempt on the ship that is aground on the Palles, or towards Ile Madame, but I do not think you will succeed; and I am anxious that you should come to me, as I wish to send you to England as soon as possible. You must, therefore, come as soon as the tide turns."

I felt deep regret at what must be considered as the evasions of this letter. First, Lord Gambier ordered me to come out of the anchorage and join the fleet! but evidently not choosing to take upon himself the responsibility of ordering me out, in opposition to my own views, he told me he would send some brigs with which I might attack vessels which his own neglect had permitted to escape up the Charente! and thirdly, I was ordered to come out as soon as the tide turned!

As the commander-in-chief's letter was thus inde-

---

\* In spite of this and other declarations arising from acts personally witnessed, though at many miles' distance, yet still within ken of the telescope, Lord Gambier, on his court-martial, stated that " I had done little beyond mischief!! "

cisive, I chose to construe it as giving me the option of remaining, and returned his lordship the following answer :—

> "*Impérieuse*, 13th April.
>
> "My Lord,—I have just had the honour to receive your Lordship's letter. We *can* destroy the ships that are on shore, which I hope your Lordship will approve of.
>
>> "I have the honour, &c.
>>
>>> "Cochrane.
>
> "The Right Hon. Lord Gambier."

At daylight on the 14th the enemy were still in the same condition, but with a number of chasse-marées quietly taking out their stores. Three of them were getting out their guns, evidently in expectation of certain destruction from the small vessels which remained after the line-of-battle ships and heavy frigates were recalled; and, had we been permitted to attack them *even now*, their destruction would have been inevitable.

In place of this, the recall signal was once more hoisted on board the *Caledonia*, to which I replied by the interrogatory signal, "*Shall we unmoor?*" considering that his lordship would understand the signal as a request to be permitted to resume the attack. I did not repeat the signal that the enemy could be destroyed, because, having conveyed to him by letter my opinion on that subject the day before, I thought a repetition of that opinion unnecessary,—the more so, as, from the enemy heaving overboard their guns, its soundness was more than ever confirmed.

In place of being ordered to attack, as from his lordship's previous letter I had every reason to expect, the recall signal was repeated, and shortly afterwards came the following letter :—

"*Caledonia*, 13th (14th) April.

"My dear Lord,—It is necessary I should have some communication with you before I close my despatches to the Admiralty. *I have, therefore, ordered Captain Wolfe to relieve you* in the services you are engaged in. I wish you to join me as soon as possible, that you may convey Sir Harry Neale to England, who will be charged with my despatches, or you may return to carry on the service where you are. I expect two bombs to arrive every moment, they will be useful in it.

"Yours, my dear Lord, most sincerely,

"Gambier.

"Capt. Lord Cochrane."

Here was a repetition of the same thing. I was ordered away from the attack, to " convey Sir H. Neale to England," or I " might return to carry on the service where I was," viz. after the enemy had got clear off, *and after being formally superseded in the service to which the Board of Admiralty had appointed me, by a senior officer whom I could not again supersede !!!*

There was, however, no evading Lord Gambier's letter this time without positive disobedience to orders, and that was not lightly to be risked, even with the Board's instructions to back me. I therefore returned to the *Caledonia,* and at once told Lord Gambier that the extraordinary hesitation which had been displayed in attacking ships helplessly on shore, could only have arisen from my being employed in the attack, in preference to senior officers. I begged his lordship, by way of preventing the ill-feeling of the fleet from becoming detrimental to the honour of the service, to set me altogether aside, and send in Admiral Stopford, with the frigates or other vessels, as with regard to him there could be no ill-feeling; further declaring my confidence that from Admiral Stopford's zeal for the service, he would, being backed by his officers, accomplish results more creditable than anything that had yet been done. I apologised for the freedom I used, stating that I took the liberty as a friend, for it would be impossible, as matters stood, to prevent a noise being made in England.

His lordship appeared much displeased; and making no remark, I repeated, " My Lord, you have before desired me to ' speak candidly to you,' and I have now used that freedom."

Lord Gambier then replied, " *If you throw blame upon what has been done, it will appear like arrogantly claiming all the merit to yourself.*"

I assured his lordship that I had no such intention, for that no merit was due, and told him that I had no wish to carry the despatches, or to go to London with Sir Harry Neale on the occasion, my object being alone that which had been entrusted to me by the Admiralty, viz. to destroy the vessels of the enemy.

His lordship, however, cut the matter short by giving me written orders immediately to convey Sir Harry Neale to England with despatches. In obedience to this order we quitted Basque Roads for Plymouth on the following morning.

These matters are officially on record, and therefore do not admit of dispute. I will not comment further upon them, but will leave them to the judgment of posterity. I will even go further, and acquit Lord Gambier of all blame up to this period, except that of an easy disposition, which yielded to the advice of officers interested in my failure that calm judgment which should characterise a commander-in-chief, and which, had it been exercised, would have rendered, as Napoleon afterwards said, the whole French fleet an easy prey.

As much misrepresentation was made at the time relative to the damage inflicted by the explosion-vessel under my immediate command, and as the same misrepresentation has been adopted by all English historians, it will be necessary particularly to advert to this. As mere assertion on my part may be deemed egotistical, if not partial, I will adduce the testimony of Captain Proteau, who commanded the enemy's frigate *Indienne*, and was *close to the boom* at the time it was destroyed by the explosion-vessel. The point here alluded to is the statement of the commander of the *Mediator*, that HIS VESSEL BROKE THE BOOM BY HER WEIGHT!! and Lord Gambier, without any personal knowledge of the fact, was thereby led to endorse his statement.

The captain of the *Indienne*, on the other hand, states that when the explosion-vessel blew up she was " *at the boom*," or, nautically speaking, " *brought up by the boom*." His words, are " *flottant à l'estacade*."

It will be best, however, to extract the passage entire :—

"Nous distinguâmes, à 9 heures et demie, sous notre bous-
soir de tribord, un corps *flottant à l'estacade*. L'explosion
s'en fit tout-à-coup, et vomit quantité de fusées artificielles,
grenades et obus, qui éclatèrent en l'air sans nous faire le
moindre mal, cependant nous n'en étions qu'à une demie
encâblure." — *Captain Proteau's Journal*.

As the *Indienne* was only half a cable's length from
the boom when the explosion took place, the testimony
of her captain on this point ought to be decisive.

Lord Gambier stated in his despatch, and afterwards
in his defence, that the explosion-vessel blew up at
half-past nine, whilst at three-quarters past nine (*a
quarter of an hour later*), the *Mediator* and other
vessels came up, and were fired on by the French
ships !

Lord Gambier, being himself more than a dozen miles
from the scene of action, made this statement on the
authority of Captain Wooldridge, who commanded the
*Mediator*, and who reiterated in his evidence on the
court-martial the statement he had previously made
to Lord Gambier, viz. that *his ship*, and not the explosion-vessel, broke the boom : of the truth of which
statement the nautical reader shall judge on professional grounds.

Admiral Allemand, who commanded in Aix Roads,
thus describes, in his despatch to the French Government, the boom which had been laid down by his
directions : — "Elle (the French fleet) étoit flanquée
*d'une estacade à quatre cents toises au large, qui avoit
huits cents toises de long*."

The boom formed two sides of a triangle, with the apex towards the British fleet, thus,—

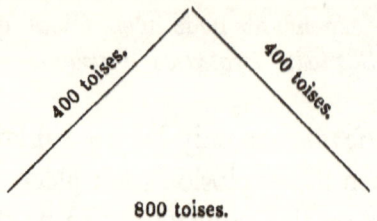

That is to say, each wing of the boom was more than half a mile long, and the distance between the extremities of the base was nearly a mile. This formidable obstacle was composed of large spars, bound by chains, and moored along its whole double line with heavy anchors at appropriate intervals, forming the most stupendous structure of the kind on record.

The statement of Captain Wooldridge to Lord Gambier, therefore, amounts to this,—that his ship, the *Mediator*, an Indiaman of 800 tons, broke up a double boom, each side of which was upwards of half a mile in length; tore up, at a single blow, a double line of heavy anchors more than a mile in extent; and snapped many miles of iron chains and lashings connecting the spars together!!!—though her contact could not have been more than a few feet, the collision necessarily taking place on one wing of the boom only. This was Captain Wooldridge's own version to Lord Gambier. To the nautical reader it is unnecessary to write one word of comment; so much so, indeed, that

I will not insult the common sense, even of the unpro-
fessional reader, by any attempt at further explanation.

Yet this statement was made by Captain Wooldridge,
not only to Lord Gambier but to the officers composing the subsequent court-martial; more strangely still,
it was *accepted by those officers*, though every one present
must have known that the *Mediator* would either have
been brought up on her first contact with the boom,
or, if she were weighty enough to overcome the obstacle,
must have passed through or over it, by pressing it
beneath her bow into the water.

It was not even pretended by those on board the
*Mediator* that any shock was felt! a pretty clear proof
that, when she passed over the place where the boom
*had been*, no such obstacle existed. That a vessel
could have broken up a boom of such magnitude is
too absurd for reflection. Nor, had not this version of
the matter appeared in every naval history since 1809,
should I have deemed a statement so truly incredible
worthy of notice.

Even the explosion-vessel did not break the boom
by actual contact. It was the combined effect of the
explosion upon the boom and upon the surface of the
sea that shook it to pieces. The huge waves caused by
the explosion lifted the boom along its entire length,
and the strain so loosened the chains which bound the
spars together, that the latter floated out of the fasten-
ings, and were carried away with the tide, the chains
sinking as a matter of course. It is certain that at
daylight the next morning not a vestige of this formi-

dable boom was to be seen; no one pretended to have seen so much as a single spar of it; though, had the *Mediator* broken through it, as falsely alleged, the whole length of the boom, except the part ruptured, must necessarily have remained at anchor!!

# CHAP. XXII.

## ARRIVAL IN ENGLAND.

SOON after my arrival in England it became known that a vote of thanks to Lord Gambier would be proposed in the House of Commons. I felt it my duty to wait on Lord Mulgrave, and apprise him that in my capacity as one of the members for Westminster, I would oppose the motion, on the ground that the commander-in-chief had not only done nothing to merit a vote of thanks, but had neglected to destroy the French fleet in Aix Roads, when it was clearly in his power to do so.

Lord Mulgrave entreated me not to persist in this determination, as such a course would not only prove injurious to the Government, but to myself, by raising up against me a host of enemies. The public, said his lordship, was satisfied with what had been done, and gave me full credit for my share therein, so that as I should be included in the vote of thanks, the recognition of Lord Gambier's services could do me no harm.

I told his lordship that I did not recognise Lord Gambier's services at all, and as for any thanks to myself, I would as soon be without them, being conscious that I had not been enabled satisfactorily to carry out the earnest wishes of the Admiralty by the destruction of the enemy's fleet; the greater part of which had been permitted to escape, and no doubt could be placed in a condition to effect the very mischief which the Board had been so desirous to avert. I begged his lordship to consider that in my professional capacity as a naval officer, I neither did offer, nor had offered, any opinions on Lord Gambier's conduct, but that my position as member of Parliament for Westminster forbade my acquiescence in a public misrepresentation.

Lord Mulgrave replied, that I was even now accusing Lord Gambier in my professional capacity: the public would not draw the distinction between my professional and parliamentary conduct. I expressed my regret for the public want of discrimination, but told his lordship that this would not alter my determination, at the same time requesting him to consider that as a naval officer I did not presume to accuse my superior in the service; but that, be the consequences to myself what they might professionally, I should pursue in Parliament whatever course I deemed right towards my constituents and the public.

Soon after this conversation Lord Mulgrave sent for

me, and again entreated me, for my own sake, to re-consider my resolution, saying that he had reported our former conversation to the Government, which was highly dissatisfied therewith. His lordship further assured me that he was anxious about the matter on my account, as such a course would certainly bring me under high displeasure. To this I replied, that the displeasure of the Government would not for a moment influence my Parliamentary conduct, for which I held myself answerable to my constituents.

His lordship then said, "If you are on service, you cannot be in your place in Parliament. Now, my lord, I will make you a proposal. I will put under your orders three frigates, with *carte blanche* to do whatever you please on the enemy's coasts in the Mediterranean. I will further get you permission to go to Sicily, and embark on board your squadron my own regiment, which is stationed there. You know how to make use of them."

I thanked Lord Mulgrave for the offer, at the same time expressing my gratitude for his anxiety thereby to preserve me from the evils of acting contrary to the wishes of the Government; but I told his lordship, that, were I to accept his offer, the country would regard my acceptance as a bribe to hold my peace, whilst I should regard my acquiescence in the same light. I must, therefore, decline the proposal.

The anxiety of the then Government was, no doubt, to convert the little that had been effected in Aix Roads into political capital, as a victory which merited the thanks of parliament; my tacit acquiescence in the object of Government would have subjected me, and rightly, to a total loss of political confidence in the estimation of those with whom I acted. No man with the slightest pretensions to political consistency could, therefore, have decided otherwise than I did, even with the kind warning of Lord Mulgrave, that evil consequences to myself would follow, a prediction subsequently verified to the letter.

The upshot of the matter was, that on Lord Mulgrave communicating my determination to Lord Gambier, the latter demanded a court-martial.

As soon as my fixed resolution of opposing the vote of thanks became known to the Government, the Board of Admiralty directed Lord Gambier to make a *fresh report* of the action in Basque Roads! requiring his lordship to call upon various officers for further reports as to the part they took therein!

Accordingly, on the 10th of May, Lord Gambier forwarded *a new despatch* to the Admiralty, *in which my services were altogether unrecognised !! !* Notwithstanding that, in Lord Gambier's previous report, he had written as follows : — " I cannot speak in sufficient terms of admiration and applause of the vigorous and gallant attack made by Lord Cochrane upon the French line-of-battle ships which were on shore ; as well as of his judicious manner of approaching them, and placing his ship in a position most advantageous to annoy the enemy and preserve his own ship, which could not be exceeded by any feat of valour hitherto achieved by the British navy."

Still more singularly, in the second despatch, which

is too long for insertion*, Lord Gambier inadvertently confirms the fact that *no attack on the French fleet would have been made at all,* had it not been for my having commenced an attack with the *Impérieuse* alone, which movement, as has been said, was executed literally *by stealth,* under the fear that the signal of recall would be hoisted by the commander-in-chief!

It having, for reasons described in a former chapter, become imperative on Lord Gambier to send us assistance, he, nevertheless, construed this into an *intention,* on his part, to attack the enemy. " *Observing the* Impérieuse *to advance, and the time of flood nearly done running,* the *Indefatigable,* &c. &c., were ordered to the attack!" It is not very probable that, had Lord Gambier intended an attack, he would have let the flood-tide go by, without taking advantage of it in a channel which was afterwards declared unsafe from want of water!

This passage alone of Lord Gambier's second despatch ought to have decided the result of any court-martial. The Board of Admiralty would not, however, see anything inculpatory of their former colleague; but, on the 29th of May, ordered me, through their secretary, to become the accuser of the commander-in-chief! "I am commanded by their Lordships to signify their directions that you state fully to me, for their information, the grounds on which your lordship

---

* The letter in question will be found at p. 7 of "Minutes of a Court-Martial on Lord Gambier, taken in short-hand by W. B. Gurney," and, as therein stated, revised by his lordship.

objects to the vote of thanks being moved to Lord
Gambier, to the end that their Lordships' objections
may be of a nature to justify the suspension of the
intended motion in Parliament, or to call for any
further information."—(Signed) " W. W. POLE."

This command was manifestly intended to entrap me
into the position of Lord Gambier's prosecutor, and
was, moreover, an improper interference with my Parliamentary capacity, in which alone I had declared my
intention to oppose an uncalled-for vote of thanks
to the commander-in-chief.   I therefore wrote to the
Secretary of the Admiralty the subjoined reply.

" Portman Square, 30th May, 1809.

" SIR,—I have to request that you will submit to their
Lordships that I shall, at all times, entertain a due sense
of the honour they will confer by any directions they may
be pleased to give me; that in pursuing the object of these
directions, my exertions will invariably go hand in hand
with my duty; and that, to satisfy their Lordships' minds in
the present instance, I beg leave to state that the log and
signal log-books of the fleet in Basque Roads contain all particulars, and furnish premises whence accurate conclusions
may be drawn; that, as these books are authentic public
documents, and as I cannot myself refer to them, anything I
could offer to their Lordships on the subject would be altogether superfluous, and would appear presumptuous inter-
ruptions to their Lordships' judgment, which will, doubtless,
always found itself upon those grounds only that cannot be
disputed.

" I have, &c. &c.
" COCHRANE.

" The Hon. W. W. Pole,
     Secretary to the Admiralty."

This reply, though plain, was respectful; but, as I had afterwards good reason to know, was deemed very offensive; the result being that, *after two months' delay* to enable Lord Gambier to get up his defence, a court-martial was assembled on the 26th of July, on board the *Gladiator*, at Portsmouth, the Court being composed of the following members: —

PRESIDENT — Sir Roger Curtis, Port-Admiral.

ADMIRALS — Young, Stanhope, Campbell, Douglas, Duckworth, and Sutton.

CAPTAINS — Irwin, Dickson, Hall, and Dunn.

It may perhaps be asked in what way a court-martial on Lord Gambier can so far concern me as to occupy a prominent place in this autobiography? The reply is, that, notwithstanding my repudiation, I was regarded at the court-martial as his accuser, though not permitted to be present so as to cross-examine witnesses; the whole proceeding being conducted in my absence, rather as a prosecution against me than Lord Gambier; and that the result was injurious to myself, as Lord Mulgrave had predicted, involving the punishment of not being employed with my frigate at Flushing, there to put in execution plans for the certain destruction of the French fleet in the Scheldt; so that, in order to punish me, the enemy's fleet was suffered to remain in security, when it might easily have been destroyed.

The reader must not imagine that I am about to inflict on him the evidence of a nine days' trial; but without some extracts therefrom, it is impossible to comprehend the matter. Let him bear in mind that

Lord Gambier relied for justification on three points : — 1st, That, had he sent in the fleet, its safety would have been endangered by the fortifications of Aix, (which he had previously spoken of as being dismantled); 2nd, Want of water to navigate the fleet in safety ; and 3rdly, From the fire of the enemy's vessels driven ashore (though lightened of their guns and stores).

CAPTAIN BROUGHTON (of the *Illustrious*).—"I was in Basque Roads, in the *Amelia*, on the 17th of March, and when within gunshot of the Isle of Aix observed the fortifications as being under repair, from the quantity of rubbish thrown up. I thought the fortifications on the island were not so strong as we supposed, and so reported to Lord Gambier. This was on the 1st of April. I did not notice any furnaces for heating red-hot shot. We were just out of gunshot, — *they fired at us from both sides, but none reached us.*"

In reply to the question, " whether everything was done that could be done to effect the destruction of the enemy's ships ? " Captain Broughton said : —

" It would have been more advantageous if the line-of-battle ships, frigates, and small vessels had *gone in at half-flood*, about 11 o'clock. There were *nine sail ashore*, and if the British ships had been ordered in, it would have been more advantageous. There were only *two* of the enemy's ships at anchor, and the *fleet*, had it gone in, would have been exposed to *their* fire; but I conceived they were panic-struck, and on the appearance of a force might have been induced to cut their cables, and escape up the river. A ship or two might have been placed, in my opinion, against the batteries on the southern part of Isle d'Aix, so as to take off their fire, and *silence them*. I told Sir Henry Neale, on board the *Caledonia*, when the signal was made for all captains in the mooring, that '*they were attackable from the confused way in which the French ships were at the time;*' viz. from having run ashore in the night, in order to escape from the fire-ships, which they imagined would explode.

" As the wind was north-westerly and northerly, ships might have found safe anchorage in what is called, in my French chart, le Grand Trousse, where there is thirty or forty feet of water *out of range of shot or shells in any direction.* When we first came into Basque Roads, if the charts were to be believed, *there appeared to be water enough in that position. I do not know anything of any shoal water. I sounded from the wreck of the Varsovie to that anchorage, and found no shoal there.* Two ships of the line would have been sufficient to have silenced the batteries on Aix, and five or six of the least draught of water to attack the enemy's ships. The discomfited French squadron would have made very little resistance. The loss would have been very little, as few of their ships were in a situation to fight their guns."

Here a distinguished officer shows that two ships could have silenced the batteries; that, in case of damage, there was plenty of water for them to retire to out of reach; and that the French ships, being ashore, could not use their guns.

CAPTAIN PULTENEY MALCOLM (of the *Donegal*).—" I saw the enemy's three-decker on shore. Till about noon she was heeling over considerably, and appeared to me to be *heaving her guns overboard.* She got off about two o'clock; *all the ships got off, except those that were destroyed.* Had it appeared to me that there was no other chance of destroying those ships but by such an attack, I CERTAINLY THINK IT OUGHT TO HAVE BEEN MADE. *Had they been attacked by the British ships, in my opinion, they could not have been warped off from the shore, as it was necessary so to do, to lay out anchors to heave them off.*"

*Question.*—"Would you, had you commanded the British fleet, have sent in ships to attack the enemy's ships on shore?"

*Answer.*—"The moment the two ships quitted their defensive position, the risk was then small, and OF COURSE I WOULD HAVE SENT THEM IN INSTANTLY."

This evidence is pretty decisive, but its plain tendency was attempted to be neutralised by the question whether there would have been *risk of damage*, had the British fleet been sent in to attack the enemy's ships when ashore! The great point of defence throughout was risk to the ships, as though the chief use of ships of war was to save them from injury.

CAPTAIN F. NEWCOMBE (of the *Beagle*).— "Can you state any instance of neglect, misconduct, or inattention in the proceedings of the Commander-in-chief, between the 11th and the 18th?"

*Answer.*—"None; save and except, had the Commander-in-chief thought proper, from his situation, TO HAVE SENT IN VESSELS EARLIER THAN THEY WERE SENT, though there might be a great risk in so doing, there was a possibility of annoying the enemy more than they were annoyed."

CAPTAIN GEORGE FRANCIS SEYMOUR (of the *Pallas*).—"I saw the *Impérieuse* inform the Commander-in-chief, by signal, that if allowed to remain he could destroy the enemy: there was every prospect of preventing them from getting off, as it would prevent their carrying out hawsers to heave off by. From what I afterwards saw, I think the ships might have floated in sooner—they might have come in with the last half of the flood-tide."

PRESIDENT.—"How much sooner would that have been than the time they actually did join?"

*Answer.*—"At *eleven o'clock.*"

*Question.*— "What time did the line-of-battle ships join?"

*Answer.*—"*Within a short time after two o'clock.*"

*Question.*—" Is your opinion formed from information obtained since the 22nd of April, or on that day ? "

*Answer.*—" It was formed from the depth of water *we found* ON GOING IN."

This evidence, coming from an officer of Captain Seymour's character and standing was so decisive, that it was subjected to a severe cross-examination, of which the subjoined is the substance :—

" It is impossible for me to foretell the event of such an attack, it so much depending on fortuitous circumstances. I cannot say that the line-of-battle ships *should* have gone in; I was not in possession of the Commander-in-chief's information. *I state the fact, and leave the Court to judge.* I mean to say, *there would have been water enough for the line-of-battle ships to have floated in.* As to the opposition they would have met with, the Court has as much before them as I have."

If the reader will refer to Lord Gambier's expression, in his second despatch of the 10th of May (see page 407), it will be evident that no attack whatever was intended; " but observing the *Impérieuse* to advance," it became imperative to support her, *i. e.* when the *flood-tide* " *had nearly done running.*" This is the true explanation of the British ships having been sent in *at all.* I repeat, that the advance of the *Impérieuse* thus forced on the little that was done. Had an attack been seriously intended, the time at which the British fleet should have gone in was that pointed out by the preceding officers, viz. when the French ships were aground, and the whole within reach of destruction ; instead of when the few, which were unable to get off by any exertions, were assailed. To have rested a case upon the danger to the British fleet from the fire of the ships *ashore*, with their guns thrown overboard to lighten them, was a course of defence which, for the honour of the British navy, is elsewhere unparalleled.

There is no necessity to adduce further extracts on this head; and I have purposely refrained from introducing my own evidence; but the *animus* by which the Court was actuated in the case must not be lightly passed over.

One of the principal witnesses was, as a matter of course, the Captain of the Fleet, Sir Harry Neale. This officer, though thoroughly conversant with both the acts and intentions of the commander-in-chief, was directed by the President openly, *not to state the opinions he had given to Lord Gambier on public services!* By Admiral Young Sir Harry Neale was told *to say nothing but what he was directed to detail!* This would be incredible were it not printed in " Minutes of the Court-Martial, revised by Lord Gambier!"

SIR H. NEALE (Captain of the Fleet).—"There were continued conversations between the Commander-in-chief and me. I have given him my opinion *on different services;* some of *those* he may have approved, and *some he may not have approved.*"

PRESIDENT.—" I apprehend *these* are *not* to be stated!"

Yet Sir H. Neale carefully marked the distinction between private conversation and the *public service,* by using the term " different services;" he being evidently ready to tell all he knew as regarded the public service. He was, however, stopped by Admiral Young, in one of the strangest injunctions which ever fell from the lips of a judge.

ADMIRAL YOUNG.— " If you are directed *to detail* any circumstances, you are *then* to say all you know of the circumstances you *are directed to detail;* but if you. are asked a specific question, your oath, I imagine, will *only* oblige you to answer SPECIFICALLY and directly, and as fully as you *can the question which is proposed to you!*"

So that Sir Harry Neale was cautioned that, if he was *not* directed to detail circumstances, he was not to relate them, however important they might be! And if asked only a specific question, he was merely to answer *specifically;* though the Court could know nothing of the facts, unless they permitted the witnesses to tell the truth, and the whole truth, in the very words of the oath.

But as Sir Harry Neale was known to be a man not likely to be thus peremptorily silenced, half a dozen insignificant questions were, therefore, only put to him by the Court, with the exception of one or two leading questions from Lord Gambier.

# CHAP. XXIII.

## LORD GAMBIER'S DESPATCH.

ITS OMISSIONS AND SUPPRESSIONS. — MOTIVE FOR LORD GAMBIER'S MIS-
STATEMENTS. — MR. FAIRFAX REPORTS THAT THE MEDIATOR WENT IN
FIFTH, NOT FIRST.—REASON OF THE CONTRARY ASSERTION.—NAPOLEON
ATTRIBUTES THE ESCAPE OF HIS FLEET TO THE IMBECILITY OF LORD
GAMBIER. — MISMANAGEMENT OF THE FIRESHIPS.—LORD GAMBIER'S
DELAY AND MISDIRECTION.—HIS PERVERSION OF FACT.—HIS MISPLACED.
PRAISE.—THE DESPATCH FAILS TO SATISFY THE PUBLIC. — CRITICISED
BY THE PRESS. — ADMIRAL GRAVIÈRE'S ACCOUNT OF THE TERMINA-
TION OF THE ACTION.

THE despatch brought to England by Sir Harry Neale
set out with the perversion, that the fireships, "arranged according to my plan," were "led on in the
most undaunted and determined manner by Captain
Wooldridge in the *Mediator*, *preceded by some vessels
filled with powder and shells, as proposed by Lord
Cochrane, with a view to explosion!*"

The omission of the fact that before Captain
Wooldridge "led the fireships" I had myself preceded them in the explosion-vessel, and that, even
before the *Mediator* proceeded on service in obedience
to the signals made by my order from the *Impérieuse*, every explosion-vessel under my personal com
mand was half-way towards the French fleet; the

suppression of my name as having anything at all to do with the attack by means of the explosion vessels, notwithstanding that by going first I ran all the risk of being boarded by the French guard-boats, and myself and crew murdered, as would have been the case had we been captured, showed that the object of the commander-in-chief was to suppress all mention of me, my plans, or their execution, as entitled to any credit for the mischief done to the enemy.

The despatch leads the reader to infer that the success subsequently obtained arose from the " undaunted and determined manner in which Captain Wooldridge led the fire-ships," from " Admiral Stopford's zealous co-operation with the boats," though not one of these ever stirred from alongside the *Cæsar*, anchored full four miles from the scene of action, and from the plans of the commander-in-chief himself.

That this suppression of all mention of the success of my plans in driving the whole enemy's fleet ashore, with the exception of two ships of the line, was deliberately intended by the commander-in-chief, is placed beyond question by the contemptuous manner in which he speaks of the means which really effected the mischief,—" *some vessels filled with powder and shells, with a view to explosion.*" That these means, conducted by myself, not Captain Wooldridge, *did* drive the French ships ashore, has been admitted by every French and English historian since that period ; and that this was done by my personal presence and instrumentality is a historical fact which nothing can shake or pervert. The only person ignoring the fact was the commander-in-chief of the British force, who not only gives me no credit for what had been done, but does not even mention my name, as having, by the above means, contributed to the result!

The sole conceivable motive for such a suppression of the success of my plans must have been that, having neglected to take advantage of the helpless condition of the French ships driven ashore, it was desirable to conceal the whole of the facts from the British public, by ascribing the success gained to other, and totally different causes, and thus to convert a deep discredit into a great victory!

The despatch goes on to state that, " the *Mediator*, *by breaking the boom !*" opened the way for the fire-ships, " but, owing to the darkness of the night, several mistook their course and failed."

At the conclusion of the last chapter, such reasons have, I think, been given why the *Mediator* could not have broken a double boom nearly a mile in extent as ought to have set the question for ever at rest.    But as that statement, notwithstanding its impossibility, is endorsed by the commander-in-chief as the groundwork of his despatch, it will be necessary to refute his lordship's statement also, and that from the evidence of an officer upon whose testimony he must necessarily rely, viz. Mr. Fairfax, the master of the fleet, who was deputed in the *Lyra* to observe the effect produced by the fire-ships, and, as a matter of course, reported to the commander-in-chief the result of his observations, which were as follows :—

" When the explosion-vessel blew up, she was about two cables' length from the *Lyra*. The *Lyra*, as well as the other explosion-vessel, is marked in the chart produced by. me. When she blew up, the fire-vessels *all* seemed to steer for that point. *I hailed four of them, and the Mediator*, and desired the *Mediator* to steer south-east, or else she would miss the French fleet."—*Minutes*, p. 177:

In another place Mr. Fairfax states that the night was so dark that it was difficult to make out exact positions, but the testimony of Captain Proteau, of the *Indienne*, that the explosion took place *at the boom*, "*à l'estacade*," is indisputable, as the *Indienne*, by Captain Proteau's testimony, was lying so close to the boom and the explosion-vessel also, as only to escape the effect of the latter by her shells going over. The spot, therefore, where the explosion took place is historically beyond doubt.

The testimony of Mr. Fairfax, then—and it must be borne in mind that I had no worse enemy in the fleet than that person — is this :—1st, The explosion took place ; 2ndly, *all* the fire-ships steered for the point where it had taken place ; 3rdly, Mr. Fairfax hailed *four* of them ; 4thly, the *Mediator* then came up, *steering in a wrong direction*, so that in place of " leading the fire-ships in the most undaunted and determined manner," as vouched for by the commander-in-chief, the master of the fleet, who was on the spot, vouches that she was the *fifth fire-ship which came up*, and that had he not set her right in her course she would have " missed the French fleet ; " *i. e.*, she was behind the other fire-ships, and *steering outside the boom, which lay in front of the French fleet !*

It would, I think, be superfluous to say another word

about this extraordinary story of the boom, nor should I have condescended to notice it at all in connection with the despatch, but that the commander-in-chief makes it the groundwork of his report to the Government, for the unworthy purpose of altogether omitting my name as connected with the explosion-vessels, and for leading the public to infer that these produced *no effect whatever, either on the boom or the French fleet!* which is indeed the main object of the despatch.

It was, however, necessary to give some reason why the French fleet ran ashore, and as it was not considered expedient to give me the credit of causing it to do so by the terror created from the explosion, the commander-in-chief, despite his own judgment as a seaman, appears to have caught at Captain Wooldridge's story of breaking the boom, and other subsequent exploits just as unfounded; though the master of the fleet must have reported that some time after the explosion-vessel had done its work *he fell in with the Mediator, steering in a wrong direction, and set her right in her course ! ! !*

I forbear to speak of having myself encountered the *Mediator* after passing several other fire-ships, as that would be assertion only. Of the effect produced, and by what means it was produced, the subjoined extract from the *Times* newspaper of May 4th, 1809, will furnish some idea, as coming from French sources : —

" Some letters have been received from the French coast, which bear testimony to the destructive result of the late attack on the enemy's fleet in Basque Roads. 'Your *infernal machines*,' says one of the letters, 'have not only destroyed several of our ships, but they have rendered almost all the remainder unfit to put to sea again. They have proved the destruction of more than 2000 of our people, (?) and *petrified the rest with fear.* The mouth of the Charente river is completely blocked up with wreck.'"ᵇ*

Yet two days after the departure of the *Impérieuse*, the commander-in-chief addressed another despatch to the Admiralty, from which the subjoined is an extract:—

" *Caledonia*, April 16, 1809.

" It has blown violently from the southward and westward ever since the departure of the *Impérieuse*, which has rendered it *impracticable to act in any way with the small vessels or boats of the fleet* against the enemy. I have the satisfaction to observe this morning, that the enemy have set fire to their frigate *L'Indienne*, and that the ship of the line which is aground at the entrance of the river—supposed to be the *Regulus*—there is every reason to believe will be wrecked."

The Emperor Napoleon himself is, moreover, an authority on the subject, not to be passed over.

" Some conversation now took place about Lord Cochrane, and the attempt which his lordship had made to capture or destroy the ships in the Charente.

" I said it was the opinion of a very distinguished officer, whom I named, and who was well known to him (Napoleon), that if Cochrane had been properly supported, he would have destroyed the whole of the French ships.

" 'He would not only have destroyed them,' replied Napoleon, ' but *he might and would have taken them out,* had your admiral supported him as he ought to have done. For, in consequence of the signal made by L'Allemand' (I think he

* That is of the boom, for no ship had been wrecked at the mouth of the Charente.

said) 'to the ships to do the best in their power to save themselves — *sauve qui peut,* in fact — they became panic-struck,
and cut their cables.   The terror of the *brûlots* * was so great,
that they *actually threw their powder overboard, so that
they could have offered very little resistance.*'

"'The French admiral,' continued Napoleon, 'was an
*imbecile,* but yours was just as bad.  I assure you, that if
Cochrane had been supported, he would have taken every
one of the ships.  They ought not to have been alarmed by
your *brûlots,* but fear deprived them of their senses, and they
no longer knew how to act in their own defence.'"—*O'Meara's
Napoleon,* vol. ii. p. 291.

Were it worth while, numerous testimonies of the
like character could be gathered from French official
sources, but it is necessary to mention some other
points of the despatch.

The commander-in-chief's assertion, that, "*owing to
the darkness of the night, several fire-ships mistook their
course and failed,*" was true enough, but not the *whole
truth,* which was, that, from their clumsy management
—neither going in the right direction, nor being kindled
at the right time or place — *not one out of the twenty-
three fire-ships took effect!*

The despatch goes on to state, that at daylight Lord
Cochrane signaling that seven of the enemy's ships
were on shore, and might be destroyed, the commander-in-chief " *immediately* " † ordered the fleet to
unmoor and weigh, *intending* to proceed with it to
their destruction ; but the wind blowing fresh *from*

---

* Napoleon, like other French writers, includes the explosion
vessels under the general term *brûlot.*

† Four hours afterwards.

*the northward* \*, and *the flood-tide running* †, rendered it too hazardous to enter Aix Roads, wherefore the fleet again anchored about three miles from the forts on Isle d'Aix.

This was, indeed, all that the fleet collectively did, or that the commander-in-chief intended it to do. Seeing, however, the "*enemy warping off their ships*," and that, whilst the fleet was unmooring and anchoring again, "*they had succeeded in getting off all but five of the line!*" the commander-in-chief "gave orders to Capt. Bligh of the *Valiant*, with the *Revenge*, frigates, bombs, &c.," — to attack those that remained aground? Nothing of the kind, but — "*to anchor near the Boyart Shoal, in readiness for an attack!!*" An odd way truly of preventing the five remaining enemy's ships, then throwing their guns overboard for the purpose of lightening themselves, from warping off!!

"At twenty minutes past two, P.M.," continues the commander-in-chief, "Lord Cochrane advanced in the *Impérieuse*, with his accustomed gallantry and spirit, and opened a well-directed fire on the *Calcutta*, which *struck her colours to the Impérieuse*." Lord Gambier afterwards *denied this*, though almost the only part of the action which he was near enough to see with his own eyes! Indeed, the terms of the despatch are decisive of having been detailed from his own personal observations!

But now comes the monstrous part of the assertion; viz. "The ships and vessels above-mentioned *soon*

* And therefore a fair wind.
† Consequently favourable for the fleet to enter Aix Roads.

*after* joined in the attack on the *Ville de Varsovie* and *Aquilon*, and obliged them to strike their colours," &c. Instead of "*soon after*," the *Valiant, Revenge*, &c., remained at anchor near the Boyart, till my signal " In want of assistance," had been wrongly interpreted as a signal of " distress." But for this, it is clear that not an anchor would have been weighed. Yet the commander-in-chief made the act of sending in these ships, *when it could no longer be avoided*, appear part of a previous plan to attack the *Ville de Varsovie* and *Aquilon*, and that they were sent for this purpose *soon after* my attack on the *Calcutta* and them simultaneously!

This is not only a perversion of fact, but a suppression of it ; for the commander-in-chief must have seen that the *Impérieuse* was engaged with the *Aquilon* and *Ville de Varsovie*, as well as with the *Calcutta*, before the *Valiant, Revenge*, &c., were ordered in to our assistance, as requested by my signal. And here it must be distinctly understood, that *had not a portion of the fleet been compelled by this justifiable device of my signaling* " *In want of assistance*," *to come to our supposed aid, no attack would have been made.* To avert this disgrace, I resolved, if necessary, to sacrifice my ship.

Throughout the whole despatch, there is not a word to indicate that the terror caused by the explosion vessels had anything to do with the success gained. On the contrary, the success is attributed to causes purely imaginary. Great credit is given to me "for the vigorous and gallant attack on the French line-of-battle ships ashore," and for " my judicious manner of approaching them, and placing my ship in a position most advantageous to annoy the enemy, and *preserve my own ship!* which," continued his Lordship, " could not be exceeded by any feat of valour hitherto achieved by the British navy ! "

The plain fact is, and it will by this time be evident to others besides nautical men, that the just quoted piece of claptrap was considered in the light of a sop to my supposed vanity, sufficient to insure my holding my peace on the subject of the fleet not having even contemplated an attack till forced into it by my signal being mistaken for being " in distress."

Instead of being praised for what my plans really effected, I was praised for what was neither done nor intended to be done. Instead of adopting " a judicious manner of approaching the enemy, so as *to preserve my ship,*" I drifted the *Impérieuse* in like a log with the tide, and stern foremost, for fear of being recalled, and then went at the enemy with a determination, not to preserve, but *to lose* my ship, if the commander-in-chief did not relieve her before she was riddled with shot; this being my only hope of forcing on an attack of any kind. My motive was, no doubt, fathomed from seeing me attack three line-of-battle ships simultaneously. Not a moment was to be lost, and for the first time, since the French ran their ships ashore in terror, two British line-of-battle ships, and some frigates, approached the spot where the enemy's vessels had been lying aground *ever since the previous midnight*, helpless, and, as every French authority admits, hopeless of escape, had the slightest effort been made to prevent it.

In place, then, of attacking these with a single frigate, in such a way as to "*preserve my ship*," I here avow that I rushed at the enemy in the bitterness of despair, determined that if a portion of the fleet was not sent in, the *Impérieuse* should never again float out; for rather than incur the stigma which would have awaited me in England, from no fault of mine, but because it was not expedient that plans which had been partially successful should be fully accomplished, she should have been destroyed.

This despatch, inexplicable as it was felt to be, naturally suggested to the public mind in England, that, despite its assumption of a great victory, the result of the victory was by no means commensurate with the tone of exultation assumed. The French fleet was *not* destroyed; and it was equally manifest, that if but little had been effected, it was owing to the time which had been suffered to elapse between my first signals and the tardy aid reluctantly yielded in support of them. By that kind of intuitive perception characteristic of the British press, it was agreed that there had been mismanagement somewhere, but *where* was not to be gathered from the commander-in-chief's despatch, in which everything "by favour of the Almighty," * as the despatch most reprehensibly set forth, had succeeded.

It is not surprising, then, that the press began to

---

* There is something very revolting to a truly religious mind in these derogatory phrases, which couple the beneficent Author of our being with the butcheries of war. Under no circumstances are they defensible. But when the name of the great and merciful

criticise the despatch on its own merits. The following remarks are extracted from a *Times* leading article in the paper of April 25th, 1809, by way of specimen :—

"None felt more joy than ourselves at the destruction of four French vessels in Basque (Aix) Roads. We have, however, been given to understand that there are some people conversant in these things, whose satisfaction is not quite so complete as was our own on the result of the action.

\* \* \* \* \* \*

"Lord Cochrane's first signal, as we learn from the *Gazette*, to the admiral of the fleet, was that 'seven of the enemy's ships were on shore, and might be destroyed.' The question which hereupon naturally suggests itself to the mind is, 'Why, then, if seven might be destroyed, were there only four?'

"The despatch proceeds. 'I *immediately* made the signal for the fleet to unmoor and weigh.' Indeed! Had Admiral Lord Gambier to unmoor at the time he received this intelligence? Did he not expect this might be the case? Or with what view was Lord Cochrane sent up the Roads? We are not much acquainted with naval matters, and therefore ask for information. To reason by analogy, if a military commander, knowing the enemy to be near, should send forward a detachment to reconnoitre and to attack, if possible, he would at least keep the rest of his troops under arms, that he

---

Creator is made subservient to an attempt to palm off as a great victory that which, in reality, was a great disgrace even to the human means available, there is something shocking in the perversion of language which should only be uttered with the profoundest reverence, and on occasions in strict coincidence with the attributes of the sacred name invoked. In this case *fireships* had been denounced as horrible and antichristian, yet *explosion vessels* — engines of destruction tenfold more diabolical — had, "by favour of the Almighty," succeeded !

might be ready to advance at a moment's warning, and to sustain his own party when necessary."

\*        \*        \*        \*        \*        \*

The best account I have ever seen of the termination of the action, is written by the venerable and gallant Admiral Gravière, who was present at the attack. It will be found in the *Revue de Deux Mondes* for 1858. From this, though incorrect in stating that I commanded a division, I make the subjoined extract, which shall close the subject :—

"Un esprit de vertige semblait s'être emparé, dans cette affreuse nuit, et dans les journées qui suivirent, des plus braves capitaines. Des vaisseaux que l'ennemi n'avait pas même attaqués furent abandonnés par leurs équipages, et des hommes héroïques partagèrent la faiblesse commune.

"*La mollesse de Lord Gambier*, le courage et le sang froid de quelques-uns de nos officiers, préservèrent seuls l'escadre Française d'une ruine totale."

END OF THE FIRST VOLUME.

www.ingramcontent.com/pod-product-compliance
Lightning Source LLC
Chambersburg PA
CBHW030328120726
47901CB00007B/1720